Tap-Dancing on Quicksand

by Killarney Greene

 FriesenPress

Suite 300 - 990 Fort St
Victoria, BC, V8V 3K2
Canada

www.friesenpress.com

Chapter graphic courtesy of Freepik.com

ISBN
978-1-4602-7871-0 (Hardcover)
978-1-4602-7872-7 (Paperback)
978-1-4602-7873-4 (eBook)

1. FICTION, THRILLERS, SUSPENSE

Distributed to the trade by The Ingram Book Company

This book is dedicated to my mom and my amazing family, and to my dearest and closest friends.

ALL THE WORLD'S A STAGE
—WILLIAM SHAKESPEARE

Acknowledgements:

Jessica MacIvar, my niece, for her fabulous front cover illustration. Linda Shore for her encouragement, support and tech savvy assistance. Rebecca Fenn for her patience, guidance and expertise in the publishing process. Elizabeth Seguin for her brilliant editorial skills and suggestions.

To the residents of our town, my heartfelt thanks for being the wonderful people you are. There is no place on earth quite like this community where we are surrounded by Nature's wonders, and embraced by our magical, mystical mountains.

Chapter One:

The Stage

THE LATE AFTERNOON SUN'S RAYS CASCADED THROUGH THE DRESSING ROOM WINDOW AND PUDDLED ON THE COUNTER AMID THE COSMETIC CLUTTER. Sunbeams bounced off the crystal perfume bottles, shattering the air with splinters of light. Impatiently, Jessica yanked the curtains shut. The harsh glare distracted her from the grim task of scrutinizing her complexion in the mirror.

There was nothing wrong with the mirror. Neither lint nor dust marred its surface; but the face reflected there transformed Jessica's glowing expectations into dismal despair. Never, never, should she have listened to that woman, she reproached herself. For all the treacherous twists of destiny in Jessica's life, she should have known something like this would happen.

"That old biddy probably had plastic surgery to look so good!" she muttered under her breath, as she examined her face. "Botox treatments, too!"

Scarlet splotches on her forehead, cheeks, and chin made her dearly regret that she had surrendered to her female vanity and disregarded the little reminder that "if it works, don't fix it". The beauty regimen she had used throughout her adulthood had been quite sufficient until she had watched a late-night talk show two weeks earlier and envied the flawless, peaches-and-cream complexion of a fifty-year-old motion picture star. The program's hostess had cajoled the movie personality on national TV into revealing the secret behind her wrinkle-free, radiant face. The recipe for eternal youth, the celebrity had crooned, was to never miss a morning and evening application of a special skin freshener plus moisturizer—available only at "better stores"—followed by a rare collagen booster which, as far as Jessica was concerned, was available only on the black market.

Scribbling down the ingredients for such a refreshing, youthful-looking appearance, Jessica had realized that at thirty-five it might be a little late for the tiny crows' feet around her eyes and the bit of a droop under her chin. But she had tried it anyway. She wanted so much to look dazzling for the grand opening of the Terrace Lodge Resort Hotel. For two weeks she hadn't missed a liberal slathering on of the combination, only to awaken on the morning of the gala affair wishing for innocuous wrinkles instead of flaming red splotches.

She had to do something with the blemishes! She couldn't bear to be dissected by the female guests who would be analyzing her hair, her face, her gown and jewelry, and even the tiniest flaw in her complexion. Ripping open her cosmetic bag, she searched frantically for her blemish concealer stick. Where was it? She tore open the counter drawer, rummaging through her jars, bottles, and tubes. Ah! There it was! Relieved, she smudged the erasing stick over each angry splotch and with deft fingers blended over the patches with liquid make-up. She stepped back from the mirror to inspect her handiwork. Fabulous! Perfect! Now for the rest of her makeup. With her high cheekbones and fine features, she had celebrity-stunning beauty but, like many women, was far too critical of herself and was never satisfied with her looks.

Her nose was too long, her cheeks were too plump, her forehead too high, her ears too big, her breasts too big or small—depending on her mood—and her hair needed a trim. But for tonight, she calculated, she would present an impressive appearance. She grinned at her reflection, revealing an alluring smile with beautiful teeth.

"Jessica, dear, will you be much longer?" chimed a female voice from outside the dressing room. "Julian's impatient to get going."

"I'm coming, Mother Lydia! I'm coming!" Jessica responded, clenching her teeth. "Tell him I'll be a few more minutes. Technical difficulties!" God! When would she ever grow to love that woman?

Lydia watched as Jessica stepped with one well-shaped leg into the opening of her dress and wiggled it up over her hips, shuffling and shrugging the top over her strapless, black lace bra.

"You look lovely, my dear," beamed Lydia, zipping up the black sheath-style gown while her daughter-in-law maneuvered the off-one-shoulder top into place. "You are so adept with make-up. One would scarcely notice those ugly little blemishes."

"It comes from years of practice, Mother Lydia," smiled Jessica, thinking the older woman really did look like a mother-in-law with her crisp L'Oréal-brown curls hugging her head, her judgmental air, and her hands folded in front of her bosom as if she was praying.

Grudgingly, Jessica admired Lydia's elegant and stylish gown of lavender silk, cut high at the neck to hide her sagging skin.

Lydia, with her arrogant, stately carriage, wore clothes well. In fact, Lydia would likely look fantastic in a flour sack. Jessica stepped in front of the full-length mirror to admire her own dress, which glittered with black sequins and beads. She looked fine. Fine enough for the Terrace Lodge Hotel owner's wife.

Directing her blue eyes to meet Lydia's hazel squint, she declared flatly, "We mustn't keep the dear man waiting, must we?"

As Jessica swished from the room, she tossed her head, her shoulder-length glistening blonde hair leaving a Joy-perfumed essence in her wake. Pausing at the top of the staircase, she struck a pose for Lydia's benefit, and then tapped her way down the gray marble steps in her black be-jeweled high heels and into the waiting arms of her husband.

Standing six feet two, Julian towered over his wife who barely came up to his shoulder; his dark brown hair coiffed perfectly to reflect his image of the owner of the Terrace Lodge Hotel. A tinge of gray at his temples added to his facade of sophistication and maturity. At forty-two, he was, shall we say, a great package of male virility and leashed sexual magnetism. Any woman with blood in her veins would most certainly have taken more than one lingering look at him; perhaps even harbored a fantasy.

Kissing her lightly on the cheek, he whispered, "You look smashing! Any plans for after the party? That dress is...uh... quite enticing!"

"I can always swing naked from the chandelier in the hotel lobby," she murmured, peeking up with adoring eyes at his handsome face. His warm brown eyes crinkled as he chuckled.

"Now that would be a great act!" he grinned, turning as his mother reached the bottom step, and Binkie, their housekeeper

-turned-nanny-for-the-night, entered the foyer. "I'm not sure how late we'll be, Binkie," he said, his rich voice echoing in the marble walls of the cavernous foyer. "One never knows about these functions. It could be all night. Go to bed whenever you want."

"Never you mind, Mr. Julian," grinned Binkie, her gray head bobbing in time with her words. "Rob and me will be just fine. Little ones are so precious." She ducked around her employers to open the heavy oak door for them.

"I'd like to look in on Rob before we leave," Jessica suggested, hesitating as Julian herded her and his mother through the entrance.

"He doesn't need his nap interrupted," clucked Lydia, draping her mink shawl around her shoulders.

Julian stood firm while his wife searched his face for the answer to her suggestion. Just as she suspected, he agreed with his mother.

The silver limousine hummed at the curb. Kenneth, the aged chauffeur, opened the door, and Lydia slid into the maroon leather interior. Jessica followed carefully in her snug gown, and Julian slipped in beside her. The door closed with a soft thud.

"A sip of sherry on the way?" Julian asked, reaching for the bar.

"Please, darling," whined Lydia, her voice grating on Jessica's nerves like fingernails on a chalkboard.

"Why not?" whispered Jessica. She always spoke in hushed tones in these elegant vehicles. They reminded her of hearses, demanding reverence.

While the car wound its way down the driveway to the street, Julian poured smoothly and handed the first small goblet to his mother. She barely touched the amber liquid to her lips, savoring the flavor. Jessica tossed hers back in two swallows, its warmth oozing its way to her stomach, lulling the apprehension in her heart. How would she ever survive the next few hours? She just had to measure up to Julian's high standards of performance and style. After all, this was the biggest grand opening in Riverbend's history.

"Really, Jessica!" snapped Lydia. "You drink like a trucker! Can't you practice some restraint?"

"I'm a wee bit nervous, Mother Lydia," Jessica explained and turned to Julian's frown with a weak smile. "Can I have another splash? I'll just sip this one." Secretly, she wished she could chug-a-lug the whole bottle and wash down a handful of Valium. She might not make a classy entrance, but at least she'd be relaxed. She also wished at that moment that she *was* a trucker—she'd like to mow Lydia down!

Too soon, the limousine glided onto the private driveway of the Terrace Lodge Hotel. It was early June, but it looked like Christmas, with the pine and birch trees bordering the drive bedecked with twinkling white lights. It was Tivoli Gardens in the mountains of America.

When the car stopped at the hotel entrance, Kenneth opened the door, and Julian led the way for the two most important women in his life. As Jessica emerged, he brushed her cheek with his lips while press cameras flashed. When Lydia stepped from the limousine, he took her hand and kissed it, and the reporters jostled for position with their cameras, snapping pictures of the three. The crowd gathered on the front terrace clapped and cheered as Julian entered the spacious lobby, a woman on each arm. Jessica wished she'd had the seamstress allow a little more room in the hipline of her creation; she could sense every man's eyes focused on her behind.

The cocktail hour was in full swing when they entered the cavernous lobby; the floor gleaming with polished slate quarried from the mountains in which the hotel was built. Three huge stone fireplaces were ablaze, emitting a cozy warmth. On the plush carpeted areas, massive sofas with plump, overstuffed cushions invited guests, with designer casualness. Heavy mahogany tables with bronze and brass-based lamps stood strategically beside the sofas and chairs. Suspended from the ceiling, enormous chandeliers shimmered over the guests who, glasses in hand, chatted and laughed, while others mingled through the crowd to find old friends, neighbors, and business acquaintances.

Lydia stopped to visit with her bridge partner. With Jessica in tow, Julian wound his way through the press of humanity, introducing her to a blur of faceless people. He laughed, joked, slapped men on the back, and gave his radiant smile to more women than Jessica had even suspected he knew. He was a born PR man—confident, charming, and able to make those he talked with believe they were the most important people in the world. She was grateful, however, that he always introduced her as "my wife" rather than "the wife", "the little woman", or "my other half". But she noticed he said it in much the same way as he said "my house", "my car", or "my hotel". Scanning the crowd, she hoped to see Rosalind or Mary-Beth, two of her closest friends who had been invited.

"Darling, let me get you a drink. The ribbon cutting won't be for another half hour or so, and I've got to talk details with Lincoln first," Julian said as he vanished, reappearing a few minutes later with a martini. "This should hold you for a while. Make sure you don't guzzle it! Just sip it!"

Noticing his own glass held only ice cubes, she estimated he was probably on his third drink. Julian was one of the chosen few who could down drink after drink and, like magic, have only ice cubes as evidence. In a moment he was gone. Perhaps never to be seen or heard from again, she thought, vaguely wishing it was true.

Was it a measure of his confidence in her or his lack of caring, which prompted him to abandon her on such a night, leaving her to chat up a storm with virtual strangers?

Gripping her martini, she searched the crowd for Rosalind; she needed a friend. In years gone by, meeting new people in large social gatherings had given her fresh opportunities to use her natural friendliness and quick wit. What was happening to her? Panic rose in her throat, but the mixture of gin and vermouth washed her fear down to the pit of her stomach where it belonged, out of sight. Better to have anxiety gnaw at her insides than have it register on her face.

As she wove her way through the glitzy crowd, she almost collided with an obese, and very pregnant young woman whose plump cheeks dimpled into a grin.

"Oh, my dear Jessica, how are you?" the mother-to-be chirped. "Isn't this exciting? What an opening! The lights outside are such a spectacular idea! Was it yours? I might have known! Who else would make it look so festive? Just imagine! Christmas lights in June!"

Jessica waited for the merry chatter to end. "Why, Roxanne, what a surprise! I certainly didn't expect to see you here! Lincoln said you were ready to pop at any moment. Wasn't that baby due last week? And speaking of Christmas, I love your outfit. All you need is a star on your head, and you'd look like the sugar plum fairy! You look delightful even with that baby hiding under your muumuu."

Roxanne was Lincoln's over-pregnant, ever-pregnant wife, and Lincoln, Julian's right-hand manager at his two hotels in town, had been appointed executive manager of the new Terrace Lodge Hotel. Roxanne had all the taste of Tugboat Annie, her wardrobe consisting of gaudy, flowered, beribboned, and sequined-to-death muumuus, usually stained with baby spit-up. But tonight her muumuu sparkled and twinkled with glued-on flash and glitter, without a trace of a child's gooey residue. Jessica was not overly fond of Roxanne and thought the woman outspoken rather than well spoken. On their first meeting, Roxanne had hinted that Jessica's svelte figure was attributable to bulimia or anorexia rather than to a good diet and exercise.

"The doctor thinks we probably had the conception date off by a week or so, which is possible. Lincoln's so horny he has to have it all the time, so who knows when I got knocked up this time?"

"Well, I hope you have a nice time tonight. Maybe a bit of dancing later will help start things moving."

"Oh, Lincoln doesn't dance! Besides hotels, he's into building remote control boats...and screwing, of course!"

"Admirable hobbies, I'm sure," replied Jessica, wondering how to disengage herself politely from this pathetic beached whale. "Gosh, I've got to run. I see a few people I want to thank for coming. Have fun! The dinner menu is terrific! You'll love it!"

Threading her way through the crowd, she admired the agility of the waiters who wove their way amongst the guests, balancing trays laden with drinks and canapés. She spotted Julian and Lincoln conspiring beside a fireplace, and noticed Julian, as a waiter passed by, expertly snare a drink from the tray without even looking. He should be in fine form for the ribbon-cutting ceremony, she thought, as she walked across the carpet to interrupt their conversation.

"Just checking," she smiled at her husband. "We have only a few more minutes. Will the bagpipes still be part of the opening? I mean...can I still count on that being the signal to go to the dining room entrance?"

"Yes, Jess." He sounded impatient. "We've gone over it a thousand times. Why don't you find Mother and go over there now, and I'll meet you?"

As she headed for the place where she last saw Lydia, she felt Lincoln's eyes on her rear end, undressing her. She shuddered. How could Roxanne stand it? On the other hand, how could Lincoln stand it? Bedding Roxanne had to be like mating with a hot air balloon. The thought of their lovemaking sent shivers through her. Finding Lydia was a welcome diversion from the repulsive idea.

The first whine of the bagpipes startled her. This was the big moment! But she calmed when she heard the lilting tune, "Comin' Through the Rye". The piper, in his blue plaid kilt, opened a path to the door of the dining room, as the guests parted to let him pass. Julian, with Jessica and his mother, stood at the entrance behind a long crimson ribbon strung between two brass posts standing ten feet apart.

A curtained plaque hung to the left of the massive mahogany doors, the centers of which contained stained glass panels of wild roses. The piper stopped at the ribbon, then retreated to the far side of the curtain, his mission completed. As the pipes sighed to silence, the chattering din subsided until everyone was hushed, waiting.

"First of all, I want to thank all of you for coming," Julian began, his face aglow with pride. "This is, indeed, a joyous moment for me, as well as for my family. I have long dreamed of having a resort on the shores of our gorgeous Emerald Lake. It will certainly add to the tourist industry of Riverbend and will be something of which we can all be proud. I want to thank the representatives of the many foreign countries interested in tourism for attending our gala. Their presence assures their fellow countrymen that the Terrace Lodge Hotel will always be a resort where they will be welcomed and where they can experience nature at her best. And of course, included in the package of this marvelous setting is a world-class golf course. My father always wanted to accomplish building this hotel on the tranquil shores of our pristine lake, so these premises will be dedicated to his memory. Mother, will you unveil the plaque?"

Everyone focused on Lydia, who stood beside the curtain with the pull-string in her fingers. Tears glistened in her eyes.

"My husband would have been so proud of this moment," she faltered, then tugged the string, opening the curtain to reveal an engraved pewter plaque. "It reads," she said, her voice quivering as her son held the microphone toward her, "In loving memory of Richard Julian Bothwell for his efforts to increase commerce in Riverbend and for his dream of the Terrace Lodge Resort Hotel."

Silence. Then a pair of hands clapped. Soon everyone in the cavernous lobby was clapping, amid thunderous cheers of congratulations. Julian smiled and nodded to Jessica, introducing her to the crowd and saying that with her ribbon cutting, "the Lodge was officially open".

"Please join us for a fabulous dinner with dancing afterwards," she warbled into the microphone, and she nervously reached for the gold scissors, which the maître d' held on a crimson velvet cushion. Holding her breath, she snipped the ribbon. The satin whispered apart, floating in two segments to the floor.

Press bulbs flashed, illuminating the faces of the family. This grand opening was news in Riverbend. Hot news! The town had its share of gossip, fires, funerals, scandals, and tragedies, but this hotel opening was headline stuff, which could be savored over morning coffee without sending chills up one's spine. Many of the guests were principals of the community: the mayor, councilmen, the police and fire chiefs, members of Riverbend's Chamber of Commerce, the hospitals' directors, bankers, lawyers, realtors, business owners, architects, builders, developers, school board members, various charity board members, travel agency owners and managers, ministers, and a priest or two.

Jessica smiled at her former boss, who owned the travel agency where she had been working when she met Julian. She and Julian had also included neighbors from Sherwood Park, the most prestigious and exclusive part of town. Also invited were old friends, school chums, and other business acquaintances. Julian, Lydia, and Jessica had squirreled themselves away in Julian's office at the Talisman Hotel and had brainstormed lists of invitees. Lincoln, of course, had helped. The list consisted of four hundred guests, and since partners were included, more than seven hundred people were expected. Nearly all the RSVP's were returned in the affirmative, such was the community support for Julian. An active member on the boards of several charities, he always donated generously and campaigned tirelessly for the impoverished, the disabled, the sick, and the mentally challenged. Everyone in Riverbend, it seemed, adored Julian.

Smiling, he raised his wife's hand to kiss it and embraced his mother's waist. Together, the family was solid and radiant as they posed for the evening's last formal photos.

Then the piper puffed into the bagpipes, wheezing them into a rendition of "Lach Lomond". His kilt swinging in time with the music, he led the family to the head table, followed by the other guests of honor. Behind them, some singing the words of the Highland favorite, the remaining guests surged into the dining room, seeking their assigned tables. Outside, the sun had begun to set behind the mountains, its glow reflected in the darkening waters of the lake.

With pleasure and pride, Julian took his seat between his wife and mother. The other dignitaries found their place cards, each with a fresh orchid attached. Alongside each card was an 18-carat gold key chain for the men or a crystal perfume decanter for the ladies, each monogrammed with "TLH". Julian had spared no expense.

Jessica stroked his hand under the table and flashed a smile at him. She knew how hard he had worked to make his vision a reality. Almost from the beginning of their relationship, he had been talking about it and discussing plans and making deals with architects, builders, town planners, and developers. The result was splendid: The three-story, low-slung river-rock-walled structure sprawled along the shore of the lake. With one hundred rooms and suites, some with balcony views of the lake and mountains, it was sure to attract tourists worldwide. It boasted three dining areas, two coffee shops, a lounge, and a shopping galleria, which included a barber shop and a beauty salon. It also had thirty outlying cedar cottages and cabins tucked into the woods, where guests could experience peace, privacy, and tranquility.

To enhance their encounters with nature, Julian had added

canoes, paddle boats, and row boats so guests could enjoy the rare beauty of the mountains from the lake, which reflected the snowy peaks, lush forests, and skies with clouds billowing overhead as sunbeams sparkled on the emerald waters. The enchanting color came from minerals leached from the rocks by streams, which fed the lake, as they cascaded down the mountains.

He winked at her and then leered teasingly at her sensuous figure in her black beaded-and-sequined gown. Julian appreciated her taste, elegance, and style. From her dress, to the diamond drop earrings, to her diamond-studded watch, she appeared flawless. He didn't seem to notice her complexion camouflage, but sensing her discomfort, he squeezed her hand and murmured, "Still want to do the chandelier act? I can announce it!"

"Oh, my God!" she laughed. "Wouldn't that look great on the front page of the *Riverbend Review!* I can see it now!"

"Relax, darling," he soothed. "Just look gorgeous as you always do. All these people are here to have a good time, not to see you. And you don't have to do or say anything that you don't want to."

"May I have another drink? It might help," she suggested.

Raising an eyebrow at her, he waved at a passing server and ordered three gin and tonics. "Make mine a double."

Lydia busied herself smiling, waving, and chatting as the people she knew passed by the table. Lincoln and Roxanne seated themselves beside Lydia as Jessica thanked God, Providence, or good planning that they weren't beside her.

The banquet was superb: vichyssoise, followed by Caesar salad with Jessica's own special dressing, rack of lamb with artichokes and parsleyed potatoes, and for dessert, a tantalizing

Blitz soufflé. The huge, cavernous ceiling of the dining room was festooned with thousands of strands of tiny lights, which sprinkled the diners with fairy godmother dust.

The eagle eyes of the maître d' and his assistants watched over the food and beverage service at all the tables. For a gathering so enormous, timing was of the essence; nothing had been left to chance. Julian had been in the industry too long and had worked in every department since his teens—when he had helped to unload taxis at his father's first hotel—to leave any detail unnoticed or forgotten. The previous day, he and the dining room and kitchen staff had gone through two dry runs to practice for the celebration. He had even prepared for the worst-case scenarios that could occur and had hired extra staff to wait in the wings. To encourage his employees' attendance, he had added the promise of a generous bonus to their paychecks.

Julian was a considerate, conscientious employer, who was more than fair to his workers. A master manipulator, he moved his people into positions where they would prove most effective. He was a hands-on employer, and regardless of which of his three hotels he was visiting, he would tour the building and the grounds and greet any employees he met, always thanking them for a job well done. However, he was intolerant of nonsense, tardiness, and sloppy work habits. He would issue one warning, and if the errant worker didn't mend his ways, Julian sent him packing.

Candles glimmered on each table, and every table had two silver ice buckets chilling bottles of Dom Pérignon. During dinner, a live orchestra played soft music as the sun went down, leaving a crescent moon in its wake. Out on the terrace, alongside the dining room, soft lights glowed from lanterns hanging from wrought iron posts. Jessica planned to stroll on the stone patio after the meal; the air would be refreshing and she could enjoy the reflections of the lights of the hotel and the moon on the lake's surface.

Rosalind, her dearest friend, seated close by, gave her the "V" for victory sign. Rosalind was better than gin and tonic any time. Jessica glanced at Julian's glass of ice cubes again. Where did he put it? He'd already drained a bottle of champagne by himself. Her stomach tightened when she heard him order another drink, and she worried that his speech at the end of the meal might need some on-the-spot editing. But she cheered herself with the thought that most of the time he really could hold his booze and rarely displayed drunken, obnoxious behavior in public. He reserved inebriated belligerence for his wife in the privacy of their home.

While the staff removed the dessert plates and served coffee with liqueur, Julian rose to thank the guests for attending and to acknowledge the community support for his project. Turning to Jessica, he thanked her for patiently listening to his plans and frustrations about the Terrace Lodge Hotel. Introducing the dignitaries at the head table, he promised that none would make a speech; this announcement bringing much laughter from everyone, including the politicians. After all, this was to be an evening of revelry and celebration, not a campaign platform. At the end of the introductions, Lincoln offered a special toast to Julian. The guests rose to clink glasses and cheered and whistled their congratulations to the man who was such a caring and generous member of their mountain town. Julian beamed with joy at the overt adulation. Lydia, teary-eyed, searched her purse for a tissue. Jessica's eyes were brimming as well, and she saw that Julian's eyes too were moist. It was a precious moment. Leaning toward him, she hugged him.

"I love you so much," she whispered. "And I'm so proud to be your wife."

As he kissed her, the crowd hollered and clapped. What a man! What a couple! What a dream!

One dance after the banquet, and Julian was off to "talk business" while Jessica entertained herself with Rosalind and Mary-Beth and with table-hopping to exchange niceties with friends who had joined their happy occasion. Once in a while, she listened to the romantic music and caught herself reminiscing about Carter and the way he used to crush her against his male hardness when they danced. She hoped Julian would return for another waltz, but he emerged from the percolating partiers only once or twice to check on her—making sure, she suspected, that she wasn't flirting. She actually cringed when any man nodded or smiled at her because of all those stories Julian had told her of unfaithful wives and how it could start with only a glance across a table—and because he had vowed to kill her if he ever caught her making eyes at another man.

At 2 AM, Julian re-appeared, his face flushed, his tie undone. "I'm tired and hot! Let's get the hell out of here!" he slurred, and he lurched slightly as he half-dragged her from the ballroom, while Rosalind and Mary-Beth shouted happily after her: "Lunch! We have to get together for lunch!"

Jessica waved goodbye to her friends and glanced with envy at the couples still swaying on the dance-floor, feeling much like a child at a carnival who hadn't been permitted to ride the carousel.

Julian plunged into the limousine while Jessica was still asking about Lydia. Shouldn't they wait for his mother?

"I sent the old bag packing at ten! Whining old bitch! Crying about Dad and how late it was getting!"

17

Jessica slid in beside him. Rarely had she ever confronted him with any of her unhappiness because she knew exactly what he'd say: "What do you have to be miserable about?" Or, "You ungrateful bitch! You should be the happiest woman in the world!" Or, "You're not upset. It's only your imagination!"

But suddenly, she wanted to risk telling him she was far from pleased. "We only danced once, Julian. And then you were off with your pals. You said such nice things about me in your speech, and then you turned around and abandoned me! I'm really hurt!"

"I don't like to dance when it's crowded. You know how hot and sweaty I get!"

"I don't think it's too much to ask for more than one dance with the man I married," she insisted. "We never have fun anymore, Julian. With you, it's nothing but work all the time!"

"Fun!" he hissed. "You want fun? At your age? My God, Jessica, grow up! You're thirty-five! The time for fun is long past! Now shut up and leave me alone!"

He hunched into his corner of the leather-upholstered vehicle while Jessica stared unseeingly out the window, a tear trickling down her camouflaged cheek. Why did her life have to end because she was thirty-five? Did wanting to have fun mean she was childish and irresponsible? She didn't want to be a little girl with gray hair and wrinkles, but she did want to be an adult with some laughter and joy in her life. Did being thirty-five, a wife and mother, mean her life was to be sober, nose-to-the-grindstone, cold, calculated, and analytical, with no sparkle or lightness of heart? Did marriage mean that her wings were clipped, and she would sit, like a budgie in its cage, watching the wild birds fly free? Did thirty-five mean waiting around for the end? The way Julian had walloped her with her age, it sounded like a death sentence with as much charm as cancer.

Keys in hand, Julian stumbled up the stone steps to the front door, which gave way without pressure--or keys. It hung slightly ajar. But he was instantly sober when he saw his dog sprawled on the foyer floor. Cuddles, his beloved toy poodle, always bounced at his arrival, and her high-pitched yelping never failed to set Jessica's teeth on edge. Now she lay lifeless on the floor at their feet, blood seeping from her nose. A note was tied to her collar. Scrawled on it, in black ink, were the words: "We'll be back!"

"My God!" yelled Julian, bounding up the stairs two at a time.

Jessica screamed for Kenneth to help, and the chauffeur, just pulling away from the curb, jerked the limo to a stop and then hobbled into the foyer as fast as his arthritic joints would allow.

Jessica scrambled after Julian, choking on her hysteria. He slammed open the door to Rob's room and struck hard against the switch. The lamplight bathed their son in a soft glow. He had his thumb in his mouth and stirred slightly, dreaming. Julian dashed to the housekeeper's room and flung open the door. Binkie was cuddled beneath her blankets, unaware of the night's mischief.

Jessica hung over the side of her son's crib, thanking God over and over that he was safe, and then stifled a scream. Rob's teddy bear was gone! Sinking to her knees, she gripped the side of the crib, whimpering in terror, muffling her sobs with one hand. She couldn't wake Rob up like this; it would alarm him. She crawled into the carpeted hallway to the staircase and huddled on the top step, hugging her knees to her heaving chest.

Julian hurled himself from Binkie's room, tearing down the stairs. Kenneth stood helplessly in the foyer, watching as Julian raced from room to room, shouting, "Goddamn those bastards! Goddamn those fucking bastards! If I get them, I'll kill them! I'll toast them in hell!"

"Mr. Bothwell, sir. Ought I call the police, sir?" offered the chauffeur. "They'd better come, sir."

Pausing in his fury, Julian knelt over the inert form of Cuddles. The little dog was still breathing. Kenneth watched sadly as his employer sobbed over the curly white bundle. With tears streaming down his face, Julian nodded. "When you've called the cops, get a vet. They can't have killed my dog, too!"

"Julian," whispered Jessica, as she knelt beside her husband, trying to comfort him, "Rob's safe. So is Binkie. Cuddles will be fine, too." She spoke of the dog with mixed emotions. She loathed cruelty to animals more than most other human failings, but she also resented the tiny poodle, which seemed to take such pleasure in peeing on her hardwood floors and carpets. Her heart broke at the creature's helplessness. And now she couldn't bear her husband's grief. She leaned over and kissed his forehead. He slipped his arm over her shoulder and together, they sobbed, tears of outrage, fear, and frustration, mingling with tears of sorrow.

All three—Julian, Jessica, and Kenneth—looked up when Binkie, at the top of the stairs, clutching her robe to her throat, called weakly, "What's happening? Has someone been murdered?"

In less than seven minutes, two patrol cars swung up the drive, sirens wailing, lights flashing. It took the officer in charge less than a minute to determine what had happened. The prowlers had gained entry, a daring chance, through the patio's French door. The lock had been jimmied.

"Once inside, it took only seconds for them to make sure the alarms weren't working," the policeman said, his gray eyes scanning the anxious faces of the victims.

Jessica couldn't resist an accusing glance at Binkie, who cowered against the wall, still clasping her robe.

"I'm sure I turned on the alarms," the poor woman sobbed. "Really I did. And I left all the lights on! Oh, it's all my fault! If only I hadn't gone to bed!"

The officer shrugged his shoulders. "They could've cut the wires to the alarms. With professionals like this, that is more than likely what they did. We'll check that out. And...if you'd been awake," he nodded at Binkie, "...any heroics, and this could have turned into a bloodbath. As it is, it's unpleasant, but everyone's alive. And..." the officer continued, "even if the detectors were on, they knew how long they'd have. If I recall the log at headquarters right, you people had two alarms about three weeks ago. Isn't that so?"

Julian hugged Jessica as she sagged against him.

"Christ!" he swore, disbelief in his voice. "That's right! They were just a few days apart. Once in the afternoon and the other about seven in the evening. Jess had the cops here, and we didn't know why the alarms had been triggered. We figured it was a short or something. The security guys checked it out. Said everything was okay."

Jessica's flesh crawled. Someone had furtively been surveying their property. Some bastard had been creeping stealthily around her yard, concealed in the bushes.

"They doubtless tripped the alarm to see how quickly we responded. They timed it and learned exactly how long it'd take us to get here. Since your property is more isolated and has so many trees hiding it from the street and your neighbors, it's an ideal target. Plus, they presumably knew about tonight's celebration. They almost certainly watched as you left and knew who'd remain in the house. More than likely, even at the Lodge, they kept an eye on you. In an upper-class neighborhood like this, it pays for them to take their time to check out a place thoroughly."

"I'll say it pays!" stormed Julian. "Christ! I'm surprised they didn't take the pool table and all the groceries! What the fuck did they do? Drive up with a moving van?"

The list of missing items was long: one stereo system plus the CD collection, three televisions with their DVD and Blu-ray players, four clock radios, the heirloom silver service, the coffee maker, the food processor, five Limoges figurines, Julian's rocker from the family room, the computer from the den, two Tiffany lamps, three fur coats and a fox jacket from the refrigerated cedar closet, and Jessica's jewelry from her dressing room. They even took Rob's beloved antique rocking horse.

Jessica shuddered to think that someone had been tiptoeing through her home, prying into her possessions and rummaging through her dressers. Julian's closet had been ransacked; all carried out in silence! Binkie hadn't heard a thing! Someone had violated Jessica's privacy. People she didn't even know, people who didn't give a sweet continental about her or her family, had defiled her home! A sadistic criminal had lifted Rob's teddy bear from his crib. It had reappeared in Jessica's dressing room, but nevertheless, it was an audacious and sadistic prank. Someone had spied on her son and had watched him as he slept. Had the intruders considered kidnapping the child? Her stomach heaved at the thought.

"We'll dust for prints, Mr. Bothwell," the officer said, "but considering the professionalism and boldness of this job, I'd guess it'll be futile. Did you have your things serial numbered or ID'd?"

Julian's angry rumble supported his answer. "What in fuck's name do we have to do? Chain things down? Bolt them to tables like we do in hotels? Of course I didn't do that! Why should we have to? This is supposed to be a free country, for Christ's sake! I guess it is! For those who just come in and take things! I'm having this whole place re-wired! I want it wired for sound, for smell, for houseflies! I'll have the goddamned place wired for mind-reading!"

⁂

The morning sun winked through the trees surrounding the pool and patio. Julian was hunched over the table under the umbrella. He was not happy.

"Listen, Jess, you have to take shooting lessons! I don't give a damn what you say! It's either that, or I hire an armed guard to march around this place day and night! And you'd better get to like Dobermans because I'll have them all over the lawn!"

Jessica quickly calculated how long it would take a Doberman to devour Cuddles for lunch. Recovering from a serious concussion, the white poodle was curled on Julian's lap, casting baleful glances at her mistress.

"But I hate guns!" she pleaded. "I'm terrified of them! I hate killing! I can't even stand it when you're out hunting!" Scowling and determined, she hugged her terry cloth robe more tightly as she slid further down into her chair.

"Jessica, please...just consider it. With me gone on trips

a lot..."

"I can't handle a bow and arrow," she protested. "I'm not even good at swatting flies! How in the name of God am I supposed to fire a bloody gun! I couldn't kill anything if my life depended on it!"

"What about Rob's life, Jess? Do you give a damn about him? Those guys could have taken him the other night! You have to face facts, darling. It could have been more of a disaster than it was. What if you and Rob were here alone, and someone tried to pull that shit?"

A cold finger touched her heart. Yes! If Rob's life hung in the balance, she would defend him fearlessly. She could tear someone apart if Rob's life were at stake. If someone threatened her family, she could fire a gun!

"You make the arrangements," she stated flatly.

⁂

The shop was musty. Antique glass and wooden cases lined with red velvet displayed a formidable array of handguns. There was enough firepower in the cases alone to stage a revolution in Riverbend. Jessica scanned the walls. Racks of rifles lined three of them. The fourth wall, of grime-covered glass, was the storefront window with "CUSTOM GUN" gold-lettered in old English script. Glancing above the racks, she saw the trophy heads: a pair of wild sheep with their magnificent curled horns; a buffalo, which would no longer partake in a stampede; a moose glowering beneath his antlers; a snarling tiger; an elk, his fourteen-point rack the excuse for his death; a reindeer staring with sightless eyes; a lion baring its useless fangs; a doe (Bambi's mother?) with woeful brown glass eyes; a wolf, with his mournful cry silenced forever. Saddest of all, a brace of waterfowl hung together from a leather thong: a Canada goose, a mallard, a canvasback, and several others, which Jessica couldn't name. The only thing missing, she thought bitterly, was the head of the hunter, complete with his red cap.

The shop was as silent as a morgue—a hushed quiet broken only by their footfalls creaking the ancient floor boards, which were oiled planks reeking of creosote. A beaded curtain, somehow out of place, hung over a doorway at the rear of the store, separating it from the business end of the building. Through the beads emerged a hobgoblin of a man, gnarled hands supporting his hunched back and bowlegs with a lob stick cane.

Jessica gripped Julian's arm. "God!" she whispered. "This is worse than TV! Is it legal to have a place like this?"

The old shopkeeper hobbled over, squinting at them through square spectacles that clung to his purple-veined, bulbous nose. Grimy fuzz balls grew in his ears. "What can I do for you folks?" he croaked, suddenly seized by a paroxysm of coughing that left him gasping.

Perhaps he'd die before Julian could buy the gun, Jessica hoped.

"Goddamn cigarettes!" he wheezed. "Now what can I do for you?"

"We're looking for a handgun for my wife," said Julian. "Something for protection at home."

"Oh! A wee bit of security," he cackled. "There's nothing like a gun for reassurance."

"We need something that'll be the right size and weight for her, but one that packs a punch," Julian added.

"We have a beauty right here," the troll offered. "It has lots of stopping power, but the recoil ain't bad for a woman. With practice, she can stay right on target."

Jessica glanced sideways at the revolver. It was cold gray steel with as much personality as a viper. She shrank, cringing from the idea of handling an instrument of death. But deep within her, she knew she'd fire it only to scare off an intruder. She wouldn't actually point it at anyone.

"Or the lady might like this one...It's a wee bit smaller, could be a problem in the thumb area with the recoil, but with a little padding, she can practice all she wants. It's an efficient persuader. One slug would stop anyone."

"I think we'll look around first," said Julian.

One step behind him, Jessica clung to his jacket. "Can't we just leave? This place gives me the heebie-jeebies."

"We leave when we get your gun," he stated, sauntering past the cases, pausing occasionally to peer at a weapon, and then moving on. He gestured to Jessica. "Here's something I think is perfect for you. The grip is small enough for you to handle easily, and the barrel is shorter for fewer distance mistakes."

"What do you mean by that?" she asked.

"Well, the shorter the barrel and the steadier the aim, the better chance you'll have of doing some damage. With a longer barrel, if you flinch the tiniest bit, you could miss by a mile because the bullet has farther to travel down the barrel."

"Oh, that certainly makes sense to me," she observed, not understanding, and neither wanting nor even attempting to do so. "Just what I wanted: a new food processor, a coffee maker, golfing lessons, and now a bloody gun! Now can we go home?"

"Can we see this one?" Julian asked, pointing to a small revolver.

"A fine one for the lady," the old man grinned, revealing

nicotine-stained stumps of teeth. Jessica shuddered. "Perfect to keep in a drawer beside the bed."

The wrinkled gnome removed it from its case, handed it to her, and said, "Its balance is perfect. The handle's a bit smaller to fit a lady's palm. Not as much pressure in the "V" of the thumb. Trigger squeezes real nice."

She felt as though she were holding a live grenade. "Is it loaded?" she asked, wishing she could toss the ugly thing across the counter and flee.

"Nah, it ain't loaded! Try the trigger," the salesman coaxed. "This one you can fire without bullets. Some guns need bullets to work. This is perfect for practicing dry runs, just to get used to firing it. Go ahead and pull the trigger."

For its size, the revolver was heavy. The steel glinted in the dusty light. Holding it by its handle, she gingerly touched the trigger with her index finger.

"Squeeze gently," the old man urged. "Just squeeze, and you'll hear the click."

She felt the cold, hard, smooth metal. Heavy and deadly. A lethal device. Breathlessly, she squeezed the trigger. It seemed forever before she heard the click. She had triumphed, had actually pulled a trigger—something they didn't teach in aerobics class.

"Would you like to look around some more?" Julian asked. "There are a few ladies' guns that have scroll work on them. They're more feminine looking. You might feel more comfortable with something that has some decoration."

"Will they fire cloisonné bullets?" she snapped. "And will having roses and violets painted on them help my aim? I'll take the one we looked at!"

"I guess we'll take this one," Julian said, pulling a roll of bills from his pocket. "Can we register it here, or do we have to go through all that bureaucratic mumbo-jumbo like I did when I bought my gun a few years ago?"

The storekeeper shook his head. "Just sign this certificate and receipt. I'll put the serial numbers on them, give you copies, and that's it. How about lessons? Do you have a gun club or instructor?"

"I've lined up an ex-cop friend of mine," Julian answered.

"Wise move," the old man chuckled. "You sure as hell don't want to teach your wife to shoot any more than you'd give her driving lessons. Shooting's got a lot more hazards!"

He tucked the revolver back in its case, placed it in a red velvet bag, and drew the strings shut. Jessica was the proud owner of a Smith and Wesson, .38 snub-nosed revolver. It wasn't quite the same feeling walking out with a gun as she would have felt had she just purchased a brand new Mustang GT.

⁂

Confronted by the man's bulk, Jessica trembled. She looked up as Julian introduced Casey Corbett and marveled that he'd once been the best detective in the biggest city in the state. He had moved to Riverbend, he said, "To get away from the shit of the big city where all you do is exist!" What he wanted now was peace and quiet, time to watch the grass grow, and to see the changing seasons in the mountains surrounding Riverbend.

Jessica held him in awe. She was one of that rare breed of early twenty-first century American women who admired police officers and silently congratulated them for the job they did. She couldn't believe that he was going to teach her how to shoot! She wouldn't have been more impressed if Chevy Chase had driven up and offered to give her acting lessons.

Beneath a soft sheen of blondish gray hair, Casey Corbett was great looking in a hard, commando sort of way. But Casey's eyes told the story. They were pools of slate, nothing registering in them as he scowled down at her. She found no life, no humor in those eyes. Perhaps they had witnessed too much evil, too much hate in humanity. Jessica was scared. Casey intimidated her, and she was terrified of the weapon she was about to fire.

The whole thing was bizarre. She didn't belong here. She belonged at home knitting and sewing and baking cookies and playing with Rob. Then she remembered she hated knitting, never sewed, and despised baking.

Leaving her in Casey's care, Julian waved and left for his hotels.

"So what's the idea here, Jessica?" Casey queried. "My pal, Julian, says you want to learn to fire a gun."

"Well, that was Julian's idea," she offered. "All I want to do is protect my son and me. I guess he told you about the fracas at our place last week."

He nodded. Didn't he ever smile?

"Well," she stumbled on, trying not to trip over her words, "all I really want is to know what to do with a gun in case someone breaks in when I'm home alone. I don't want to hurt anyone. I just want to look as if I know what I'm doing."

"You're wasting your time, my time, and Julian's money if that's all you want," Casey grumbled. "Just take this thing home and practice in your kitchen. Pretend it's a frying pan if you want. Get to know how it feels in your hand and bury it in your dresser drawer. Then if someone breaks in, you can look like you know what you're doing. But I'll tell you this!" He peered into her startled eyes. "You'll end up dead!"

She was stunned. Her game plan had crashed and burned.

"Look," he said, "it's like this: There are no nice rules when it comes to protecting yourself. You're not going up against Santa Claus who's breaking into your house. You either want to learn to shoot to stop, or you want to learn how to crochet!"

"All I want to do is disable the guy!" she snapped. "Show me how to shoot this goddamned thing so I can hit his knee or shoot his hand off! Anything to get him out of my home!"

"You actually believe that if you splinter his kneecap or take a hand off, he'll leave?" He laughed. "You watch too much TV, woman! The guy'll kill you!"

Jessica cursed Julian in her mind. Why hadn't he told the ex-cop why she was there? She wasn't enrolled in Martha Stewart's cooking school, but she didn't want murder lessons either!

He softened at her look of dismay. "Look, Jessica, let's go and have a cup of coffee and discuss this. I think you need a lesson or two in toughening up before we tackle this shooting thing."

He led her to a snack shop tucked into a corner of the range. Windows along one side offered a view of the firing area. The walls were sound proofed. They were alone. She sipped her coffee and lit a cigarette. Tension held her in its icy grip. Casey Corbett lounged back in his chair, puffed on his cigarette, and squinted at her through the smoke. Feeling as if he was studying her soul, she squirmed slightly and tapped the ash from her cigarette, not knowing what to do or where to look. Casey leaned forward, his arms on the table, directing his gray eyes at her.

"I'll tell you something, sweetheart, that may change your mind about shooting to stop. In one of the last cases I had, a young guy held up a liquor store. The old lady behind the counter had a real gun. She didn't know the thing he had was only a toy. She gave him her cash, but as he ran from the store, she fired at him. Knocked him flat. Didn't kill him, or really disable him because she got him in the leg. She rushed to see—at least this is how we figured it from the surveillance camera they had in the place—about getting her money back. He grabbed the gun and blew her brains all over the place. Messiest goddamn thing I ever saw. Her husband told us later neither of them knew much about guns, but they kept it as a deterrent in case they were robbed. Now the kid's doing time for robbery... and *murder!*"

Jessica stared at Casey, her eyes round with horror.

"D'ya want to know how much he got away with?" Casey barked.

"Fifty-nine lousy bucks! She shot him to get her fifty-nine bucks back, and now she's dead!"

"Holy shit!" Jessica swore. "This is serious stuff!"

"You bet it is! With guns, there's no fooling around!" He leaned closer over the table. "See, Jessica, it's like this: The public thinks we cops shoot to kill. Not so. We're trained to shoot to stop criminals. Unfortunately, sometimes a bullet does kill someone. But it's not intentional. And, sad to say, we do have some renegade cops who didn't learn about the shooting to stop part. I won't teach you to murder someone. All you'll learn is how to stop someone who's out to harm you or your kid."

She trembled and gazed down.

"It's a mean old world out there, Jessica. You read about it, see it on TV. But not until it's under your nose, right in your own backyard, your own home, do you really believe it! Christ, woman! Your house was robbed! How close must it come before you realize this isn't tiddlywinks?"

"Okay," she sighed. He sounded sincere, as if he really cared.

31

"I'll learn to shoot this damn thing. Where do I start?"

He grinned at her, his eyes sparkling. "With that little number in your handbag," he said.

⁂

A deep breath. Hold it. Arm steady. Be calm. Squeeze the trigger. Keep squeezing. Pull twice. Click, click! Jessica exhaled happily. She repeated the process while relaxing in her deck chair in the sunshine beside the pool. Click, click!

"Jesus, Jess!" Julian exploded, as he tried to enjoy his morning coffee and read his *Wall Street Journal.* "You're driving me nuts with that goddamned clicking!"

"You're the one who wanted me to take shooting lessons!" she argued back. "I'm just practicing my dry runs! Casey told me to do this for two weeks, so I won't flinch when I pull the trigger! Then I can fire real bullets."

"You haven't flinched once since you started pulling that trigger, Annie Oakley! Go tell Corbett you've passed with flying colors!"

"Look, Julian, he's a pro. The best of the best. I'm going to do this right, even if I have to practice dry firing in my sleep! Rob's life and mine might depend on my ability to shoot. You learned how to do it, didn't you? You know what's involved!"

"We sure as hell didn't go click, click, clicking all over the place! We practiced at the range or in the bush!" Julian grumbled, sipping coffee and turning to the financial page of his newspaper.

"Where did you meet Casey, anyway?" she asked. "You never mentioned him until the subject of shooting lessons came up."

Julian thought a moment. "Think I met him a few years back

when he was in town for a pit-stop. The city and his job were getting to him. I met him in the Mayfield bar, and we chatted. Anyway, we continued to keep in touch whenever he was in town, and now he lives here."

"He seems like a good guy, a good teacher. I already know how to sight a gun. I didn't know I was to line up my finger with something to get used to the idea of sighting." She didn't mention she'd been practicing on Cuddles.

"Well, you'll be getting into some fun stuff later. But I hope when you start firing live ammo you won't hang a target in our back yard."

"I thought one in the family room would be perfect," she laughed, winking at him.

He softened, grinning. "You're really something, Jess. Go ahead and drive me nuts. But don't bring that thing into our bed. You can drive me crazy in bed, but not with that god-damned pistol."

She left her deck chair and strolled toward him. Running her fingers through his hair, she kissed him.

"Did I tell you today I love you?" she murmured, nibbling his ear.

He caught her hand and kissed it. "Not so far, but it's nice to hear."

"Anything special on your agenda today?" she asked. "I was hoping we could do something."

"Not today, Princess," he said. "I'm meeting the guys from Japan, trying to work out a mutual tourist deal. Big bucks involved. I might even have to go to Japan next week to meet with some high-level officials."

"You spend more time in Japan than you do here," she complained. "Rob and I never see you. I feel like I'm married to a phantom." She sat down facing him. "I love you. I adore our life...we have such a lovely home...but I miss you. Don't you understand that?" She blinked back tears.

"Jessica, we've been over this before," he groaned, irritated. "Hotels are my life. You and Rob are the delicious icing on the cake. Without the cake, I wouldn't have either of you. I'd have absolutely nothing. You know the hotels and the tourist industry are what pay the bills so we can afford this lifestyle. Be patient, sweetheart. There will be a time when I won't have to work this hard."

"I know, darling," she sighed. "I only wanted to tell you how I feel. Couldn't we have something special...just for us? How about dinner tonight? Maybe I can arrange a really great dessert...me! Done up in strawberries and whipped cream! We haven't really seen each other since that awful break-in. I'd love to fulfill your wildest fantasy tonight...if you have the time."

"I'll make time," he smiled. "I can't promise dinner, but I'll be home early. You make yourself beautiful, and I'll do the rest." Getting up, he bent over and kissed her. "I promise, darling. I'll be home early, and I'll do a number on you that you'll never forget. You'll be walking funny for a week after I'm through with you."

"Promise?" She looked up at him, searching his face.

"For absolutely sure."

His kiss was warm and hungry, his tongue seeking. She responded, her whole body yielding to his touch.

God! She wished it would be true! How she hoped it would be true!

⁂

After his limousine pulled away, she gazed around the sumptuous foyer of their home. Gray marble imported from Italy graced the walls, the floor, and the staircase. Paintings adorned the walls with mirrors reflecting light from the stained glass windows on both sides of the entrance. It looked like a palace. Suspended from the ceiling, a huge, hand-cut crystal chandelier sparkled and shimmered.

Luxury living was a delight, but Jessica found it barren without the man she loved. Something was wrong. She felt she was in freefall from a plane, and the parachute wouldn't open. But then...she did have a lively imagination.

How to spend the day? Perhaps call Rosalind for lunch. Possibly check out the firing-range, familiarize herself with it. Maybe she could meet Casey there and fire a round or two if he was confident in her ability to dry fire. Binkie could care for Rob; she was coming to clean anyway.

Casey's recorded message said he'd return any calls. Faintly disappointed, she phoned Rosalind who said she'd love to meet for lunch. How about the Wharf? A terrific setting for a luncheon. Rosalind said she'd bring Mary-Beth; the poor darling needed support in her recent separation and pending divorce. Jessica hung up. Great! Just what she needed, a sobbing friend. Well, she knew Mary-Beth had tried. It was too bad her husband had had lovers on the side, and certainly too bad they'd been men! Mary-Beth could have contracted HIV for God's sake! What a mess! And she, Jessica, hadn't suspected a thing! Wonder what else I'm missing out on, she pondered as she climbed the stairs to her dressing room to change for lunch.

☆☆

The Wharf, which was situated on the bank of the river, was crowded, but they didn't mind waiting in the lounge. The maître d' would call them as soon as their table was ready.

Mary-Beth looked as if she had been hit by a mallet, dragged through a trench, and then had her ash-blonde hair styled by an airplane propeller. Leading the way to a corner table, Rosalind ordered a straight double scotch for their ailing friend. Jessica sipped her soda and lime and Rosalind tossed back her martini, then ordered another.

Leaning across the table, Jessica gripped Mary-Beth's hand.

"I'm really sorry about what's happening to you," she sympathized. "Is there anything I can do?"

"Can you kill him for me?" Mary-Beth sobbed. "You're taking shooting lessons. You can do it!"

"I'm not exactly into Murder Incorporated. Maybe we can come up with some more positive alternatives."

"If I had the money, I'd hire an assassin! Honest to God I would!" wept their stricken friend. "I'd like him to die slowly and painfully! I want him to suffer! That's what I'm doing! Oh, Jess! I loved him so much! We had such a good life! Why couldn't I hold him? What's wrong with me? Maybe I'm not enough of a woman! Maybe if I'd been a better lover, he'd never have done what he did! Oh, God! This hurts so much!" She sniffled and dabbed at her eyes with a tissue.

"First things first, Mary-Beth," soothed Jessica. "Have you had an HIV test?"

Her friend nodded. "But the tests take forever! I could be dying right now and not even know it!"

"I think killing's too good for the bastard!" said Rosalind in a stage whisper that could be heard across the lounge. A few heads turned to stare at the threesome.

Jessica was aware of the eavesdroppers. "Keep it down, Rosalind, for God's sake! You too, Mary-Beth. We need to talk about this stuff, but we'll be arrested for conspiracy to commit murder if we're not careful!"

Rosalind was insistent, but she lowered her voice to a soft hiss. "I pray to God he doesn't have AIDS, but I think Ebola would be a nice touch. Maybe leprosy. Is there any way we can contaminate him?"

"Let's get practical here," Jessica demanded, losing patience. "We can sit here all day and discuss ways to seek revenge, but that's not going to help Mary-Beth one bit!"

The poor woman downed her scotch and begged another from a passing waiter. In a few minutes, Mary-Beth was going to be beyond all reason or help.

"I hate him so much! How dare he treat me like a piece of shit! I wish I could hurt him the way he's hurt me!"

Jessica reached over and grasped Mary-Beth's hand. "The best revenge of all, Mary-Beth, is to live well. You have to look after yourself! And remember, loose lips sink ships. Wars have been lost because someone blabbed, and the wrong people got hold of the information. Right now you're really hurting, and we're here for you, but keep a button on your lip!"

Mary-Beth stared across the table, and Jessica could tell her words hadn't registered, but Rosalind arched an eyebrow and studied her quizzically.

"Where on earth do you get those ideas?" Rosalind asked. "Are you planning something I should know about?"

Allowing a smile to play across her lips, Jessica swirled her drink with a straw. "I never divulge my trade secrets. Besides I'm thinking about nothing more than showing Julian a good time tonight, my dear."

It was their shortest luncheon on record. Halfway through her third double scotch, Mary-Beth gagged and threw up. The Wharf staff were understanding and helpful as they cleaned up the mess, and the maître d' even carried Mary-Beth to Rosalind's Corvette where she whimpered and drooled and passed out on the front seat. Rosalind tucked a borrowed tablecloth around her. "I'll wash the cloth and return it," she called after the maître d' as he hurried off.

"Don't bother," he replied over his shoulder. "Keep it!"

"Well, I guess we're off the social register at the Wharf," sighed Jessica. "Too bad. I really liked it here. Will you be all right driving her home?"

"I will be if she doesn't throw up again. If she does, I'll drown her husband in my pool!"

"I'll follow you, okay?" Jessica suggested.

"Just as far as the turnoff to my place. I'm taking her home with me. She needs some TLC, and Harry and I can look after her for a day or two."

Tossing her mane of naturally curly auburn hair over her shoulder, Rosalind climbed into her car, and careened off the parking lot. Jiminy! thought Jessica, we women sure allow funny things to happen to our heads when we give our hearts to men. For some of us, being in love isn't "happily ever after". It's agony!

※

It was two o'clock when Jessica found Binkie busy cleaning the kitchen windows while Rob napped. Checking her phone messages, she was pleased to see Casey had returned her call. She dialed him back.

"Hi, it's Jessica calling."

"Yeah?" His voice was gruff.

"I have a few free hours this afternoon, and I was wondering if we could meet at the range. Just to kind of see how I'm doing."

"It hasn't been quite a week. Got your dry firing down pat?"

"Sure do!" she replied, smiling to herself.

"How's your sighting?"

"Pretty good, I think. But I won't really know that until I use real bullets, will I?"

"For someone who didn't want to do this, you're turning into an enthusiastic pupil." He sounded skeptical.

"Well, I really hate to admit it, but this is kind of fun...and... if I use live ammunition today and get within ten feet of the target, then I can surprise Julian."

"How does three o'clock sound?"

"I'll be there!" she laughed. She couldn't wait to get to the range. She'd surprise the hell out of everyone.

Scampering up the stairs to change, she stole into Rob's room to peek at him as he slumbered, one arm thrown over his teddy bear.

"Sleep tight, Pumpkin," she whispered as she touched his cheek and stroked his blond curls. "I love you."

Off with her dress and into her jeans. Yanking an old sweater from her drawer, she pulled it on. Hair tied back with a ribbon, she was off, her Smith and Wesson in her large leather bag. She flew down the stairway and into her old Fifth Avenue. It was a great car. Fast! Sometimes too fast. She had the speeding tickets to prove it! Cranking up the stereo, she blared her way to the range, thumping one hand on the steering wheel in time to the music. It was a great day! Great to be alive! She was going to be a success at the range, and she would surely get laid that night by the best lover in the world! What more could a rich young woman want?

Casey was waiting at the range when she screeched to a halt beside his car, kicking up a spray of dust and gravel in the parking lot.

"Christ!" he swore. "If you shoot like you drive, you're a goddamned hazard!"

"Didn't want to keep you waiting." She flashed a bright smile at him.

They walked to the firing line, and she reached into her bag and lifted out the revolver. She gripped it in one hand, supporting it with the other, arms straight out in front of her. Just the way he had shown her.

"Not bad," he said with no enthusiasm.

"I practiced in front of the mirror. Drew a bead on myself."

"Well, let's fire a few rounds to get you used to the recoil. It shouldn't be too bad with your thirty-eight." He showed her where to stand on the firing line, pointing out that she had the lane to herself and to never use anyone else's target. "Safety is your first concern here. Remember that! Always check to make sure that no one's in your line of fire, and always keep your eyes on what's going on around you. That means in every direction. Don't ever fire without your ear protectors, and here...use these goggles."

"Will I have time for ear muffs and goggles if I'm being robbed?"

"Right, Jessica! Here! Use them! Where's the ammo?"

Her magical bag produced a whole box of shiny new shells.

"Let's see you load."

Releasing the cylinder, she fumbled six shells into the mechanism. Loading was not something she had practiced a whole lot. Closing the cylinder with a soft click, she maneuvered the goggles over her eyes. Then she donned the ear muffs.

"Don't worry about the target," Casey cautioned. "Concentrate on the firing."

She lined herself up, back straight, shoulders taut, left hand supporting, right index finger on the trigger, left eye sighting. She saw the target—an outline of the upper body, the "x" area, the place where a bullet would stop an intruder. Slowly now. Her finger gently squeezed the trigger. Gentle but firm. Steady. Keep pulling. She braced herself for the split second it would take the gun to fire. BAM! She felt the jolt, but didn't waiver. Turning her head, she looked at her instructor. He nodded. No smile, no sign of success. She lined herself up again. BAM! BAM! Six rounds.

She took off her equipment. "Well? How'd I do" Was it okay? Do I pass?" she gasped.

"Holy shit!" he yelled. "Where'd you learn to shoot like that? You're a natural, Jessica! A natural!"

"Maybe I was a hit man in my last life," she laughed. "Can I fire another six, and then really try for the target?"

The six bullets exploded from the thirty-eight, with Jessica holding steady on all of them. Now for the target. No fooling around. Concentrate on the target! Aim right for the middle of the "x" area. The guts. She stood so still it looked like the target was moving. Only a trick of the imagination. Steady on the target. BAM! Five more rounds burst from the revolver. Her arms ached. Stepping back from the firing line, she saw that Casey was already reeling in the target. Closer it came. She didn't want to look. What if she'd missed with every shot?

"I don't believe this!" he hollered. "You're dead on with all of 'em. Eighteen shots! Looks like you hit the target every time!

Some in the chest, some in the gut! One bullet shot the guy's balls off!"

"Yahoo!" she yelled. "I did it! I did it! I knew I could do it! Thanks, Casey!"

She jumped and grabbed him around his thick neck, kissing his cheeks. "You're the best teacher anyone could ever have!"

"Hey, lady, wait! I haven't taught you everything yet! This is just a beginning! But what a start!"

"Can I buy you a Coke to celebrate?"

"Great idea! But first pick up the casings...that's a rule!"

"Can I keep the target? I want to show Julian. He won't believe it when he sees this. I'll keep the casings for souvenirs. Maybe have them melted down for a paperweight when I get enough. My first shots! I'm impressed!"

Taking their Cokes out to the parking lot, they stood in the late afternoon sun, leaning against Casey's car.

"Okay, Jessica, we start on Monday at 9:00 AM. We do the left hand shots first...until you do that easily. So practice dry firing with your left hand. Then we do the kneeling positions, the crouch, and the flat-on-your-belly routine. All with either hand. Then we do it all over again with obstructions. You have to be prepared for anything...anything!"

"We're going to do all that on Monday?" She was shocked. She might be off to a good start, but that was expecting too much.

"No!" he laughed. "We'll do what we can on Monday. Then we'll go from there. It's going to take a while before we get all the positions. But maybe we can discuss setting up a schedule of sorts on Monday."

Sipping her drink, she watched as he dragged on his cigarette. What a tough guy. Just the sight of him, his bulk, his stance, his no-nonsense scowl would stop a culprit in his tracks. But she had seen him laugh. He did have a heart.

"Julian tells me you met when you stayed at the hotel," she ventured, brushing a wisp of hair back from her forehead. She wanted to know more about him.

"Yeah...he's right about that, but I knew who he was before..."

"Oh?"

"Long time ago...I'd just finished high school and came to Riverbend to work for the summer at his dad's first hotel. The Mayfield. Lots of big city kids did that. Extra money for college and beer. I knew who Julian was even back then, but he wouldn't remember. He was younger than I was, and we didn't hang out together at all. I was here only a few weeks. Hated being a waiter, didn't work out as a bellman. I don't score high on PR work. Went to construction after that...then onto police work. Years after I worked at the Mayfield, my kid sister worked at the Bothwells' other hotel, the Talisman, for two seasons. I guess she liked it. I never really asked her. Never had much of a chance to ask."

Something in Casey's eyes and voice alerted her not to pursue the topic. She sensed he was a very private person.

"How about you?" he asked. "What brought you to Riverbend?"

"City-life sucked me dry. No time to live—what with fighting heavy traffic all the time and endless line-ups for everything. I don't do well in crowds. I needed a place that was large enough to provide a few amenities, but small enough to get from one side to another without hiring a jet. Being in the mountains appealed to me. Then I met Julian. And now I'm taking shooting lessons. And I'd better get home. Binkie will want to leave soon."

She reached out and grabbed his hand. "Thanks, Casey! I'll

never be a killer, and I probably won't ever have to use this revolver. But I *love* shooting guns!"

Casey watched as she climbed into her car, then spun out of the lot in another cloud of dust and gravel. He puffed thoughtfully on his cigarette. A very nice lady, he contemplated. Yeah, a very interesting situation.

As he eased himself into his old gray Chevrolet, his face registered a worried frown.

Chapter Two:

The Setting of the Stage

OB DRIFTED OFF TO SLEEP AS JESSICA RUBBED HIS BACK WHILE HUMMING A TUNE. As soon as she was sure he was out for the night, she slipped off her jeans and sweater, tossed them into a hamper, and then slid into her bath, bubbles frothing about her, caressing her skin with their tiny pops. As she sipped her champagne, she pointed a toe toward the ceiling, admiring the line of her leg. Not a bad body for thirty-five. As the bath and champagne relaxed her, she thought of Julian and his delicious lovemaking. Never in her life had she been made love to as magically. The anticipation of his arrival in their bedroom made her shiver with ecstasy. Sober, he was a marvelous lover, and he'd promised to be home early. That meant he wouldn't stop for ten nightcaps. A tiny doubt whispered to her that he might forget his promise, but she dismissed the negative thought as she reminisced about how they met...

Hers was a love story many women would have died for, and if their self-esteem was a notch higher, would have killed for.

He had walked into the travel agency where Jessica worked to arrange a Caribbean Cruise for two—a three-week extravaganza with stops in the Bahamas, Jamaica, Puerto Rico, the

45

Virgin Islands, Antigua, Barbados, and Trinidad. It was a luxury cruise of the highest order, the most expensive any travel agency had to offer in that area. As Jessica played with the computer, lining up the holiday with the dates he preferred, she felt him studying her. When she glanced up to ask a question or offer a suggestion, his eyes never left hers. They were marvelous eyes, deep brown, warm, penetrating, and inviting. He was, without a doubt, easy to look at. She guessed he was slightly over six feet tall and forty-ish. His sensuous lips smiled often, revealing perfect teeth. Jessica knew that some lucky woman on the trip would be in for the time of her life.

"This is a wonderful vacation for you and your wife." She smiled into his dancing eyes. "Sounds like a second honeymoon!"

"Actually," he replied, "I'm taking my mother on a holiday to celebrate her sixty-fifth birthday."

"Lucky mother!" Jessica beamed, convinced he must be divorced or, at the very least, separated. Perhaps gay.

"Maybe when I get back, I'll take you on a cruise," he laughed.

"Only if it's to Hawaii." She handed him his itinerary. "Your tickets will be ready in a day or two, Mr. Bothwell, or we can phone you."

"I'll probably have them picked up as I may be out of town. Thanks for your help and advice."

Then he was gone.

"Do you know who that was?" asked the agency owner when Julian disappeared.

"No. Should I? I mean...I wish I did! I've never seen a man quite like him. He's enough to make me give up celibacy as a way of life."

"He owns the two biggest hotels in town—the Talisman and the Mayfield."

"No kidding! And he's taking his mother? Not a wife?"

"That's the picture, Jessica."

"I don't think I will turn my body over to science when I die," she mused. Then she forgot him.

"Letter here for you," the agency owner said two months later, handing Jessica a heavy parchment envelope bearing the seal of the Hyatt Regency Hotel, Trinidad. She watched as Jessica slit the envelope. "Maybe it's from your admirer."

"Who on earth would that be?" wondered Jessica.

Enclosed were three postcards, all with the same message:

Having a wonderful time. Wish you were here.

Signed, Julian Bothwell

"I'll just die if he shows up here!" uttered Jessica. "I can't believe this!"

"Neither can I," commented the older woman, who was pushing sixty and attempting to look thirty. "You young chicks have all the luck. The last time a client hit on me, he was eighty-one, poor, and using his life savings to take him back to Iceland to see his homeland before he died. He asked me to wait for him, but he never re-appeared, thank God. Perhaps he passed away."

Two weeks later, Jessica's office phone rang, and a woman asked her to please hold the line for a call from Mr. Bothwell.

"Hello? Jessica Foley? This is Julian Bothwell. In case you don't remember me, I'm the one who booked that three-week Caribbean cruise. I sent you some postcards."

"Of course, I remember you." She smiled into the receiver. "Thank you for the cards. That was very thoughtful."

"How about dinner tonight?"

He certainly didn't waste time, she thought, wondering what to wear. She'd have to go shopping after work. A nice little black dress would be perfect. She'd wear her gorgeous crystal watch with the matching earrings.

"I'm not sure about this evening," she replied. It would not do to appear overly anxious. "I do have another engagement. May I take a rain check?"

"Is there any way you can break it? I'm leaving for Germany for two weeks in the morning."

"Well...this person is a good enough friend. I'm sure he'll understand."

"That'd be great. May I have your address? I'll pick you up at nine, and we can have a late dinner at the Diplomat if that suits you."

"It's one of my favorite places. I love their piano bar."

"Address," he reminded her.

"Oh, that'd be helpful," she laughed. "905 Bradmore. Apartment One."

Hanging up, she sat with her head in her hands, unable to believe his call. Her mind, her heart, and her hormones all vied for first place. Steady, she reminded herself; this guy might be after only one thing. She'd been wrong in affairs of the heart before, and she'd lost badly. She couldn't bear another relationship that ended in heartbreak. Time for a reality check, Jessica, she reminded herself; all he asked was to take you to dinner.

At nine sharp, her doorbell rang. Grabbing her evening bag and tossing her shawl over her shoulder, she opened the door and faced a complete stranger. Was he canvassing the neighborhood for charity?

"Are you Miss Foley?" the elderly man asked, and she nodded.

"Mr. Bothwell is waiting in the limo for you."

She looked past him to the street. Sure enough, a silver limousine was at the curb.

"I'm so sorry," she apologized. "I'm just not used to luxury."

"That's okay, ma'am," he replied graciously. "Mr. Bothwell does like to do things in style."

He took her arm, escorted her down the steps, and held the limo door open as she slipped into its lush leather depths. Julian smiled at her.

"I'm glad you could make it."

The limousine whispered onto the street and wound its way through light traffic. Offering her a drink from the bar, Julian expertly poured a scotch-on-the-rocks for himself and a Perrier for her.

"You don't drink?" he asked.

"Of course I do," she replied. "But not with strangers. Once I get to know you better, I may let my hair down and indulge in something stronger than water."

The car pulled up at the Diplomat, a stately old building, which in the thirties and forties was a country retreat for the wealthy from the city that was 250 miles from Riverbend. The inn had gradually fallen into a sad state of neglect and had been ready for the wrecking ball when a visionary purchased it and turned it into a fine dining and entertainment center. It still had a few luxury suites for those who could afford them. Painted white, the building boasted a porch with mighty pillars. The window frames, shutters, and roofing were black. The double entry doors were crimson red, which added a delicious touch of panache.

Inside, two crystal chandeliers shimmered in the gloom, illuminating the ebony-walled entry foyer. Paintings of wildflowers in gilded frames adorned the walls. Brass candelabra, set between the pictures, added to the luxurious ambiance, and music tinkled softly from the piano bar.

The maître d' welcomed them. "Mr. Bothwell, sir, it's good to see you. Your suite is ready, so we need only to know what time you'd like to dine. Allow me to show you the way."

He led them past the first dining room where guests conversed in hushed tones. It was a place that welcomed romance and intrigue. Jessica was disappointed that they didn't stop at the piano bar with its delightful music. The second dining room had a live orchestra, which played lusciously romantic tunes, and she had been looking forward to dancing with this handsome, virile man. Perhaps they would start their date in the lounge in front of the roaring fireplace.

Down the hall, they followed the maître d' up a few stairs, around a corner, down another corridor. Their leader paused at a doorway recessed into the wall, and then stood aside as Julian ushered her into the room. She stepped gingerly over the threshold and looked around, not believing her eyes at the sight which met them: a huge sofa, plush lounge chairs, dim lamps, a full bar, a table set for two with candles flickering on a snowy white cloth, silver goblets, crystal glasses, Dom Pérignon chilling in an ice bucket, and a king-sized bed partially hidden in an alcove. A boudoir for two. Blatant seduction, if she read it right.

"Let me know when you'd like to dine, sir," the maître d' reminded Julian. "May I prepare a cocktail for you?"

"No, no, I'll do that. Dinner right away will be all right for me. I'm really very hungry. Chateaubriand for two will be great. How do you like your filet cooked, Jessica?"

"Medium rare will be fine," she answered, wondering how she was going to escape intact from this compromising situation. She pictured the indelicate persuasion. "Just remove your clothes, please, then I'll have my way with you, and you can go home because I have to catch a plane in the morning." That had to be the price for all this.

As the maître d' disappeared, she eyed a lounge chair with room for only one on it, but she remained standing, unsure what to do. Should she just rip off her clothes or run like hell?

Julian sensed her discomfort. "Sit down, Jessica," he suggested. "Why not get relaxed? Let me fix you a drink. Now that you know me better, I can make you something stronger than Perrier over ice."

"A martini would be nice," she said, as she curled into the chair, crossing her legs. He'd have a tough time prying them apart. "Maybe throw in a Valium or two instead of olives."

He was silent a moment, then laughed, turning his head to look at her. "Are you unhappy you came here tonight?"

"Not unhappy. Slightly unnerved is more accurate. I wasn't expecting anything like this. I mean...the bed and all...it could lead me to misunderstand your intentions."

"Yes, I can see that it could, but let me assure you. I like privacy at times, and I wanted some privacy with you this evening. You intrigued me from the moment I saw you, and I'd like us to find out a little bit about each other."

He handed her a generous martini and settled himself on the sofa so that he was facing her. She wanted to slosh the drink back to quiet her heart, which was thumping its way out of her chest. God! The guy was handsome. Dark complexion, tall, long-lashed brown eyes, wavy brown hair that looked like he'd just had it styled, and a smile so attractive it could charm the stripes off a tiger. And he wasn't married. He had taken his mother on a cruise!

Was there something wrong with him? There had to be. If

he was attracted to her, something had to be awry. She, in her past, had always managed to link up with the losers: the men who were Peter Pan; the ones who drank too much; some who gambled away all their money; men who weren't there for her emotionally or who tried to control her, own her, and bleed her dry. She always ended up hurt, damaged, and scarred. The only one who had seemed to have his act together was Carter. But he had returned to his ex-wife while Jessica died a thousand deaths.

And now here she was with Julian.

She was really going to take a reading on him. She wasn't going to wear her heart on her sleeve this time. This man wasn't going to use her and dump her, no matter how brilliant his mind was, how kind he was to his mother, how good-looking he was, how wealthy and successful he was, or how talented or acrobatic he may be in bed. She wanted to know about his past, check his credentials and, if need be, ask for letters of reference.

"So...tell me about you," Julian said, lounging on the sofa. "How long have you lived in Riverbend? How do you like your work? Are you making a career in the travel industry? Are you currently involved with anyone? Ever been married? If so, do you have children? Do you like children? Do you like animals? What do you think about our environmental problems? What are your views on the world's economy? What's your education? Do you have any hobbies? Do you put out on first dates? And, if I asked you, would you let me make mad passionate love to you?"

She was stunned. She was supposed to be the one asking the questions. She laughed.

"Those were the questions I was going to ask you...all except the last two. And I can answer both of those with 'absolutely no'!"

"And why not?" he queried, sipping his scotch and looking directly into her eyes.

This was a time for truth. No more hedging and pretending her thoughts, beliefs, and feelings didn't count. "Several reasons, actually. First of all, I believe that sex between two people should be an act of deep sharing and caring, and one doesn't really have that on a first date. Secondly, there are some pretty nasty diseases out there. And last...I'm not really into sex that much. I'm looking for emotional security and stability in a relationship, which only comes through time and knowing the person you're with. And I don't believe in sex as a form of enter-tainment or recreation. I believe it's an act of commitment and love and should be special and sacred for both people. I've also come to the conclusion that women need a reason to make love. Men just need a place."

"Interesting," he observed, as he tossed back his drink, rising to pour another. "How's your martini? Ready for a freshen-ing up?"

"Yes, please, but much lighter this time. And how about you, Julian? Tell me something about yourself."

"I will...in time. Right now, we're discussing you."

She sipped thoughtfully, seeking the proper words. "Well, I moved here a little over a year ago from Boston. I like smaller places rather than urban nightmares, and I love the mountains, so Riverbend is perfect for me...I'm very happy here.

"Besides leaving the city, I jettisoned my electronic devices for keeping in touch with half the world's population. I aban-doned Face book, texting, tweeting and twittering. I just grew weary from being distracted by the incessant interference and being available 24/7. I do, however, have a plain ordinary cell phone for my personal use in emergencies, especially for mountain driving, and I kept my PC. Some people might consider me odd for having gone off the digital grid, but at least my personal life is not in chaos. I treasure the peace of mind I have now. With the Internet, and all our seemingly miraculous electronic gadgets and widgets, we're all wired for sound, with no real connection to others. So I just unplugged myself, and have never been happier. I keep in touch with my friends and sister by phone or e-mail."

"Hmm," Julian responded, leveling his eyes at her. "I find that especially interesting. Please continue."

God, she thought, I feel like I'm giving him my resume for a job.

"I really enjoy my work, and right now, it's my career. I've never been married, but I've had a few close calls. I've never really thought about having children...haven't seriously considered it.

"I adore animals, and I loathe any form of animal abuse. Hunting as a sport is despicable to me, and I wouldn't eat wild meat unless I was on the point of starvation. As a matter of fact, I don't think hunting is a sport at all. If I were asked what I consider sport, I'd have to say there should be an evening up. The hunter would have to leave his rifle and clothes in camp, take only a hunting knife, and then go looking for a cougar. That'd be sport for me...when the stakes are even. My God! It disgusts me the way men go into the bush armed with camouflaged combat gear, complete with night vision equipment, just to bring down a moose, or elk, or deer. That isn't sport! It's murder!"

He was nodding, tight-mouthed at her remarks. "You certainly have strong views on that topic! Well, I'm one of those murderers you're talking about. I like going into the bush and bringing out the very animals you mentioned. For me, there's nothing better than venison. And the way I hunt is probably more humane than what happens to cattle in feed-lots and slaughter houses."

"I'm not very informed on that subject. Actually, I prefer not to be because the knowledge would probably be unbearable."

"And yet you eat steak? Filet mignon?"

She was caught for the hypocrite she was. "Yes, and I feel guilty about each delicious bite."

"So what's your education? Do you have any hobbies?"

"University degree in Education, but teaching is a very dangerous, stressful profession right now, so I switched careers when I came here. My hobbies are people...my friends. I love to read, go to movies, listen to music. Cooking is not my forte, and I don't sew, knit, or crochet. I love riding horses and do that often. I like short hikes, but not long overnight hauls into the bush. Canoeing is fun. And I've taken men off my list of things to do."

"Really?" He seemed surprised. "Any special reason?"

"No reason other than I took stock of myself and came to the conclusion that I had thrown so much of myself into my relationships with men that I had nothing left for myself. So I live quietly alone and enjoy my girlfriends. I have a few male friends as well, but they are just friends...nothing more. So there, you have my credentials.

"Now, about you, Julian. I already know that you own two hotels in town, and that you're a good son to your mother, and that you're absolutely divine looking. But you could be a serial killer under your handsome, charming veneer. You could have a wife secreted somewhere and are just playing cat and mouse with me."

As she spoke, he listened carefully to her every word, studying her expressive face, and the way her blonde hair glistened as
it fell against her neck. He laughed at her last sentence.

"For sure, I'm not married! Never have been. I'm much
too busy for deep entanglements. And yes, I own the hotels.
Actually, my father built and owned them until he died seven
years ago. Right now I'm busy with plans to open a resort on
the shores of Emerald Lake, which was a dream my father
always had. So I'm following through for him."

"What about your mother? Does she live with you?"

"No, she doesn't. After Dad died, she gave the house to me.
She didn't like rattling around in that big place by herself, so
she moved into a condo in town. She and I are pretty close. We
always have been."

Little red lights flickered in Jessica's head, and a tiny gong
rang in her mind as she listened to the way he spoke about his
mother. Nonsense, she thought, he's just a devoted son. On the
other hand, she had heard that if one wants to know how a
man might treat a woman, one had only to observe how he
treats his mother.

"What are your views on sex? I mean...you asked me some
very personal things. Now it's my turn."

"Well," he chuckled, his brown eyes twinkling, "I'm not into
kinky stuff at all. I draw the line at hanging by my thumbs
from the ceiling, and I don't fancy women who are loose with
their favors. Let's eat," he said, as he rose to respond to the soft
tap at the door.

They watched as the waiter prepared a Caesar salad: a
pinch of this, a dash of that, freshly squeezed lemon, a smidgen
of crushed anchovies, a whole fresh egg, crispy greens, and
Parmesan cheese. Jessica found the taste irresistible; just enough

garlic to keep evil spirits away. The steak, which the waiter had expertly carved for them, was delectable, sizzled to perfection. Julian ate daintily and sparsely. No wonder he was so slim. The champagne enhanced the meal, but while she sipped, she noticed he gulped, refilling his glass often.

Relaxing with heated Grand Marnier after dinner, she observed that while he drank copiously, he didn't even seem slightly tipsy. When he invited her to join him on the sofa, she wondered what his ulterior motive might be. Was this an advance warning of seduction? If so, she would set him straight in no uncertain terms. Even though she had expressed her views regarding sex on first dates, she had encountered several men who really interpreted "no" as meaning "try harder". He was very appealing, and she would have loved to lose herself in his arms. But she knew if he held out the bait, and she nibbled it, it could be the crashing end to a great beginning. However, all he wanted to do was talk.

At eleven o'clock, he said it was time to leave since he had his early morning flight. Phoning Kenneth to pick them up, he touched her arm as they left the suite.

"I've enjoyed meeting you, Jessica. For me, this has been a memorable encounter. I hope I can see you again."

"Call me when you get back from your trip," she smiled. "And thank you for a wonderful dinner." And for not raping me, she thought. But was she really so grateful that he hadn't even kissed her?

Sleep was out of the question for her that night. Thoughts of Julian sent shudders of desire throbbing though her veins.

Damn it anyway! She had her life under control. No deep relationships with men had meant, for her, a measure of stability and emotional security. Loneliness, sure, but that was preferable to living on the edge with men who kept her guessing and off balance; men who were there for a while and then vanished, pursuing their own interests while she waited for them to call. Did other women experience that? Did they spend night after night crazy-glued to the telephone waiting for that one special call?

She remembered how enraged she'd feel if it was only a girlfriend who phoned (and heaven help the unsuspecting telemarketer who had Jessica's name on her list!) instead of that hunk she'd met at a party or bar the night before. She'd be disappointed if it wasn't the man who had given his word to contact her in a day or two. God! She'd wasted days, months, and years of her life on men who never worked out.

Her last big romance had gone down in flames when Carter's ex-wife had called to inform her that Carter was safely ensconced in her loving arms once again and wouldn't be needing Jessica's shoulder to sob on any longer. Jessica had hated Carter for the cowardly worm he was and had decided that she had had enough emotional turmoil and heart-wrenching agony. She needed a sabbatical from men. She had always sought their love, acceptance, affection, approval, and praise, but now she sought that from herself. And it was working! It had worked for almost two years.

And now Julian had upset her applecart, had started her blood pulsing with desire. It had been ages since she had known that longing to have someone love her and hold her close. It had been a long time since her body had throbbed with yearning to have a man make love to her. She thought her sexual desire was buried in a trunk, dusty and covered with cobwebs. It was a good thing she hadn't placed bets on her vow to never get involved again.

The ten days he was in Germany seemed endless. She talked to Rosalind about it.

"Well, honey child," smirked Rosalind, "you could do worse than have a crush on Julian. He's quite a catch. Just don't get your hopes up. He could prove troublesome. I should know. I grew up here and went to school with him."

"Yes, but this guy doesn't seem to have time for his women. I could be stuck on the back burner."

"That's what I mean, but I'd rather be stuck on his back burner than the one I've got. Harry's a completely predictable bore. If that man moves around at all, it's to fine-tune his drink, the TV, or the garden hose. Just watch your step with Julian."

And then he called.

It was 2:00 AM when her phone jangled, jarring her awake.

"Jessica, it's me, Julian. Sorry to call you so late. It's morning over here, but I wanted you to know I'm thinking of you. How about dinner when I get back? This time, I won't hide you in a suite. We'll go dancing at the Diplomat."

❈

What a romantic courtship! Straight out of Harlequin books. He took her to dinner-dances at the Diplomat, and as they swayed to the orchestra's melodies, he held her close, but always tenderly.

Bundles of flowers arrived for her at the travel agency, and he had gardenias delivered to her home.

They went to movies, on long drives through the mountains

at sunset, and on walks through the woods.

One cool evening, bundled into warm jackets, he took her canoeing on Emerald Lake at midnight under a full moon, while mist wafted in ghostly swirls from the ebony water. The air was so quiet that they could hear soft chomping from far across the lake. Signaling her to absolute silence, he expertly guided the canoe toward the sound. The craft crept forward slowly, noiselessly, until out of the mist, they could see a beaver snacking on floating water plants. In awe, Jessica watched as the small creature nibbled his way through a clump of succulent greens. Then, sensing their presence, with a slap of his tail he vanished.

It was a magical, enchanting time. Until he took her to meet his mother.

Mother Bothwell received them in her living room and served tea and tiny sandwiches that tasted like Bristol board smeared with creamed cheese.

"So...you're the bewitching creature Julian's been talking about," sniffed Lydia, while she poured tea.

"I'd no idea I was bewitching," said Jessica, wondering what would happen if she spilled tea on Lydia's snowy white sofa or snowy white carpet. Balancing the tiny china cup on the saucer, she hoped that her shaking hands didn't clatter them together. The room was as silent as a tomb.

"Well, my dear," chirped Lydia, "it's always a pleasure to meet one of Julian's female friends. Heaven knows, I've seen them come and go."

Jessica felt as secure as someone in a hot tub with a blue shark. She tried a limp smile at Lydia, but she was sure she had cream cheese glued to her teeth. Glancing at Julian for support, she wondered how he could feel so close to his mother; she was as cuddly as a snapping turtle.

The visit was short. It was unfortunate they couldn't stay longer, Lydia complained, as she walked them to the door. Who would eat all the sandwiches she'd spent hours making?

"Feed them to Cuddles," recommended Julian. "I'll take a doggie bag."

Standing on the step of her townhouse, Lydia waved goodbye, blowing kisses to her son.

"I certainly hope you like her," said Julian, as they drove away from the curb. "She's quite a woman!"

"A delightful person, I'm sure," replied Jessica, crossing her fingers, and praying to God for forgiveness for her tiny fib. "I don't think she really liked me."

"Oh, that's just the way she is when she first meets someone. Once you get to know her better, she'll warm right up to you."

A grizzly with cubs would seem friendlier, she thought.

Mother or not, Julian continued to court Jessica, proudly escorting her through his two hotels and introducing her to the managers of the departments.

Then he gave her the royal tour of Sherwood Park, an exclusive neighborhood built near the outskirts of town on a series of rolling hills. The houses were almost obscured from the tree-lined boulevards by towering oak and elm, their branches forming leafy cathedrals over the quiet streets. A vast array of bushes, trees, shrubs, hedges, stone walls, and latticed fencing, further hid the magnificent homes. Julian turned off Sherwood Boulevard and followed a broad sweeping, circular drive. Finally, he eased the midnight blue Mercedes to a stop in front of a gray stone mansion, its white marble columns supporting a large entry porch.

"Well, this is where I live," he grinned, while Jessica stared at the imposing structure.

"Let's go in," he said as he opened her car door. "I'll show you around."

Holding her breath, Jessica mounted the flagstone steps to the massive carved oak door, which Julian held open for her, and entered the foyer. It was made entirely of pale gray marble, polished to a dull sheen, with a spectacular curved marble staircase that swept to the second floor. Oak railings guided one's ascent or descent. As Julian led the way, Jessica stumbled along, trying to listen while he told her how his mother had designed and furnished this sumptuous sixteen-room home with the fortune his father's hotels had thrust upon the family. There were four bedrooms, one of them with a second adjoining bedroom—a nursery plus room for a nurse, a den, library, four baths, two powder rooms, a sunroom, a family room, a living room, the kitchen with its eating nook, and a formal dining area. While Jessica noted that much of the house was slightly dated, she was delighted to see that Lydia had installed sparkling white cupboards in the kitchen, and the counter tops gleamed with black granite. Many of the cupboards had glass doors.

Jessica's eyes grew bigger at the lavishness and size of the home, and she wondered aloud, "You live here alone?"

"Sure do! Absolutely love it!"

"Who cleans this place? Looks after the upkeep?"

"Oh, I have a housekeeper, Binkie, who comes every day. There's always something to do. I also have a handyman who does all the repairs when I call him in, and a gardener who looks after the yard. I don't have the time to do too much around here, except sometimes I tend to the roses."

Jessica was overwhelmed with the structure and its decor. Oak wainscoting adorned the walls of the den, library, and dining room, with hardwood gracing the floors. Ceramic tile in the kitchen, sunroom, and eating nook felt cool under her bare feet, as she padded along with Julian while he pointed out the paintings, bric-a-brac, carvings, wall hangings, and furniture his parents had scavenged the world to import when they had traveled abroad.

When they entered the master bedroom, which, like the other bedrooms opened onto a hallway that overlooked the immense foyer, Jessica wondered if it was here that Julian might make an advance on her. But he was involved in displaying the features of this haven from the cares of the world.

The king-sized bed did not appear over-large in the room, which was carpeted in dusty blue plush broadloom. The navy spread and drapes, with matching upholstery on the sofa and chairs in the sitting room, lent a soft, restful atmosphere. The sitting room also had a stone fireplace which, Julian explained, his mother had had built to ward off the chill of wintry evenings when she retired to read. And tucked into a corner, stood a wet bar, complete with a tiny fridge, plus ice maker.

Off the bedroom, a French door with frosted glass led to a dressing-room which was, Jessica noted, almost the same size as the living room in her own apartment. It had walls of closets and a vanity with sink. Another doorway opened from the bedroom to reveal a bathroom with a massive soaker tub and shower, a marble counter housing double sinks, and a commode recessed behind a frosted glass-block wall.

"Well, what do you think?" Julian asked as they descended the staircase to the foyer.

"It's certainly bigger than my apartment," she laughed. "But I must say I'm impressed."

"I have more to show you," smiled Julian as he gently took her elbow and guided her around the marble staircase and the massive stone walls supporting it. Tucked under the stairwell and set into the marble wall was a French door. Julian flicked on the lights, and a soft glow illuminated another flight of steps leading into the depths of the house. Opening the door, he led the way down. The stairs were of bamboo-colored hardwood with a slim slice of hardwood on the edge of each step to make descending them safe. The steps were also wide making them more secure. He gently took Jessica's hand to guide her as she grasped the railing for support. At the bottom of the stairs, he turned on several switches bathing the room in lights from lamps, with a large shade over the pool table at the far end of the room. Jessica's eyes grew round with the size and lavishness of this enormous room which must have measured thirty by forty-five feet. The floor had the same pale hardwood flooring except for the area surrounding the pool table, which was carpeted in broadloom, a soft beige shade to complement the hardwood. The walls were a neutral sandstone shade.

"Dad wanted to develop this lower part of the house. He and mother used to love throwing parties, and he wanted plenty of room for his guests. That far wall is right beneath the library and den," he explained. "Dad also had huge steel columns installed beneath the marble staircase and foyer to support the tremendous weight of the stone. A must-have for him was the entire house being built with twelve-foot ceilings, so that is why the windows down here are so much larger than regular basement windows. He had them triple paned and he added shatter and bullet proof glass to discourage break-ins.

"We used to have a real fireplace down here, but it made such a tiresome mess hauling wood down and cleaning the bloody thing out, that Dad had an electric insert installed."

Jessica was in awe of this spectacular room with its tasteful, comfortable furnishings and beautiful artwork. An enormous television screen dominated one wall, and Julian said that sometimes he and friends enjoyed hockey, football, and baseball games down here. There was also a full bar as well as a small functional kitchen which caterers used for large gatherings.

Julian was obviously impressed that he had impressed his girlfriend.

"Come on, I'll show you the rest of the wonders of this part of the house. He pointed out Cuddle's kennel tucked under the stairs. There was room enough for a pack of poodles, with a large, comfy doggie bed, dishes for water and food, and a special spot for overnight 'calls of Nature.' The kennel was spotless. "Cuddles is well-trained" he explained, "and rarely makes a mess."

Leading her through another French door way, halfway down the wall closer to the pool table, he opened it to reveal a hallway. Jessica commented, "Your parents certainly liked French doors."

"They add depth as well as elegance to a room, and they can also let you see if someone else is on the other side. Makes for fewer collisions at a party."

The hallway came to a T-intersection, and this new hall ran the breadth of the house, and had doors to various rooms. He led her to the far end, and opened the door to show her an exercise room, with a weight bench, leg press, Bow-Flex trainer, a treadmill, and a slant board, plus a chin-up bar.

"No wonder you're so slim and in such good shape," commented Jessica.

The next two doors, which had "HIS" and "HERS" signs on them, opened to reveal two enormous washrooms, each with three stalls. The marble counters housed three sinks and there were stacks of hand towels, monogrammed with the Bothwell insignia, piled neatly beside each. A huge mirror hung over the sinks and on the counter at one end stood a delicate bouquet of silk wildflowers, which added a touch of class.

"With the two powders rooms off the main floor hallway—you remember where I showed you the laundry room around the corner from the kitchen—guests here never have trouble finding a place to freshen up. And there's always the main bath on the second storey."

"Julian," commented Jessica as she closed the door of the ladies' room, "this is just an observation. But does Binkie do all the cleaning after one of your entertainment nights? Just straightening things up would take her days."

"No, no!" he laughed. "Binkie has a handpicked staff to help her. She is the original fuss budget when it comes to keeping things clean, and she brings in people to help. She's a real drill sergeant, and within a day or two everything's ship-shape. She also brings in staff twice a year for spring and autumn cleaning, and that's when they do all the chandeliers as well...Come on, I want to show you the rest of this place." Opening a solid door, he stood back as Jessica peeked inside. A huge freezer with stacks of wire shelves met her eyes, and there was side of meat hanging on a hook.

"This is where I keep the venison I hunt, and beef, bacon and other meats I order from the butcher. He cuts and wraps and labels everything and then delivers it for me."

The next door opened to a cold room, for food stock, plus a small freezer for left-overs, baked goods and frozen desserts. One wall was devoted to shelves for various wines. The next door of solid cedar opened into a huge refrigerated cedar closet for Lydia's opulent fur collection—coats, jackets, stoles.

"Wait until you see this last place, he told her, a mischievous grin on his face. Another cedar door. A sauna, plus a room for toilet and shower. "I just love Saunas," he explained. "I couldn't imagine a home without one!" Jessica thought, they remind me of very hot, stifling coffins. Aloud she said, "How delightful."

The last door opened into the plumbing section, with two huge boilers, one to supply hot water for the house, and other to heat the house. "Dad simply hated oil and gas furnaces, and insisted on hot water heating."

"Well, what do you think?" he asked as they made their way upstairs.

"Your home is absolutely amazing. It makes me feel very much like an unsophisticated country mouse," she laughed.

"I love your sense of humour," he chuckled. "And you are far from being unsophisticated. And you're about the cutest, sweetest country mouse I've ever encountered."

Once on the main level, he guided her to the kitchen and through the sliding doors onto the patio. An enormous pool met her eyes, inviting her with its tempting coolness.

"You might just as well have the entire tour," he smiled. "I spend early mornings out here, weather allowing. I usually have a swim, then grab a shower, dress for the day, and have coffee at the table under the umbrella. I seldom use the bathhouse, but guests make good use of it. Over there against the fence and hedge, is the gardener's shed." Painted white, it complemented the bathhouse with its color, and black shingles. Both buildings had garden boxes beneath the large windows, and they were crammed with floral displays, and trailing ivy.

"The gardener comes twice or three times a week to keep this acre of land under control. Mom and Dad picked this parcel of land because of its size and seclusion. Mom designed the walks and flower gardens, and of course she just had to have a hammock for summer days, and she and Dad both sipped cocktails on the lawn swing beneath that gorgeous oak tree. Mother installed a second lawn swing for people to use at their garden parties which happened once or twice a month all summer long. Mother had that gazebo built with latticed walls for vines and climbing roses. It's a great place to read and relax."

Jessica's head was spinning as she admired the roses Julian was so proud of keeping tuned up, and the spacious expanse of lawn, punctuated by shrubs, a fountain, and more flowers than she had seen in her entire life. Giant hedges kept the property totally invisible and private from its neighbours, and the enormous trees emanated a subtle sense of pristine personal space.

"Your gardener is a busy man," she observed. "Just raking the yard in the fall must be daunting."

"Well, let's go in and have a drink in the sunroom where you can do nothing but watch the sparkles from the sun catchers," he laughed, as he hugged her shoulder.

⁂

Impressed with the house she was, but she was even more impressed with his restraint in never making a pass at her. For the three months he had been escorting her to the sights and entertainment spots of Riverbend, he had never so much as kissed her. The only physical intimacy he had displayed was to touch her arm or hold her gently as they danced. His gentle hug around her shoulders in the garden was the first and last. She began to have doubts about him. Perhaps he was gay. Maybe Lydia had put a hex on him. Was he afraid of women? She began to doubt herself. Maybe she wasn't his type; perhaps he wanted her only as a friend.

One evening, as they relaxed in her living room after a candle-light dinner of Kentucky Fried Chicken and potato salad, for which she had spent six days preparing (by cleaning the apartment from top to bottom—scrubbing sinks, washing windows, having the draperies dry-cleaned, and polishing all the doorknobs for her boyfriend's first visit to her modest home), she snuggled up to him on the sofa. Gently, he put an arm around her, and as she turned her head to look up at him, he bent to find her mouth with a gong-ringing, open-mouthed, tongue-seeking, Bergman/Bogart kiss. It was one of those kisses that never ended. She would have preferred to smother rather than be the first to pull away. She couldn't remember who broke the spell, but when they recovered from the intensity of their passion, he gasped, "I think we should start making plans for that Hawaiian cruise."

"What a jolly good idea!" she smiled, wondering if she had done something wrong to discourage his passion. She could have sworn their kiss would lead to something more.

"Uh...Julian," she whispered shyly, "do you...do you think we'll ever make love?"

"That's why we should go to Hawaii," he smiled down at her, chuckling. "I want to have you in one of the most romantic places in the world before I ravish your body from head to toe."

"Can we leave right now? Tonight?"

"Do I detect a sense of urgency here?"

"More like an emergency," she murmured and meant it.

"God, Jessica, you're beautiful!" He breathed into her hair. "You definitely are bewitching me! They miss me at the hotels these days, you know. I scarcely know what's going on. Those places could be in bankruptcy or burned to the ground, and I wouldn't know."

"Don't let me keep you from your work," she purred.

"It's my pleasure," he replied. "Start arranging for that trip tomorrow. Make it for two weeks, including a short cruise, which should be easy for you to take off...and leave the seduction to me."

Lighting a cigarette after he'd gone, she vaguely puzzled over who possessed all the control in their relationship. To hell with control, she thought. If control makes him happy, then he's got it. If this is his idea of control, I love it!

⁂

The suite at the Halekulani Hotel on Oahu was resplendent with bouquets of island blossoms in pastel vases on every table and on every bureau. Two crystal goblets, their stems tied with ribbons, sat beside a silver ice bucket in which two bottles of champagne were chilling. The balcony opened onto the ocean; its waves sloshing and sliding in an unchanging, soothing rhythm onto the beach and back to the sea. A sea breeze riffled Jessica's blonde hair as she gazed at the beauty of it all: the ocean beneath a cerulean sky, the vast golden stretch of beach, the magnificent hotel gardens, the palm trees gently waving their fronds, and lovers strolling hand in hand on the sand.

Stepping onto the balcony behind her, Julian wrapped his arms around her waist, as he gently hugged her. She felt the hard line of his readiness against the small of her back and thrilled to his kiss as she turned to face him.

With his mouth on hers, he asked, "Would you like dinner first?"

"What do you think?" she whispered against the warmth of

his lips.

"We should have some preliminaries first, don't you think?" he murmured. "Maybe a shower, maybe you in a negligee, maybe me in bed waiting for you."

"This will be the fastest shower in history!" she squealed, laughing as she freed herself and dashed inside. Grabbing her suitcase marked "x", she rifled through the sensuous nightgowns and sexy Frederick's of Hollywood lingerie she had so gleefully packed and found what she had purchased in an exclusive boutique for this moment.

Taking it with her, she sang out, "I'll be gone just a few minutes!"

"I'll meet you in bed!" he laughed. "We're lucky this suite has two bathrooms or we'd have to shower together!"

"Let's save that for later," she called over her shoulder as she vanished into the bathroom.

She was prepared. Off with her make-up. There was nothing as yucky as old foundation on pillowcases and mascara streaked on a lover's face. How could he kiss her with lipstick and other cosmetics all over? Trying to turn on the water, she fumed at the inventor of complicated taps, wondering how they worked. Finally she triumphed, and the spray was glorious. Peeling off her clothes, she knotted her hair and tucked it under a plastic cap. She didn't want to wait an hour while her hair dried.

Then came a generous soaping, particularly of all areas where a female scent might lurk. Next she towel dried and slathered on her Silken Veil lotion, a delightful scent guaranteed to drive men crazy. She brushed her hair and applied a hint of blush to her cheeks. On with the nightgown and bed jacket of spun silk so fine that it whispered on her skin. It was black. Men loved black. A trim of gold thread at the plunging neckline enhanced her cleavage. Thank God her breasts were still firm. She studied her reflection in the mirror. "Julia Roberts, eat your heart out!" She looked delicious!

Quietly opening the door, she slipped into the room. Julian was lying on the turned-down bed, a towel around his waist. He was bronzed and muscular, a modern Apollo, gazing at her with a rogue smile. Was that a critical eye or one that appreciated her?

"You're absolutely gorgeous," he whispered. "You look good enough to devour."

Letting the jacket and nightie slip to the floor, she slid onto the bed and into his arms. She sensed his hunger for her, a desire matching her own.

"I think we waited too long," he breathed as he caressed her. His hands were like fire on her breasts. Then he began kissing them, sending thrills throughout her body. "I'm a bit too anxious. I may come before we even get started. This one will be for me, but I guarantee you'll love the second time. I don't think we'll have to wait for me to get hard again. I've been aching for you since I met you."

She slid her hand down between their bodies to touch him, and his hard, pulsing readiness met her searching fingers. She gasped.

"Am I too big for you?" he asked softly. "Can you take me? I don't want to hurt you."

"I want you inside me!" she pleaded. "I need you so much!"

"Not until you come first," he murmured, slipping his fingers inside her. His hands were magical, and her orgasm sent shudders vibrating through her so intensely that she thought she'd die of ecstasy. Entering her, his body melded with hers. Lifting himself to look into her eyes, he moved in rhythmic strokes, filling her completely. She gazed up at him with tears of joy trickling down her cheeks. He lowered himself to wrap her in his arms, then paused inside her, kissing her lovingly, longingly, deeply, his tongue playing with hers in a moment of total oneness.

"Oh, God, Jessica, I adore you! I've never met a woman like you. I don't ever want to let you go," he gasped, and she felt herself jolted by the rising intensity of his desire, his breath rushing fiercely in her ear.

She felt him tremble and shudder with his orgasm. He didn't go soft, and he didn't withdraw. He held her, loving her with his hardness. Softly and slowly, hard and fast, but always tenderly. She clung to him, her fingers caressing his back, her mouth fused to his. Then she kissed his face, his neck, and his chest. Nuzzling her breasts, he tasted them with the tip of his tongue. She whispered that if he maintained a steady rhythm, she could follow him and climax simultaneously with him. He adjusted his rhythm to hers.

"Take your time," he smiled down at her. "I'm fine. I won't come until you do. I was a bit quick before, but this is all for you."

"Oh, Julian, I've never felt like this before. I don't know what you're doing to me," she moaned, her eyes closed in passion.

"I'm loving you, my sweet, and I'm loving the most beautiful woman in the world," he murmured, covering her face and throat with gentle kisses. "Just take your time."

She was lost. She was in love with him. She never wanted the moment to end. This was bliss, the kind she only dreamed about. When she came to him, he held her in his arms, cradling her, kissing her.

"Keep coming to me," he breathed, as her body quivered

beneath his. "Take all the time you need."

And then he climaxed. They clung together, their passion spent, but needing to bond. He lifted his head to peek at her.

"You're quite a woman!" he laughed. "I don't know if I'm man enough to keep you satisfied!"

"I'm so happy now!" she smiled up at him. "And very satisfied. That was so-o-o-o good! Thank you!"

"Thank *you*!" he grinned. "If you weren't here, these moments would never have happened!"

Afterwards, they lay in each other's arms. Afraid to break the spell, she would rather have died of a ruptured bladder than leave him to go to the bathroom. Not speaking, they lay there, caressing each other. The sun set as they cuddled together. And they made love all night long. The sun rose, and he stirred, his arms around her, cradling her.

"Jess," he whispered in her ear, "are you awake?"

"Mmmm," she responded drowsily.

"I think I'll order up some breakfast. "Are you hungry?"

"Famished," she replied, yawning and stretching. "Dying for coffee."

When he'd called room service, he suggested they eat on the balcony.

"What a smashing idea!" she agreed, slipping into a white terry cloth robe. "Then can we come back to bed?"

"Is that how we're going to spend the next two weeks?" he laughed.

"I can't think of a better way." She looked up at him, mischief dancing in her eyes. "At least until the ship sails."

That first breakfast she would never forget. Halfway through his papaya, he asked a penetrating question.

"I don't know why we never discussed this before, but are you on some kind of birth control?"

"Divine intervention, I suppose...No." She flushed and swallowed a gulp of coffee, giving her a moment to think of a response. "My doctor told me I'd never have children. There's something wrong inside. My cervix is upside down, or my ovaries are inside out, or my fallopian tubes are completely blocked...I'm not exactly sure what. But I've never used birth control, and I've never been pregnant."

"I think I can make you pregnant," he said, his eyes never leaving her. "In fact, I hope you're pregnant now."

"Why on earth would you want that to happen?" She put down her coffee cup and reached for a cigarette, her fingers shaking as she lit it. "I'm not wired for kids. I've never really wanted any. Besides, I'm not into being a single mother."

"I want you to have my baby, Jessica," he said in a hushed voice, his eyes intent on hers, "and I want you to marry me."

"God, Julian! I'm thirty-two. And you're pushing forty. We're a bit too old to start a family, don't you think? But, if you want an answer to your proposal that I marry you, I have news for you...I'd love to be your wife! But children? I'll have to think about that."

⁂

On the first evening of the cruise, as they stood at the railing of the ss *Constitution*, watching the moonbeams dance on the waves and lights flicker on the shores of Maui, Julian enveloped her in his arms.

"I adore you, Jessica. You mean more to me than anything on earth."

"Next to your hotels," she laughed. "I love you too, Julian. I've never been happier in my life or felt more secure."

Music from the ballroom drifted on the warm sea breeze as he embraced her. Turning her gently, so that he was looking into her eyes, he said that he had something important to tell her.

"There are a couple of things you have to know about my past." He hesitated, "...Riverbend is not all that big a place. Some people have memories going back further than recorded history, and they have tongues that wag at both ends—whether it's the truth they're gossiping about or not. I want you to know the truth in case someone wants to fill you in on details about me."

She studied his face in the shadows. The only thing he could say to destroy her love was an admission that he was a new Jack the Ripper. She knew the worst thing he could say was that he'd been married six times before and wanted to give her a chance to renege on her promise to marry him.

"Jesus, Jess!" he choked. "This is just so hard, but you need to know... You're such an honest, truthful person. I'm so ashamed of this. It really hit me like a freight train when it happened."

"Oh, sweetheart," she said softly, brushing his cheek with her fingertips, "it's okay. Just let go of it. Secrets can kill us, but remember the truth sets you free. Besides, it can't be worse than the pain you're suffering now."

"Well, I was engaged once...a long time ago...nearly fifteen years ago. Her name was Tiffany. I'd known her a long time, but we didn't actually start dating until I was twenty-three. She was a terrific lady. You'd have liked her, I know."

Right! thought Jessica. She would really appreciate having all his previous girlfriends file by! What woman wouldn't? His following words made her want to have her thoughts crucified.

"Well, anyway, she died."

"Oh, my God!" she gasped. Would her rival be a ghost? People who were alive she could deal with, but phantoms were out of her league.

"It happened in the wintertime. I was driving her and my best friend to the city. We were going on a bit of a spending spree for our wedding that spring to find new furniture for the house we'd bought and gifts for the bridesmaids and ushers. Stuff like that. Riverbend is okay for some things, but if you really want to shop, the city's the place to go. Halfway there, we hit a blizzard. Storm warnings were out, but who pays attention to them if you really want to do something? And so often weather reports are dead wrong! Besides, we were young and bulletproof; none of us took the warnings seriously.

"The storm was awful, and in the blinding conditions, the car went off the road. We were all shaken up, but nothing worse than a few cuts, bumps, and bruises. The car's battery cables snapped on impact, so it was disabled. Even if we could've dragged it out of the ditch, it wouldn't have started.

"Anyway..." A long sigh escaped his lips. "God! I hate talking about this...I knew there was a village a few miles back. I could go for help and leave Jack with Tiffany. I didn't want her trying to hike through the blizzard and cold, and I didn't want to leave her alone. Jack gave me his jacket for extra warmth; Tiffany gave me her scarf and some big fuzzy mittens she always wore. Since I was the one to face the elements, I had to keep warm...

"It was one hell of a storm...and cold! It took me forever to reach the village. Not one car went by on the highway. And then, when I finally found someone to help, when we got back, they were gone...both of them... from hypothermia. It was so awful! That was so terrible! My fiancé and my best friend! I blamed myself and hated myself for it. I wish to God I'd died too! For years that haunted me. After that, I hardly took a woman out.

"Later, I ran around a lot, but I never got close to anyone. I was afraid. That's what Mom meant when she said she'd seen women come and go. But you're different, Jessica. That's why I never touched you for all those months we dated. I had to make sure I loved you. Now I'm sorry I waited so long."

Folding herself into his arms, Jessica wrapped her arms around him to assure him of her love and comfort.

"Thank you for telling me, Julian. You're absolutely right. I certainly would've wanted to know. I love you and admire you even more for your courage in disclosing this to me."

"There was a big inquest," he continued. "People wanted to find out what really happened. That was terrible too. Tiffany's parents and Jack's blamed me for the accident. They blamed me for leaving them to die! I was going for help, for Christ's sake! It was a total nightmare! For a long time there were some pretty malicious, vicious rumors going around!"

"That must've been dreadful for you," she said softly. "I can't imagine how horrible that was."

"There is one other thing I have to tell you, and then all the skeletons are out of the closet."

Now what? She speculated: Perhaps he had a child hidden somewhere. Maybe he'd had a homosexual relationship.

"This happened when I was eighteen. I hung out with a girl from the city when she came here to work for the summer. We weren't going steady or anything like that. I think she thought we were, but I told her lots of times not to get stuck on me. That upset her. Anyway, she got pregnant, and then went absolutely bonkers! Hysterical! She said I was the one who knocked her up. She screamed it all over town...and then went to my parents. Her parents got involved too. Nice people. They were reasonable.

"We all decided the best thing was an abortion. Back then, it wasn't easy, but my dad had some connections. She went to some guy in the city, and he solved the problem. The only thing was...something went terribly wrong. The girl died. Bled to death in her own bed. Her mother found her in the morning. That was pretty rough on everyone. And then, when Tiffany died too, it was too much for me. I suffered some very negative notoriety in Riverbend for quite a while. I guess you could say I'm not a good risk as a partner."

"That's not true, darling." She spoke very softly, soothingly, as she smoothed his hair ruffled by the breeze and kissed his cheek. Sympathy for him tugged at her heart, and tears welled in her eyes. "I've never had a better partner in my life...I'm sorry you had to suffer so much pain and torment, but that's in the past. It's all over now. We have a bright, sunny future ahead, and I love you more than you'll ever know."

"Thanks for the vote of confidence." He managed a weak smile.

Other than the trauma of Julian's disturbing confessions, their trip was enchanting. They danced under the moon and played under the sun. They laughed, dined, swam, and indulged their love and passion for each other. And she did become pregnant later—six months before their marriage. The joyful, unexpected result was Rob. Jessica had never for one moment regretted her relationship with, and marriage to, Julian. At least, she had no serious regrets. And now she was making herself irresistible for a delightful night in her lover's arms. She still had the hots for him, even after nearly three years.

There were, however, two tiny clouds of uncertainty on her

sunny horizon. Number one was her mother-in-law. On her wedding day, while hugging and welcoming her as a daughter, Lydia had hissed in her ear, "Remember what I told you when I first met you? I've seen Julian's women come and go. I wish you the very best, my dear." Even though she knew what lay behind Lydia's thoughtless remark, she felt as if she were Snow White and had just been offered the poisoned apple by the wicked queen who was disguised to look like everyone's favorite grandmother.

Number two was Julian's drinking. He sometimes became very inebriated and verbally abusive. Twice he had slapped her around. She smiled when she recalled their wedding night. At the time, she was devastated, but time has a way of finding humor in situations. He'd been so drunk with happiness and jubilation that he had passed out while making love to her, abandoning her to the TV and re-runs of season one of *The Walking Dead*, or *Peter Popoff* and his miracle spring water, paid programming, or reading the Gideon Bible.

☆☆

Dismissing those old clouds, she chose her nightgown. Julian loved her in black, and he admired her in the gown that tied under her breasts, making them plump and emphasizing her cleavage. It had a narrow skirt, slashed on both sides to the hip. Teasing her about the slits, he said it gave him reasonable access. That gown worked every time.

After making the rounds to check on all the alarm systems, she peeked in on Rob, tucking his quilt around him, and then slipped into bed. Maybe she would read or watch TV while waiting for her husband. She prayed he'd be early and that he'd be sober. It was 11:00 PM.

She had dozed off, but was jolted rudely awake by the first savage smack across her face. She shrieked as Julian dragged her from the bed by her hair.

"You fucking slut!" he yelled. "Who are you dressed up like that for?"

"Julian!" she screamed. "What's wrong?" It had to be a nightmare! She'd wake up to find herself in his loving arms, being comforted and reassured. But it wasn't a nightmare.

"You bitch whore! I knew you were screwing around! But I never dreamed it'd be in my own bed!"

"Julian is this some kind of joke? If it is, it's not one bit funny!" she cried, as she scrambled from the floor and clung to the dresser. Like a shark after blood, he lunged at her, his face ablaze with rage. His fist struck the side of her head, and his backhand across her shoulders knocked her to the floor.

"Shut up, you bitch! I'm sick of listening to you! You're nothing but poor white trash! Get the hell out of here! Get out of my house!"

Entwining his fingers in her hair, he jerked her to her feet. My God! This couldn't be happening! She knew he was drunk. His face was florid and puffy, and he reeked of scotch. She had seen him in drunken, intolerable states before, but this was the worst. Horror gripped her heart.

"Darling," she crooned, reaching for him, hoping to snap him into reality, "it's me, Jessica...Please come to bed. You'll feel better when you've slept this off."

"You stupid dumb bitch! I'm not drunk! I just caught you! Sleep in the garage! Sleep in the car! And that gown...I'll fix it!" With a twist of his hands and a yank, he shredded it down the back.

Rob screamed from his room, and she flew to him, gathering him up and trying to comfort him as he sobbed.

The door to her bedroom crashed shut with Julian shouting, "Don't you dare come in here! I'll kill you if you do! You leave in the morning!"

Crying, terrified, and bewildered, she held Rob close as he clung to her. She sat in the rocker, hugging him tightly until he fell asleep, his thumb in his mouth, and an arm clutching his teddy bear. Tucking him back into his crib, she pulled the covers over him and kissed his cheek.

"Sweet dreams, little one. I love you."

On tiptoe, she crept to the door of her bedroom and listened. Julian was snoring. Furtively, she opened the door and stole into her dressing room to find her warmest robe. Shivering with cold and fright, she pulled off the shreds of what used to be Julian's favorite gown. Even Binkie's nimble fingers wouldn't be able to repair it. She left the tatters on the floor and wrapped the robe around herself. Creeping softly past the bed, she could see through the gloom and shadows that Julian was spread-eagled across the blankets. He was naked, and drool and foam spluttered from his mouth each time he snored. Disgust and revulsion tore at her stomach and anguish at her heart.

Dazed, she faltered down the staircase to the kitchen. A cup of coffee and a cigarette might clear her head, make her feel better, and help her to see some sense in the horror, the madness. Had she done something to anger him? Perhaps she shouldn't have suggested he come home early. Maybe the nightgown triggered him. Where could she go in the morning? Rosalind's place was out because Mary-Beth was there. It seemed their luncheon had taken place ten years before, not just a few hours ago. Compared to what was happening in Jessica's life, Mary-Beth's troubles seemed like a birthday party. It was all so crazy!

The grandfather clock in the foyer chimed 3:00 AM. She took her coffee and ashtray into the living room and sat in her favorite rocker in the corner with its surrounding windows revealing the patio and pool from one angle and the spacious expanse of their yard from the other. Remembering her revolver in the glove compartment of her car, she wondered if it would be a deterrent if Julian attacked her again. No! She would never be able to point it at him. She doubted if she would ever be able to use it against anyone. But she decided to get it anyway. Since sleep was out of the question, she might as well practice some dry firing with her left hand. Sadly, she thought of her triumph at the range; she hadn't even had a chance to tell Julian about it.

Why had something so ghastly happened? She sat in the dark living room, sipping coffee, thinking, and clicking the trigger.

The sky lightened and pinked; the sun's rosy hues glowing through the sheer curtains over the windows in the corner where Jessica sat. Her coffee was cold, the ashtray was full of butts, and her revolver lay on the table. Staring into a vacuum, she heard the clock chime 7:00 AM. Dear God! What would the new day bring?

Binkie wouldn't be in until noon. That meant she could keep herself busy with Rob, a ploy to distance herself from Julian if he ever woke up. What shape would he be in? Should she start packing? He'd made it clear that this was his house and that he wanted her out of it. Where would she go? She had several thousand dollars in the bank, enough to get her back east and to set herself up in an apartment with Rob. Maybe she could go back to teaching. Or should she just board a slow boat to China?

Tears blinded her. My God, what had happened?

She should have paid more attention to the fact that he drank too much. Actually, she had, but it didn't seem to have the same effect on him as it did on other men she had known. At first, he just became tipsy, scarcely ever staggeringly inebriated. He had overindulged a few times, but he had slept it off. On occasion, he had been verbally obnoxious, but he was contrite and apologetic the next day, and on two occasions, he had struck her across the face. However, both times, Jessica believed him when he said he had smacked her because she wouldn't stop nagging him. But last night's attack was insanity! Her mind felt as ragged as her nightgown.

She stirred, groaning as she stood up, her body screaming from the assault. She shuffled to the garage to put the revolver away and then entered the kitchen. The blushing sun peeped in the windows, and as she glanced out across the patio, she saw that the pool was glittering in the early morning light. Perhaps a swim would refresh her.

As she stepped out onto the patio, the tiles, icy from the cool night air, made her feet tingle. She headed into the bathhouse for a quick change into a bathing suit. The yellow bikini would be fine. Pattering to the edge of the pool, she stepped in, the freezing water stimulating every nerve. Julian had refused to have the pool heated. "It gets your blood going!" he had insisted. It could also stop your heart, she reflected.

Julian always dove in, but she preferred the inch-by-inch approach. It kept one in suspense, scarcely breathing. Finally, she eased into an easy sidestroke across the pool. Nothing too noisy; no splashing lest she awaken the slumbering ogre. Back and forth she stroked, up and down the pool. Her body felt alive, her mind dead. One more length and she'd go in and warm up with a fresh cup of coffee.

Returning to the kitchen, snuggled in her robe, she gazed out the window while waiting for the coffee to brew. What a glorious day, she mused. There were birds twittering in the bushes, a bold robin pecking for a worm, and a squirrel scampering across the lawn and scrambling up a tree. Dew sparkled on the grass and twinkled on the shrubs. Everything looked so perfect, so serene and happy, yet her life was in shreds. Nothing had changed in the garden, but everything had altered inside her home.

She heard a thud above her—either Rob climbing out of his crib, or perhaps it was Julian falling out of their bed. If it was indeed Rob, he'd surprise her with how grown-up he was; if it was Julian, he'd terrify her with how infantile he could be She sipped her coffee, hearing a rhythmical swish, swish, swish; the unmistakable sound of Rob's sleepers with his little feet in them. His grin peeped around the corner. Seeing his mother, he squealed with delight. She opened her arms wide to receive and embrace him. Swinging him up onto her lap, she covered his face with kisses and held him close.

A breakfast of oatmeal with cream and brown sugar would be a great start to what could prove to be an eventful day. While she whipped things together, Rob opened the basement door for Cuddles, and the little white bundle of fluff bounded in, springing up onto Jessica's legs and pirouetting around the kitchen with her insistent yip.

"Shut up, Cuddles! You'll have your master down here, and then we'll all catch the devil!"

She filled the dog's dish with Puppy Chow. Cuddles rarely ate anything else, other than her favorite canned dog food and leftovers from Julian's plate, when and if he made it home for supper. Pouring the hot oatmeal into two bowls, she added fresh strawberries, cream, and oodles of brown sugar.

She heard the clock chime 8:00 AM. When would Julian be up? She wished she hadn't eaten breakfast. How silly of me, she thought, as she felt the oatmeal crawling into her throat.

After changing Rob into soiled clothes from the hamper, since she didn't dare risk disturbing the dormant volcano by going upstairs to Rob's room, she, Rob, and Cuddles paraded out to the patio. This was a delicious morning for enjoying coffee under the umbrella, while Rob and Cuddles romped around the yard. Even though Cuddles was not her favorite pet, she loved the way the dog and Rob played. The poodle had never once nipped her son; she was as gentle as cotton wool. It was her high energy level and acting as though she were part pogo stick that rattled Jessica's nerves.

Lighting a cigarette, she tried to think of how to deal with Julian when he arose. She'd turned off the phone so that it wouldn't jangle him awake. Maybe he'd sleep off his rampage.

She studied an ant as it picked its way across the patio tiles and the crevices between them, carrying home a bit of breakfast for her nest. How hard those little suckers worked, she mused. But then again, they didn't have to worry about VISA bills, shooting lessons, and drunken husbands. She envied the ant's simplicity of life. Maybe that's what she ought to do—join a commune. Bees buzzed round the roses, packing their tiny pouches full of pollen and humming home with it. Sparrows chirped from the tree branches, and a dove bathed itself in the birdbath, preening for the day. So much love all around her, so much beauty, and so much lavish luxury. These might be her last few hours in her garden, she realized.

Rob spotted Julian before she did, running into his arms to be swung high overhead. Then Julian lowered him, crushing his son to his chest.

"Hi there, Springer!" he laughed. "What are you up to?"

Gently lowering Rob to the ground, Julian walked toward his wife, a sick smile twisting his mouth. As he took her hand, he kissed her on the cheek, before seating himself on the chair beside hers. "God, Jess, I'm sorry about last night! I know I promised to be home early, but Lincoln and a few of the guys had some business to discuss, mostly about building a new hotel in California, and we had a bit too much to drink. I'm sorry. You must have felt pretty hurt, when I promised..."

She was dumbfounded. "Have you never heard of an invention called the telephone? And I hope you build that goddamned hotel right on top of the San Andreas Fault!"

His face clouded with genuine bewilderment. "Hey, Hon, what's wrong? I said I was sorry!"

"Sorry doesn't make up for this!" She turned her face so that he could see the welt across her cheek. "Sorry doesn't make up for this either!" Standing, she lowered her robe so that the welts and bruises on her back and shoulder were visible.

"What in hell happened to you?"

"You don't remember?" Her eyes flashed dismay, hurt, and anger.

"What am I supposed to remember?" he floundered.

"Wait here! I have something to show you! Get Rob's play pool out and let him play in that while we talk. This is serious!"

She tore up the stairs to the dressing room where the nightgown lay in tatters. It was unbelievable! He couldn't remember!

When she returned, Rob was splashing in his pool, with Cuddles bouncing in and out, yapping and shaking water off in tiny sprinkles. It was a perfect picture of a happy family enjoying a morning on the patio. She hurled the gown at him.

"What's this supposed to mean?" he demanded, befuddled by the ragged garment.

"You ripped that to pieces last night! Batted me around! Look at the welts on my head where you yanked my hair! You smashed my face, karate-chopped me across my back, and threw me out of our bedroom! You said I was unfaithful! You threatened to kill me!"

Tears rolled down her cheeks. "It was so awful! I'd rather have a burglar attack me! That I can understand! But this...!"

She collapsed into her chair sobbing, burying her face in her hands, her hair tangled and snarled over her shoulders.

"Oh, my God, Jess! It can't be true!" he cried, stunned.

"It is true! You were a maniac! I was terrified for my life! You swatted me around like I was trash!"

His face was drained of color, expressionless. He rose from his chair. "I need a coffee. How's yours?"

"Fine!" she snapped, huddling into her chair, hugging her robe tightly. In spite of the promised heat of the day, she shivered.

Returning with his cup, he took a swallow. "Jesus, Jess! What can I say? I'm sorry! If it happened, I can't remember! I can't remember a thing from the time Kenneth picked me up from the hotel. There has to be some mistake. Maybe you dreamed it!"

She stared at him with reddened eyes, her face wet from weeping. "Do those marks look like my imagination? You beat me up! You said I was making out with someone else in our bed! Oh, Julian!"

He grabbed her hand. "Come here," he said softly. "Come and sit on my lap. Just let me hold you."

Reluctantly, she followed him to his chair and gingerly sat

on his knee. His arms around her felt like home. Burying her face in his shoulder, she wept.

"Is Mommy okay?" asked Rob, pattering over. "Is Mommy crying? Why?"

"Oh, sometimes mommies cry—just like little boys do. And sometimes daddies cry, too," offered Julian. "I want Mommy to know how much we love her."

"Don't cry, Mommy," piped Rob. "I love you."

She peeked at Rob through her tear-soaked lashes and reached out for his chubby hand. "I love you, too, sweetheart. I'll be fine. I'm just a little sad right now. You go and play with Cuddles."

Julian hugged her close. "Oh, Jess, my darling, I must've been hammered. I don't remember a thing except that I was coming home early, and then it got later..." He broke off in torment.

"Julian, I love you so much, and now this has happened! I can't take it! We used to be so sweet and loving. Maybe you drink too much, and it does weird things to your head."

He nuzzled her neck and brushed her cheeks with gentle kisses, tracing her tears with a finger. "Whatever happened last night will never happen again! I promise! Please, darling, don't hate me!" he managed, his voice cracking with emotion.

"Hate you? I love you! You're my life! You and Rob are what I live for!"

She gulped and hiccupped from the intensity and depth of her grief. "And I didn't show you how well I did at the range!"

"You went to the range? I didn't think you were ready for that!"

She nodded, brushing away her tears, and brightening. "I did well! I hit the "x" area with all eighteen shots! One slug blew the guy's balls off!" She laughed through her tears. "I wanted so much to surprise you! And now our whole world is falling apart!" She broke into fresh tears.

He cradled her while she sobbed, his own eyes stinging with tears. His were ones of shame, guilt, and remorse. If he'd had a hangover when he awoke, there weren't words to describe what he felt now. He searched his memory. Nothing. Just getting into the limousine. After that...zero! But he had to believe the marks. His wife didn't fabricate things. She might have a vivacious imagination, but she wasn't into masochism.

"Look, Jess, I have a few things I want to clear up this morning. Do you have anything planned for this afternoon?"

"Nothing," she snuffled.

"Why don't we go to the beach today and take Rob? We can have some fun. I'll be back by two o'clock. No later, I swear. Then tonight...how about you and me going to bed early and making up for some lost time?"

"But your favorite nightie's wrecked! You hate the others!"

"Don't wear anything," he whispered, as he tickled her throat with his tongue. "That's the best, sexiest outfit of all. Let me have this one chance to make it up to you."

⁂

Binkie helped her pack the picnic hamper with salad, sandwiches, pop, fresh strawberries, plates, plastic glasses, and only one bottle of white wine.

When the clock chimed two, Jessica dashed upstairs and tugged on a pair of jean shorts and a tank top, the kind that showed off her trim figure. She slipped on a pair of sandals and knotted her hair on top of her head. With Rob ready in his sunsuit, she gathered up towels, the beach blanket, picnic hamper, a tablecloth, and they were ready to go.

Where was Julian? Three o'clock came and went. Another broken promise. Why did he bother making them at all? If he wasn't home in fifteen minutes, she was leaving for the beach and Julian be damned! Wandering out to the pool, she stared at the water while fears vied for position in her mind, but she chased them away. Go bother someone else, she thought, as if she were swatting mosquitoes.

She sensed his presence before she heard his steps. He was jingling car keys.

"Ready?" he asked, as he nibbled the back of her neck.

She felt like slapping him and asking what took him so long. Instead, she smiled, and in her most cheerful voice, said, "Sure am." She was the perfect domestic diplomat.

He tossed the car keys to her. "You drive!"

The keys were unfamiliar. "Whose car am I supposed to drive? These keys aren't mine, and they aren't yours, and I sure as hell am not driving the limousine!"

His eyes spelled mischief. "You'll see," he grinned, as they walked through the house gathering their picnic gear.

She opened the front door.

"Oh, my God!" she squealed. "Whose is that?"

A red Ford Mustang GT gleamed at the curb. Tinted windows. Sun roof. Shimmering chrome. She dashed around the car.

"What a beauty! Oh, my God! My God!" She tore open the door. Midnight black leather upholstery. Arm rests. Floor module. Enough dials to fight a war. There was even a child's car seat installed in the rear. "Is it mine?"

"Only the best for my woman!" he laughed, as he hugged her waist. "Go ahead. Get in."

"Does it have peace offering written all over it?" she asked.

"Sort of," he smiled.

⁂

The lake was glass, the sand spun gold. Not a cloud blemished the sky, and there were few sun-seekers. It was too early for the tourists, but in another week, the beach would be jammed. Jessica and Julian lolled on the sand while Rob played in the shallows with his plastic boats.

Putting his arm around her, Julian whispered, "Do you think we can find the time we missed last night?"

She eyed him suspiciously. The Mustang was a super way of saying he was sorry, and she wanted to submit to his suggestion, but what next?

"Without the nightie, of course," she murmured.

"There's a little something in the trunk of your new car that I'd like to see you in." He smiled as he touched the bruise on her cheek. "You'll never know how much I regret last night. But we have the rest of our lives to be loving and kind to one another."

Chapter Three:

Crazy-Making

LAST NIGHT WAS CERTAINLY OVER, NOTED JESSICA, AS SHE UNTIED THE GOLD RIBBON AROUND THE GOLD-PAPERED BOX. Inside, wrapped in tissue as fragile as a robin's egg, was a beautiful gown of black raw silk, even more elegant than the old one lying in rags in the rubbish. Slender straps held up the bodice, which was sheer, the skirt falling in folds to the floor. The short lace jacket had chandelle feathers over the shoulders. It was a creation designed in heaven. Pirouetting in front of the mirror, she admired the effect—sensual, alluring, and tantalizing. A splash of Joy perfume, and she stepped out of the dressing room.

Julian waited in the doorway where he lifted her into his arms and carried her to their bed. Flames crackled in the fireplace, and two flickering candles graced their night tables, offering a warm glow that shimmered in his deep brown eyes. As he placed her tenderly against the pillows, he kissed her longingly, hungrily.

"How about a sip of champagne," he asked, his fingers tracing across her shoulders and down to her breasts. "A celebration of our love."

"How about you inside me?" she suggested, as she undid the towel at his waist and ran her fingers teasingly down his belly to his erection.

"Just a sample of things to come," he smiled, lifting her gown's skirt, "and then we'll have a real session."

He lifted himself onto the bed so that he was above her and then slowly lowered his body to meet her as she guided him with her fingers. Tilting her pelvis, she arched up to welcome him. Slowly, lovingly, they clung to each other, and the previous night hadn't happened at all. He withdrew before they forgot the champagne, and they laughed because they realized that just as they were getting started they quit.

"Listen, woman," he breathed in her ear, "I haven't seen you in this outfit yet. Do a little dance in it so I can admire the woman I adore."

This dance-thing was not the highlight of any of their love-making, as far as she was concerned. She loathed showing off her body in the bedroom by attempting to imitate a stripper. Looking sexy at the beach, wearing elegant garments to parties and functions, and tearing around the yard in shorts and a halter-top never for a second embarrassed her. But to strut her stuff in the bedroom for him always caused her anguish. It was not something she had discussed with him, because to discuss it would be more painful than the performance. She found she couldn't move her feet; she didn't know what to do with her hands. She wanted to run and hide and call up some professional burlesque queens. She was totally shameless in bed, but to frolic like an exotic dancer and have him watch her was not on her list of sensual teasers. But she did it anyway. With a few twists and turns, a couple of bumps and grinds, she peeled off the jacket and then slithered out of her gown. Diving under the covers, she begged for some champagne.

He was already pouring. As they entwined their arms in a toast, he whispered in her ear, "To the most beautiful woman in the world, the one I adore and cherish."

Tears of joy brimmed in her eyes. "Oh, Julian, I love you so much! You're the star on my Christmas tree."

The evening was long and mystical, their lovemaking exquisite. Long after Julian had fallen asleep, she lay curled against him, her head on his chest, listening to the beating of his heart. She knew, without a doubt, there was no other place she would rather be.

☆

BAM! BAM! BAM! Six shots. Reload. Another six, and Casey reeled in the target.

"I've never seen anything like it, Jessica!" he boasted for her. "You're just as good with your left hand as you are with your right."

"I practice dry firing a lot when I have nothing else to do." Like sitting in the dark after Julian almost beat me to death, she thought. But that was over. It wouldn't happen again.

"I never told you I took a course in private investigation," she said, picking up the spent cartridges.

"Hah! You've got to be kidding!" he laughed.

"Truth! I swear to God and on a stack of bibles! It was only a two-week introductory course, but...oh, Casey! I loved it! I relished every second and was furious if they ended classes five minutes early. It was fascinating, and I learned so many interesting things. Like stuff you can use against your friends. Tidbits to hang your enemies with."

"So what happened? Why didn't you continue and get your license?"

"You're not going to believe this," she replied, hanging her head and peeking up at him through her lashes. "I didn't have the nerve for it. I just knew I couldn't cut it. My imagination runs rampant, and I'd be an absolute wreck on a stakeout at 3:00 AM in some back alley. I'd have to have all the car lights on and the radio blaring to survive in the dark. I'm still spooked by that break-in at our house! And I couldn't possibly work undercover. They'd have me drawn and quartered before I could even get started. I'd be a crack shot, but I couldn't do any mean, nasty stuff, like hunt down and spy on a wife who's living in terror of an abusive husband finding her."

"I hear you," he sighed. "I've had to do some lowdown shitty things I don't even want to think about. But you're right about one thing. You're a crack shot!"

All at once he scowled and looked at the ground, deep in thought. She searched his face. What was he thinking? Pursing his lips, he looked at her sideways. "I guess now we get down to work, Jessica."

"Isn't that what we're doing?" she inquired. "I thought I was working *damn hard!*"

"Yeah," Casey agreed, "but this is only an appetizer. You can fire a gun, load it, and clean it. You can shoot like no one I ever saw before! But you have to be prepared for anything if someone breaks into your home. Your prowler is going to be armed with a knife, gun, anything to protect his ass! You have to be as cool, calm, and cold, as the bastard who's in your house. If he's sneaking around, you have to do it, too. You have to be able to fire around furniture, or doorframes, or corners with either hand. And we have to talk ammunition. These little jellybeans you're popping won't make a damned bit of difference unless you get the guy dead in the heart or head. Otherwise, they just pass clean through. You might wound him mortally, but he can still come at you, this time with nothing to lose. The bullet can puncture a lung or his liver, but he can still take you with him. We have to talk about using hollow-point bullets."

"So we're back to talking murder!" she snapped.

"No, Jessica! We're not into assassination. We're here to teach you how to shoot to stop!"

"So what are hollow-point bullets?"

"They explode on impact. Make a small hole going in and tear a big hole exiting. That's why they stop."

"I think I'm going to sick, Casey. And if I shoot a burglar and kill him, I'll be up on murder charges!"

"If you don't, we'll all be attending your funeral. Haven't you ever heard it's better to be tried by twelve, than carried by six?"

"Never! What's that supposed to mean?"

"It's better to be tried by twelve jurors, than carried by six pall bearers."

"Why don't I just join the French Foreign Legion and get it over with?" She tried to smile, but didn't quite make it.

⁂

The room was dark. A vanishing dream tugged at Jessica's mind as it misted its way into nothingness. Slowly she awoke, aware that Julian was groping for her breasts and sliding his free hand between her legs. She buried her head deeper into her pillow and inched away from him, tightly closing her legs, trapping his hand. Her body language screamed, "Screw off!" She loathed sex before she was awake in the morning. It used to thrill her, but it had become a nuisance. She adored his love-making at night, but in the early hours of the morning when she was still sleeping, it was irritating.

Why did men always wake up with a hard-on and expect their drowsy women to respond with fervor? Wide-awake now, anger bubbled in her blood. Persistent, he forced his fingers into her vagina. Damn! Why did her body always betray her? She was wet! She had hoped she'd be as parched as the Sahara Desert.

Pulling himself up behind her, he pressed his erection against her, nuzzling her neck. Okay, Julian, she thought, I'll relent. Just get it over pronto and let me go back to sleep. Moaning, she arched her back to receive him as he entered her from behind. Thrusting, he came in seven strokes. No preliminaries, no words of love, no kisses. She thanked Providence, or whatever might be responsible, for his having relieved himself so quickly.

Mornings were not her sensual time. In the early days of their union, she was eager all the time, but as time passed, she wasn't in heat every moment. Mornings were for waking up with coffee to get her heart started.

Without a word, he pattered into the adjoining bathroom. She could hear him brushing his teeth, the hum of the electric razor, and the shower running. Eyes wide open, she cursed him under her breath. This was an issue of which he was well aware; they'd discussed it several times. But, she reflected, men seemed to have a very short memory about when it might not be a good idea to pursue a sexual urge.

The clock said 6:30 AM. Dragging herself up, she grabbed her robe and sleepily made her way down to the kitchen. Should she say anything? No, it was better to leave it alone. Since the beating and their night of love following the horror, she figured that some things were better left unsaid—especially since he wasn't drinking. He had actually been home before ten for six nights in a row, and it was peaceful to have him sober. Don't say a word. Not one bloody word. And try to smile.

"Breakfast?" she smiled, as he entered the kitchen, and she rose to pour two cups of steaming black coffee.

Dressed in a dark blue business suit with a sparkling white shirt and a navy tie with red dots, he was handsome. He played the role of hotel-owner well.

"No, I'll grab something later. Thanks for the coffee. And thanks for the loving. What a great way to start the day!"

"My pleasure," she managed, feeling like a call girl as she hid behind a puff of smoke. He paid the bills; she came across. Things weren't supposed to be like that. "Will you be home early?"

"I can't say," he said, drinking his coffee. "We have three proposed tour packages to finalize for some European companies. And a couple of travel agency executives are here for a few days, so I might be entertaining them. I'll call you later."

Walking him to the front door, she watched as he entered the limousine and the silver car vanished down the drive. I love him so much, she thought, but something isn't right with this picture.

*

The phone rang at 11:20.

"Jess, Rosalind here. We have an emergency on our hands. Mary-Beth's going berserk on us. We have to take her to lunch and talk some sense into her."

"What's wrong with her, other than her goofy husband?" asked Jessica.

"She's sure she's losing him because she isn't enough of

a woman."

"I'm relieved she doesn't think she isn't enough of a man, or we'd really be in trouble. God! Why do we women always think it's us? It's not her! It's that nitwit that she married. It isn't her fault that he likes scoring with men rather than with her."

"Just tell her that! You'll never guess what she's planning!"

"Being a bridesmaid when he marries his boyfriend?"

"No!" Rosalind barked. "Get sensible! She's going in for breast augmentation!"

"Is she crazy? That's pretty drastic!" Jessica was shocked.

"I know. That's why we have to talk to her *now*! Before she sees the plastic surgeon."

"Okay. Let's meet at one o'clock. Where? The Wharf?"

"Not unless we bring a pail for her to throw up in. How about the Diplomat instead?"

"Perfect! It's dark and quiet at lunch. We can really talk there. See you at one."

Doesn't that beat all, Jessica pondered, as she readied for lunch. A breast amplification to keep a homosexual at home.

Why do women think so much depends on breast size? She was more concerned with the size of her brain, than she was with her bust measurement. Besides, she wished hers were smaller. They looked great in a plunging neckline with the right bra for uplift and cleavage, but other than that, they were a nuisance. There had been times in her life when she had despised her breasts, especially when some lecher leered at her or some disrespectful date tried to fondle them. She'd even asked one lascivious creep if he'd like her to cut one off for him and hand it to him as a souvenir.

Men seemed to have a breast fixation. In some other cultures, breasts were considered "just another thing", but men of capitalistic social orders seemed to have a lewd obsession with them.

Many women were fanatical about their size. There was no doubt about that. They were always too small for the women who were flat chested and always too big for those dragging around boulders in their bras. Wasn't anyone satisfied? She certainly wasn't surprised when her own sister had had hers reduced. She sympathized when Sue-Bell had told her she'd given her plastic surgeon orders to scrape them off until her ribs were visible. The poor woman had endured distress both physically and emotionally; men were always declaring open season on her because she packed such a set. They weren't interested in her head or her heart; they were fascinated with her chest.

Jiminy! she thought. We're dumb! The whole planet is being eaten alive with pollution and overpopulation, and we're worried about the size of body parts!

⁎⁎

Henri, the maître d, smiled at Jessica at the Diplomat entrance. His skinny black moustache wiggled over his upper lip. "Ah! Madam Bothwell, so nice to see you. You are meeting Monsieur for lunch? He waits for you in the lounge."

Think fast! "Oh! He's here already? No, no. I can find my way. Actually, I'm meeting two friends...ladies...so will you please arrange a table for three by the window?"

"But of course." The maître d' bowed. "I'll see to it right away."

Jessica crept into the lounge, and through the gloom, she saw Julian hunched over the bar. Damn this small world, she thought, as he downed at least a double scotch. He was with two other men, and she guessed they were engrossed in some kind of plotting because they were busily scribbling on napkins and nodding and shaking their heads. How many deals were hatched with pens scratching on serviettes? she wondered. Watching from her dim corner, she decided to leave well enough alone. She backed out of the lounge and turned into the dining room, almost stumbling into Henri who stood directly in front of her.

"I have your table ready, Madame. Your friends are waiting." Smug. Arrogant. He had caught her spying on her husband. Upstairs/downstairs. The hired help loved gossip! Measly, mousy little man, Jessica thought. For the first time since she had met him years earlier, she felt loathing for Henri.

"Thank you, Henri," she muttered, dodging around him in a flutter. Then, collecting herself, she was all business. "By the way, don't mention to my husband that I'm here. He's involved in a very important project, and I don't want to interrupt him."

"Ah, yes, I understand," he whispered conspiratorially as he pulled out her chair for her.

Turning to face Henri, she minced her words "Thank you, Henri. That will be all for now!"

"Well, Mary-Beth, you look a lot better than the last time I saw you. How are you?" Jessica said blithely, trying to calm her mind from the sight of Julian drinking.

"Wretched!" snapped the unhappy woman. "I can't sleep! I can't eat! I can't stop thinking about how much I love him! But I'm not giving up without a fight!"

"Mary-Beth," soothed Rosalind, "the bastard's not worth it. He's gay, and that's that! Nothing can change that fact. It's not *you* he's dumping. It's all women. He's into guys, plain and simple."

"I know I can keep him, Jessica! I'm going to have my breasts enlarged. He's always said he likes big boobs."

Jessica admired Mary-Beth's petite figure, her nicely rounded bosom, her lovely face. She was an adorable looking woman. Tiny and elegant.

"Look, Mary-Beth," said Jessica, "I don't think this idea of yours is the answer. Haven't you been watching TV lately or reading *Time* magazine? Silicone implants are dangerous! They can poison your whole system. You can *die* from them! It's like hoping, praying, and planning for the chemical pollution of your body!"

"The surgeon I talked to doesn't use silicone," she argued.

"What's he going to use? Cotton balls or balloons?" countered Jessica.

"He's going to use something filled with a saline solution," Mary-Beth said authoritatively. "If the implants break, it won't matter. I'll just get a new one."

The waiter came with their drinks—Rosalind's martini, a single scotch for Mary-Beth, and Jessica's soda water with a lime twist.

"We'll order later," Rosalind told him. "And Mary-Beth, don't you dare get drunk and throw up here!"

"Speaking of drinking," Jessica whispered to her friends, "Julian's in the bar talking business. I just wanted you to know in case he sees us. I didn't want to disturb him. You know how serious he is about his hotels."

"Back to the topic," pleaded Rosalind. "Getting a new transplant isn't like changing a tampon. This is major surgery. And for what? A man you have to mutilate yourself for isn't worth it. David isn't going to hang around and admire your breasts anyway. You've got a great chest, and you look divine in that sweater."

"At least it would give me a fighting chance!" cried Mary-Beth. "I knew you wouldn't understand!"

"Mary-Beth," reassured Jessica, "we do understand. We're women too, don't forget. I've got okay breasts; at least Julian thinks so. But I'm pretty sure he didn't marry me for my measurements. And I'd hope he'd stand by me if I lost one to 'you know what'."

"You want to cry about chests, Mary-Beth?" asked Rosalind. "I'm flat as a pancake. Harry doesn't give a bloody hoot. I'd like to look as great in a sweater as you do, but I'm not going to put my life on the line for a great set of knockers!"

"I'm not putting my life on the line! It's my marriage I'm trying to save! I'm sure implants will make me more of a woman and give me a fighting chance to make my marriage float instead of heading for the rocks!"

"Well, if having big breasts is a measure of how much of a woman one is, I guess I rate a zero!" retaliated Rosalind. "That's what you're saying, Mary-Beth. Thanks a whole hell of a lot!"

"Obviously, you're going to do what you're going to do," said Jessica. "I want you to know I'm your friend. I don't support this idea one bit, but I support you. I think this scheme of yours is crazy, and I think you're wrong about yourself. But there isn't one thing Rosalind or I can say that will make a damned bit of difference. Please study up on this 'little operation' beforehand. Get a few facts straight. And that doesn't mean going to strip-joints and interviewing dancers. Those gals get implants so they can make big bucks from screwy guys who have their heads full of gibberish!"

Rosalind stared at Jessica. "You're giving up on her? Just like that?" She snapped her fingers.

"No, I'm not giving up on anyone. Mary-Beth's in full control of her faculties. They're just a bit out of whack. She has all her marbles, but they aren't lined up right. However, this is America, and she has the right to make her own decisions."

"Christ!" muttered Rosalind. "You're both nuts!"

"Shall we order lunch?" suggested Jessica, as she watched Julian totter from the lounge. Glancing at her watch, she saw that it was slightly after two. Now where would he be off to in that condition? He never went home that early in the day. He'd probably sleep it off in his office in the Talisman's palatial suite of rooms. Suspicion and fear nibbled at her insides, but she dismissed them as she surveyed the menu.

Never letting on to her friends what she had just witnessed, she said to the waiter, "I think I'll try the chicken breast in wine and mushroom sauce."

Wickedly, she whispered to Mary-Beth, "See what great breasts did for the chicken? Maybe smearing yours in sauce would save you the trouble of having surgery."

Mary-Beth glared at her and polished off her scotch, while Rosalind stifled a laugh.

⁂

Midnight! He still wasn't home. Jessica prowled the house, checking the door and window locks, something she had done ever since the break-in. All the alarms were set, except for the motion detector; she could turn that on from the bedroom. Opening the basement door, she sent Cuddles down to her kennel. Satisfied the house was secure, she climbed the stairs, looking in on Rob before she settled into her own bed to wait. To wait for what?

She picked up her newest paperback novel, *The Red Dragon*,

hardly a comforting book to soothe jumpy nerves. When she found herself reading the same paragraph ten times without grasping a word, she knew she was wrecked. Pattering down to the living room, she paced the floor in the dark. Something like dread tingled in her blood. Heart pounding, she decided a drink might calm her frayed edges. A splash of Rémy Martin. That ought to do the trick. Carrying it back to the bedroom, she tried to make herself comfortable under the blankets. She sipped the cognac and heard the clock strike 1:00 AM.

Shortly after, she heard the soft hum of the limousine. He was home! The door of the house opened, and then closed with a loud thudding crash. The footfalls on the staircase sounded erratic, out of rhythm. Then he stood in the doorway of their bedroom, clinging to the frame and staring at her stupidly. His face was red, splotchy, and bloated; his eyes were glazed and his nostrils flaring.

"Hi," he slurred. "Still awake? Did your friend just leave?"

She felt like the wife in *The Shining*, when Jack Nicholson chopped a hole in the door with an axe, and hollered, "Wendy, I'm home!"

Silence. What was she supposed to say?

He lurched forward swiftly and unevenly, glowering at her.

"I asked you a question, you dumb bitch! Cat got your tongue? Where's your fucking friend?"

"Which one are you referring to? I have lots of friends," she dared.

"Smart-assed, aren't you, you fucking cunt? If women didn't have cunts, there'd be a bounty on all of you bitches!"

"Nice talk from such an important man," she countered. "Is that how you make all those deals? Is that how you talked to the town council when you wanted the land for the Terrace

Lodge?" She knew she should shut up, keep quiet. She stared back bravely at his puffy, twisted sneer.

He staggered closer and towered over her, rage flaming in his eyes, a dragon breathing fire. Her body tensed as he lunged at her, but she was faster and flew to the other side of the bed, jumping to her feet. She had to get out, but he blocked her escape to the door. She knew she'd never make it to her dressing room or the hallway. Forget the bathroom; she was on the wrong side of the room! Speed and agility were on her side, but rage and brute force were on his.

"Julian, for God's sake, let's talk about this in the morning!" Reasoning with a drunk was always a last resort; totally useless, but worth trying.

"You fucking whore!" he bellowed, cornering her against the bar. His fist smashed into her face. White-hot pain flashed through her head, and paralyzing terror gripped her.

"So help me, I'll kill you! I'm busting my ass to make a living, and you're fucking around!" he stormed. "You're nothing but a useless slut! You're no better'n Tiffany! She was a whore, too!"

Dazed, she sagged against the bar. Yanking her arm, he dragged her to the floor, and with his fingers snarled in her hair, he wrenched her head back and forth and then backhanded her across her face again. She felt her nose crackle and break, blood spurting at once. And then he was on top of her, one hand at her throat as he landed punch after punch to her jaw, her face, her chest. She believed she was about to die. He was totally insane.

Screaming, she pleaded for him to stop. She tore at his shirt, his jacket, anything to stop him. But he had her pinned to the carpet. Rob screeched.

"When I'm through with you, I'm going to kill him too! That little bastard isn't even my kid!"

Horror clawed at her heart. And then, suddenly Julian seemed to sag, and let her go. Exhausted, he staggered to his feet.

"You bitch!" he rasped. "You're dead meat if I ever catch you fucking around on me again!"

Totally incapable of more than drawing breath, she heard Rob howling. She watched as Julian ripped off his clothes and fell face down on the bed, mumbling and muttering to himself.

Aching, she staggered to her feet and stumbled into the bathroom to survey the damage in the mirror. Rob wailed from his crib. Later, she thought, I'll go to him later. I have to stop this bleeding first. I'll terrify him if he sees me like this.

Splashing cold water over her cuts, bruises, and throbbing nose, she watched the red water escape into the drain. So much blood. But even a little blood looked like a hemorrhage when mixed with water. It probably wasn't as bad as she thought. Dabbing at her cheeks and forehead with a cold cloth, she examined the havoc. One eye was almost closed; finger marks like neon lights glared from her throat; red welts and purple bruises covered her chest; one cheek looked like a flaming balloon; and her nose was puffed and crimson, with red mucous draining from her nostrils. Her breasts throbbed. The cold cloth felt like fire as she squeezed her nostrils together to staunch the flow of blood. Her head pounded from his yanking her hair, and the roots themselves seemed to sizzle. Gingerly, she pinned her hair up so its weight wouldn't torture her scalp.

Rob was still whimpering from his room; she had to go to him. As she pulled on her robe and passed by the bed, she looked at Julian. Drips of spittle bubbled at his mouth as he snored, and his pillow was soaked in saliva. She shuddered. This madman was someone she didn't know.

Rob reached out to her as soon as she turned on the light

in his room. It was a miracle he hadn't climbed out of his crib when Julian was raging. Picking him up, she held him close as she eased herself down the staircase, gripping the railing with one hand while she measured each step, her knees buckling.

Just to the kitchen. If she could make it to the kitchen, she'd be fine. The pool and patio lights were on—a rule following the break-in—and they bathed the room in a ghostly glow. Putting Rob in his chair, she poured juice for him and pacified him with soft murmurs of love. His terror subsided, and he ceased sobbing. She was operating on automatic pilot, her brain dead. Easing herself onto a chair beside the telephone, she dialed 9-1-1.

"This is Jessica Bothwell," she whimpered into the phone. "My husband has beaten me very badly, and I don't know what to do."

"I'll have the police there in five minutes." The operator sounded efficient. "Name again, please, and address."

"Fifteen Sherwood Park Boulevard. I'm Jessica Bothwell. Tell them *no* lights or sirens, please. That's important. Tell them to knock. I'll be waiting."

The house itself felt chilled and mute, and gloom shrouded her as she waited. Julian would kill her for what she'd done, but he was going to kill her anyway. Dragging herself up, she reached for her cigarettes, inhaling the smoke. God! She shouldn't have called the cops! What would she say?

She heard the knock. Flipping on the kitchen lights, she shambled through the foyer to open the door. Two huge men in uniform stood on the porch, determining her identity, and confirming that she had made an emergency call.

"Come in," she lisped through swollen lips, her tongue thick and raw.

Warily, they stepped into the foyer, eyes darting up the

stairway, into the darkened living room, toward the kitchen.

"We can talk in the kitchen," she offered, pointing the way.

Their boots sounded hard on the stone tiles as they followed her. Tearfully, she described what had occurred and to their questions replied that there were no firearms or ammunition in the house as her revolver and Julian's were locked in their respective cars in the garage. She added that Julian had passed out in their bedroom. They both left the kitchen when she told them how to reach her room. Hands on their unfastened holsters, they inched their way up the staircase as she watched from the foyer. It was like a scene from a crime movie, but it was happening to her! The two officers breathed more easily as they descended the stairs, returning with her to the kitchen. Rob's eyes were round as he studied the policemen with curiosity.

"I think you need to go to the hospital to get checked out," said the oldest of the pair. "You're messed up pretty badly."

"I can't leave my son," she sobbed.

"We'll take him too. Just get yourself ready. We'll look after Skipper for you," he said with concern and kindness.

"I'll just put on my coat. This isn't a social call. I'm sure they've seen worse messes than me," she said dully, shrugging her coat on over her robe.

Grabbing her purse, she shuffled to the door. The oldest officer helped her into the back seat, fastening Rob in with a seatbelt. Slowly, the cruiser moved down the drive onto the street. As they drove, the younger man asked her more questions about the assault. She answered them all, recalling every detail of Julian's rampage. Strange that she remembered. It happened so fast, like a prairie thunderstorm. Then it was over.

The hospital emergency room was empty. No small miracle. True to their word, the policemen took Rob and amused him while the nurse and intern attended to Jessica. They were compassionate and professional. X-rays were necessary to determine the extent of the damage. Ice packs soothed her cheek and nose. She felt numb, drugged.

"No bones broken," the doctor observed, while he studied the X-rays. "There's a bone chip in your upper left cheek, which will disappear over time. But you're going to have black eyes for a while. You've sustained some serious bruising. Your nose isn't broken, but from the damage, it probably feels like it is. Use ice packs to relieve the discomfort and reduce the swelling.

"Would you like to press assault charges against your husband? You've been severely beaten. It might be a good idea."

"I'd like to, but I'd better not," she replied. "It won't help. It'll only make matters worse."

"If you change your mind, we have the X-rays and report here. It helps in court," he said gently. "Good luck."

The drive back to the house seemed endless. The police officers tried to be comforting. The one in the passenger seat leaned around to look at her while he spoke in low tones. He seemed kind and concerned.

"You know, Mrs. Bothwell, any time a relationship needs police intervention, it's a good indication there's something wrong. You aren't alone. We see this kind of thing more than most people think. We are obliged by law to lay charges against your husband, even if you decide not to do so. But because of his position, what we'd like to do is talk to the Chief in the morning about this. He might be able to intervene in a meaningful way, considering who your husband is. We understand you're in a very delicate situation."

She felt helpless and hopeless. "What can I do?" she sniffled, tears splashing over her cheeks, stinging her ruptured skin.

"Talk to your husband. Try to reason with him. Maybe you'll have to leave him. We don't know the answers. Here's our card. Show it to him in the morning and let him know how serious this is. We'll talk to the Chief. We're sure he will investigate this, considering how bad your injuries are."

Right, she thought. Trying to reason with Julian was like trying to reason with a hyena over a fresh kill. He might listen if he was sober, but with him drunk, having a sensible conversation was like swimming up Niagara Falls.

"Would you like to spend the night at a friend's place? There's also a shelter for battered women in town. It might be better than staying at home. He could get ugly again."

"No, thanks. He'll probably sleep through the night now. He'll be all right in the morning."

They helped her into the house and waited until she turned off the porch lights before leaving. Struggling, she carried Rob to his room. What a darling. Not a peep out of him except for one of concern.

"Is your face hurt, Mommy?"

"Yes, sweetheart, it's hurt." Why lie to him? "Now you cuddle down and go to sleep."

With a grin, he curled under his blankets.

One task was left before she could lie down and die. Digging in her purse, she found the card the officer had given to her. "Victims of Crime" was the caption, with the file number and the date written beneath it. She dropped it on the bathroom counter where Julian would be sure to see it. She didn't even look at him as she left the bedroom. She'd sleep in the nanny's room, which adjoined Rob's.

Managing to reach the nanny's room, she let her coat and robe fall from her shoulders to the floor. To hell with being tidy.

To hell with everything. Weeping, she sank onto the bed and prayed to die. The hell of the dead couldn't be as bad as the anguish of the living. She didn't remember falling asleep. She didn't even hear the clock chime 4:00 AM.

⁂

The sun streamed in the windows, pouring light over the soft blue carpet. Jessica stirred. Her body had been run over by a tank. Where was she? She was facing a wall and couldn't understand why she was staring at wallpaper covered with blue cornflowers. Raising herself into a sitting position and squinting against the bright sunlight, she looked around. Why was she in the nanny's room? Memories of a nightmare flashed though her head. A phantom had ravaged her, beaten her, and left her for dead. Then she remembered that it wasn't a nightmare.

What time was it? Where was Rob?

Easing her broken body from the bed, she picked up her robe, and pulled it over her bruises. She shambled into Rob's room and found his crib empty. Venturing out onto the landing, she listened for any noise. Nothing. From her vantage point, she could see the grandfather clock indicating it was 11:20. Where was everyone? She stumbled awkwardly down the stairs, each step jolting her body into more pain. In the kitchen, she discovered a note on the fridge:

Have gone for a drive with Rob. We love you.

Hope you had a good sleep.

All my love, Julian

Wonderful! she thought bitterly. A love note from the man who had wanted to murder her the night before. Sinking into a chair, she lit a cigarette and leaned over the table, her head in

113

her hands. Everything was growing crazier by the minute. That Julian had taken Rob for a drive was not unusual, so Jessica was unconcerned about the outing. Once or twice a month, he took Rob for breakfast at one of his hotels. He was very proud of his son, and the dining staff always made a great fuss over the little boy, much to Julian's joy. What concerned her was Julian's reaction to the card she had left on the bathroom counter.

Unaware of how long she had been sitting there, not thinking, and staring into empty space, she heard a car door slam. That would have to be Binkie. God! She didn't want anyone to see her! Hastening to her feet, she opened the French door to the patio and huddled herself into a deck chair under the umbrella, wishing herself invisible.

Tiny feet scampered across the patio, followed by heavier, slower footsteps. Rob was beside her, eyes dancing, cheeks glowing, grinning. "Hi, Mommy! Here!" In his hands, he held a giant bouquet of tiger lilies, a long orange ribbon trailing from the shiny wrapping.

"Thank you, darling," she whispered. "What beautiful flowers! They're the prettiest I've ever seen. How did you know I adore tiger lilies?" Tears stung her eyes. She couldn't cry again, not in front of Rob.

She sensed Julian behind her, but she didn't turn to look at him. He could damn well sit down and face her, see the devastation of his own personal nuclear hell.

"Hey, Rob!" said her husband. "Go play ball with Cuddles. Mommy and I want to talk a minute."

He sat down across from her while Rob and the dog chased across the lawn, laughing and yelping. She didn't look at Julian. Her very soul had been ripped down the middle, savaged, and thrown onto a slagheap. Anger, terror, grief, and bewilderment

114

simmered and seethed in her stomach.

He leaned over and said so quietly that she had to strain to hear him, "Jess, what can I say? Christ! Were the cops really here last night? I saw the card."

She nodded, refusing to look at him, refusing to shed one more tear.

"I've taken the day off. I called and told Binkie not to come. I just want to stay here and take care of you."

She shrugged, staring at the ground.

"Jess, please listen...I'm never going to drink again. I swear it! I can't remember a thing from suppertime on last night! I had dinner with those guys from Europe. I can't even remember coming home...I love you, Jess." His eyes were filled with pleading as she lifted her head to glare at him.

"You said I was screwing around!" she snarled. "You said you were going to kill me! Then...then you said you were going to kill Rob, too! You said he wasn't even your son! And you said I was no better than Tiffany! What in hell is that supposed to mean? I'm *not* Tiffany! I'm Jessica!"

"Oh, my God!" He looked as if he'd been struck by lightning. "Jesus, Jess, I love you!"

"This is how much you love me!" she shot back, anger bubbling from her pores. "Two black eyes worth! A bone chip in my face and bruises all over! Even my hair hurts! That's how much you love me! And please, don't show Rob how much you love him! One loving smack from you could kill him! I'm not your personal punching bag, you bastard! I'm your wife!"

"I honestly can't remember!" he cried, tears brimming in his eyes. "What can I do?"

"I think we should split! I'm too scared to ever trust you again! I want to get away from you!"

"Come on, Jessica, not that! We love each other! Let's try to work this out! I need a chance!"

"You've had your chance! And you bloody well blew it! Loving you could be fatal for me! And for Rob! Loving you is dangerous, Julian!" She glowered at him, her emotions snarled and seething.

"Why don't you get dressed, and maybe we can take Rob to the lake. It's a great day for the beach," he suggested.

"I'm not going anywhere looking like this! I don't even dare let my friends see me like this! I'm a Halloween freak! And if you think I'll condone your vicious assault by being seen in public with you, you had better think again!"

"Please, Jess, it'll do us both some good."

She couldn't believe the seeming naiveté of his proposal. Was he really so obtuse?

"Let me ask you something, Julian! I'm taking shooting lessons to protect us from prowlers. What must I use to protect myself from you?" She glared at him, her fury sparking from her one good eye. "Do I need combat gear? What am I supposed to do when you come home like you did last night? Where am I supposed to go? Even the cops don't want to help! They've referred this situation to the Chief! You're such an important man! You could probably get away with murder!"

The dam broke. Tears gushed and spilled down her cheeks, and she sobbed into her hands. Rob, stopping in his play to observe his parents, saw her. Running on his short, chubby legs, he scrambled to her, putting his hands on her arm.

"Mommy! Mommy! Don't cry! I love you! Please, don't cry!"

"Oh, my darling, I love you, too," she wept, hugging him close. "I'm just very sad, but I'm okay. You play and have fun with Cuddles."

But I want you to play, too," he begged.

"I will later, sweetheart."

Off he scampered. Watching him, her heart broke.

"My God, Julian! Look at that! Not yet three and he's worried about his mother! What are we doing to each other? And to him?"

"It's not what we're doing to each other at all, Jess," he said. "It's what I'm doing to you! I've made this mess...I have to fix it... Please, please forgive me."

"I want to," she sniffled, "but I'm scared to."

⁂

The afternoon and evening wore on, and Julian was restless; reading or watching TV was of no interest to him. Nor could the pool entice him. All he did was mark time, waiting for this new nightmare of his creation to pass. Every time he looked at Jessica, fresh waves of shame washed over him. He knew she wasn't unfaithful. That had never entered his mind. Well, it had, but he always knew it wasn't true. Jessica wasn't like the others. She was fresh, clean, beautiful, and innocent, like a daisy or a prairie lily.

He thought about his deal with the Europeans. They were striking a very hard bargain at the table, and things were not clicking the way they were supposed to go. His hotel venture in California didn't look quite as sunny as it did in the beginning. Life could be a bitch at times!

His mind wandered back to Jessica. She was fun, warm, and loving. She sparkled like a mountain spring in the sunlight. He adored her, and now she was hiding in the bedroom, staring at the television. He knew she was cowering from him for what he had done.

Bathing Rob, he watched his son playing with a yellow rubber duck and floating plastic boats among the bubbles. Free from worries, free from cares. Childhood was a time to be cherished. He couldn't wreck his son's childhood the way his father had trampled his. Jessica was right; Rob didn't need to have his family in turmoil. Drinking was at the bottom of his rampages. Liquor, therefore, would be out of his life.

And...Tiffany? A name from out of the past. That was something he had to bury. When Jessica had said he'd compared her to Tiffany, he felt as if he had just jumped from a highway overpass with a bungee rope that was too long. Tiffany was dead, cremated, forgotten. At least, she *had* to be forgotten!

It was after eleven o'clock before he felt like going to bed, and he hauled himself up the stairs and entered the bedroom. Jessica was propped against her pillows, face wrecked and blackened, eyes staring at nothing, not even acknowledging his presence. Stripping down to his shorts, he climbed into bed beside her.

"How're you doing?" he asked.

"Okay," she replied.

"Anything good on TV?"

"I dunno. I'm not watching it."

"Can I get you anything? A drink? Something to eat?"

As an answer, she lifted herself and tossed two of her pillows onto the floor, keeping her favorite to snuggle into. Rolling over, she turned her back to him. Flicking off the lights and TV and uncertain what to do, he gently slid across the sheets and folded his arms around her. He felt her quiver and knew she was crying.

"Why didn't you just kill me and get it over with?" she sobbed, her impassioned plea hanging in the dark air.

"Oh, my God!" he whispered to the shadows.

⁂

The days struggled by. Rosalind called. Would Jessica and Rob like to come over and play in her pool? Why didn't they get together for lunch? How about a movie? No, Jessica wasn't feeling well and wasn't herself at all. No, nothing serious. Only a flu bug.

Mary-Beth phoned. She had some exciting news she was absolutely dying to share. Could she come for coffee? No, it wasn't a good time. Jessica had a touch of something or other. Julian relayed their messages to Jessica.

Casey called. Had Jessica forgotten her lessons? Julian made her apologies for her. Yes, he'd convey Casey's wishes for a speedy recovery from whatever was ailing her, and yes, he felt confident that she was looking forward to getting back to the range.

After five days, Julian returned to work. But he wasn't drinking and was home early every evening to care for Rob while Jessica hid from him on the patio, in the library, in the sunroom, watching TV, or burying her nose in a book.

Each day she looked in the mirror. Would the bruises and black eyes never heal? Another goddamned day cooped up in the house or yard. She wanted to get out, drive her Mustang, go to the range, see her friends, play tennis, and attend her aerobics class.

She had sworn Binkie to silence. The first morning that Julian returned to work, when Binkie came to clean, she'd been shocked to see Jessica's appearance.

"It was the craziest thing, Binkie. I slipped in some milk

spilled on the floor, and I went out of control. I smashed into the corner of the cupboard. Hit headfirst. I guess it's true what they say about most accidents happening in the home."

Binkie raised her gray eyebrows. "You did all that damage from fallin' into a cupboard?" she asked, shaking her head. "I've heard some tall tales in my time, but yours beats all. Miss Jessica, I've known you for over three years, and we've never lied to each other. And I've worked for the Bothwells for nearly thirty. I've seen lotsa stuff in this here family, and I don't believe your story for one minute. I *know* what happened to you! Believe me, old Mr. Bothwell was a mean man, and your Julian's cut from the same cloth. I seen Miss Lydia black 'n' blue many times. I also know Mr. Julian can be as charmin' as they come, but I know underneath them nice words, there's a rattlesnake."

That was certainly a new slant on things, contemplated Jessica. "Please don't say anything, Binkie. Please, don't say a word."

⁂

For days and days, she remained by the pool, reading, doing crossword puzzles, giving Rob swimming lessons, playing in his sandbox with him, doing needle-point and anything to keep busy while the bruises and welts healed. She still loved Julian, and he *was* trying. Maybe she should give him another chance. Maybe their marriage was worth salvaging.

And then it struck! Out of the blue! She'd been tending to her flower garden when a dull current of horror spun through her body. It attacked her feet first, then crawled up her legs, and wound its icy fingers around her guts. It slithered its way up her spine, spiraling into her head. Her brain felt as if it would explode. Her heart thumped and pounded erratically. Every nerve screamed with agony as panic and hysteria gripped her. She couldn't breathe, and she felt as if she was choking. Gooseflesh chilled her to the bone. She was locked in a dark freezer and couldn't get out.

Fleeing into the house, she bolted up the stairs, but the phantom stalked her steps. Terror was her reality. Throwing herself onto the bed, she huddled into a ball, panting to regain her breath, trying to swallow her horror. Anguish gripped her in its frigid fist, twisting her brain into knots. Convulsing with cold, she rolled herself into the blankets. Her mind was out of control, and she gulped for air as if she was drowning.

Binkie knocked at the bedroom door. "You okay, Miss Jessica?"

"No, I'm not! Come in!" she screamed. "Something terrible's happening to me! I don't know what it is!"

"Should I call Mr. Julian?"

"Please!" she pleaded, as another attack convulsed her.

Binkie hustled to the telephone on the night table and dialed. She had a short, terse conversation three times.

"Mr. Julian's not at any of the hotels. I tried all three," Binkie said, as she sat on the bed and massaged Jessica's back. "You'll be fine, Miss Jessica. You're just hurtin' real bad, is all."

Jessica hurled herself away from Binkie's gentle hands. "I've got to get help!" she panted. "I'll call Rosalind!"

The phone rang and rang. Please, dear God, let her be home! On the fifth ring, Rosalind answered.

"Roz, it's Jess. Something terrible's happening to me! Can you come over? I need you! I need you!"

"I'll be there in five!" Click. Dial tone.

She heard the door chimes, Binkie opening the door, loud

voices echoing in the foyer, then footsteps hammering up the stairs to her room.

"What's going on?" Rosalind demanded in that deep, loud voice she had. She belonged on a parade square. "Good Christ! What happened to you?"

"Please, Roz, help me," Jessica whimpered. "Please don't let me die!"

Sucking in her breath, Rosalind digested Jessica's plea, then dashed to the landing. "Binkie! Come and help me with Jessica!" she hollered. "I'm taking her to the hospital! Where's Julian? Need I ask? He's out doing business!"

Rosalind had never seen anything like it. Her friend was ashen, her teeth were chattering, and she was shivering. And she had all those horrible bruises, with her eyes almost closed shut and framed in murky purple. It was clear why Jessica wouldn't see anyone.

Rosalind called the hospital. A commanding, demanding woman, she declared stridently, "This is Rosalind Rodgers. I'm bringing a friend in...Mrs. Julian Bothwell. She's in bad shape. I want a doctor and nurse available immediately. We'll be there in five minutes!"

Together, Rosalind and Binkie half-carried, half-dragged Jessica to the Corvette and piled her into the passenger seat. While Binkie wrapped a blanket around the stricken Jessica, Rosalind started the engine. Slamming the door, Binkie stood back as the car careened down the driveway. Rob hovered in the doorway, alarmed.

"Where's my mommy? I want my mommy!"

The little boy burst into tears as Binkie hugged him and carried him into the house.

At the hospital, a doctor and nurse were waiting with a

wheelchair for Mrs. Bothwell. They told Rosalind she could wait in the lounge.

"Wait nothing! I'm coming with her! She needs me!" Rosalind's eyes were ablaze, her face grim.

The medical team had seen sharks before, and they didn't want this one bearing down on them. Rosalind was "more than welcome to attend the examination".

After helping Jessica to undress and don an examination gown, Rosalind stood close by, supportively, while Jessica went through a number of routine tests.

"How did you get all those bruises on your upper body and face?" the doctor asked, his tone compassionate.

Jessica glanced at Rosalind who scowled back, one eyebrow raised, and one foot tapping on the floor, with her arms folded across her chest.

"I'd rather not say," Jessica mumbled.

"Cut the crap, Jess! Tell him! He can't help if he doesn't know the truth!"

Tears glistened in Jessica's eyes, and she trembled as she replied, almost inaudibly, "My husband beat me up."

"I see," the doctor said softly. "Well, it seems to me you're suffering from an extreme anxiety attack. Have you had them before?"

"Not like this. This is the worst. I think I'm going to die," she murmured, her voice breaking.

Nodding, the doctor inhaled deeply and spoke with empathy. "Something in your life is causing you considerable anguish. Pressure and anxiety build up to such a degree that your body can't handle it, except in an episode such as you're experiencing. I'll give you a shot to make you more comfortable and prescribe a mild tranquilizer as well as sleeping pills. These aren't addictive if you take them as prescribed, cautiously. If you don't need one, don't take it. These can be helpful, if you take positive steps to relieve whatever may be causing you to suffer from negative emotions. I'd suggest you make arrangements for counseling to help you through your crisis. If you need to see me again, please call me."

He handed her the prescription slips as well as his card, and she noted her hand trembling as she took them.

Rosalind didn't say anything as she led her friend to the car. Once seated, she reached over and hugged Jessica. "You're my dearest, most wonderful friend. Why didn't you tell me what was happening?" she moaned sympathetically.

"Rosalind, I couldn't! I was so ashamed! I feel awful! Look at me! I'm wrecked! I couldn't tell anyone! Only Julian knows, and he'd kill me if I told anybody! Roz, I'm so goddamned afraid!"

"Look," Rosalind said, her anger rising along with her determination, "you need a break from that house, from Rob, and from Julian. Why don't you take a little trip to the city for some R and R?"

Jessica's voice was low and dull. "I'll think about it. I need some time to heal from my bumps and bruises. I can't go anywhere looking like I've tangled with a freight train."

"Okay, I buy that," Rosalind agreed. "But as soon as your wounds heal, off you go to the best hotel to pamper yourself. Between Binkie and me, we can take care of Rob. Now let's pick up those prescriptions."

When Rosalind drove up to the house and parked, Julian, who was waiting on the porch, dashed to Jessica's door and helped her out. Binkie had contacted him and told him of the emergency.

"Darling, what happened?" he asked, worry and concern

etched on his face.

"I'm not exactly sure." Her voice was barely audible.

Rosalind marched right up to him, and looking him straight in the eyes, announced, "She's in serious condition, Julian! She's suffering from third-degree anxiety attacks, the very worst kind. She needs plenty of rest and TLC! I know that you'll see to it that she gets it!"

"Why of course," he agreed quickly. "Are you alright, darling?"

Jessica nodded, choking back tears.

"Thanks, Rosalind, for your help," said Julian, an arm around his wife's shoulder. "I appreciate all you've done."

"Right!" she snapped as she got back into her car. "Call me tomorrow, Jessica, with your progress report. If you don't phone, I'll be over here banging on your door!"

Mission accomplished, she squealed the Corvette down the drive.

Julian helped Jessica into the house.

"What in hell are anxiety attacks?" he wanted to know.

"It means," she replied, as she climbed the stairs to their bedroom, with Julian following, "that something is troubling me. The doctor isn't sure what's at the bottom of it. But the stress of what's disturbing me builds up, and my body can't handle it, and blows its stack, so to speak. Something like a pressure cooker blowing its lid."

"Do you mean this whole thing is in your head?" he asked, somehow dodging responsibility for her condition.

At the top step, she turned to face him, her eyes narrowed, her demeanor bristling, "Julian, what I experienced was *not* in my head!"

"Well, you know how you blow everything out of proportion. You know how you worry and fret over every little thing. You have a very dangerous imagination, Jess, and this is what it's doing to you. What are you supposed to do get rid of these so-called anxiety attacks?"

"The doctor gave me prescriptions for tranquilizers and sleeping pills. Besides trying to relax, all I can do is try to figure out why I'm so uptight."

"It doesn't sound too serious to me," he commented with a shrug, as she turned the handle to open the door to her dressing room.

"No, Julian, I guess it isn't too serious. Not to anyone but *me!*"

In her dressing room, she stripped and put on a cozy flannel nightgown. With fall approaching, the nights were cool. Besides, she was chilled to the very marrow of her bones, and she wasn't exactly into tantalizing her husband. As she climbed into bed, Julian handed her a Valium with a glass of water. Leaning over, he ran his fingers through her hair.

"I love you, Jess. You stay in bed, and I'll look after Rob. Binkie wants to go home, but I can play nanny and make supper."

As she snuggled under the covers, the old familiar feeling drifted and floated its way through her being; the Valium plus the shot at the hospital were casting their magical spell. Closing her eyes, she let her mind wash upon serene, sandy shores. It had been a long time since she had taken any kind of mood-altering drug, other than the occasional drink of alcohol. This little gem was her vacation from cares and worries.

She was confident that she wouldn't become addicted because she had learned a lot about the nature of addiction years earlier, when she had allowed Valium to do a number on her while she was in the throes of a love affair turned sour. Thirty days in a treatment center had certainly opened her eyes to the subtlety of drug dependence. That knowledge would prevent her from getting hooked again. "Be cautious," the doctor had said. She'd be prudent, and the pills would help. She needed them because she was stressed-out, strangling on something.

Julian and Rob marched into the room together, Julian carrying a tray with a red rose in a vase, a glass of champagne, a medium-rare steak cut into bite-sized pieces, and a fresh fruit salad. Jessica hoped Julian hadn't had the foresight to put poison in anything. Her trust in him had been through a wood chipper.

Rob hovered by the bed. "Are you feeling better now? Can we play tomorrow?" he asked in his baby voice.

"I'm lots better now, Love-Bug. And, of course, we'll play. Maybe we can go to the park," she told him, smiling sweetly.

"Let's get you ready for bed, young man," grinned Julian, grabbing his son's hand. "We'll let Mommy eat her supper while I read you a story."

She picked at her meal. Even though it was delicious, she wasn't hungry. With a sip of champagne, she washed down another Valium. She promised herself she'd start taking them as prescribed tomorrow. Right now, it felt so good not to be afraid, not to have terror stalking her steps.

When Julian came in to claim the tray, she was dozing, but she jerked awake, startled.

"Well, everything's quiet in the house," he beamed. "Rob's in bed, Cuddles has had her exercise, the kitchen's all cleaned up. Why don't we snuggle and watch TV?"

Sure, she thought, with another Valium, I could snuggle with Attila the Hun.

And so they cuddled together to watch a movie, while Jessica's perception blinked on and off with the show, snippets of scenes invading her peaceful space. With another sip of champagne, she swallowed the sleeping pill, savoring its charms as the effects swirled throughout her body, caressing her mind and lulling her frizzled nerves. A month's supply of pills sat in her night table drawer. That was long enough to get to the bottom of her nightmare. And she knew she wouldn't become addicted in a month; it took much longer than that.

Julian watched as she dozed off, her head on his chest, his arm around her. What was distressing her? He knew! She was terrified of his drinking, and the horror he had inflicted upon her. Well, no more shit! There was too much at stake. He had his hotels; his business was successful in spite of a few setbacks; he had a beautiful home, a luxurious lifestyle, a fabulous wife, and a terrific little boy. But Tiffany! That was troublesome! What if Jessica remembered what he'd said? Damn him and his drunken mouth! Not to worry. He could explain that away. He'd done it before, and he could do it again. He also knew that if Jessica decided she couldn't handle their relationship, he'd never let her leave. He'd make this marriage work...even if it killed them both.

※

The days floated by in her Valium haze. Jessica counted the pills every time she took one, aware that she was doubling and even tripling the dosage. She panicked when she realized she'd never be able to make it through the month. Maybe she'd be able to beg more pills from the doctor. Perhaps he'd understand her terror and her dire need for the pills in order to cope.

Warily, she watched Julian, wondering if he'd verbally assassinate her, physically batter her, emotionally shred her, and spiritually annihilate her. Instead, he was loving and generous, sweet and tender, kind and considerate, the way he was when they had first realized they were soul mates. But her unhappiness and despair clung to her like saran wrap. Fear was the color of her prison.

✢

Surveying her face one morning, she breathed a sigh of relief that she could finally escape from the house. With Rob and his toys piled into the Mustang, she headed for the lake and the beach.

The sun sparkled on the wavelets as Rob played in the shallows, but already the kiss of autumn was in the air. The trees, still lush and green, hinted that winter was coming by waving a yellowed leaf or two. With her son, Jessica scooped out a trench for the moat around their sand castle. Laughing with him, they skipped stones across the water. His plunked, but hers danced over the surface, sending up showers of droplets that glittered like diamonds.

A loon swam out of the rushes, oblivious to their presence. Holding hands, they stood back to watch the loon bobbing on the water. Suddenly, it flapped its wings and ran along the surface of the lake, churning up the water in its pursuit of its prey. A fish glistened silver before the loon snared it. Lunch! Rob giggled and clapped as the loon triumphed. Oh, nature and its wonders!

Jessica watched her son in his freedom and his joyous childhood, envying his pure, untarnished view of the world. Had she ever felt like that? she wondered. Now she felt old and trapped.

Hope filled her when the doctor welcomed her into his office. Of course, he understood her pain. Of course, he could understand why she "occasionally doubled up the dosage". Of course, he'd help her through this rough period, until she felt better able to cope. No, he had no problem giving her another prescription. How were the sleeping pills working? He was glad to hear that she was resting at night. Oh, she needed a re-fill of that prescription, too?

Clutching her bottles full of re-fills, she hid them between the mattress and box spring of the king-sized bed. The secret knowledge of having them there comforted her. And she would definitely try to cut down. Of course she would.

⁂

Rosalind called. Was Jessica up to having lunch? Mary-Beth was absolutely bursting at the seams to tell them her news.

"Would you mind picking me up?" Jessica asked. Other than driving to the lake and visiting her doctor, she preferred not to use her car. It terrified her. Her confidence at the wheel had vanished. She couldn't negotiate through traffic, maneuver around corners, and burn rubber on the thoroughfare as she had earlier.

"No problem," said Rosalind. "I'll be there at one."

Dressing for the important lunch, she examined her face. No amount of makeup could return the sparkle to her eyes. Even though the bruising was gone, her mind and heart bore the scars of that terrible night.

Damn it, Jess, she thought. Julian's been a darling for weeks. It's time to live and laugh again. Bury the past and get on with your life.

Mary-Beth radiated all that Jessica wished she could feel. She envied Mary-Beth's dazzling smile and her clear twinkling eyes. The maître d' at the Wharf seated them, took their drink orders, and arched an eyebrow at Mary-Beth who ordered a virgin piña colada.

"We're in the Wharf's good graces again," explained Mary-Beth. "I came and apologized for my antics the last time we were here. God! The things I do for posh places and atmosphere!" She giggled.

Giggling? thought Jessica. This David-thing is sending her into her second childhood!

"Okay," Rosalind said, as they sipped their drinks, "out with it!"

"I can't believe what's happened!" bubbled Mary-Beth, tossing her blonde curls, as she wiggled with ecstasy. "You are going to simply die when I tell you! But first, what's wrong with you, Jess? You aren't your usual perky self. You seem down or something."

Jessica looked at Rosalind and hoped she would understand the lie. "Oh, I had the flu, and I've been stuck in the house, and Julian and I had a bit of a spat. I'll be fine. It's just bad timing for me today, that's all. Now come on, we're tired of trying to guess what's exciting in your life. The only thing we could come up with is that you're considering having a sex change so you and David can be together," she teased, and her whimsy sent Rosalind into a fit of laughter.

Mary-Beth blushed, compressing a grin. "That's awful, Jessica! What a terrible thing to say!"

"Well, you were so unhinged about David, we figured you'd do something desperate," smiled Jessica. "But from the look on your face, I'd say you've experienced the second coming of Christ!"

Mary-Beth shook her head vigorously. "Okay. Here's what happened...I went to see this plastic surgeon in the city. He gave me the low-down on the whole deal about having my breasts enlarged. Expensive as hell, but it was worth it, if I could keep David. I was willing to go up to a double D to save my marriage. You remember how unglued I was?"

Her friends nodded, holding their breaths.

"Well, this doctor...oh! He's so terrific! He told me to really consider this and that implants can be dangerous. He wouldn't commit himself to my project until I'd thought about it for thirty days. I was really impressed because he was so sincere. I thought plastic surgeons took on anything to make a buck. That night, I got a call at my hotel. I'd told him where I was staying, and that I'd phone him the next day to arrange my next appointment. Anyway, he said he wanted to see me..."

Rosalind furrowed her brow. "This guy sounds like a predator to me. Don't tell me you actually..."

"Give me some credit for brains, Rosalind! I might be blonde, but I'm not stupid! Don't jump to conclusions!"

"Go ahead, Mary-Beth," encouraged Jessica. "This sounds fascinating."

"This sounds God-awful," moaned Rosalind, shaking her head.

"Okay," continued Mary-Beth, ignoring Rosalind, "he called. He'd like to meet me for drinks at my hotel. I was concerned, but I knew I was safe in that busy place; and I thought that if he tried anything peculiar, I'd nail him with a charge of molesting a patient. I know the ropes, ladies!" She grinned as she stirred her drink. "I agreed to meet him in the lounge. Anyway, we had a couple of drinks, and he said that if I went through with the operation, it'd be a waste. He said as far as he was concerned, my breasts were perfect, and it would be a crime to inflate them. I told him about David, and he said as much as I loved my husband, putting my life on the line wasn't worth it."

Rosalind interjected, "Jessica and I both told you that!"

"I know," conceded Mary-Beth, "but I did what I had to do. God! To think I would've mutilated myself to please a man who prefers men! I crawl with gooseflesh every time I think about it! Anyway, Orville...that's his name..."

"Orville?" croaked Rosalind, rolling her green eyes. "Anyone with that name can't be all bad!"

Mary-Beth glared at her. "For heaven's sake, Rosalind, stop interrupting me! I'm trying to tell you something! Orville said my breasts were perfect! They're the exact dimensions for my frame, and they're beautiful..."

"Oh, God!" groaned Rosalind. "What else did you show him in the examination room?"

"Nothing!" snapped Mary-Beth.

With a brilliant smile, she batted her eyelashes at the waiter while he filled their water glasses. Perturbed, Jessica watched her shamelessly flirt with him when he returned to take their orders. What in heaven's name was the woman on? Jessica wished she could look as fresh and act as fresh as Mary-Beth. She recalled how she used to feel full of fun and reckless in safe situations, but now she was paranoid in her own house. If burglars weren't breaking in, her husband was smacking her around. Calling a halt to her introspection, she brightened for Mary-Beth's sake; she didn't want to spoil her friend's surprise.

"Well," continued Mary-Beth, as she swirled her creamy drink with her straw. "Orville thought I should really re-consider my position.... And then he told me a little about himself. He's divorced...no kids..."

"Thanks be to God!" gasped Rosalind.

"And..." Mary-Beth said, as she glared at Rosalind, "...he said before I left the city, he'd like to treat me to dinner. So

I accepted, and he told me he found me most attractive and wanted us to become better acquainted, on one condition..."

"Which is...?" prompted Jessica.

"That I not have a breast augmentation!"

"And what about David in all this?" questioned Jessica.

"Oh! Him! That's all over. I don't need that perversion in my life!"

Jessica was amazed that in such a short time, Mary-Beth had been transformed from a woman attempting to patch her life together with scotch tape and safety pins to a woman in charge of her own destiny.

"David's gone now, and he and his lover are together. I'm happy for him that he has what he needs. But the very best part is that Orville is taking me to Tahiti for Christmas." She squealed her news. "And if everything goes okay in the next few months, we might even get married!"

Rosalind stared at Mary-Beth, then at Jessica. The waiter served their lunch in silence. The air was charged with unuttered thoughts while Mary-Beth waited for her friends' comments on her tidings.

Jessica was speechless, but knowing that Rosalind was bursting to voice her opinion, she interjected first.

"I think your surprise is, uh...a surprise! It certainly wasn't what I was expecting, but I'm thrilled for you, Mary-Beth!"

"Are you sure this bimbo is on the level?" queried Rosalind, whose mind was as instinctively suspicious as a mouse's would be if it were scurrying across a field with an eagle gliding overhead.

"I'm positive! I checked him out while I was in the city. He even showed me his divorce papers, and he took me to see his penthouse...and he never touched me once! We want to really get to know each other. And you'll get to meet him and give him the third degree before I do anything silly like get married." She felt a little deflated because her great announcement hadn't been met with cheers and applause.

"Do you know what I think?" asked Rosalind as she cut into her quiche.

Both Mary-Beth and Jessica braced themselves.

"I think this is the greatest news I've heard in years! Let's celebrate! How about champagne? You're paying, aren't you, Mary-Beth?"

⁂

Julian slid his fingers across the white tablecloth at their table at the Diplomat, reaching for Jessica's hand. With his brown eyes glimmering in the candlelight, he gazed into hers as he lifted her hand to his lips and kissed her fingertips.

"Happy Anniversary, darling." He placed a small black velvet box in front of her. "Three wonderful years. Thank you, precious."

Jessica sipped her Chauvenet Red Cap, her favorite bubbling wine. Teeny swallows. She knew that combined with the one Valium she had popped when she excused herself to go to the powder room, the mixture could be tricky.

Gingerly, she picked up the tiny package. It opened easily to reveal a burst of crystal fire. A huge heart-shaped diamond solitaire set in a platinum ring dazzled her eyes.

"Three carats," he smiled at her. "One carat for each year."

"Julian, it's gorgeous!" she wept, trying to hide her tears.

"What's wrong?" he asked.

"I didn't get you anything!" she sniffled. "I didn't know if we'd be celebrating this year or going through divorce court."

"Darling, don't even think things like that. I'll never let you go. You mean too much to me. And don't worry about not buying me anything. I have *you*! What else could I ever wish for? *You're* my anniversary present!"

He slipped the ring on her finger where it blazed in the flickering candlelight.

"Oh, Julian, I love you so much! All I could ever hope for I have with you."

"Come on. Let's dance before they serve our dinner," he chuckled.

He led her to the dance floor of the Diplomat, and they swayed to the melody of "I Had the Last Waltz with You". Relaxing in his arms, she dismissed the terror that had haunted her. After three years of marriage, Jessica decided that what had happened four weeks earlier was a small price to pay for the joy she knew could be hers in the warmth and safety of his loving embrace.

Lifting her chin so that their eyes met as the music ended, he whispered, "I love you. You don't ever have to be afraid again. I adore both you and Rob. You're the two most important people in my life."

Later, in the haven of their bedroom, she surrendered to the delight of his lovemaking. As she lay curled in his arms after their desire was spent, she banished the fear from her heart. The nightmare was over.

⁂

Their honeymoon lasted for three months, until the last week of November. She had cut down on her intake of Valium so much that she was pills ahead instead of behind. With Julian home nearly every evening, not off to Japan or Europe every other week, and not drinking, she relaxed. She didn't need Seconal at night. They made lazy, tingling, silky love, laughed again, shared jokes, went for walks with Rob and Cuddles in their lavish neighborhood, went out to dinner and movies, and made plans to go skiing when the snow in the mountains was deep enough.

They went to the range together, and she proudly demonstrated her skill, while Casey admired her proficiency and told Julian his wife was the star of the range. And while Julian watched Jessica, Casey quietly observed Julian.

She awoke on the last day of November and knew what she wanted to do the moment she peeked though the curtains of her bedroom. The lawn was dusted with snow as flakes danced outside the window. The tingle of Christmas coursed through her veins. She adored the lights, the trees, the presents, and the joy. As a child, she had greeted the season with the innocent eagerness of the young. But somehow, Christmases past that were supposed to hold such wonderful memories, in hindsight, didn't.

As she watched the snowflakes, she leaned against the sill and thought of those long-ago Christmas Days when they were supposed to have such a happy family. But she and her sister had argued all day over whose gifts were nicest and best, while her mother tried to take family pictures and her father snarled and accused his wife of being silly and sentimental. Her mother had cried that only her family didn't get along on Christmas, for God's sake! She repeatedly asked the children where she had gone wrong to deserve such a fate. How could they have turned out to be such squabbling brats when all she ever wanted was a home full of love and joy and peace?

She recalled all those years when her mother had slaved for days to prepare a feast that was devoured in fifteen minutes. Her mother fretted, worried, and cleaned for weeks because everything had to be perfect for the sweet Baby Jesus and Santa Claus. While Jessica and Sue-Bell scrubbed their old dolls, their mother washed, starched, and ironed all the toys' dresses, so that all the dolls would feel as beautiful and special as the new ones that Santa was sure to bring.

With those memories tugging at her heartstrings, Jessica's eyes brimmed with tears as she thought of her mother and how hard the dear lady had tried, year after year, to match to reality the fantasy of her dreams about Christmas. Jessica could not remember a single truly joyous holiday season—at least not the kind promised by the merry tunes that trilled over the radio. Not one Christmas had been free from strife, panic, and worry. Her mother had wrung her hands in despair, while her father silently observed the frantic activity and then retreated from the rest of the family to his study with his books and opera music.

Through it all, Jessica remained determined that one day, when she was older and married and perhaps had children of her own, she would have Christmases that were joyful and magical.

Thinking of her mother, she choked back a painful lump rising in her throat. Jessica's mother had died of a broken heart and shattered dreams at the age of fifty-six, a year to the day after her husband left her for an ashram in the Himalayas to find himself. His wife had never recognized that he was lost. Jessica still hated her father for that. Neither she, nor her sister, had heard from their father since he vanished on his pilgrimage.

With the leaden sky billowing forth snowflakes, Jessica decided to do her Christmas baking. She was one of those women who loathed cooking and never touched flour except to make Christmas treats. She and Julian always invited friends and acquaintances in on Christmas Eve, and she liked to have some of her own home-made goodies to serve besides the delicacies supplied by the catering firm attending to their parties.

"Merry Christmas, Mom," she whispered. "I love you."

She skipped down the stairs to the kitchen to take stock of her baking supplies. Tearing open cupboards and drawers, she was satisfied that she had everything she required. As she whirled around, organizing everything exactly the way she preferred in order to make the joyous task easier, she tripped over Cuddles who danced at her feet and Rob who begged for some breakfast. With the meal over, she encouraged Rob and Cuddles to frolic in the family room, out of her kitchen, and then put on her favorite Christmas music CD to listen to the energetic selections that inspired her. Humming as she studied her recipe books, she picked out the things she liked best.

Beyond her windows, the snowflakes continued their silent ballet to earth. What a great day to stay indoors and bake! With the snow and dark sky, she felt cocooned and cozy in the kitchen, enveloped in a magical dream of how wonderful their Christmas would be. Remembering the previous year, she smiled to herself; how delicious it had been making love beside the tree after everyone had left the party.

By five that afternoon, every counter was piled high with her efforts: shortbreads decorated with red and green cherries to make them look like poinsettias and wreathes; rum balls; mincemeat tarts; butter tarts; brownies; date bread with nuts; banana loaf; cherry bread; fruit cake; and also gumdrop cake and Rice Krispies squares for the children's party she and Julian hosted every year for the employees' kids. She also called Julian to make sure he'd be home for supper before she made one of his favorite meals—pork hock stew with dumplings. As it bubbled on the stove, the delightful aroma permeated the air.

Jessica might not have liked cooking, but she was a whiz at it, always preparing delectable meals with the best of ingredients. She knew a lot about nutrition, and she created meals with Rob's growing needs in mind. She wanted him to get off to a great start in life with food that was filled with nutrients, and she wanted her family to get the best nutritional bang for their buck.

All day, Rob scampered in and out of the kitchen, licking spoons, pots, and mixing bowls; snacking on fresh vegetables chopped for the stew; and sampling cookies and tarts.

For hours, the kitchen buzzed and hummed as the treats piled higher. With the last cookie off the sheet, Jessica sat down to admire her work. Full of pride at her accomplishment, she knew Julian would be impressed.

❆

"Good Christ, Jess, what in hell are you going to do with all this stuff? There's enough here to last for years! And you know I hate shortbreads with cherries and all that gunk on top! Mother would never dream of wrecking cookies like that! Who do you expect to eat all this shit? Me? You know I'm trying to keep my weight down! We might be having people in on Christmas Eve, but we're not inviting all of Riverbend! And why did you make so much goddamned stew? You know I hate leftovers!"

Merry Christmas to you too, Julian, she thought.

Not saying a word, she packaged her offerings and carried them to the freezer in the basement. Choking on her hurt and anger, she sat down to help Rob with his supper, and then turned to find her own meal cold and tasteless. Julian wolfed down his stew, sopping up the gravy with the dumplings. The perfect gentleman, who performed in public with exquisite taste and impeccable manners, was a slob at home, humming away to himself as he enjoyed the delicious stew. Jessica swallowed her fury with every mouthful, as she watched Julian heap sugar into his tea and snare four butter tarts...to help keep his weight down.

As she scraped her meal into the disposal, Julian flipped on the TV in the family room. Rob followed him, and Jessica waited for the call, which was sure to come. She rinsed the dishes and loaded the dishwasher. It took every fiber of her being and every shred of patience she had left over from the day's frantic activity to not slam the machine's door shut and smash the dishes to smithereens. As she wiped clean the counters and tables, she heard what she had been expecting.

"Jess, come and get this kid! I'm trying to watch the news! How can I relax with a kid and a dog crawling all over me?"

"Right, darling!" she snapped, as she rescued him from Rob. "You relax and unwind after your exhausting day at the office, while I get him off to bed! Do you think you'll be able to tolerate Cuddles? Or would you like me to euthanize her? I wouldn't want your relaxation time to be interrupted!"

"Get off it, Jess!" He glared at the TV, hiking up the volume to tune her out.

She marched Rob militantly upstairs to a warm bath. Resentment throbbed in her veins, but she kept a lid on her anger. Suddenly, she loathed Rob. The little boy had been into everything all day, while she had labored with her baking. She'd managed a three-ring circus for nine hours. Her fingers yearned to strangle the tireless child who still demanded her time and attention, when all she wanted to do was sit and unwind like Julian. Capping her rage, she dried, lotioned, and powdered Rob and put him to bed, smiling and gritting her teeth through *Peter Rabbit*. Rob reached for a hug as she pulled the covers over him, while she fought the urge to smother him with the quilt. Turning out the light, she went to her dressing room to change into her lounging pajamas.

As she stripped, the horror struck, choking her. With blood thrumming in her ears, she sagged against the counter. My God! She'd been so busy and purposeful all day that she'd forgotten to take her Valium. How silly of her! Gripped with fear and panic, she washed down three. A bath would calm her. Running a tub, she soaked until she was floating and serene, her breathing normal, her heart beating slowly and easily.

In her silk pajamas, she curled herself on the couch in the family room, drawing an afghan around her shoulders. Julian stirred in his new leather recliner and lit a cigarette, hiding behind a blue haze.

"Jess, I'm sorry I was so hard on you about the baking and the stew. I just wish you'd practice a little more restraint."

Rule #697: When trying to please one's husband, always practice restraint—except in bed.

Wickedly, she thought, Yes, Julian. No Julian. Anything you say, Julian. And after that, screw yourself, Julian.

She gave up trying to make him disappear into a puff of smoke with her poisonous glances. She also gave up watching TV while he blip, blip, blipped his way through dozens of channels with the remote control. How could she concentrate on any program with a madman at the helm? Did every man consider the remote control his sacred possession to blip from one channel to another, regardless of who else might be present? She was sure it was a male trait spawned by an errant chromosome.

With fury festering in her brain, she stomped up the stairs, crawled into bed, took two Seconals, and dozed off reading a magazine. She awoke, as she so often had, with Julian all over her, pawing and fondling her. She longed to scream at him to leave her alone and to "practice some restraint". In her drugged state, she choked down the rage, the humiliation, and the self-loathing for not ordering him to leave her in peace and jack off! By the time he was finished and had rolled over, she had worked herself into a wide-awake, glassy-eyed, foul humor. Yanking her magazine from the night table, she fumed down the stairs to the living room.

Up early, without having really slept, she made coffee and sat down with Julian, who was concealed behind *The Wall Street Journal*. Stock markets interested him since he had several large investments. He mumbled and grumbled about stocks tumbling, his cigarette sending up smoke signals.

"Is something bothering you, darling?" she purred, well aware that he hated losing money. "You seem a little agitated."

"As a matter of fact, there is!" He peered around the side of the paper, scowling. "You know damned well I can't tolerate the top being left off the toothpaste. You're doing it deliberately to get my day off to a bad start! You'd better stop doing it right now! I'm onto your lousy little game, and it sucks!"

So, he'd developed a new tactic. She couldn't believe he was capable of such pettiness. She also couldn't help herself; she laughed. He glowered as he noisily folded the paper.

"Darling," she snickered, "I had no idea I was driving you crazy. But if I ever wanted to, now I know how. Thanks for telling me."

"Fuck you!" he spat. "I'm glad I can leave you laughing. But watch your step, Jess! You're treading on thin ice!" And he hurled himself from the table, smacking the paper down.

She stared after him, dazed at his belligerence. Well, she thought, I guess we're back to "Operation Trench Warfare".

⁂

Every second he was at home, Jessica tiptoed through a minefield, never knowing what might set him off. He began to stay out later, with excuses that he was attending hospital board meetings, working on a charity campaign for Christmas, and spending extra time at the hotels as the busy holiday season approached.

The nights became lonely and terrifying. She swallowed more pills. The bottles grew emptier every day, while her heart stopped every time she counted the tiny pieces of serenity. She knew she'd never make it through the holidays without more pills.

Dr. Morton was miffed when she requested another prescription renewal. Holding her breath and clinging to a chair in front of his desk, she listened to his reluctance.

"I'm not at all sure about this, Jessica...All right, I'll give you another supply, but if you want more when this is gone, I'll be making an appointment with a psychiatrist."

"For yourself?"

"No!" he barked. "For you!"

She was startled by his vehemence. For a moment, chastened, she wet her lips. "Dr. Morton, I wouldn't ask if I didn't need them. There's some connection between my anxiety and my home life. Without the pills, I can't function or sleep. I don't know what to do. Until I find a solution to my problems, I'd appreciate artificial help."

"Okay. But this is the last prescription I'm giving you."

Promising not to double up, promising to come up with another way out of her difficulties, promising not to become addicted, she clung to the small prescription slip as she escaped to her car. She would have promised a pint of her blood every day for those pills. But in her heart, she knew she was addicted, that she would double up, that she'd never have the courage to stand up to Julian.

⁂

Christmas Eve. The house pulsed with music, bubbled with people, twinkled with tree lights and tinsel, and glimmered with the magic of the season. Jessica, dressed in a crimson jumpsuit designed with long sleeves and a plunging neckline, mingled with the guests, while the caterers side-stepped and wove their way through the crowd, offering champagne, rum and egg nog, punch, canapés, and Jessica's goodies.

Lydia touched her arm "What a lovely party, my dear. I must say, you know how to entertain. You seem to outdo yourself every year! Are you still planning on coming to dinner tomorrow? I have your gifts under my tree."

"The plans haven't changed, as far as I know...Oh, excuse me. Julian's waving at me," she said, relieved to get away from

145

the woman.

She threaded her way through the laughing guests to her husband, who, glass in hand, was grinning. Lincoln was snickering beside him.

"Jess, darling, Lincoln's told me the most amusing joke," he managed through his laughter. "How do you paralyze a woman from the waist down?"

"I've no idea." She stared at him.

"Marry her!" he smirked. Considering the past few weeks, she wasn't surprised that he found it humorous. She didn't laugh or even smile.

"You're well aware of my environmental concerns and my hope that we can rid our planet of all the pollution." Her voice was monotonic, no hint of mirth. "What do you call two thousand men at the bottom of Lake Superior?"

Lincoln and Julian, still chuckling like schoolboys, shrugged their shoulders.

"A *start!*" She hurled the words at them like a sack of rotting fish. "Now excuse me, I have more people to visit with."

Turning, she bumped into Roxanne.

"Oh, Jessica," gurgled Lincoln's wife, "you're absolutely the most fantastic hostess! The waitress told me you made all the sweets! How quaint!" Her plump cheeks glowed with too much champagne, and her caftan, awash with red and green swirls of sequins and glitter, made her resemble a tipsy Christmas tree. "I just don't understand how you keep your figure and make these yummy sweets and all. I wish I could knock off about two hundred pounds, but the weight's welded on!"

You might try an extended vacation on a desert island, Jessica thought. Aloud, she said, "Why, Roxanne, you're perfect the way you are!" She hoped the remarkable fib would win her points when she said her prayers about having enough pills to get through the holidays.

✿

The guests drifted home. By 1:00 AM, Jessica was saying good night to the last couple.

"Merry Christmas!" she waved as their car pulled away.

As the caterers packed up the last of their equipment, Jessica sipped on her rum and egg nog, hoping that once everyone was gone, she and Julian would be able to cuddle in the glow of the tree and watch the embers in the fireplace blush, flash, and burn out.

While Julian poured another scotch, she admired the tree. It had taken hours to decorate. True to her environmentally conscious self, it was an imitation blue spruce. She couldn't bear to chop down a tree as Julian had suggested. The decorations twinkled and shimmered in the lights, and she had twirled strings of pearls and crystals through the branches so that the entire tree glistened.

She heard Julian say good night to the caterers. On cat feet, he was behind her, offending her nostrils with the stench of his scotch.

"That goddamned tree looks like it's going to topple, Jess! Did you have to be so bloody extravagant? Christ! You always do things way over the top! You always go overboard! I'm sick of it!"

"Sweetheart, I did my best. I love the tree. Why don't we play Santa and put Rob's presents under it?"

"Fuck you! Do it yourself!" His eyes were glassy, his stance unsteady. "Why don't we just have a good fuck under the goddamned thing? Then I can go to bed!"

Alarm bells rang in her head. "Why don't I tuck you into bed?" she asked softly. "We can cuddle there, and you can go to sleep." The silk gloves approach.

"You stupid bitch!" he slurred "Are you deaf as well as stupid? I said I wanna screw under the fuckin' tree!" He grabbed at her as she backed away.

"Not tonight," she whispered. "Maybe tomorrow."

He snared her by the neckline of her jumpsuit and it ripped as he pulled her to him, crushing his scotch-reeking mouth on hers.

"You're sure a cold bitch!" he sneered. "Wanna know what I think? Anybody who's as cold as you are is getting tail somewhere, and it sure ain't at home!"

"That's ludicrous!" she countered, trying to claw her way to freedom. "We never make love because you're out until all hours! I'm home with Rob every night waiting for you, and you never come home!"

"What's there to come home to? A goddamned iceberg! And I'm working, you stupid cunt! Making the bucks while you spend them!"

"You call what you do work?" she retaliated. She knew she should shut her mouth, not say a word, but anger smoldered in her heart, and it had found expression. She felt powerless to resist its force. "All you do is drink, entertain your henchmen, and scheme and plot about who you can screw for another damned dime! You're nothing but a legalized crook!"

It wasn't going like last Christmas at all.

"At least I bring home the bread!" he garbled, yanking her by her shredded jumpsuit.

"Shut up, Julian! I'm sick of hearing how great you think you are! You're nothing but a powerhouse and a bully! All you want to do is control people!"

"You're nuthin' but a money-spending machine!" He smacked her on the side of the head. "Christ! You spend it faster than I can make it! You're fuckin' around, you bitch!" Another crack on her cheek.

Struggling, she freed herself, side-stepping out of his path as he lunged at her. Like a linebacker, he tackled the tree. It shook and quivered and tumbled over, spilling ornaments and lights and ropes of crystals, tangling him in a tinsel web. The blown-glass balls popped and crackled as they splintered, and the lights sparked and fizzled as they shattered. Perhaps, she hoped, while she asked heaven's forgiveness, he'd electrocute himself.

Scrambling to his feet, bound in bobbles, bangles, and beads, he nailed her to the floor before she reached the staircase. With one hand, he held her by the throat, and with the other, he hammered her face as she screamed and cried. One of his blows hit home and sent her dizzily into blackness. Satisfied he had silenced her, he pulled himself up the stairs to his bed.

"Women!" he muttered, as he flopped onto the comforter. "Like my daddy always said, 'If they didn't have cunts, there'd be a bounty on 'em!'"

Dazed, Jessica raised her head to see if her attacker was gone. As she shook her head, she raised herself to her knees and looked around. Her tree, her work of art, was crumbled and smashed. The presents were strewn and broken. Rob's new rocking horse was splintered. The boxes were crushed, nametags littered the carpet, and bows and ribbons lay scattered in silent testimony to the devastation of her favorite celebration.

It was her fault, she decided, as she picked herself up. "If only I'd buttoned my lip, this never would have happened," she whimpered, as she picked up a tag signed, "All my love, Julian".

This was not like last Christmas at all. Popping two Valium, she turned to the task of restoring sanity to the madhouse of her living room.

Rule # 994: Never argue with your husband.

The next morning, she dialed Lydia's number. "Merry Christmas, Mother Lydia. Jess here. I'm sorry we won't be able to make it for dinner. Julian's sick in bed. Probably something he ate last night."

When she looked at herself in the mirror, a bruised and welted face stared back at her with vacant eyes. Thank God for Rob and for Chevy Chase in *Christmas Vacation*. She and Rob giggled through two runs of the movie, while Jessica soothed her battered face with ice packs.

Julian sulked and simmered through a hangover in bed.

Chapter Four:

Desperate Attempts

THE WIND THRASHED THROUGH THE YARD AND SCREAMED AROUND THE HOUSE. Frost crept up the windows while Jessica gazed at the moonscape her patio and garden had become. Drifts of snow were packed along the cedar hedges, which separated the Bothwells' property from that of their neighbors. Thank God the holidays were over. She had escaped the New Year's Eve party at Rosalind's by explaining that the flu had her in bed again.

"This is the worst attack I've had," she had pleaded. "I can't come, Roz. Besides, Julian has something going on at the Lodge."

"Worse than what attack?" Rosalind clipped. "Flu or Julian?"

"What do you think?"

"Jess, you're going to get yourself killed. You've got to do something!"

"I'll get through this. It was my own fault. I didn't shut up. I should have kept my mouth closed."

"Nonsense! It wasn't your fault. Julian has an ugly temper. I've known him longer than you have, and I've seen some of his shenanigans."

"Please, Roz, let me heal, and I'll be over to see you."

"Any more nonsense over there, you call me. I'll come and get you. I don't want to hear about your murder in the paper!" Click.

Lydia had phoned on New Year's Day. "We missed you at the Terrace Lodge last night. What a wonderful party! Julian said you were unwell. My, the two of you have had a bit of bad luck with him sick at Christmas and now you..."

"It's just the flu. You know how susceptible I am to bugs. If anyone sneezes, I end up with pneumonia." She hated the lies. What else could she do?

"Well, I certainly hope you'll make it to my anniversary party. You know, if Julian's father had lived, we'd be celebrating forty-seven years this month."

"What a tender touch, Mother Lydia, still celebrating your wedding anniversary even though he's been gone all these years."

"He was a special man, my dear, and I still miss him. Doing up a party makes him seem still close to me."

"I'm sure I'll feel the same way about Julian if I outlive him," she said, praying she *would survive* to outlive him.

She stared out the window at the blowing snow. She thought about Julian's contrite apologies for the Christmas catastrophe, and how he'd sworn off drinking again and proven it by not having so much as a beer for days. Occasionally, he was home early, but he was non-communicative, preferring to fall asleep in front of the television in the family room. He played with Rob and built houses and bridges with him using Lego and wooden blocks; took Cuddles for walks; even had supper a few times with Jessica. But there was no physical intimacy, no communication. Every night, she fell asleep alone and woke up with him gone to work. She seemed to wander in some kind of purgatory, unsure of what she had done. Was he punishing her?

Was he unsure of himself, having broken his promises about his drinking and abusive behavior so recently and so often? Maybe he was waiting for her to give him a signal that she forgave him, and she was willing to get on with their life together. After all, she had avoided him as much as possible, vanishing to put Rob to bed and then escaping to the bedroom immediately after supper.

They had to talk, she decided, but when? Mornings were not conducive to an intimate dialogue, because he was too rushed. He was too busy during the day. And she felt uncomfortable about the evenings because he might not be home early enough, he might be too tired, or he might not appear sober. She wanted him alert, attentive, and anxious for a discussion.

She still loved him and knew that, given a chance to salvage what they once had, they could build a new and better relationship. She clung to the memories of their promises to each other that they would never go to bed angry with each other; that they would always be open and honest about their feelings; that they would always communicate; that if one of them needed to talk, the other would make himself or herself available to listen; and that they would cherish each other and their relationship. They were, after all, best friends. Had Julian forgotten those promises? Was she the one who had to grovel this time?

An idea exploded in her head. She called the Talisman. Yes, Mr. Bothwell was in. Breaking the connection, she phoned Binkie to look after Rob. Jessica would drop him off at her place on the way to the hotel. Dashing down to the refrigerated cedar room where she stored her fur coats, she grabbed the champagne mink, which Julian had presented to her as a token apology for the Christmas calamity. She loathed the fur industry and the suffering it caused, but for her purposes, the mink's glamour was ideal.

Flying up the stairs two at a time, she scrubbed under a shower, washed her hair, blow-dried it, and let it fall straight over her shoulders. Makeup, fastidiously applied, concealed the yellow remnants of her bruises. Pearl button earrings and a matching necklace added a touch of elegance and class. Draped in the champagne mink and wearing her up-to-the-knee leather boots, she surveyed herself in the full-length mirror and decided she looked like the kind of woman she would like to encounter if she were a man. Perhaps she could even tempt him to come home with her.

She called for a taxi; anyone in his right mind wouldn't be out driving on such a day unless he was being paid.

Bundling Rob into a snowsuit, she experienced a rush of happiness spiraling through her being. Why hadn't she thought of this before? Julian wouldn't be able to ignore her this time.

Entering the lobby of the Talisman, she held the soft lapels of the coat close to her throat. The cold wind had blown up the lining as she exited the taxi, making her skin tingle with its icy crispness. Her high-heeled boots echoed on the marble floor as she proceeded to her husband's office.

"Oh, Mrs. Bothwell, we weren't expecting you!" Julian's secretary, Avis, scrambled to her feet to bar the way to Julian's door. "Mr. Bothwell's busy right now. He's in a meeting."

"Is he in the boardroom or his office?" Jessica inquired.

"The boardroom," Avis gasped. "That is, I think..."

"Well, I'll wait for him in his office," Jessica broke in.

"No...I'd forgotten. He's interviewing someone," quavered the secretary.

"Then I suppose you and I will get to know each other better," smiled Jessica, perplexed at the secretary's discomfort, but determined to accomplish her mission. This was too important to be discouraged by a mere paid employee. "I'm sure I can wait right here." She plopped herself down on the antique rocker, carefully arranging her coat so that it covered her legs to the tops of her boots.

"Please let me take your coat, Mrs. Bothwell. I can hang it up for you."

"Oh, no! I'll keep it on. This was a Christmas gift from Mr. Bothwell, and it's the first time I've worn it. I'm enjoying how luxurious it feels." She took her cigarettes and lighter from her purse. "You can be a dear, though. Please bring me an ashtray and order up some coffee."

The secretary produced an ashtray from her desk drawer and phoned the kitchen for coffee. A waiter arrived to serve the steaming brew from a silver engraved pot with an elegantly curved spout, pouring it into a white china cup decorated with the hotel logo. Jessica riffled through a magazine and then took another from the coffee table. As the number of magazines dwindled, the ashtray filled with cigarette butts, and the coffee pot emptied, Jessica sat sweltering in her coat. A glance at her watch indicated that she'd been waiting for almost an hour. Maybe it hadn't been such a good idea to come here today. Perhaps fate didn't want her to see her husband.

Hearing the office door open, she turned her head to see a tall, redheaded, young woman emerge, her face aglow as she said goodbye to Julian.

"Thanks for the opportunity to be of service," she gushed as she blew him a kiss.

Julian exuded a radiance of health and well-being. How seldom he radiated anything at home, except for a desire for space and silence.

"Take care, Amber. How about next week, same time?" Jessica heard her husband say, before he stepped back into his office, closing the door.

As the secretary busied herself with her files and computer screen, intent on her office duties, the redhead breezed from the office, smelling like a hothouse rosebush. Jessica noticed she had a figure that would stop a hearse and probably wake the dead.

Blushing, and avoiding Jessica's eyes, the secretary buzzed Julian's office. "Your wife to see you, sir." There was a pause as she waited for his reply. She wore a deeper shade of red as she told Jessica to wait another five minutes.

Jessica stood up. "Wait? Not on your life? I've waited too long as it is! And that looked like quite an interview sailing by!"

With determination, she strode to the door, flinging it open. Julian was re-arranging his tie as he turned from the window.

"My, my, my, the interviewees are becoming more attractive all the time," Jessica sang as she closed the door and settled herself in a chair alongside his desk. "And just what will Amber be doing? Collecting stamps from all your mail?"

He didn't miss a beat, his expression inscrutable. "No. I thought she'd make a great singer in the lounge at the Terrace Lodge," he replied smoothly. "She's a woman of many talents." He leveled his eyes at her, defying her to plunge into a debate.

"So it seems," she purred. Don't blow it, Jessica.

"And what brings you out on this stormy afternoon? I was going to cut things short and perhaps head home."

"Maybe the same thing that brought Amber out in the storm."

"Look, I don't know what you're thinking, but you can cool it with Amber! She's a masseuse and comes once or twice a week."

"So your secretary tells me she's an interview? Come on,

Julian, I wasn't born yesterday."

Julian shrugged, still smiling, "Darling, if I wanted to mess around, I sure wouldn't be doing it in my office. Credit me with some brains!"

"Hmmm...That's true," she conceded, unsure of herself.

"So why are you here? I sure as hell hope you didn't drive!"

"Taxi," she smiled, wishing he'd ask her to take off her coat. "Gosh! It's sure warm in here!"

"Take off that damned coat! I know it's cold outside, but there's no blizzard in here!"

"Can you help me with it?" She stood up, undoing the buttons. "Are the days of chivalry over?" She peeked up at him, mischief dancing in her eyes.

Suspicious, he asked, "Is that a trick question?"

"Darling, I never ask trick questions. Please help me with my coat."

As he slipped off the fur, he found she had nothing on but her earrings, pearl necklace, and diamond watch. With her knee-high boots, she looked a little like a number from the drag, which was her intention.

"Holy shit, Jess!" He attempted to cover her with the coat. "What if Avis barged in? What about Lincoln?"

"I locked the door, precious," she whispered. "There isn't anyone in here but you and me."

"Jesus H. Christ, Jess, what is this?" he gasped, visibly ruffled.

"*Us* for beginners! I don't see you in the mornings these days; you're busy all day, and we don't, or can't, talk at night. I couldn't get your attention if I shaved off my eyebrows and set my hair on fire! So, I thought this might..."

"Okay! So I'm paying attention! What's so damned important?"

"*Us*, Julian! *Us!* Ever since the holidays, we haven't discussed anything about what's happening to us!" she implored.

"Here! Put your coat on! I can't listen or talk with you hanging out all over the place!" he said gruffly.

As he poured the mink over her shoulders, she heard herself mew, "Please let's talk when you get home today. I'll put Rob down early, make a special dinner, and maybe we can discuss the things that are driving a wedge between us."

Even as she uttered the plaintive, begging words, she hated herself. He had rejected her body, was less than happy to see her, and she was responding with love and neediness.

"You come here stark naked with a dinner invitation?"

She swallowed hard. "I came here to tell you how important you are to my life and that we need to talk."

"Okay. I concede Christmas was a shambles. The whole holiday season was a disaster. What do you want me to do about it? Apologize?"

"You've already done that verbally. I don't want apologies! Words mean absolutely nothing! We've been living on apologies and chicken soup for ages. It's time for some action!"

"Action? You want action? I can lay you right now on this desk. Is that the kind of action you want?" Was this woman never satisfied? Money! He could offer her money. "Do you want a nice fat bank account?" He sneered. "Will that satisfy you? The way you spend money, you need accounts at every store in town!"

"I don't want money, charge accounts, fur coats, or diamonds, Julian. I want you!"

He sighed with exasperation. "You still haven't figured it out, Jess. I need to work to give you the kind of lifestyle we have."

"All I want is you, Julian. Just a few hours a week. You

managed it in the fall. Why not now?"

Tears brimmed over her lashes.

"For Christ's sake, don't start bawling! You know how involved I am in community affairs. They take up a lot of my time."

"Maybe you should add me to your list of charities."

"Don't be absurd, Jess!"

"God, Julian, doesn't anything register with you? You brag about me all over town. You're so proud of me, you can hardly wait to invite people to our parties. You keep Rob up until all hours so everyone can see him. Then after everyone leaves, you re-decorate the living room with my blood! We need to talk about this stuff, Julian. It's killing me!" She sniffled, probing through her purse for more tissues.

"So you came all the way down here through a mean blizzard just to tell me this? Okay, okay. I get the message, loud and clear. You go home, Jessica. I'll be home early, and we'll talk." He interrupted himself to signal Avis for a cab. "On the spot, Avis, Mrs. Bothwell needs to leave!"

He turned off the intercom and gave her a smile, his arms reaching out so she could curl into them. "I never told you how luscious you look in mink, darling. And your outfit underneath makes you irresistible. I promise, I'll be home early. Put on something that I can peel off piece by delicious piece." He nibbled her ear, sending shivers of ecstasy through her body, while another part of her psyche looked on in disgust.

"I love you," she whispered. "I don't want to lose you."

"Nothing can come between us, I promise," he said, sounding wooden, false.

"Only your hotels," she added bitterly as she straightened his tie.

There was a tap-tapping at the door. Through the heavy oak, they heard Avis announce that the taxi was waiting. Julian kissed his wife passionately and opened the door for her.

"No later than seven," she murmured as she slithered through the doorway, clutching her mink and her purse.

Her mind went into overdrive as she wondered what she could do to surprise him once Rob was asleep in his bed.

⁂

Seven o'clock came and went, quickly followed by eight, nine, and ten. At eleven, the supper she had so cheerfully prepared was glued to the pots and roasting pan. One last peek to make sure the chicken was cremated, and then she scraped and scratched the crusted remains into the trash. What she really felt like doing was packing it all in a box and delivering it by taxi to Julian in the lounge at the Terrace Lodge Hotel where he was sure to be. There was nothing like cremated chicken and scorched potatoes to mix well with his scotch.

Checking on Rob, she pulled his covers up under his chin and popped two Valium before she ran a bubble bath. Considering the level of her stress, she took another two. While she watched the tub fill with froth, she sipped champagne from an ordinary tumbler, hoping it would ease her desire to strangle Julian. With enough pills, soon she wouldn't feel anything.

Soaking in the water as the bubbles snapped and emitted a floral fragrance, the realization drifted through her mind that she was really hooked on the calm, floating feeling the pills gave her. But who the hell cared? It was better than being stressed out all the time and feeling as if she was walking on the edge of a precipice that was about to crumble beneath her feet.

Scarcely drying herself, she yanked on a flannel gown. The nights were frosty, and Julian certainly wasn't there to warm her. Reaching under the mattress, she retrieved her sleeping pills, requiring no more than the remaining champagne to swallow three. Carefully, she replaced the containers. If Julian ever discovered her secret stash, he'd have a seizure. Screw Julian!

Pulling the quilt around herself, she nestled into the pillows, closing out the hostile world. Calm, peaceful dreams lapped at the fringes of her mind, and a gentle brook meandered its way through her being. She strolled strong and free through pastures bright with daisies and scented with clover. She skipped along a woodland path, with sunlight filtering through the trees, and falling in golden splashes on the loamy earth. She stood on the crest of a windswept hill, the breeze ruffling her hair. Stretching her arms skyward, she reached for the billowing clouds racing overhead. She didn't remember passing out.

⁂

"Miss Jessica! Miss Jessica!" Someone was tugging her arm, shaking her shoulder. "Miss Jessica! It's me, Binkie!"

Her lashes fluttered open. Where was the pasture? Where were the daisies? Where was the windswept hill? Slowly her mind wandered back to her bed. Staring around, she checked to make sure it was her room.

"What time is it?" she groaned.

"Goin' on eleven. Mr. Julian called me to come in early. You looked like you'd sleep all day. You okay, Miss Jessica?"

"Yes," she yawned, stretching. "Where's Rob?"

"Downstairs gettin' in a heapa trouble in the kitchen. He sure likes pots 'n' pans. Coffee's ready. Would you like some?"

161

"Sounds like a divine idea. I'll be down in a few minutes." Reality pushed the clover and the clouds into the recesses of her mind.

Binkie rushed to save the kitchen from Rob as Jessica eased herself from the bed. She felt like someone who had spent three months at sea and wasn't sure how her legs would work on dry land. Using the furniture to balance herself, she made it to her dressing room. The mirror revealed puffy eyes with dark circles and ashen skin where the dark circles ended. What a ghastly sight!

She gasped and spluttered as she splashed icy water on her face, hoping the cold would freshen her complexion. Scrubbing a towel over her skin, she touched up her cheeks with blusher—anything to add color and make her appear healthy. Her mouth tasted like used kitty litter. Gargling with Listerine, she felt her tonsils shrivel. She struggled into a robe and shambled down to the kitchen.

"Please close the blinds, Binkie." She uttered the words slowly and softly; a normal voice would clatter in her head. "I've got a beast of a headache and the glare from the snow blinds me."

The phone rang, jarring every nerve.

"Hello," she whispered.

There was silence before a man's voice exploded, "Christ! You sound like you're ready to croak! This is Casey."

"Oh, hi Casey."

"Thought I'd meet you at the range. Streets are clear. Sky's blue. A great day to be at the range."

"Not today, I'm afraid. I can't seem to get rid of this flu." She coughed convincingly.

"You better have a doctor check that out, Jessica! Look, I'm leaving town tomorrow for a few days. I'll call you when I get back. By the way, how's my pal, Julian?"

"Oh, he's ticking right along. He wouldn't get sick if the bubonic plague hit town. Germs take one look at him and invade me instead."

He laughed. "Don't count on that, Jessica. There's one big microbe out after him. Talk to you later." Click.

It was a thoughtful Jessica who sat drinking her coffee. Now what did Casey mean by that? And why did he always ask about Julian? If they were such good buddies, why didn't Casey call Julian himself?

Rosalind's idea about a trip to the city sounded better all the time. There was something going on just beyond the perimeter of her conscious awareness. With Lincoln going on many overseas trips to negotiate arrangements with the Europeans and Japanese, Julian was home more, but Jessica wasn't so sure that was a good idea any longer. He wasn't exactly at home; more precisely, he was "in town".

The day before, she'd humiliated herself again, hoping to talk to him, and once more, he'd disappointed her. A crawling sensation engulfed her. Suddenly, she felt "watched". Thinking back to those times when Julian was away, she remembered her discomfort and the feeling that she had eyes and ears monitoring her every move. She used to attribute those feelings to the fact that her home had been under surveillance before the break-in and believed it was a hangover reaction to that event. But now she wasn't so sure. Julian had told her many times, in the middle of a heated argument, that he knew everything she did from morning 'til night—how many phone calls she had made and to whom, where she went, and what time she did something.

Was her home bugged? Was Casey keeping an eye on her for his pal? Worse, was Binkie a spy? Anything was possible at the

Mad Hatter's Tea Party.

Damn! She should have paid more attention at the Private Investigator's Course. She'd tossed out all her books and notes and doubted she'd recognize a piece of bugging equipment if it bit her on the ankle. To her dismay, she knew there could be a surveillance device in every phone, in any of the crystals of the chandeliers in the foyer and dining room, behind every picture, under any bed, secreted in any light switch, in any of Rob's toys, and even in Cuddles' collar. The list of possible hiding places was infinite.

On impulse, she called out to Binkie who was polishing the dining room furniture. The short gray lady chugged into the room.

"Does Mr. Bothwell ever talk to you about how we spend our days when you're here? I mean, does he like to pry?"

The little lady shook her head. "No, ma'am. The only time he ever talks to me at all is if'n he goes out at the same time I comes in. He hardly never speaks to me, Miss Jessica."

Her wide-eyed expression told Jessica that this little old elf of a woman wouldn't be capable of telling a lie...unless absolutely necessary.

⁂

It was a very contemplative Jessica who showered and blow-dried her hair. The wheels turned in her head, but nothing meshed. Some gear wasn't working properly. The shower refreshed her and even her headache abated. Although her thoughts were still snarled, and her insides quivered, she felt more human than when she had first awakened. Wrapped in her terry robe, she wandered into the alcove off their bedroom, opened wide the curtains, and gazed out at the snow-covered backyard. Even in the sunlight, it was bleak.

What was going on? Why had Casey's remark so disturbed her? Why now did she recall those feelings of being observed? Why did she feel as if she was tap dancing on quicksand?

She thought about how her father used to bully her, not unlike Julian. Her father had told her often how much he loved her, but his actions didn't correspond with his words. His love filled her with guilt and shame. Her father! Why did she have to remember that now? She stared at the swirling snow as it whipped across the patio and shivered.

Like a spider, her mind darted along the dragline to the core of the web, long abandoned, and clotted with dust and debris. Silken-bound carcasses clung to the feeble strands. The corpses were the remains of her childhood, which she had bound and gagged with their secrets. Secrets that no one imagined and that she had vowed never to divulge, even under severe torture.

She choked back tears of guilt and shame. How she had loved her father! She had done her best to please him, but somehow had never measured up to his impeccable expectations. She had become accustomed to cringing at his scowl of disapproval at her small accomplishments: a gold star for her first attempts at printing; an "A" average in grade school; a standing ovation for her piano recital in high school. When she had delivered the valedictory address at commencement exercises, he told her she had talked far too long and had bored everyone.

But the worst punishment was his never believing her. He called her "Liar!" at every opportunity. If she arrived late for supper by two minutes, her explanation that she had stopped to wash her hands first elicited a snapping "Liar!" If her younger sister tumbled and bruised her knee, Jessica's account of the event prompted another "Liar! You pushed her!" He hadn't even believed her when her beloved pet Irish Setter, Shamus, had broken his leash and bounded in front of a car that smashed him into a screaming, dying mass of blood and bone. "Liar!" her father had shouted. "You let him run loose!"

Mourning the death of her beloved pet, she'd been as defenseless as a child of seven could be. Her mother had stood silent while her husband rained his wrath on their daughter. His wife pinched the flesh on her forearms until the tiny punctures bled; it was her way of distracting herself, knowing that to express one word on Jessica's behalf would only invite more abuse.

But he could love his daughter, Jessica discovered. On the night Shamus died, he crept into her bed to hush her tears. Brushing her pale blonde hair with his stubby fingers, he told her he loved her so dearly he wasn't able to let anyone else know. As he hugged and caressed her, she sobbed her grief onto his hairy chest, while he did things she couldn't remember. All she recalled was the scent of his cologne, and that her bedroom wallpaper had pictures of "Mary and her Little Lamb" on their way to school. And she remembered Shamus and his glistening copper coat soaking up his blood while his life oozed away in the middle of the street.

It was their very special secret, he had told her on subsequent nights when he held her while she trembled from the nightmares that plagued her. As they lay together in her bed, he soothed her fears and lulled her with his fondling fingers. But she loathed it when he grunted and shuddered, and she felt the hot sticky goop that came from him. He always wiped it away with a tissue, telling her that it was his "love-juice" and that because he adored her, he couldn't help it. But long after he stole back to his own bed, she lay awake in the darkness, guilt and shame shrouding her tiny body, and acid eating her insides. It was their secret, he said, because if she told anyone, they would hate her, and worse, they would call her a liar.

Recalling the ugly past with its muted memories, Jessica shook her head, chasing the spider spinning into the deep caverns of her mind. She needed a distraction to lure her head from its morbid mode! She dashed to the phone.

"Rosalind," she said when her friend answered, hoping her own voice sounded upbeat and not anxious, "anything special on your agenda today? How about I pick you up and take you to Pierre's? I saw a stunning dress on sale there. It's raw silk and one of a kind. I want it. I need a lift. Retail therapy! Then let's go for a late lunch. I have to talk to you!"

She bought the dress at a bargain price of only eight hundred and ninety-five dollars.

"Well, what's up, honey-child?" asked Rosalind, as they drove from the parking lot at Pierre's. "You've been as jittery as a jackrabbit with a fox in the vicinity ever since we left my place."

"It shows?" Jessica eased the car onto the street. "Let's wait 'til we get to the Wharf, and I'll tell you. Right now, I need to concentrate on the traffic."

The maître d' greeted them with enthusiasm, knowing they always spent a bundle and left generous tips. Leading them to a window table, he took their orders for two double martinis.

"You aren't turning to drink, are you, Jess?" questioned Rosalind, her brows knitted in a concerned frown.

"No, but what I'm going to tell you takes my being uninhibited. But I'll only have this one because I'm driving."

She stared out the window at the skaters on the river. The town had plowed a small portion of the frozen river for a rink and at night provided romantic colored lights in the pines along the bank.

"Isn't this gorgeous, Roz? How lucky we are to live in such a beautiful place. Riverbend is a dream come true!"

"Are you sure this dream isn't turning into a nightmare for you?"

Rosalind's green eyes penetrated Jessica's.

"I'm not sure, actually," she sighed. "There are so many things that don't add up."

"This sounds mysterious," Rosalind said, lifting her glass to Jessica's in a toast. "To our friendship! May it outlast us both, no matter what!"

"No matter what," repeated Jessica. "Oh, Roz, I'm going to cry. I know it!" she blinked back sudden tears.

"Okay kid, fire away. What's been happening in paradise?"

"Well, paradise is fast becoming a sink-hole. I'm going to wake up some morning and find the whole place buried in mud."

At Rosalind's horrified expression, Jessica explained, "I'm speaking colloquially, Roz! For God's sake, you can be so thick! It's how I feel! I sometimes feel like I'm buried in mud! I never told you what happened at our place after the Christmas party. The tree was a shambles by the time Julian crawled out of it. He knocked the whole thing down, decorations and all..."

Picturing the scene, Rosalind laughed until tears rolled down her cheeks. "Oh, God, that must've been cute! I'm sorry, Jess, but I can just see sedate, never-does-anything-wrong Julian wrapped up in tinsel!" She wiped her eyes. "Is my mascara running?"

"Not yet! But it will be if you don't stop laughing! This is serious!"

Rosalind stopped at once and sat quietly, subdued and attentive. She patted Jessica's hand.

"Well, after he crawled out from the mess, he smashed me

around and then blackened my eyes. The only good that came out of it was that we didn't go to Lydia's for dinner."

"Saints be praised. At least you were spared that! But I'm concerned, Jess. I'm very worried about you with that violence."

"I'm worried, too. The whole thing becomes crazier by the minute. Yesterday, I decided to visit him at his office because God knows we can't talk at home. He's too busy reading the stock reports. He's too tired. He has to watch the hockey game. He comes home too late. So I went to see him at the office. I waited for over an hour, and what struts out of his office? A stacked redhead, blowing kisses at him. He told me she only comes to give him a massage..."

"Did he say what she massaged?" Rosalind probed as she played with the olive in her drink.

"No! But I have a pretty good idea! Anyway, he helped me take off the mink he bought me as a peace offering after the Christmas debacle. And what did I have on? Nothing! Did he notice? I could have tattooed graffiti all over my body, and he wouldn't even have blinked! Do you have any idea what it's like having a -22° wind blowing up your behind?"

"Can't say that I do."

"All he did was cover me up with the coat and treat me like a leper. He was afraid that his secretary or Lincoln might barge in. But while Beulah-Boobs was in there, Avis stood guard like a Doberman protecting her puppies. The only thing he did was promise to come home early last night to talk things over. Did he? Not on your life! But he manages to get his screwing in the morning, or he just helps himself when I'm sleeping! I hate my life, Roz! Paradise is turning into Hell-on-Earth!"

Rosalind lit a cigarette and pondered her friend's plight. "Why don't you do what I suggested before? Go to the city, and get away from all this," she urged. "You need a break from Julian, and it'll give you a new perspective on things. It'll give you a chance to think things through without the interference of your home-life. Treat yourself to a manicure and to having your hair done. Swim in the pool, have a steam bath, get a massage, do some shopping, and go to the theatre. Stay a week. Binkie and I can look after Rob."

"God, Roz, how do you do it? You seem so normal and so in control. You never get bent out of shape like I do."

"I just accept my lot in life, my dear. I wanted to marry money and I did. I love Harry, even though he's boring and completely predictable. He treats me well, and I treat him the same way. We don't bounce off each other. We made a pre-nuptial agreement that we wouldn't embarrass or humiliate each other and that we'd be loyal and faithful. So far it's working. I love the lifestyle money can buy and he loves to see me happy. We have separate TV's and separate bedrooms, and we accept each other. Next to you, he's my very best friend, and I'm his. Some things we do together—like making love, playing golf, going to the theatre, dining out, and going to the cabin. Other things we do separately. He likes to garden and go the racetrack. I like to cook and entertain. I have a nice life. I truly appreciate it, and I never take Harry for granted."

Rosalind studied her long red fingernails and tossed her mane of long auburn hair over her shoulder, while Jessica stared at her, transfixed with awe and amazement. Rosalind made it all sound so normal, so uncomplicated.

"Do you know what I think Julian is doing?" whispered Jessica. "I think he's bugging the house."

Rosalind stared at her in disbelief and then shook her head. "You really do need to take a break."

✽

"You want to do what?" Julian peered at her over *The Wall Street Journal*. "You want a mother's holiday? You've got to be joking! You're on a holiday every day of the week! When Binkie's here, you're out every minute. And now you want a vacation? You need a holiday about as much as that dippy ex-Duchess of York!"

It had started out badly. She composed herself.

"But Julian, it might do me some good. You're always off to Europe, Japan, or somewhere else. And don't tell me you're working every minute. You get wined and dined and God knows what else! All I want is a few days in the city."

"Forget it, Jess! Keep this nonsense up and I'll fire Binkie, and you'll really need a holiday then!"

This wasn't working. Maybe she could appeal to his sympathy.

"Please, Julian! I'm a wreck! I don't know why. All I know is I'm coming unraveled. I need some time away from Riverbend. And Rob won't be any trouble. Rosalind and Binkie have already discussed baby-sitting arrangements for him."

"I said forget it!" he boomed, slapping his paper down on the table, slopping coffee all over the cloth. "One more word about breaks or holidays and I'll have your credit cards cancelled, and you'll find yourself without your bank account—and off the joint one. You'll be down on the drag with a little tin cup!"

She covered her face with her hands and wept.

"Tears won't save you either, Jessica! Just grow up! You can't leave Rob every time you get a little upset. What kind of uncaring mother are you anyway?" the surly dictator shouted in unending hostility.

"What kind of father are you?" she screamed at his disappearing back. "Rob never sees you!"

The very floor vibrated as the oak door crashed behind him. Looking through the foyer windows, she watched as he jammed himself into the back of the limousine.

"Have a nice trip!" she hissed under her breath. "You forgot your bloody paper to read on the way to your fucking office!"

⁂

Rob screamed and yelled from the kitchen, and Jessica's head was bursting from the racket and from her frustrating argument with Julian. Fury bubbled from the pit of her being, carrying with it explosive anger and blistering rage. With measured steps, she pounded back to the kitchen. The energy of her rage seethed hotter with every heartbeat. Its power was fierce enough to enable her to pick up Rob in his high chair and heave them both through the window.

Sensing her son's distress because of his parents' argument, but knowing she was incapable of handling it calmly, she ignored his cries. Instead, she stood at the French door overlooking the snow-covered backyard. She had to calm herself before she struck out and did something she would regret forever. Count to ten, she told herself. Do not do anything until you reach ten. Count slowly; breathe deeply. Do not scream; do not smash the door; do not break anything. Count to ten. That accomplished, she turned her attention to Rob and, pasting a smile on her face, walked to him and touched him softly on his cheek.

"You're upset," she murmured. "Mommy's not mad at you. I'm not happy with Daddy, but I love *you* very much. Here, let me help you finish up this bowl of cereal."

Lovingly, carefully, she spooned the mush from the bowl and coaxed him to eat. Gradually his sobs subsided, and together they cleaned out the bowl. Then Jessica helped him from the highchair and cradled him on her lap while she sat and sipped her cold coffee and thought about how easily child abuse could happen. Had she not taken the time to count to ten and breathe slowly, she could have simply duplicated with her son how Julian dealt with his wife. That must never happen, she vowed. I am my child's protector, not his tormentor. With a hug and a cuddle, she kissed the top of his head.

"Go find Cuddles and play with her. I have something I have to do."

She tossed the phone book on the table. Ministers. She was searching for ministers. Where was the bastard who'd officiated at her marriage to this psychopath? In a way, he was responsible for the stew in which she found herself. Maybe he could help. She'd sell her soul to the devil if it would help save her life! "Babbitz". There it was. "Reverend Selwyn Babbitz". What kind of name was that? It sounded like a disease for God's sake! Something you got from drinking swamp water. Who cared? He was the guy who had fatally tied her to Julian in unholy matrimony.

She dialed the number. Five rings. Maybe he wasn't in. Please, God, let him answer. Ring seven and a pacifying voice answered.

"This is Reverend Babbitz. May I help you?"

"You'll never remember me," she began nervously, her heart jack hammering in her chest. "I was only in your church once... to get married, but I need help desperately!" she cried, trying not to sound so hysterical that he'd cross her off as a nut, but not so composed that he might believe she wasn't really in need of emergency comfort and solace.

"What's your name? Perhaps I'll remember you," he suggested.

"Jessica Bothwell. I'm married to the town's hotel tycoon."

"Of course, I remember," he assured her jovially. "You were married in the fall. A lovely ceremony. Reception at the Mayfield."

"May I see you? I need some spiritual direction. I'm swimming in a river full of piranhas, and I can't find my way out."

"Like much of mankind," he sympathized sadly.

"Can I please see you *now*? I need help! Another hour of this nightmare, and I won't need any help at all! I'll be totally crazy!"

"My schedule is quite full this morning."

"Please!" she begged. "I promise I won't stay long. I only need some guidance and advice. I'm a fast learner!"

"If you can be here in fifteen minutes, I'll have coffee with you. Maybe that'll help."

His home was on the other side of town. No matter. Even if she had to run red lights, she'd be there.

Rob squawked, screamed, and fought as she dressed him in his snowsuit; totally uncooperative.

"Please, Rob, please help Mommy. I'm going to get God's help in ironing out this lousy mess. If you don't stop screaming and jumping right now, Mommy will be upset."

That didn't work. The child had had enough of a shake-up already with his parents' dispute that he wasn't prepared to co-operate with anyone, least of all his mother, who radiated anger, frustration, and intolerance.

Forcing Rob into his car seat in the back of the Mustang, she buckled him in while he continued to screech and holler. She revved up the engine, and backed out of the garage. Careening around the drive, she sheered several inches off the snow banks. Who cared? She had to save her life! And Rob's!

The car screamed around corners, and she double turbo-charged it onto the freeway. Two exits and turn left, go straight for three blocks, and then hang a right, and it was the second house on the right. She jerked to a stop in front of a modest bungalow. A man waved from the front window and then vanished to open the front door.

"How nice to see you, Mrs. Bothwell." He grinned broadly as Jessica and Rob mounted the front steps. The Reverend bent forward to look at Rob. "And who is this wee person?"

Rob stared up wide-eyed and curious, his nose running from having cried so much. Jessica yanked a tissue from her pocket and wiped his nose while she gently nudged him up the step.

"This is my son, Rob."

The Reverend welcomed them into his home. "Perhaps Rob would like to play with the other children while we talk in the study...Donna-Lee, can you take wee Rob into the playroom with the others. I'm sure he'll have fun with some little ones his own age to play with."

A pale and frail Donna-Lee emerged with a toddler on each hip, and one well on the way. From the noise, laughter, and chatter, Jessica knew she was in a busy house full of loving chaos.

"Do you run a day care center here?" she asked as Donna-Lee guided Rob to another room.

"Oh my, no!" Reverend Babbitz said proudly. "We have seven little ones of our very own! And we'll have nine two months from now. We're expecting twins this time. We already have two sets."

"How delightful!" she said, wondering if the good reverend was holy or horny. Nine children! Her worst-case scenario.

"Let's go into my study. We can talk undisturbed here. What do you take in your coffee?"

"Black is fine."

"Well, what seems to be the problem, Mrs. Bothwell?" he asked as he handed her a cup of steaming black brew, and seated himself in a chair opposite hers.

She bit her lip, realizing she couldn't quite address the issue directly. She decided to test the water with just a toe. "Nothing really, except that my husband doesn't understand I need to get away for a few days to clear my head. I'd like to take a couple of days in the city without having to worry about Rob. And please call me Jessica."

"Well, Jessica, if we keep in mind that God gives us children as treasures to hold in our tender care, then we don't have selfish notions of trying to run from these responsibilities, which are entrusted to us. Donna-Lee would no more want time for herself than dropping off the face of the earth. She is a very holy, Christian woman who takes great delight in her seven blessings from God. Do you have other children?"

"No, thank God, unless I count my husband, and then I have two," she replied, feeling like a heathen and a pagan and guilt-ridden by his assessment.

He gazed at her while he drank his coffee. "Well, what I'd suggest is that you read the Bible together once a day and look for God's blessing on every page. It's there, you know, if you look."

"Julian reading the Bible would be a joke, Reverend Babbitz. *The Wall Street Journal* is his Bible."

"Hmmm...Extreme materialism. And what else is bothering you?"

"What else?" Her voice went up five decibels. "Do you want

to know if I'm having other problems?"

He nodded kindly. God, he seemed so young, so untainted by life, and so untouched by corruption.

"Well," she stumbled on, plunging into deeper water, "my husband sometimes smacks me around. Especially if he's been drinking."

"Oh, we have a drinking problem to contend with, too?"

She nodded, tears sprinkling her lashes.

"Does your husband know it's against God's laws to be drunk?"

"He knows it's against the state's laws, too, but that doesn't stop him! If God Himself were to materialize in front of him, my husband would drink a toast to the holy angels, and invite everyone to join the party."

"My, my, my, we certainly have a problem on our hands, don't we? I have to run," he said as he glanced at his watch. "An appointment at the hospital. I always visit twice a day. I'm a fisher of men, and God's children are often in hospital and need God's blessing. Why don't you stay and visit with Donna-Lee? I know she'd love to have you stay. Maybe she can help, where I can't. You know, a woman's perspective and all."

Donna-Lee welcomed Jessica into the living room, where Rob and two other toddlers played in a pool of sunbeams on the floor. The rest of the children seemed to be in the basement, whooping, hollering, and throwing toys. Once in a while, Jessica heard a screech as a toy hit a moving target, but Donna-Lee didn't seem to notice. Jessica got the impression that if there wasn't any blood, there wasn't any emergency. Donna-Lee, with her youngest baby nursing at her breast, seemed calm and serene and emanated a soft glow of perfect inner peace. Jessica was sure she was on something. Either that or she was still dazed from finding herself with an estimated nine children to care for in two month's time.

The soft, plump sofa pillowed her as the sun streamed through the sheer drapes onto the geraniums bursting with life in the window. Jessica would have liked to sit there forever, except that the children's screams and bellows grated on her nerves like fine ground glass. However, she felt a warmth and joy surrounding her, wrapping her in a love that seeped into her pores. A leather-bound Bible lay on the scarred coffee table.

She told Donna-Lee about her wanting to escape to the city for a few days, and how Julian forbade her to do it, and how hopeless and trapped she felt. Donna-Lee said she understood, but as she calmly scraped Arrowroot gunk from the green shag carpet, Jessica was sure the minister's wife couldn't begin to relate. As the children clanged toys, bumped heads, hollered, and whacked the coffee table with a battered plastic clown, Donna-Lee simply smiled, making no attempt to interfere, and Jessica became more convinced than ever that Donna-Lee didn't relate at all. Perhaps she was gassed on grass. As she sipped her coffee, Donna-Lee pursed her lips to form a crimson rosette and looked at Jessica, who wore her skepticism like a badge. Donna-Lee smiled. How could anyone, marveled Jessica, especially a woman who bred kids like rabbits, be that calm?

"I can see you're a bit skeptical about my knowing what you're experiencing," Donna-Lee remarked in her soft musical voice. "With all the children coming so quickly, I thought I was going crazy. But I finally resigned myself to this bedlam and bent myself to God's will. I came to see that what I wanted for my life didn't matter. It was what God wanted for me that was important. My realization certainly didn't come over-night. My husband talked to me endlessly about it. We read the Bible together all the time, and finally I was blessed with clear, unquestioning sight. I began reading the Bible on my own and became involved in prayer and Bible study groups. Why don't you pray? Read the Bible and come to our study groups. We have sitters so Rob would be no problem. It'll help. I know it will!"

"If my prayers counted for anything," said Jessica, "I'd be up for sainthood right now. I've prayed until I'm blue in the face. I've prayed to God and every saint and angel there can possibly be in heaven! But that doesn't stop Julian from battering me when he's drunk. It doesn't save me from his verbal abuse!"

"Oh, my dear," whispered Donna-Lee, "that does change the picture a little, doesn't it? It isn't just a matter of dealing with your little one? Oh, dearie me! Well, all I can suggest is that you keep on praying. Maybe God will do something about the drinking and the violence." Her face brightened as a thought skipped through her head. "Sometimes God works through people. Have you called the police?"

Jessica nodded.

"Didn't they help?" Donna-Lee asked, wiping baby spit-up from her shoulder.

Jessica shook her head, not trusting herself not to cry if she talked about her despair.

"And you still love him, don't you?"

"Yes," she whispered, "but sometimes I think maybe I should just divorce him."

"Oh, my dear! That's drastic! If you do that, may God have mercy on your soul!"

"I don't want to *murder* him!" Jessica cried. "I just want a divorce!"

Donna-Lee smiled serenely, showing patience for this novice

in God's ways. "But that would mean your marriage vows were a lie."

"His vows haven't meant much to him, either. He seems to have forgotten about love, honor, and cherish."

"Have you forgotten the 'obey' part?" Donna-Lee asked quietly as she bobbed the baby on her knee.

Exasperated, Jessica fumed, making wild gestures. It seemed she was a fallen sinner no matter what she said. "*Obey*? If you had to live with him, you wouldn't obey him either!"

"Well, we do have to accept what God gives us," the unruffled woman chided, nodding in her supercilious manner.

The conversation was heading into uncharted waters, and Jessica didn't have all her scuba gear. She rose to leave, holding Rob's hand.

As she bundled him into his snowsuit, Jessica looked at the pale young woman holding another of her babies to her breast. "I do hope our discussion is confidential," she said with soft emphasis. "I've said some things that could prove troublesome... if word got out."

"May the blessing of our Lord, Jesus Christ, flow from heaven to surround you," Donna-Lee murmured in Jessica's ear.

Never having had anyone wish that for her before, Jessica had the strangest feeling, almost as if she didn't deserve any blessings.

So could prayer and bending, *crumbling* to God's will take away all her anger and despair? Why hadn't she thought of that? Of one thing she was certain: The Reverend Babbitz and all the little Babbitzes had seen the last of her. She didn't believe that the Creator would be crazy or cruel enough to keep her trapped in a cycle of rage, brutality, terror, and hopelessness.

✲

She swallowed two Valium, mustered her courage, and marched into the kitchen where Julian was enjoying his morning coffee, while he perused the newspaper. Pouring herself a cup, she sat down.

"Good morning," she said conversationally, "I trust you slept well."

"As well as can be expected, considering the iceberg you've become."

"Can we talk, Julian? I know you have to get to work, but I need to talk about what's happening."

He lowered his paper. "If it's about Christmas and that other shit, we've talked it to death. I don't like post mortems."

"No, it's about us. We're not getting along well at all. We never see each other, and when we are together, all we do is argue."

"Yes," he agreed, "things have deteriorated badly. But it isn't only me, Jess. You're as cold as a blizzard wind. I can't even touch you anymore."

"That's because everything else is so wrong. I can't snuggle up to a cactus. I can't get turned on if you've just given me another inventory of my failings as a wife and mother. You complain about everything I do wrong, and then you expect me to be a sex goddess. I miss the physical side of our relationship too, but I miss all the good things we had together even more. Maybe we should talk about separating or something..." Her voice trailed off as she watched him.

Slowly, he folded his paper, and placed it on the table. His face darkened, and his eyes narrowed until they were no more than glittering slits. Almost in slow motion, he leaned across the table, his jaw clenched, and he cupped her chin in his hand. He raised her face with a slight jerk so that he was staring directly into her eyes.

She felt as if she was confronting the face of Death itself as he hissed in a voice that was scarcely more than a whisper. With every word perfectly enunciated, he said, "Get this through your head, because I will *not* repeat it! We will not get a divorce *ever*! If you try to leave, I will find you. You've probably heard that little saying: If you love something, set it free. If it comes back to you, then it's yours; if it doesn't, hunt it down, and kill it!' That's what I'll do, Jessica. I'll hunt you down, and I'll kill you. And I won't stop with you. I'll kill your brat, too. You can't hide from me, Jessica. *Anywhere!* So you'd better shape up, or you'll find yourself at the top of the endangered species list...And one more thing...I haven't told you that I met with the police chief. He called me shortly after that little incident with the cops. We had lunch, and he told me not to worry about it—that the log with your call on it has vanished, and that the hospital records of your visit have disappeared. The doctor you saw was transferred out shortly after your social call. I certainly hope there won't be any more calls to the police just because we have an inconsequential family spat. One more visit from the police, and you'll be gone...gone for good! I hope you've found our little chat beneficial." He picked up his paper. "I've got to run. Meetings all day."

Whistling, with his newspaper tucked under his arm, he strolled from the kitchen as if he had just discussed with his wife a cruise they might be taking next month. She heard the door close softly behind him.

Dazed, she stared into a void, as empty and black as deep space itself. For once in its life, her head had absolutely nothing at all to say. Only one stray thought had a voice: You might not believe in the Devil, but if you did, you're the only one in the world to know precisely where he lives.

Rob stumbled into the kitchen, rubbing sleepy eyes, while she watched him resentfully. If it weren't for Rob, she could pack her bags and flee, take her chances that Julian wouldn't find her.

"Hi, sunshine," she smiled, with a warmth she didn't feel. "How's Mommy's boy this morning? Ready for some breakfast?"

Pouring milk over Rob's Cheerios, she wished herself ten thousand miles away. Even ten thousand miles wasn't far enough when Rob spilled his bowl, and milk and Cheerios flooded across the highchair tray, waterfalled onto the table, and dribbled onto the floor. Something came unstuck in her head.

"You miserable little bastard! Look at the goddamned mess you made! Now I have to clean up after you!"

Cuddles was busy licking up the puddle on the floor, but the table swam in the mess. Rob started to whimper, his eyes wide with apprehension and fear.

His alarm startled her. Realizing he was about to scream with terror because of *her*, she controlled her urge to slap him. Count to ten, breathe deeply. Don't say a thing. Don't smash the bowl on the floor. Just breathe.

"It's okay, sweetheart. Just a bit of spilled milk."

"I love you, Mommy. Don't be mad at me."

"I'm not mad at you," she murmured as she ruffled his hair. "Look and see how happy Cuddles is. She's gobbling up your cereal from the floor!"

"Can I sit on your lap, Mommy? I feel sad."

"Why, of course! What a good idea. Let's have a cuddle

on my chair. Let's see what the dog does if I lift her onto the table." To hell with sanitary measures, she thought. Let's just get through this without bruises and blood.

Rob's mouth fell open in awe as Jessica lifted the surprised poodle and set her to work on the puddle on the table.

In less than a moment, she and Rob were sitting on her chair watching and giggling as Cuddles eagerly cleaned the delectable surface. Next, Cuddles lapped up the cereal on Rob's tray. Better than Spic and Span any time. Wouldn't Julian simply puke if he knew his coffee the next morning would be sitting on a table licked spotless by his dog!

"I love you, Mommy." Rob peeked up at her shyly. "Don't be mad at me."

"I love you, too my sweet boy. Accidents happen. It's fine. Just don't tell Daddy what I did with Cuddles. He won't think that's funny at all."

"I think it's really funny, Mommy," he giggled.

"I do too," she laughed. Soon they were both whooping with laughter. It felt so good to laugh with her son, and she squeezed him tightly to her. Thank God she had counted to ten. She put Rob down and lifted Cuddles from the squeaky clean table. Rob galloped into the family room to watch cartoons while Jessica set about making him brown toast with peanut butter and jam.

Cuddles yipped at the patio door; she needed to relieve herself, and today was not a good day to pee on the hardwood floor. As Jessica opened the door, a gust of icy wind spun into the kitchen, its blast triggering an idea. In the past, aged Inuit would simply walk away from their winter homes and wander through the drifts until the frigid temperature overcame them. It was said to be painless. Did she have the moxie to sit on her patio, half-naked, and allow nature to take its course? Imagine

Julian coming home to discover her frozen corpse decorating the patio! Knowing him, he wouldn't notice she was missing for days. She waited for Cuddles who was quick about it, the cold certainly speeding things up. The white poodle scurried back into the house, diving for her favorite scatter rug.

After serving Rob his toast in the family room, Jessica fell heavily into a chair, wondering where her life had become lost. Where had she missed the trail? With her chin in her hands, she sat pondering how to destroy herself. Her whole life was a disaster. Julian's threats had completely unglued her, and her despair led her down a lethal path. Pills? She didn't have enough. Even mixed with booze, there weren't nearly enough. Carbon monoxide? She didn't have the guts. Slashing her wrists? Too painful; one cut, and she'd quit. Driving her car over a cliff or blowing her brains out with the revolver? She'd chicken out at the last second.

In her mind's eye, without ever figuring out how she'd render herself lifeless, she pictured her funeral: Her casket heaped with daisies and tiger lilies dominated Reverend Babbitz's church, while the good minister gave solace to the crowds of mourners filing by. Julian threw himself onto her coffin, wracked with weeping, as his mother wiped away tears of sorrow, regretting her nasty words that may have contributed to this tragedy. Rosalind, Harry, and Mary-Beth, beside themselves with grief, were casting venomous glances at Julian, knowing he was fully responsible for this pitiful waste. The police chief stood close by her coffin, well aware that if he had acted responsibly, this would never have happened. Julian's secretary, Avis, dressed in mourning black, wished that she hadn't kept this poor woman waiting the day she had visited Julian's office. Hovering in the background stood Amber, knowing that she had added to

Jessica's burden. Julian was hysterical as he pounded his forehead with his fist, cursing himself for not trying to work out their problems.

But the sorrow of others in this madcap mayhem in her mind would never match her own, because she would be the one who was dead and the one responsible for her own demise.

Jolting herself from this irreverent reverie, Jessica lit a cigarette and felt herself relax. The racket in her head fell silent, and the place where emotional pain dwelled and boiled, cooled. It no longer seethed with its poisonous brew. She had to get a grip. Her child needed her, depended on her. Another few minutes, and she could truly mother Rob. Her poor little darling, the one she loved most, had been terrified of her. She had almost become worse than Julian.

She waited until he finished munching down his toast, and then poured him orange juice into his sippy cup. "Please, darling, come and sit on my lap. We need to have a talk. You can drink your juice while we chat."

Wide-eyed, he looked at her, struggled to his feet, scampered over, and climbed onto her lap. He took a sip of juice.

Cuddling him gently, she said softly. "Mommy needs to tell you she's sorry she hollered at you. I am so, so sorry, sweetheart. I was angry at Daddy and I took it out on you. You didn't do anything wrong. I did. It was wrong of me to yell at you. It won't happen again."

"I was scared, Mommy," he piped. "Cuddles was scared, too."

"I know you were, and I am so sorry. I didn't mean what I said. Please forgive me."

"It's alright, Mommy. I'm not scared now." He lifted his face to her and kissed her on the chin. "I love you."

"Oh, Rob, I'm so happy to hear those words. I love you, too."

Tears stung her eyes while she slowly rubbed his back. "Listen, sweetheart, Mommy's going to lie down on her bed. If you want, you can come and lie down too. Maybe we can cuddle and talk. Bring teddy. I'm sure he'll want to be with you."

The house was silent. The grandfather clock hadn't chimed in days, and she hadn't mentioned it to Julian. Lying on her bed in her robe, she was grateful that Binkie wasn't coming. She needed silence and space to think about what Julian had said, about what she had done to Rob, about her pills, and about going to the city to get away.

How would she ever manage without more pills? Could she cajole Dr. Morton into okaying another supply? Probably not. But then, she might be able to convince him to do so if she agreed to see a psychiatrist. Digging the vials out from under the mattress, she counted three Valium and six Seconals. She would tell him that she had willed her body to science, she thought, as she dialed his office.

"I'm sorry, Dr. Morton's out of town for several days," the receptionist said. "We have Dr. Berezowski taking his place. Would you like an appointment to see him?"

"Oh, dear, I'd hoped to see Dr. Morton. However, since this is important, I suppose I should come in. Is it possible to see him today?"

"Tomorrow at nine will be much better. We're double-booked for the remainder of today. May I ask who's calling?"

"Jessica Bothwell. I'll be there at nine tomorrow."

She hung up, hugging herself. What a deal! Dr. Morton wasn't in. She'd see a new doctor! What a stroke of luck!

A tiny shadow stood at the door. Rob. He was motionless, holding his teddy bear by an ear.

"Hi, sweetheart. Do you want another cuddle now?"

His curly blond head nodded.

"Well, come on! Where's my hug?"

He dashed to her and she folded her arms around him.

"Oh, darling, I love you so very much! More than you'll ever know!"

Holding him against her breast, she rocked back and forth on the bed, hoping the love she felt for him could seep through her and into his little body. She couldn't hurt her son any more. What had happened this morning was absolutely the last straw. She and Julian were having serious problems, and she was addicted to prescription drugs, but her son was never to feel afraid again. She could defend herself against Julian, but this small child was totally defenseless. He was her son and she adored him; and she was there to protect and defend him, regardless of Julian's twisted mind.

"Do you know what we should do today?" she asked, brightening at an idea. He peeked up at her, his blue eyes full of wonder. "Why don't we get the toboggan and go to the lake? I can pull you around on the snow, and we might even find a hill where we can go sliding."

"Can we go right now?" His face was all smiles.

"As soon as we get ready."

Yanking on warm clothes, tucking socks into boots, tying on scarves, pulling on knitted hats, they were ready. She crammed the toboggan into the Mustang, and with seat belts fastened, they were off.

She turned onto the road leading to the Terrace Lodge, bypassing the private drive to the hotel. Instead, she followed the road around the lake and stopped at the far end, where they had a view of the Terrace Lodge sprawling on the shores a mile across the ice.

"Hold the sides, sweetheart, and I'll take you for a fast jaunt. I'll be the horse, and you can be the driver."

"That way!" he yelled, his shrill voice echoing in the silence. "No! Go that way! Run, Horsey! Run faster!"

Panting with the effort of following his directions, she decided smoking wasn't helping her exertion.

"Come on, Horsey! Gallop! Go faster!"

"Okay driver, this horse has to walk. Pretty soon, this horse will have to sit down."

"That's silly, Mommy!" he giggled. "Horses don't sit down. They lie down."

"Anything you say, driver!" And she collapsed onto the soft, crystal powder. On her back, she gazed up at the puffs of clouds drifting across the blue. Oh, to be a cloud and just float around all day.

"Let's make snow angels, Mommy," Rob suggested, as he rolled off the toboggan and trudged to her side. "I learned how from Binkie. She showed me."

Binkie had played outside in the snow with her son? That little gray lady had been on her back in her yard making snow angels with Rob? And where had she been? Out for lunch? At the shooting range? Shopping? Hiding her bruises indoors? Guilt pinched a nerve.

"Okay, you show me how to do it!" she challenged him with relish.

He dropped onto the snow and rolled onto his back. With arms outstretched, he flopped his limbs back and forth, carving an angel in the white fluff. With the sun sparkling on the snow crystals, Jessica knew he had created the most beautiful angel in the world.

"Your turn now!" he ordered, clambering to his feet.

This is fun, she thought, following his instructions. She'd made hundreds of snow angels as a child, but had forgotten the joyful innocence of that time. She struggled to her feet to admire her art.

"Yours is the biggest, Mommy. Mine is nicer!" he announced.

"Do you know what? I think you're right! Your angel is simply gorgeous!" She hugged him close. "Now let's find a hill to toboggan on."

From the frozen lake, she surveyed the pine-covered slopes, and not far off, she spotted a clearing ideal for short runs. Up the slope they tramped, leaving footprints in the virgin snow.

With Rob up front, Jessica pushed off, and they flew through the drifts as Rob squealed with delight. A pine tree she hadn't calculated into their flight plan brought them to an abrupt stop, toppling them, laughing, into a pile of snow.

"Should we try again?" she sputtered, wiping snow from her face.

"Yeah!" He scampered ahead of her. Down they soared, skimming the snow like a canoe does water, tumbling into another drift.

Up they trudged and down they flew, so many times that Jessica lost count. However, when the sun dropped behind a cliff, the sudden chill told her it was time to leave.

"One more time!" he begged. "One more time!"

Will I ever have the chance to do this with Rob again? she wondered, as they sailed down the slope. If not, then it has been worth every second. I shall hold this in my heart always, as a treasured time with my son.

Chapter Five:

Roadblocks and Roses

D R. BEREZOWSKI FLIPPED THROUGH HER RECORDS, FROWNING AT HER AS SHE SAT CLINGING TO THE EDGE OF HER CHAIR. "I'm just reading this rap sheet on you," he mumbled, revealing some kind of accent. "You've had quite a colorful few months. What's happening at home?"

"I'm playing with live grenades," she replied, squirming as he arched his eyebrows and drilled his bright blue eyes into hers. "I'm scared all the time, have anxiety attacks that de-rail me, and I can't sleep. I'm willing to see a therapist or psychiatrist, if you think I should."

She knew he could see "insane", "maniac", "garden-variety cuckoo", and "nitwit" engraved on her forehead.

"Have you considered leaving him?" He twirled a pencil in his fingers. "Beating you up so that you require hospital visits and need to rely on medication doesn't indicate a healthy lifestyle."

"I know," she answered feebly. "I keep hoping things will improve."

He studied her silently for a long moment, then sighed, shrugging. "Here's what I'm going to do. Dr. Morton won't be back for a couple of weeks. I'll give you enough medication

191

until he returns. I don't know enough about your case to suggest something more constructive. But you might consider some alternatives, such as counseling."

A reprieve! Thank God she got the prescriptions! They would give her time to think, plan, plot, scheme, connive, or perhaps talk her way out of her nightmare. The doctor had said "alternatives". She might have to enter into some sort of conspiracy to escape Julian's clutches. On the other hand, maybe they could work things out. Perhaps they still loved each other.

⁂

"When are you taking that holiday for yourself?" Rosalind phoned to inquire. She didn't beat around the bush for anyone.

"Soon," Jessica answered. "By the way, listen, why don't I pick you up, and let's go skating?"

"Are you insane? I haven't been on skates in years! Okay. Why not? You take me skating, and then I'll take you skiing!"

"It's a deal!" laughed Jessica.

They parked the car in the lot overlooking the frozen river. It was a peach of a day with the sun bright on the sparkling snow and no breeze. There were few skaters, which meant fewer targets for the pair to crash into.

As they sat on the bench beside the rink to put on their skates and lace them up, Rosalind laughed. "I don't have insurance on risk-taking. If I break my neck, Harry will break yours!"

"Hey, look!" Jessica pointed. "There's an old metal chair. Perfect for you to hang onto for balance. I'll get it for you."

When she skated back with the chair, she held out a mittened hand to help guide Rosalind from the bench. Rosalind gripped Jessica's fingers as if she were about to go over a cliff.

"You talk me into the damnedest things!" she laughed as she clung to the back of the chair, easing herself onto the ice. "No wonder you're my best friend. I never know what we'll be doing next!"

For a while, they skated in silence, Jessica contemplative and troubled. Finally she spoke in a hushed voice.

"We need to talk. That's why I wanted to go skating. No one can overhear us out here. I don't want to talk about any of this stuff on the phone. You know that bugging thing I was telling you about? I think he's doing it."

"Why would he?" Rosalind frowned. "He's probably capable of it, but why would he go to all that trouble? You never say anything incriminating on the phone."

"I know that. He knows it, too. I think he wants to unnerve me. Can you come over when Binkie's not there and help me go though the house? I've already opened every phone and receiver, and I've checked out all the kitchen cupboards, the microwave, food processor, stove and fridge, the family room, and my dressing room."

"Christ, Jessica, you don't know what you're looking for!" scolded Rosalind, plopping down onto the chair. "Why don't you ask Casey for help? He probably has access to the equipment you need to snoop out those devices."

"I can't do that! Casey and Julian are as thick as thieves! The first thing he'd do is inform Julian. For all I know, Casey could have helped him install the damned things! I don't trust that man one little bit. He's a great teacher, but I wouldn't ask him for help of any kind!"

"Sometimes, I think you're Alice-Through-The-Looking-Glass. Are you sure you aren't just being paranoid? Besides, those gadgets are illegal."

"Since when did anything illegal stop Julian? He's not exactly the epitome of perfectly legal tactics. I'm still not sure how he managed to acquire all that land for the Terrace Lodge Hotel."

"What exactly are you suggesting, Jess?"

"Oh, Roz, I don't know! I get creepy feelings sometimes."

"Like when he beats you up?"

"No." She spun around on her skates, reminded of how she felt that she was being spied upon—that someone knew what she was doing, when she was doing it, and with whom. "It's not when he's rough. It's when he's nice, around, and acting like the model husband. And Roz, you and I have never discussed this before. I always wanted to talk to you about it, but it didn't seem appropriate. How well did you know Tiffany, the girl Julian was engaged to?"

Rosalind remained silent for a moment, then stood up, and braced herself on the back of the chair. She skated away while Jessica followed.

"I was wondering if you'd ever want to know. I knew her pretty well. We were good friends, and she invited me to be one of her bridesmaids. She was a really sweet girl."

Jessica digested that with a twinge of pain and asked, "What really happened to her? Lydia told me she'd seen Julian's women come and go. What did she mean by that?"

"I'm not sure," answered Rosalind, as she sat down on the chair again, facing the sun to catch its warm rays. "I know Julian was running around a lot after Tiffany died. I thought he was trying to replace her with as many parties and as much female action as he could."

"How did she die?" Jessica asked, her voice quivering, but needing to know if Julian's explanation could be corroborated.

"She froze to death. Both Jack and Tiffany froze to death on

194

that trip to the city. Julian must have told you about that."

Jessica nodded, but she needed to know more. "Why was there an inquest?"

"There usually is an investigation in cases like that." She squinted at Jessica. "Why do you want to know?"

"I guess it's because I've been doing some thinking lately. I've never told you this, but when Julian gets drunk and starts treating me like I'm his personal punching bag, he screams at me about her. He says I'm just like her, that I'm screwing around on him just like she did."

"God, Jess, does he actually say that?"

"Ever since the first time he hammered me, he's accused me of messing around. Then he started telling me I was no better than Tiffany."

Rosalind's gloved hand grasped Jessica's. "Jess, I don't believe Tiffany was ever unfaithful to Julian. She simply wasn't that kind of person because she had very high principles. But I do recall that Tiffany once told me that she might call off the wedding because she'd heard something about him, and she was afraid of him. But those of us she told all convinced her he was a great guy. I guess she believed us. My God, Jess!"

Jessica chilled at the suggestion.

"Julian is threatening to kill me if I ever leave him. Rosalind, I really think he'll do it, whether I leave him or not."

Rosalind jumped up. "Let's go to the Wharf. I think we both need a drink!"

"Please let's not talk about this in the lounge. Sometimes walls have ears," Jessica pleaded.

"And," Rosalind added, "sometimes I wish I were a fly on the wall. You worry me, Jess. I think you should pack your bags and get out of there."

Jessica realized that her fists were clenched, her heart was thudding, and in spite of the cool temperature, her forehead was beaded with perspiration. Tears stung her eyes. "I have nowhere to go, Rosalind! Julian told me I had nowhere to hide, that he'd track me down, and kill both Rob and me if I ever left him. He means it, Roz. I know he'll do it!"

Rosalind studied her friend's pale face. "Let's go and have that drink," she urged. "You don't have to worry about his bugging the house. There isn't anything going on there that shouldn't be happening, except for him. You have a lot more to be concerned about, Jessica, than stupid listening devices."

⁑

"You're going to do it anyway?" Julian exclaimed, peering at her incredulously over morning coffee. "You're going to up and run to the city. Fine mother you are! All you want to do is get away from Rob. And from me, too, probably."

You're absolutely right about yourself, she thought.

"Julian, darling," she said, reaching for his hand. "I love you and Rob dearly, but I need some time away from Riverbend. It isn't like I'm going to the Amazon jungle. I'll only be two hundred and fifty miles away. I need a change of scene. I need to think about my life, and the life you and I have together. Maybe you can do some thinking too. Right now our relationship is at a flash point. If either one of us says the wrong word, we're screaming at each other! We both deserve better than that, and Rob deserves parents who aren't squabbling all the time. Our behavior is badly affecting him, probably leaving permanent scars on his developing psyche."

Julian heard her out and gulped down his coffee.

"And just who is going to look after that kid while you dash off to meditate? I'm sure as hell not taking time off to be a sitter!"

Carefully, she explained the arrangements she had made for Rob's care.

"It sounds like you've been doing some heavy-duty scheming behind my back," he sneered suspiciously. "Okay! Go on! You wear me out! Have a good time. Just don't forget where you live! And don't forget Mother's anniversary party at the end of the month!"

"I'll probably miss it. Besides, she'd love to have you all to herself. But you can invite Amber in my place. I'm sure your mother will adore her."

Glowering at her, he snarled, "You get the most outrageous ideas in your head! One of these days, your imagination's going to explode and kill you!"

"Not that you'd notice!" she spat.

"Listen, Jessica," he grinned, with all the benevolence of an asp. "I've been hearing things about you in town. Some very unpleasant things."

"And what have you been hearing?" It had never occurred to her that she might be the target of malicious gossip.

"You know what I'm talking about." He looked smug, like a shark that had swallowed the last of a diver.

"I haven't got a clue. Who's telling stories?"

"Think about it, sweetheart!" he said with a smirk, as he pecked her cheek. "You're a very clever woman. While you're on your little trip, think about it."

And he was gone.

✵

"You're sure about taking the bus?" asked Rosalind, as she helped Jessica unload her bags for the city.

"I don't want the hassle of driving there and back. Trains are always behind schedule, and flying makes me sick. This is the best way. Besides, now Julian can say, 'Thank God and Greyhound, she's gone!'"

"Make sure you call me. I need to know you're all right. And don't worry for one second about Rob. You relax and unwind and pamper yourself with luxury."

"I love you, Roz," Jessica said, hugging her friend. "Thanks for being such a darling. You'll never know what your love and support mean to me."

Climbing aboard, she found a window seat where she could be alone and waved at Rosalind who watched anxiously from the platform.

Thank God for people like Roz, she thought, feeling guilty about her inability to tell her friend the real reason she opted for the bus. How could she say she was terrified to drive because she was buzzed on Valium? How could she admit she was hooked on pills? How could she tell the woman she trusted the most in the world that, if she drove, she'd be tempted to drive off a cliff or straight into the path of an oncoming semi-trailer? How could she explain that she was on the razor's edge of sanity? She didn't even have the nerve to ask Rosalind what stories were being bruited around town. How could she explain lying awake at night, wondering what she had done to deserve vicious gossip?

As the bus pulled out of the terminal, she waved to Rosalind who waved back enthusiastically, blowing kisses. Jessica opened her purse and took two Valium from the prescription bottle, washing them down with the cola she had taken with her. Two pills would kill the five-hour trip.

*

Her suite at the Westin Hotel was gorgeous, just the thing
for her purpose, which was to stay blitzed on pills while she
figured out a way to reach Julian and mend the tatters of their
relationship. She saw that as the only alternative, since to separate would mean her certain death...and Rob's! Every fiber of
her being believed Julian had meant what he said and that he
was *capable* of it.

Running water into the Jacuzzi, she dribbled in just enough
bubble liquid to make a tranquilizing bath. Remembering the
first time she and Julian had shared a Jacuzzi bubble bath, she
smiled; she had poured in too much bubble stuff and the whole
tub had ballooned with froth until foam reached almost to the
ceiling. That had been a bath to remember, as they probed their
way through the white fluff to make slow satiny love while the
water caressed their bodies. The memory brought tears to her
eyes. Sliding into the bubbling water, she shook the memories
from her mind and floated into a dream of how things would be
when she got off the pills and helped Julian realize how precious
their relationship was.

Things will get better, she thought. I know they will...because
they have to.

*

The headwaiter seemed surprised when Jessica requested a
quiet corner, stating that she was dining alone. She knew she
looked terrific. She was wearing that little silk number from

Pierre's—a simple black sheath with a round neckline and capped sleeves. To enhance the dress, she had put on her glittering crystal earrings and matching brooch, her diamond watch, and the heart-shaped diamond ring Julian had given to her.

"Mother's night out," she smiled, brandishing the book she had brought for company. There was nothing like a story about myth, madness, and greed to distract a busy mind. She had picked up *The Golden Spruce* by Canadian author John Vaillant because it was a story about the lumbering industry and how a timber scout had chopped down a legendary golden spruce, sacred to the Haida people, in order to make a statement about how lumbering practices were destroying delicate ecosystems on Canada's West Coast. The cover description had fascinated her and, with her own environmental concerns, she had decided to challenge her mind and learn something new rather than concentrate on her own self-involved pursuits.

"Without the kiddies, I understand." His thick graying mustache curled as he returned the smile. His mustache looked like a creepy gray caterpillar crawling under his nose. She shuddered.

He led her to a small table tucked into an alcove. It was perfect for a clandestine rendezvous, and it was perfect for her. A candle flickered in its pewter holder, the light shimmering on the china and silver.

"Would madame care for a drink? An aperitif perhaps?" he asked, as he placed a leather-bound menu in front of her.

"A glass of white Chablis would be nice," she replied.

While he rushed off to deliver her order to a waiter, she slipped two Valium out of her change purse. It wouldn't do to make a show of taking medication. The pills could have been for elevated blood pressure, cardiac arrhythmia, gastric distress or headache, but the paranoia of addiction held her in its grasp, and she imagined that anyone watching her would be certain she was a junkie. Furtively, she glanced around to see if anyone noticed her putting the pills into her mouth and swallowing them dry. That aside from her, the dining room was empty except for an elderly couple, was almost a disappointment. Oh, who the hell cared, anyway?

Within seconds, the waiter delivered her wine. As she savored its crisp taste, she felt smug that she hadn't ordered hard liquor. She knew that mixing drugs with alcohol was not clever, but at least it wasn't Scotch. The time of reckoning was closing in, but this was the start of her holiday, and she intended to relish every minute, basking in the luxury of having no arguments, no threats, no spills, and no messes.

She ordered escargots, knowing she could get away with the lingering garlic bouquet; sleeping alone had its advantages. She ordered a tiny salad and a chicken breast in white wine and lemon sauce. No potato, but extra vegetable, please. Another glass of Chablis would be nice while awaiting the appetizer.

Halfway through the escargots, she took another Valium, gulping it down with the wine. When she dribbled some escargot sauce down the front of her dress, she sensed she was getting smashed from not eating all day and mixing chemical supports. Four Valium and three Chablis later, the chicken arrived. Her book swam in front of her eyes, the print blending with the starched white cloth and bouncing off the cream sauce. Her dinner lost its appeal as her stomach lurched around the escargots and salad. She knew she was about to be sick and signaled the waiter.

"Is anything wrong, madame? Would you care for some more wine?"

"Just the check, please," she choked, striving to force down an escargot that had slithered into her throat. "Everything's fine, thank you. I'm not quite as hungry as I thought, but I'd like to pay and go to my room."

She held the napkin to her mouth. Dear God, she prayed, don't let me pull a Mary-Beth. She kept re-swallowing the escargot and salad, which insisted on returning to her mouth. The damned things wouldn't stay down!

The bill took forever. Taking her credit card from her purse took forever. A Valium fell out onto the table, and she snatched it back, tucking it into her change purse. She signed the credit voucher, leaving it on the tray. Then, with carefully measured steps, feeling as if she were wading through liquid tar, passed the maître d' who smiled, welcoming her back anytime. She managed a weak smile with paralyzed lips. Slowly, she teetered down the hall to the elevator, trying not to vomit, and trying not to look as though she was stewed to the gills.

The phone was ringing as she opened the door to her suite. Let it ring. She had talked to Rosalind before supper, so this call was only from that cursed Julian. Let him worry about where she was. She didn't give a sweet damn!

She undressed, dropped her clothes on a chair, and kicked her shoes into a corner. The nausea passed, and she stretched out on the bed, staring up at the ceiling to see how fast it was spinning. Things really were getting out of hand. She had become no better than a street corner junkie and no better than a drunk in an alley. High up in her ivory tower of the Westin Hotel, with its doormen, charming dining nooks, plush upholstery, mirrored bathrooms, and opulent décor, she was no better than a guy in the gutter screaming for a fix.

Suddenly, in a single moment of clarity that pierced her Valium haze, she knew she had to get help or she'd be lost forever!

Grabbing the telephone book, she riffled through its pages until she found what she was looking for—the Glenora Treatment Center. With her breath coming in gasps, she dialed the number with trembling fingers. A man answered.

"I'd...I'd like to talk to...to someone about a pill problem," she faltered.

"You're talkin' to him," came the cheerful reply.

Why did people at facilities like that always sound so maddeningly happy? Didn't they know that life, at best, was a rotten deal? If only they sounded mournful and sympathetic! Perhaps they should take lessons from receptionists at funeral homes!

"I think I have a pill problem. I don't know what to do."

"What're you taking? How much?" Gruff questions.

"Valium and Seconal. Sometimes up to nine or ten Valium, five milligrams each. Seconal, the lowest dosage, but sometimes I take three or four."

"Whewee! You tryin' to blow yourself away?" the man observed.

"No, just trying to make it through."

"Yeah, I know the feelin'." There it was, the mournful, sympathetic understanding.

"Listen," the voice said, "there's nuthin' we can do about it tonight. How about comin' tomorrow to talk to one of our counselors? I'll put you down for one o'clock with Dan Kennedy. Do you think you can wait that long?"

"As long as I know I can get help, I can wait. I've made it this far. One more night won't kill me."

"I sure hope not. Take it easy with those pills or one more night *could* kill you! May I have your name, please?"

"Jessica...Jessica Bothwell," she almost sobbed.

"Take it easy, Jessica. You're gonna be okay." The voice was cheerful again and positive.

She hung up.

After swallowing three Seconals, she curled under the bed covers. She'd be okay, she told herself. Fairy tales had always comforted her as a child, so she told herself the fairy tale that she'd be fine. She needed a happy ending to her crisis. Otherwise, she wouldn't fall asleep.

The phone rang. She counted ten rings. When it finally stopped, she took the receiver off the hook.

⁂

She felt like death warmed over when she awoke. Her blood seemed to have solidified in her veins; her tongue was glued to the roof of her mouth. Drawing open the drapes, she jerked them closed quickly before the sunlight poured into her room. She hated cheerful, sunny days when her insides felt like chopped liver. Had the day matched her mood, it would have been overcast with icy gales lashing the landscape.

Standing under a freezing shower, she scoured her skin with a washcloth to stir up some circulation. After wrapping herself in a terry cloth robe, she called room service for coffee, lots of it. Then, following every addict's ritual, she checked her supply of Valium. Eight pills left! And only five Seconals! My God, she was almost out! Maybe she could get a prescription filled here in the city.

Tossing the phone book onto the bed, she searched the listings for a doctor near the hotel, then phoned and made an appointment for four-thirty. God, what was she doing? Treatment Center for help and then a doctor for more pills!

Just enough, she comforted herself, to get her through until she could find her way out of this maze of madness.

The coffee arrived, steaming and black, bringing to mind her mother's kitchen, with its coffee pot always on the back burner, and its wonderful aroma. Why was she thinking of her mother now? Was it because her mother would have been happy to know that Jessica had chosen to emulate her by becoming a wife and mother, instead of merely frittering her life away? Was it because her mother would have frowned upon her being sick from pills in a fancy hotel suite? Jessica felt guilty about everything having gone to hell when it had all started out so brightly and full of promise. Did her mother turn to drugs—her life wrecked from giving her all to an emotionally absent man and two children? No! Not Jessica's mother! She kept herself busy, busy, busy! Busy with her cooking and nonstop cleaning, busy with her church groups, and busy with her endless hobbies! Keeping busy had been the gospel, according to Jessica's sainted mother.

"Keep busy and don't think about it," her mother had told Jessica, as the frail, emaciated woman lay dying in hospital. "That's your problem, Jessica. You have too much time to sit around and brood," she'd gasped, choking on the tubes running though her nose and throat.

Desperate, Jessica uncapped the Valium bottle and swallowed two pills with a gulp of the scalding coffee. God! She didn't want to end up like her mother!

⁂

The treatment center was located in the outskirts of the city, where the farms began. The taxi dropped her at the front door, and Jessica introduced herself to the shining bundle of health at the reception window.

"Please take a seat," the young woman smiled. "Mr. Kennedy will be right with you."

Jessica perched at the edge of the wooden chair, wondering if the receptionist was Miss January for Playboy's centerfold. She wished she could smoke, but "No Smoking" signs bristled on the walls.

Footsteps tapped along the tile floor. Looking up, Jessica saw a tall, slim man who was about forty approaching, his shaggy eyebrows drawn together over bright, alert eyes.

"Jessica Bothwell? I'm Dan Kennedy," he introduced himself, shaking her hand. "Why don't we go into the sitting room? We can talk privately there."

As she skittered along beside his easy strides, she wished she could scamper under the baseboards and hide. Why had she ever come here?

Inviting her to sit in a comfortable, leather-upholstered chair, he handed her an ashtray. Did she look like a nicotine addict too? He leaned back in his chair.

"So...Jessica...how can we help?" His smile was warm and pleasant.

"Well, Mr. Kennedy..."

"Please, call me 'Dan'," he grinned amiably. "I like people here to call me Dan. That way, we're all equals."

"Well," she began again, "I...uh...I think...I *know* I have a drug problem. Prescription drugs. I've been to a treatment center before, so I thought this time I'd be able to handle the pills I'm taking, but I'm in deep trouble." She described the history of her present addiction, describing her terror and the anxiety attacks, skillfully avoiding her marriage problems and never mentioning the violence.

"Does your husband know you're here? Will he be supportive of your receiving treatment?"

She shook her head. "He'd have a convulsion if he knew I came here. He knew about the first batch of pills, but I never told him I'd had the prescriptions filled again...and again...and again. He'd blow a gasket if he knew I had a problem."

"What if you do come here? Would he encourage you?"

"I don't think so. He doesn't think there's anything wrong. He hates treatment centers and counselors. But, Dan, I don't want to die! I can't go on living like this! I'm sick of crying all the time and feeling like I can't cope."

As tears began to trickle, in spite of her effort not to cry, Dan handed her a tissue and asked kindly, "Where are the tears coming from, Jessica?"

"I don't know," she sniffled. "They just come, no matter how much I try to hold them back. I guess I'm asking for too much."

"What are you asking for that seems too much?"

"Well, I'd like to be happy and not angry. I'd like to be able to cope without feeling I was paddling against the current all the time. I'd like to be free of my anxiety and be able to deal with life's problems in positive ways."

"That doesn't sound too unrealistic to me," he said. "What keeps you from being the way you want to be?"

"I'm not really sure. That's why I want to come here."

Dan leaned over, elbows resting on his thighs, fingers of both hands touching to form a steeple. "Jessica, I can't make any promises to you. We don't have a magic wand to wave over you in this center to bring you health, happiness, and an ability to cope. We can't help you have fun or give your life meaning or direction. All the answers to your problems lie within yourself.

What we do here is provide an atmosphere free from mood-altering substances and the appropriate support systems to help you discover your own unique answers to your own unique problems. You see, what might work for you would never be someone else's solution to the problem. It's difficult, Jessica, but not impossible. In view of what you're experiencing, it's in your best interests to consider treatment. All we ask is that you be open-minded, honest, and willing to cooperate with us. Do you want to apply for treatment, even if your husband is against it?"

"I don't have any choice, Dan! If I don't come, I'll die! I might even commit suicide if I feel any worse than I do now!"

"Jessica, do you understand that any addiction to any substance is merely a symptom of underlying emotional problems? Do you understand that once we have the addiction under control, you'll have to dig to discover and peel away some old habits, attitudes, and values that aren't working for you?"

She nodded.

"Do you know, beyond any shadow of a doubt, that the biggest battle you'll face when you come here is with *yourself*? It won't be with me, or with any other therapist, or with the other clients. When it gets rough and tough in therapy, and your world is turned inside out, you'll have your own room to run and hide in, but you'll be in there alone...with yourself."

"I think I knew that, Dan," she whispered, "when I called."

"Have your doctor fill in this part of the application and return it as quickly as possible. We can have you here in two weeks."

"Dan, I wish I could thank you," she began, her heart pounding. She felt grateful, terrified, exhilarated, hopeful, despairing, and anxious.

"Don't thank me. Thank yourself. And show up! You'd be

surprised at the number of people who come here looking for help and then never come back."

"You can bet on it, Dan. I'll be back!" She tried to smile.

"Do it for you, Jessica," he grinned at her. "Do it for the life you have ...which is very precious."

The doctor's office was a short distance up the street from the hotel. Walking through the frosty afternoon air, Jessica glanced into shop windows and dodged passers-by who were bent against the January wind. She realized she had taken only two Valium all day, yet she didn't even feel jangly. She felt almost normal, good about seeing Dan, and good about doing something so momentous for herself. A mouse skittered across her mind–the guilt mouse. She knew that going for more pills was something she should not be doing. But God! What if she needed them before she entered treatment? Rationalization won out, and she chased the mouse back to its hole. Finding the street number, she took the elevator to the eleventh floor.

The office was as quiet as a tomb with no other patients waiting. There was no receptionist either. She sat down to wait, flipping through a *Vogue* magazine.

"Mrs. Bothwell?" A deep voice interrupted her as she pictured herself in one of the stylish outfits. She dropped the magazine as though it was ablaze.

"Yes!" she gulped and followed the doctor, a short, paunchy man, into the consulting room.

"I'm Dr. Blackstone," he intoned, seating himself behind a massive, polished mahogany desk. Not a picture, paper, book, pen, file, or blotter littered the top. Folding his hands on the desk, he peered at her through giant horn-rimmed glasses, which magnified his eyes to the size of sunny-side-up blue eggs. His head was bald and as shiny and polished as the top of his desk. He was no more than five feet tall, and Jessica imagined him sitting on a booster seat in that giant chair with his feet dangling in mid-air.

"Now what is the nature of your visit?" he asked, his mouth twisting into a smug smile.

"Doctor, I'll come right to the point. I'm in the midst of a crisis at home, and I'm experiencing difficult marriage problems. God knows, I ought to be able to deal with it better than I am, but I'm having a lot of trouble coping. I can't sleep. I'm edgy all the time. Uptight. I suffer from anxiety attacks. I thought perhaps some artificial support would help until I get some professional advice and counseling, of course."

"Of course." He nodded.

"Well, I thought perhaps you might be able to prescribe something to help me. I need to sleep. I need to relax and unwind."

"Any suggestions?" he asked. "You're not allergic to anything, are you? No addiction problems?"

"I can't think of any allergies. Certainly *no* addiction problems, except to caffeine," Jessica giggled.

"Coffee! You and half the world," he chuckled. "Me, too. Any preference?"

"I'm not really sure. I so seldom take anything stronger than aspirin, but a friend of mine went though similar problems and she used Valium and Seconal. They helped her immensely."

"They're not addictive if they're taken on a short-term basis only," he reminded her.

"Do you think I could have a two-month supply? That should give me ample time to start therapy, and they'd help to level me out."

From his desk drawer, he took out a prescription pad. Scribbling on it, he ripped off the order, and handed it to her.

"I'm sure you'll find these helpful, Mrs. Bothwell. Good luck with the situation at home. Call me if you need further help. You'll find a drugstore on the corner."

So easy, she thought, as the elevator descended to the street level, after she had paid her bill in cash to avoid a paper trail. Walk in, tell the doctor half the truth, don't get hysterical, and you get a supply of pills from a man who doesn't even know you. He doesn't have a clue if you're going to commit suicide, peddle the damn things on the street, poison the family cat, or do a number on a rich aunt. Be grateful, Jessica. He could have said, "No!"

✻

She threw herself onto the bed. Exhaustion coursed through her in undulating waves, while dread tiptoed down her spine, its frigid fingers clutching her heart. What had she done? She couldn't go to a treatment center! Julian would simply not allow it. He'd holler, yell, and never understand.

He doesn't care if I'm well, she thought, as long as I behave as if I am. He doesn't care how I feel as long as I don't interfere with him. He doesn't care if I'm short-circuiting inside, as long as my eyes don't glow in the dark. He says he loves me, and then ignores me, or beats me into submission. What's wrong? If people in Riverbend knew how I really lived, they'd puke! They think because I'm married to one of the most important, financially influential men in town, that my life is tickety-boo. If only they knew the truth! Maybe I really am crazy. Maybe I have something that can't be fixed. Maybe I'll have to live like this forever. If I have to do that, I'd rather be dead!

Anguish tore at her soul, at her mind, and her heart. Ripping open the prescription vial, she shook three Valium into her hand and tossed them back, gulping them down with the cold remains of her morning coffee. She wanted to scream and tear her hair. She despised herself for the predicament in which she found herself. If only she hadn't encountered Julian. If only she hadn't married him. If only she wasn't hooked on pills. If only she hadn't been born. If only she was dead. She'd heard once that dying was the easy part; it was living that was the bitch. She didn't have what it took to live; she was nothing but a snot-nosed coward!

Exhausted by the effort of being "normal" all day, she took two more pills. What she needed now was to treat herself to a Jacuzzi while the chemical de-frazzler worked its way through her veins. She'd get swacked out of her skull, loll in the bath, and watch whatever appeared on TV. That would be her rest and relaxation from her turmoil. She didn't give a damn if she stayed locked in her room for three days. The maids could clean around her, and she'd have all her meals sent to the suite. What were luxury suites for if she couldn't take pleasure in their peace and tranquility, floating far above the real world on the eighteenth floor? She now had enough of a pill supply to afford to be spun out for days and still have plenty until treatment center time.

The phone rang while she lazed in the tub, the water surging around her, massaging her psychic cramps. It rang ten times, quit, and rang again. After four rings, it stopped. Julian could take a flying leap off a bridge. Let him worry about her!

Wrapping her terry robe around her goose bumps after the

steamy bath, she plumped up the pillows on the bed, picked up the TV remote, blipped though a few channels, and made friends with Diane Sawyer. Why couldn't she communicate like good old Diane? Millions of viewers understood what this TV personality said. Why couldn't Julian understand his wife?

The days and nights melded together, as she floated in and out of her fantasy of how delightful things were going to be once she was free from the pills and Julian wasn't battering her. There was nothing like Valium to take the harsh realities of life and spin them into a tempting treat of imagination and hallucination. She watched all the talk shows. Dr. Phil certainly had it together. Geraldo seemed so loving and concerned about his guests who, on one show, were battered wives. Nancy Grace appeared to listen to her guests. Was it because they were being paid to listen, to be understanding, inquisitive, and empathetic?

Christ! What had she done now? This treatment center idea would put Julian in a frenzy. He'd serve up her pancreas and liver as delicacies for Hannibal the Cannibal, complete with sour cream dip. Two Valium and three Seconals later, she forgot about Julian.

On her last evening in the city, the telephone jarred her from her murky haven. Six rings and she answered.

"Where in the hell have you been? I've been phoning for days! Aren't you ever in your room? Why didn't you return my calls?"

"Oh, Julian, how sweet of you to call!" Her brain needed airing.

"How are you? Are you feeling better?"

"I feel awful!" she cried. "I wish you were here to love me and help me!"

Would he ever hear her?

"Christ! You sound worse than before! What's going on with you? This little scheme was supposed to make you happy! It's just like all the plots you hatch! They don't work, do they?"

"Please listen!" she begged. "I love you and I need you. I've never needed you more than I do now! I want to be home with you and Rob."

"Yes, Jessica." His voice softened. "I want you home, too. I've missed you, and I love you. This place isn't the same without you."

She clung to his words as she would a life preserver: Love. Miss. Want.

"Listen," he said, "you're taking the early bus, right? Why don't I meet you at the depot and take you to lunch?"

"What a wonderful idea! I'd love that! God, I need you. I need you to love me and to have your arms around me."

"My arms will always be around you. I love you, darling. You have a good sleep, and I'll see you at noon. I'll call Rosalind and let her know I'm picking you up. I can hardly wait to see you. Hugs and kisses."

After putting in a wake-up call, she took off her robe and slid between the cool sheets. She swallowed three Seconals and snuggled into her pillow, pretending Julian was holding her, comforting her, and loving her. Maybe he had needed some time to get the picture. She fell asleep hugging her pillow. She was smiling.

⁂

She stepped from the bus into the bright noon sun. Snow

scrunched beneath her boots as she claimed her luggage from the driver, and then hauled them into the warmth of the station. Where was Julian? He'd promised to be there. Panic slashed at her heart. The depot clock said five minutes before twelve. That was the problem; the bus was slightly ahead of schedule. He'd be here in a few minutes. She could hardly wait to throw herself into his arms. Then she saw Lincoln walk through the door. As he glanced around, he spotted her wave. But he didn't smile, and he avoided her eyes as he approached her.

"Where's Julian?" Alarm tore through her. "Has anything happened to him?"

"No, he's fine. Are these your bags? He's gone skiing and asked me to come and get you."

"Skiing?" A scream of rage and disappointment registered in her brain. "He's supposed to be here for God's sake! He phoned and told me he'd meet me for lunch. I talked to him last night."

Lincoln was embarrassed and uncomfortable. "I don't know, Jessica. All he told me was to come and pick you up and take you home."

As he wheeled the car though the snow-packed streets, Lincoln didn't say anything. Jessica choked on the nausea that scalded the back of her throat.

"Did he say when he'd be back?" she croaked, swallowing bile.

"Not until tonight."

"Did he have a redheaded snow bunny with him?"

"I wouldn't know about that."

"Thanks for picking me up," she mumbled, as he handed her the luggage in the middle of a drift in the driveway.

As he pulled away, she scrambled through the drift, wondering where the guy who plowed the driveway was. With boots full of snow, she swore as she tried to get the key in the lock of the oak door. Great welcome home, she thought, yanking her suitcases into the foyer.

The house was a sepulcher with the drapes drawn and the heat cranked down to sixty degrees. She set the thermostat to seventy and heard the pipes hiss as hot water flushed through them. In the kitchen, she checked for a note. Nothing. The room was spotless, not a dish, pot, pan, or cloth out of place. She hauled the suitcases up the marble stairs. In the bedroom, everything was in order. Inspecting the bar, she found every bottle and decanter was full.

She shrugged off her coat and kicked her boots under a chair. Who cared if she had tracked snow through the house? Scrounging in her purse, she found her prescription. Two pills would do just fine. She needed something to quell the dragon of rage.

Heaving the suitcases onto the bed, she dumped the contents on the spread to sort out her clothes. The hamper was bursting when she finished unpacking. Stacking the suitcases on the shelf she had had built in her dressing room, she closed the door and forgot them. There was no sign she had ever been away...or missed. She lit a cigarette and phoned Rosalind.

"Rob's been a doll!" gushed Rosalind. "What a terrific kid! I don't think Harry's going to relinquish him without a fight. How're you?"

"Wonderful!" How could she tell her friend she'd broiled her brain with pills? "It was terrific to get away, until I got off the bus, and Lincoln picked me up. Did Julian call you?"

"Yes. He phoned last night about meeting you."

"Well, he didn't. He told Lincoln he was going skiing instead of meeting me. No explanation. Nothing! I can't figure this out."

"He's probably pouting because you did something for

yourself. Don't worry about it. Just enjoy the peace and quiet this afternoon. I told Binkie to take the day off. The last thing you need is her buzzing around on your first day home. And listen, Jess. Why don't you leave Rob here until tomorrow? We adore having him, and he's no trouble for us. Harry's having the time of his life! Enjoy your space by yourself, and we'll see you tomorrow."

Jessica slithered rather than pranced down the staircase. The slightest effort made her flesh crawl. In the living room, she opened the drapes and sank into her cushiony rocker by the window.

Well, lady, what do you do now? No child, no husband, and an empty house. You don't have to do anything more strenuous than watch the dust dance in the sunbeams. But, for heaven's sake, whatever you do, keep believing there will be a happy ending to all this after all.

Whining from the basement stairwell roused her from her lethargy, and she wandered to the door to open it for Cuddles. The perky poodle bounced around Jessica's legs, and her mistress opened the French patio door for the tiny critter to relieve herself. Once finished her duty, the dog made a beeline for the kitchen and her scatter rug, while Jessica wandered back to her chair in the living room. Within a few minutes, Cuddles joined her, lying at Jessica's feet, staring up with her dark round eyes at Jessica's misery. Once in a while, the poodle sighed, and Jessica reached down and scratched her ears. "Yes, puppy," she murmured, "we both lead a dog's life in this house."

The hours vanished and the sky blackened. Through the lights from around the empty pool, snowflakes pirouetted to the ground. Sitting in the gloom, she saw the lights from the limousine ease up the drive. Good grief! Did he have Kenneth drive him to the hill? She heard the banging and crashing as Julian replaced the skis and poles in their racks in the garage. Then, "Goodnight Kenneth. Thanks for your time."

She pretended to be lost in reverie as Julian opened the front door and flashed the lights on.

"Jess," he called, "are you home?"

"In here."

"For crying out loud, Jess, do we have to save on power?" He flicked on the lamps as he made his way to his rocker and used the remote to turn on the TV. His face was flushed from the slopes.

She watched as he yanked off his cap, shrugged off his jacket, and wiggled out of his ski pants, tossing them in a pile on the floor. And just who was going to pick them up and hang them away? He lit a cigarette. Was she supposed to go and ruffle his hair, kiss him, shake his hand, and welcome him home? She opted instead for cool sarcasm.

"How do you do? I'm so pleased to see you in my living room. I've been dying for company all day, and it was so thoughtful of you to drop by. My name's Jessica, and who might you be?"

Jay Leno smiled at her from the screen, but Julian could have been counting cash for all the attention he paid to her.

"It's been a long time since I've seen you." But she was competing with one of Leno's jokes. "Just visiting, Julian? Or do you plan on staying a few days? It was nice of you to drop in," she drawled, finding comfort in sarcasm.

"What in hell is that supposed to mean?" he snapped.

"You know what I mean! Where were you when you promised to meet the bus?" She hiked across the carpet and switched off Jay Leno.

"Hey! I was watching that!"

"That may very well be, but I'm pretty upset about your not meeting the bus like you said you would. That was a low blow, especially when you knew how much I needed you."

"I can't take any more of your sniveling and crying. Christ, Jessica, you never stop crying! You have everything a woman could want, and you're fucking miserable! Why don't you start being a wife and mother and stop worrying about yourself and all your measly problems?"

She had to take control of the situation before it escalated into a World Cup Screaming Match. Kneeling before his chair, she took his hand.

"Sweetheart," she warbled. "I want to thank you for my holiday. It wasn't the greatest, but I learned something, and it's this. Part of the reason I'm unhappy is that I've been taking pills to bail out of every crisis, and..."

"Do you mean you're still on those pieces of crap?" he interrupted.

"Well...not exactly...but I take them whenever I feel skittery like I do now." Say it really quickly, she thought, before I lose my nerve. "I went to the Glenora Treatment Center while I was in the city. I'm making arrangements to enter therapy."

Julian's scowl deepened. His brows knit together. His eyes glowed like coals. They burned bigger and brighter. He was going to explode. She was not disappointed.

"The hell you will! Over my dead body! You aren't going there...or anywhere! You don't need that goddamned place! You need to stay at home where you belong. You don't need treatment! You need a crack on the head to smarten you up! If you'd stay at home you wouldn't be so wrecked!"

"Julian, please listen to me! We're having serious problems. I want to get my head straight so I can think clearly."

"Bullshit! The only problem we have is *you* and your running off every time you can't take the heat! Keep up this shit, Jessica, and you won't have time to sleep! I'll cut off your shooting lessons! I'll bar you from every restaurant and lounge in town! I'll cancel your credit cards! I'll fire Binkie, and I'll keep you so busy shoveling walks and driveways, you won't have time to think with that hazardous mind of yours! I'll make up a schedule for cleaning rooms, washing floors, washing windows, and polishing every goddamned crystal on the chandeliers! You're going to be so fucking busy, you'll have to hire a sitter for Rob! And why don't you think about me for a change?"

"Think about *you*? That's all I've been doing, and I'm a bloody pile of rubble! You don't know the hell I'm in, and you could care less!"

"Shut up, Jess! Shut up!"

"I won't shut up!" she shrieked. "I thought marriage was a fifty-fifty deal! I guess it is! I *give* fifty per cent, and you *take* fifty per cent!"

"Stop yelling!" he shouted. "Do you want the neighbors to hear?"

"I want *you* to hear, Julian! If you can't hear me, then maybe the neighbors will!" she yelled, her throat raw.

The energy from her rage and frustration pounded through her veins and burst into her head. Running to the window, she threw herself against it, clawing at the glass.

"Hey!" she screeched. "Wake up and listen! My husband won't!"

Julian grabbed her, fisted her on the side of the head, and hurled her into her chair. Looming over her, he breathed fire.

"Stupid ass! You're going to wake up the whole town!" Then his voice hushed, and he hissed like a rattler cornered under a rock. "You grow up! Get this asinine notion of treatment out of your head! Any more nonsense and by God, I'll have you committed. Christ! I work my butt off, and all I get is this shit!"

He stormed from the room like a black cloud of thunder and lightning.

She was numb. What was she supposed to do now? The shouting match was her fault, for sure. Damn her mouth! Shame washed over her, and she swallowed three pills to sandbag the incoming tide.

Julian was gone when she awoke. The bedside clock told her it was eight-thirty. She saw no signs of life downstairs as she peered over the landing. No aroma of coffee teased her nose. Clutching the railing, she crept down the cold marble steps. The kitchen was undisturbed.

Lighting a cigarette, she poured water into the coffee maker and sat down beside the window to wait for the brew. Staring at the bleak morning, she watched a few sparrows scrapping over a morsel of food. She had saved breadcrumbs left over from her Christmas turkey and tossed them onto the patio. Where there had been only five sparrows, dozens appeared from nowhere to squabble over the tidbits. She made a mental note: birdseed. The poor little creatures had to struggle hard enough in the freezing wind without having to scratch for food too.

The coffee ready, she poured a cup, and then settled by the window to keep an eye on the sparrows. They certainly had it tough in winter's frigid clutches. Sipping her coffee and practicing smoke rings that Julian said were not in good taste for a woman of her standing, she decided it didn't matter if she blew smoke rings or puffed like a steam engine. It all came down to the same thing: Smoking was a filthy habit and said to cause cancer. Gazing into empty space, she parked herself on a cloud and listened to the doorbell chime.

Who in God's name would be out so early? She shuffled into the foyer and peeked through the window. Three prim little ladies stood on the porch gazing hopefully at the door. She opened it.

"Good morning!" the little ladies beamed, their faces gleaming and polished like bright new pennies. They clutched Bibles and books and leaflets.

"What is it?" she asked as the wind whistled through the doorway.

"Good morning!" they chorused again.

"How are you on this fine God's morning?" one of them sang.

"Tired and not awake," Jessica moaned as she clutched and sagged against the door.

"We thought we'd drop by and cheer you with God's word and assure you of His many blessings for those who follow His guidance," glowed the one in the black coat.

"The only way you can cheer me is by letting me drink my coffee to jump-start my heart," muttered Jessica, as the wind blew up her robe, freezing her legs. "I didn't know you people were allowed in this private community."

She knew they were Jehovah's Witnesses, and as cold as it was, she wasn't about to invite these three into her house. It would take an act of God to get them out again.

"Oh, my dear, we find sinners everywhere," sang one sadly.

"Prayerful attitudes will help you through the day," trilled one of the songbirds, while Jessica marveled that anyone could be so cheerful on a blustery morning at that hour. "May we come in and share God's message?"

"Not today!" She backed behind the door.

"Maybe you'd like to read the book we chose especially for you," Merry Sunshine smiled, her bun bobbing at the nape of her neck. She proffered a heavy red tome, which Jessica grasped out of curiosity.

How to Have a Happy Family Life, she read on its spine. She thrust it right back.

"What are you trying to do to me? Send me on a guilt trip?" she whimpered angrily. "My family's a wreck! I'm a wreck! Leave me alone! Christ Himself didn't bang on people's doors the way you people do!"

"Ah! But He sent his disciples!" they chorused. "Just like us!"

"I don't care! I don't need any heavies! Leave me alone!" She slammed the door. Rudeness be damned!

Agitated, and trying to catch her breath, she leaned against the door. Sneaking a peek through the foyer window, she saw her three saviors in conference on the porch. She backed away quickly lest they spot her. The doorbell chimed once more.

Flinging the door open, she was again greeted by the birds of Paradise, clustered together.

"You seem so disturbed, child," the trio's leader said. "Can't we give you some words of comfort from God Himself? The day of reckoning is fast approaching, and we're sure you'd like to save yourself by working things out with your family and with God. Armageddon is just around the corner and you must be spiritually fit."

"Armageddon!" Jessica shrilled. "My *life* is Armageddon! There isn't anything about Armageddon and the end of the world that I don't already know! My world is a catastrophe right now! If all you have to talk about is Armageddon, drop dead! Get off my porch!"

"But we just want you to be saved!" the Jehovah's Witnesses protested.

"I don't want to be gang-saved at nine o'clock in the morning while I freeze to death on my front porch! Get lost!"

She smashed the door shut. How dare those sanctimonious pea-brains preach to her! Sizzling into the kitchen, she plunked herself down at the table, gulping her coffee in one swallow.

"Sorry, God," she muttered, "I just couldn't take it!"

⁂

The wheels turned in her head as she plotted her plan of action. She didn't care if Julian ordered a lobotomy for her, she was going to Glenora. With a call to Dr. Morton's office, she arranged an appointment for the next morning. Mission accomplished, she phoned Rosalind.

"You stay there, Jess. I'll bring Rob right over. Knowing you, you aren't even dressed yet. What's happening? You sound awful."

"I'll tell you when you get here."

She went back to sitting on her cloud. As she drank her coffee, she swallowed a Valium she had dug from her robe pocket. Mother of God, she thought, I have these damned things squirreled away in everything I wear. "Be prepared", the Girl Guides said. Well, she was prepared.

When the doorbell chimed, she rushed to the door, squealing with delight as she picked Rob up to crush him against her. He sloshed a wet kiss on her cheek and snuggled his cheek against her neck.

"Rosalind, how can I thank you for looking after him?"

"Just get your head straight," Rosalind replied, stepping into the foyer. "It's as cold as Julian's heart out there!" she puffed, as she pulled off her coat, while Jessica removed Rob's snowsuit and boots.

In the kitchen, Jessica poured coffee while Rob and Cuddles enjoyed their reunion in the family room.

"You sure have a gorgeous kitchen," mused Rosalind, as she poured cream and sugar into her cup. "I've always admired all the windows and French doors."

"Lydia designed it," said Jessica. "I loved it too, the moment I first saw it. She might be a bit of a bat, but she has a great sense of design and style."

"Okay, what's happening?" Rosalind peered at her over her cup.

"God, where do I start? First things first...I'm hooked on pills."

Rosalind nodded. "Tell me something I didn't know."

"You know? How could you know?"

"I'm not exactly blind, lamb chop, and I'm not deaf either. You really slur your words on the phone sometimes. And with your eyes glazed...like they are now...I just put two and two together."

"God, Rosalind, why didn't you say anything?"

"Because I love you, and I know how clever you are. I knew you'd figure out that pills aren't the answer to anything. But if you didn't clean up your act soon, I was going to intervene. I hate to see what you're doing to yourself."

"Oh, Roz, all of this is so awful! And Julian is being mean about it! I've made arrangements to go to the Glenora Treatment Center in the city. I can be there in two weeks if everything falls into place."

"Harry and I will look after Rob, so don't even worry

about that."

"God, Rosalind, how can I ever thank you for being such a good friend?"

"Just get well. That's all I want."

✲✲

Sitting behind his desk and waiting for Jessica to close the door to his office, Dr. Morton looked as friendly as a sea urchin.

"More pills?" He sounded annoyed.

"Not today," she answered as she poised herself on the edge of her chair, feeling like a kid who's been summoned to the principal's office.

"How are your anxiety attacks?" he inquired.

"Getting worse by the day."

"And what is this application to a treatment center for?"

"Well...the pills have certainly helped...up to a point, but I can't rely on them forever. If I did that, I could end up addicted."

She couldn't bear to tell him that she already was. She knew she was protecting herself and her nasty little secret, but that wasn't the issue. The application was the point of her visit, and she wasn't about to plunge into a debate about her pill problem.

"I'm not at all sure this is what you need, Jessica. This seems a bit drastic. It seems to me you want to run away. Lots of people hide themselves in these institutions. "Institutionalized", that's what I call them."

"Dr. Morton, I've been hiding all my life!" she protested, her anxiety rising. "I don't want to go there to hide! I want to *expose* myself! I want to find out why I can't cope and why I depend on pills."

"Have you considered a vacation? It seems better than

226

locking yourself up in an institution," the doctor suggested, studying her.

"Dr. Morton, I don't want a holiday! I want treatment!"

He threw another sandbag in her direction. "I don't think this is a good idea at all. Too many people come out of those places and display absolutely no improvement."

"Doctor, I don't mean to be disrespectful, but if you won't fill out that application for me, I'll find someone else who will."

He sighed while she clung to her chair, her nerves shrilling from the anxiety of her plea. With a grunt, he spread the application open on his desk and scratched his pen in the appropriate blanks.

"Do you want me to mail this for you?" he asked wearily. "It says here the physician is supposed to forward it."

"No, thanks." She reached across the desk and snatched the application from his grasp, smiling triumphantly. "I already have an envelope addressed and stamped. I'll mail it on my way home."

"Suit yourself." Sighing, he ambled to the door, holding it open for her to dance through.

Maybe, just maybe, that light at the end of the tunnel was not the headlamp of an oncoming train.

✵

Her visit to the doctor had drained her emotional store, so she swallowed three Valium as soon as she arrived home. The pills had no sooner disappeared than the phone rang. Binkie answered it and handed the receiver to Jessica.

"Jess, I want you down here at one o'clock. Meet me in the dining room. Mom's joining us for lunch."

"Which hotel?" she asked.

"Mayfield." His voice sounded ominous.

"In whose honor are we having lunch?" she wondered.

"We have to talk about this Glenora thing. Maybe Mother can talk some sense into you."

"Can Kenneth pick me up? I don't want to drive."

"Be ready at twelve forty-five."

Great balls of fire! she thought to herself as she hung up the phone. Isn't this just terrific! This was all she needed to make this a perfect day! The doctor's signature in the morning, and Julian's and Lydia's blessings over lunch! They could threaten to boil her in oil, but she wouldn't relent. They could threaten to cut her out of the will, send her to Siberia, and take back the keys to the Mustang. There were two of them, and they wielded a lot of power, but she knew something they didn't. They didn't know she was going to Glenora, no matter what.

Hmmm, she thought, as she surveyed her closet after her bath. What should she wear for such an auspicious occasion? Should she wear that scarlet number that was cut down the front to her navel and slashed up one side to the hip? She'd certainly draw a crowd. Julian had applauded the outfit before they were married, but forbade her to wear it in public after their wedding because he said it made her look like a siren. Maybe she should appear pure, demure, helpless, and feminine. There was nothing like innocence and femininity to help her cause. On the outside, she'd appear vulnerable, while on the inside, she'd be pure steel. She chose a white silk blouse with a delicate bow at the high neckline and a simple black skirt. Tiny pearl earrings completed the air of purity.

A Valium would calm her. She didn't mind that it was her fourth pill within an hour and made her look slightly dazed. She certainly didn't want to wobble, but the drug would give her the strength to withstand their disparaging comments without blowing her stack. It would take the edge off her emotions.

The dining room was abuzz with luncheon guests, mostly business people. Lawyers were debating ways to get the guy off or hang him. Bankers were discussing interest rates and whether they'd dip or go higher. Secretaries were daintily picking at salads. A few men were swilling martinis or scotch or bourbon as they worked out complicated transactions on paper bar napkins. The maître d' took her coat, the champagne mink, and hung it up for her.

"Mr. Bothwell is waiting for you," he said as he led her to a banquette in the corner, a very private place to dine. It was perfect for lovers...or an execution.

"Darling," Jessica smiled as she settled herself beside him, "how sweet of you to invite me for lunch! And Lydia, how nice to see you! My, my, my, isn't it cold today? I had to wear my mink to keep out the chill. And darling, thank you so much for sending Kenneth. I appreciate not having to drive when the streets are so hazardous." And, she admitted to herself, when I don't dare drive because I'm seeing double from drugs.

"Stop babbling so we can get this over with!" snapped Julian.

"Oh, excuse me, darling, I thought this was going to be a leisurely lunch. How silly of me! Of course, you're busy! I keep forgetting you have three hotels that depend on having you at the helm."

Julian glowered as he tossed back his scotch on the rocks, while Lydia sipped a gin and tonic.

What should she drink, Jessica wondered. Maybe a double bourbon; with the Valium in her system, she could do a Mexican hat dance on the table. She knew she was putting herself at risk with these two vultures with her flippant chatter, but if she didn't prattle, she knew she'd short-circuit and burst into tears. She would most surely betray how she really felt, which was exposed, naked, and petrified with terror. Where was the steel she had felt while dressing for the confrontation? It had transformed into molten lead, cremating her insides.

"You look lovely, my dear," smiled Lydia, her green eyes darting around the room. Lydia had difficulty making eye contact if there was something unpleasant to discuss.

"Why, thank you, Mother Lydia. And may I say you look smashing in that dress. The color matches your eyes perfectly," replied Jessica, thinking the green on Lydia turned her into a giant, animated shamrock.

"What do you want to eat?" growled Julian as the waiter stood by to take their orders.

"Oh, my goodness, I haven't even looked at the menu. Could you give me a moment to decide? Oh, dearie me, so many tempting choices! Tsk, tsk, tsk, I can't even pronounce half these dishes; how will I ever decide?"

"Bring her a coffee!" Julian ordered. He leaned across the table. "What the hell are you on? You're acting like a spun-out, dizzy broad!"

"Oh, dear," she replied demurely, batting her eyelashes at him. "I only took one teeny, tiny Valium to calm me. I'd no idea I was creating a spectacle!"

The waiter returned with the coffee, took their orders and left.

"I've already told Mother about this lame-brain scheme of yours, Jess, so we might just as well get down to talking about it."

"You know, my dear," sniffed Lydia, "it will be a scandal if you go. We do have to keep up appearances. After all, our family has a high standing in the community, and we can't afford any unpleasant gossip. When one is a prominent member of society, one has to be prudent and always mindful of public opinion."

"How can there be gossip if no one knows I'm going?"

"Things get out, Jessica," grumbled Julian. "People talk. Rumors start. Before you know it, they'll say I drove you to it."

"Well, in a way you have, you know." She sipped her coffee.

"Now, Jessica, that's hardly fair! Julian is a wonderful husband," soothed Lydia, patting Julian's hand.

"I agree," said Jessica, realizing that her smart tongue now could earn her a swollen lip later.

"Why don't you give this problem a little time?" suggested Lydia. "You seem to be off and running without a thought as to how it might affect the rest of us. It seems to me you're being totally selfish, and I scarcely think your problem warrants a treatment center. I'm sure that with a little will power, you'll be fine. Land sakes, Jessica, we can't all run off to treatment centers with our petty problems."

Jessica sat mute and motionless for a moment before responding. "Lydia, I've considered my options carefully. I'm not sure if you're aware that I've developed a serious addiction to Valium and Seconal. I've tried to overcome this on my own with no success. When I went to the city, I went to Glenora for a consultation with a therapist. My addiction warrants treatment."

"Glenora!" Lydia was aghast. "That sleazy place! Surely, you could consider a place with more prestige. If you need help, why don't you consider the Betty Ford Clinic? At least, there you'd be with people of *our* class!"

"I don't want to go there. It's too far, and I'm not interested in hob-nobbing with celebrities. I want to be with people who are down-to-earth."

"In the gutter, you mean!" snarled Julian. "For Christ's sake, Jessica, smarten up! The people at Glenora are down and out! Most of them are druggies from off the street, hookers, and pimps!"

Jessica forced herself to stay calm and cool. "I don't think it's quite that colorful, Julian. I didn't see any evidence of that when I was there. It looked quite genteel and professional."

"Well, you aren't going! That's all there is to it!" Julian huffed as the waiter set their orders before them.

"Julian!" she pleaded. "I don't have any choice. I'll die if I don't go! I'm not doing this to shame the family. I'm going because I want to live and to make you proud of me."

"I'm already proud of you," he mumbled around a piece of chicken.

Her eyes stung with the threat of sudden tears. "Sweetheart, I know that. But I need to go and get my head straight," she said softly. "Even if you divorce me, I won't change my mind."

"Oh, Jessica," snapped Lydia impatiently. "Don't be so dramatic! Julian wouldn't divorce you...would you, darling?" She patted his arm, denoting ownership, intimacy, and motherhood.

"Of course not!" he replied, and turned to face Jessica, staring into her eyes. "We've already discussed that, haven't we, sweetheart?"

Jessica watched him. Did she detect a smirk? His eyes were expressionless, unfathomable, hiding what lay behind them. But his words made her feel like her heart had sprung a leak. The threat was there. Dear God, she had to get to Glenora to save her life, to try to save her marriage, so she could save Rob's life! She was in a vicious, unholy trap. She had to buy time. She had lost her appetite and shoved her plate aside. Lighting up a cigarette, she blew the smoke in Lydia's direction. The older woman waved the puff aside, giving Jessica a cold stare as she raised her fork to her mouth.

Jessica tapped her cigarette against the ashtray and played with the ashes, stirring them with the end of her cigarette. She had to find the right words. She didn't want to get up on her soapbox and give the speech she had rehearsed in the bathtub. Most of all, she didn't want to lose her temper. Her soul longed to scream the truth that she was caught in a wicked web of despair and that she was married to a monster.

"Julian...and Mother Lydia, I'm not very proud of my behavior lately. I'm angry, uptight, and unhappy. I cry a lot. I often feel my life isn't worth living. And I have everything to live for. You, my darling Julian, whom I love and adore! You, Mother Lydia, who have always been so supportive, and Rob, my cherished little boy. A wonderful home. Great friends. I have everything a woman could possibly want."

"Is this going to take long?" Julian interrupted.

"No. All I want to do is explain my position. I used to think I had all the answers to life. But if I do, why am I so miserable and suffering from anxiety attacks? I don't think you make unreasonable demands on me," she lied. "You just want me to be a good wife. I know that life isn't all roses, but I forgot that where there are roses, there are usually thorns. I'm a bloody disaster zone, Julian. My addiction is serious. I want to live better than we've been living recently. I know this has been hard on you. I want to get better, not only for me, but also for you and Rob. I need professional help to unravel this snarl I've made of things. I'm so tired of living in despair and chaos!"

Against her will, the tears started to brim over. Blinking them back, she puffed agitatedly on her cigarette. Was that amusement playing across his face? His eyes revealed nothing.

Absolutely nothing!

"I see," he said as he waved at a passing waiter for coffee. "Very nice speech, Jessica. Are you sure you never took dramatics at school? You could win an Academy Award with that performance."

Lydia gave Jessica a sick smile and reached to pat her hand.

"Tell you what," Julian smirked as he stirred his coffee. The smirk held all the cheer of a moray eel. "You go to the treatment center. You're obviously defiant, rebellious, stubborn, and determined to go whether it's with my blessing or not. *But*, and I mean this, Jessica, you will not receive one ounce of support from me! I will not look after Rob! I have a business to run, and I will not spend one minute looking after that kid! And don't expect me to phone you, write to you, or see a counselor on your behalf. I won't lift one finger to help you. You find your own way to the city. Hire a jet for all I care, and you pay the center's tab. Use your savings. Count me out! You're absolutely on your own! One more thing...don't tell anyone where you're going. I don't want the whole of Riverbend suspecting that I'm married to a half-baked lunatic!"

Jessica was ecstatic. She couldn't believe her ears. He wasn't throwing her a life preserver, but neither was he throwing her any lead anchors.

"Thank you, Julian! Thank you for letting me go!"

"I'm not letting you do anything, Jessica! I just know there's no reasoning with you. You'll have to go and discover for yourself that this will never work. You have this treatment thing so crazy-glued to your skull that only going there will ever root it out. You go, fall flat on your ass, and then maybe you'll come back to reality. Maybe then you'll have your feet on the ground instead of firmly planted in mid-air! I'm going to work now.

You absolutely wear me out! Now please stand up and let me out of this place!"

While Jessica stood, he pulled himself from the banquette and stomped off without another word to either his wife or his mother.

"My dear, I know how difficult this has been on poor Julian." Lydia's voice dripped with disdain, as she gazed down her nose at Jessica. "I do hope this treatment center works. But I still believe you should go to the Betty Ford Center. My goodness, who knows what kind of trash you might encounter at Glenora?"

"You know, Mother Lydia, I'm glad of one thing. I'm glad that I'm not a snob. Being one limits one's vision and one's freedom. Being a snob is worse than being trash. I hope you enjoyed lunch."

The next day, Jessica helped Julian pack. She had always helped him prepare for a trip.

"I hope this works out well for you," she murmured, as she tucked extra socks into the open suitcase on the bed.

"Why should you care?" he snarled, as he folded his suit bag and fastened it.

"Julian, that's not fair. Of course, I care."

"Yeah, right!" He glared at her. "You care so much you get blitzed on pills, and now you have to run off to a goddamned treatment center!"

"Julian, the pills are my problem! Not yours! I'm going for both of us. I want us to get back to the way we were before..."

"Before what?" he yelled. "Before you started fucking around?"

"I've never messed around! You know that! Why do you always accuse me of it? It hurts me so much when you say that, and you know it isn't true at all!"

"I know more things about you than you'd ever dream I knew! I've checked up on you. The whole town knows you're nothing but trailer trash! And while we're on the subject, you really piss me off with your nonsense. You keep doing it just to annoy me! And you'd better cut it out, or I'll make you one sorry woman!"

"Please tell me what people are saying, Julian! And what is it that annoys you? How can I defend myself or change my behavior when I don't know what you're talking about?"

"I'm crediting you with some brains, Jessica. You're bright and clever! You figure it out!"

"I don't intend to continue this conversation." She walked toward the door.

He reached out and grabbed her, crushing her body to his. His arm dug into the small of her back and she gasped in pain.

"Julian, you're hurting me!"

"You bitch whore!" he spat in her face and smacked her across the cheek with his free open hand.

With his fingers entwined in her hair, he yanked her head back with such a snap, she could swear she heard bones crunch in her neck. He threw her onto the bed, tackling her as she scrambled across the spread. He snared her by her blouse, and with one hand cutting off her breath, ripped away her blouse and bra. Gasping, and almost unconscious, she felt him drag off her jeans. He mounted her and thrust his erection into her, slamming against her with each stroke. All she could think of was, Where's Rob? I hope he doesn't see any of this! And praying, she begged to die. Finished, he pulled himself away.

"You're still a good fuck, bitch!" he rasped, as he pulled himself away, after delivering another punch to her face.

She lay there, dazed, with no feeling, no life left.

He tossed the comforter over her. "Cover yourself! Have you no shame?"

"What's wrong with Mommy?" piped a wee voice. "Is she asleep?"

"Yeah, she's sleeping. You go downstairs. I'll be there in a minute to say goodbye."

Curling under the bedspread, she prayed Rob hadn't seen her disgrace and humiliation while his father pounded her. My God! What had that poor child witnessed?

She lay still and listened as Julian dragged his luggage to the staircase and down the steps. Then silence. A silence deeper than she'd ever been able to achieve in meditation. The front door opened, and the sound of Julian shuffling suitcases on the marble foyer floor drifted up the staircase. Julian said something to Kenneth, and then she heard Rob crying. He always cried when Julian left on business trips. Listening to his sobs, she dragged herself from the bed and scrounged for some clothes. She had to go to her son, hold him, and comfort him.

The decision wasn't difficult, she realized as she ran her bath. Not difficult at all. That amazed her. She'd always believed this kind of decision meant agonizing over it for months, weighing the pros and cons, figuring out a means that suited lifestyle, habit, and personality. She had no doubt that some people really did harbor such an awful secret for days, weeks, months, or even years. But for her it was just so simple!

She had made the decision as she held Rob while he sobbed after his father left. She had no idea if the child had witnessed that terrible scene in their bedroom. She had wanted to ask him, but when he volunteered no questions or comments, she decided not to arouse his curiosity.

If she were gone, Rob wouldn't have to live in this turmoil of hatred and hostility. It never occurred to her to take the child and flee because that would be futile. Julian would ferret them out and kill them both. He had sworn to her that was what he would do. *But* if she were dead, Rob would be safe. Julian would make sure of that. And Lydia would be the doting grandmother. Even though Jessica didn't like Lydia, she knew her mother-in-law loved her grandson and would help nurture him. So while Rob ate his supper, Jessica called Binkie and asked her to come in early in the morning.

"I have a few things to do, and I'd appreciate your being here at eight."

"No problem," sang Binkie. "See you bright and early."

That took care of Rob being looked after, once she was dead. Well aware that her thinking was totally irrational, there still were logical thoughts that worked all the angles and touched all the bases. She did not want Rob to be left alone. He usually slept until half-past eight, sometimes later, but there was always the off chance he might awaken earlier. He was also a child who slept through the night. So if she took the pills around midnight, he wouldn't be left awake and alone for hours in the morning.

That last night with him was special so she ran him a bubble bath and piled him into the tub with his boats and rubber ducks. Laughing and singing, she watched him frolic in the bubbles, blowing them off his hands while she played scrub-a-dub-dub. As she toweled him dry, she admired his perfect little body, with just the right amount of padding and chubby legs. His smile would melt a snowman, she thought. What a treasure. I'll watch over him. I might not be here, but I can keep an eye on him. Maybe haunt Julian while I'm at it.

Once he was ready for bed, she sat in the rocker, hugging him close on her lap, while she read the book, *Cars and Trucks and Things That Go*, laughing as they searched each page to find the gold bug. Too soon he was yawning and rubbing his eyes, and she tucked him into his bed, kissing him goodnight. In her heart, she knew it was goodbye, and she reached down for another hug, before he turned over with his teddy bear.

"How glad I am that you have Teddy," she whispered. "He loves you so much. Teddy loves you as much as I do."

⁂

Going into the study, she found a pretty piece of stationery, one with roses and violets on it, and wrote a brief note:

To those who love me, do not grieve,
but rejoice that I have at long last
found the peace I craved. Please look
after my wonderful son. And to Julian,
you know more clearly than anyone why
I have chosen the course I have taken.
Jessica.

At midnight, she poured herself a glass of champagne and ran her bath. Carefully, she counted out the pills, arranging them in groups of ten on her counter top. She had five groups, seven Valium and three Seconals in each. With the champagne, the plot would work. There were lots of pills left over, but she preferred to drift off, not knock herself out cold. If she was going to the Hereafter, it was her one shot, and she wanted to do it her way. Besides, she'd heard horror stories about people who had been saved from suicide, only to end up on the back wards of hospitals because their brains had been ravaged from taking too large a dose. Not sure what she was doing, since she hadn't read any books on suicide, she believed the gems she had so meticulously counted out would do the trick. She didn't mind dying, but insanity was not her goal. Carefully, she hid the rest of her stash under the mattress.

Removing her clothing, she tossed the garments into the hamper and chose a beautiful nightgown of blue silk. Blue went well with her eyes and coloring and, she thought bitterly, with her bruises. Taking a gulp of champagne, she washed down the first batch of pills. They would get her through her bath.

Placing the champagne on the edge of the tub, she eased her body into the caressing foam. Wistful melancholy washed over her, and she wished things didn't have to be the way they were. The center, she was sure, would have worked, but nothing would change at home. What had happened to Julian that he wanted to destroy her? Everything had started out so well. They had loved each other, both of them basking in the sunshine of their relationship. And then he had switched from being loving, warm, and gentle into an atrocity. Something had snapped inside her after his savage attack in the afternoon, breaking her heart and shattering her desire to live. Why live when he threatened to kill her? With her death, Rob had a good chance of survival.

Polishing off the glass of champagne, she sloshed a wash-cloth over her body, relishing the touch of the course fabric on her skin. Stepping from the tub, she dried herself, and slathered lotion all over from head to toe; if she were going out, she would go out soft, silky, and scented.

Back in her dressing room, she poured more champagne for the next batch of pills. Damn! She couldn't even feel the first lot! Maybe she was doing something wrong. Slipping into her nightgown, she decided that a bit of makeup would be a nice touch. Blush on the cheeks was perfect, a wisp of blue eye shadow, some mascara. She'd only chew off the lipstick, so to hell with it. Admiring her image in the mirror, she decided she'd make a beautiful corpse. The mortician wouldn't gag when he saw her spread out on the bed. Another gulp of champagne, more pills. She began to feel woozy. Good! Brushing her hair, she thought her golden tresses had never looked better. Such a pity; hair always looked fantastic when one didn't need it at its most luminous, silky best.

She scooped up more pills, and not even bothering to pour the champagne, she guzzled it straight from the bottle. To hell with class now. Taking the last of the pills, she sloshed them back with another swig. Checking the bottle, which was still half full, she tipped it up and swallowed it down. Her knees seemed to bend backwards as she clung to the door for support. The concoction was working!

She calculated that it was almost ten feet to the bed. If she moved quickly, she could manage it without falling. Her buckling knees wavered as she directed her stumbling feet towards the bed. Gasping, she fell onto the sheets. Having already turned the blankets down, she struggled to untangle her nightgown from beneath her body before she pulled the blankets over herself. She'd never realized, until that moment, all the things involved in simply going to bed. We take so much for granted, her muddled mind murmured. Rolling onto her side, she felt the pillow cool beneath her cheek. God, it felt so good, comforting.

Gently rocking her, lovingly caressing her, the drugs worked their mischief. On the wings of a butterfly, she fluttered into the dark abyss, hovering on a cloud, dancing on a moonbeam. Her breathing slowed as the toxic brew claimed her. Her heart ceased its terrified pounding. Nothing would ever terrify her again. Her last thoughts were of God. What would she say to Him? How would she ever explain what she'd done? But then, He'd probably heard worse stories than hers and even flimsier excuses. She hoped the Creator would forgive her.

✲✲

Rosalind was enjoying her morning coffee, propped against the pillows in her giant bed, with her newspaper spread open on the quilt when the telephone rang.

Damn! She thought. Why can't people call at civilized hours? Eight in the morning was not a civilized hour for her.

"Yes!" she barked into the phone, expecting some sales pitch.

"Miss Rosalind? It's about Miss Jessica! Can you come right away? She's on the floor, and she's been sick all over!"

"Who is this?"

"It's me, Binkie. Please come, Miss Rosalind! I can't wake her up! I think she's dead! Please hurry!"

"I'll be right there!" gasped Rosalind and hung up.

Christ! What was going on now? She yanked on her jeans and a sweatshirt, dragged a brush through her disheveled auburn hair, grabbed her fur jacket and pulled on snow boots. Diving into her Corvette, she pushed the remote to open the garage doors. If that damned woman has killed herself, I'll never forgive her, she thought as she pulled out onto the street, careening through a stop sign. If she hasn't, I'll kill her myself.

Damn you, Jessica, I love you!

Binkie was standing in the open doorway as Rosalind screeched to a halt at the curb and, flinging the car door open, burst onto the porch.

"She's upstairs, Miss Rosalind!" Binkie cried. "Please hurry!"

Pounding up the stairs two at a time, Rosalind dashed to Jessica. Sweet Jesus! What a mess! Bile dribbled from Jessica's mouth and was smeared on the carpet. Her nightgown was soiled with vomit and perspiration. She had obviously been in physical torment during the night. Vomit was caked in the pillowslips and sheets and a hateful-smelling mess covered the front of Jessica's gown. Rosalind's nostrils flared at the stench. She could see streaks of vomit on the bathroom door and more drying on the tiles.

Jessica's skin was ashen and bruised and mascara streaked her cheeks. Rosalind touched her. Clammy. She felt for a pulse. Slow. Feeble. Jessica's breathing was irregular and shallow and a soft mewing accompanied each exhalation.

"Call 9-1-1!" Rosalind ordered. "Where's Rob?"

"Eatin' breakfast."

"Keep him busy! Don't let him see this! Sweet Mother of God! What's been going on here?"

"I dunno. Mr. Julian's gone. He left yesterday for Europe."

Rosalind had become a whirlwind of activity, her face flushed, hands flailing.

"He's fucking lucky he's out of the country. If I get my hands on him, I'll rip off his pecker! Grab me a blanket, call an ambulance, and then go look after Rob. I'll take care of Jess."

Binkie skittered off for a blanket, tossed it at Rosalind, called 9-1-1, and beetled out of the room and down the stairs. She was relieved that she didn't have to look after Jessica. It was enough to make anyone throw up.

Tucking the blanket around Jessica, Rosalind placed a cushion beneath her head, repeatedly begging Jessica to wake up.

"Don't you dare die!" she cried. "Don't you dare die! You're my best friend. Please don't die! I love you, Jess! Please don't die!"

Rushing to the bathroom, she wet a washcloth and tried to clean Jessica's face, and to rub the vomit out of her tangled strands of hair.

The sirens wailed to a stop as the ambulance pulled into the driveway. Binkie met the attendants at the door, and they stampeded up the stairs and into the room, brushing Rosalind aside. Stethoscopes bristled and blood pressure cuffs appeared from nowhere as the men went to work on the devastation that was Jessica.

"What happened to her? Suicide? Battering?"

"Both, I think. I'll check her dressing room," offered Rosalind.

She found the empty pill and champagne bottles, and the note. Bringing the evidence, she showed it to the paramedics.

"What a combination!" one of the men remarked. "But it looks like she threw most of it up. That's probably why she's still alive."

They lifted Jessica onto the stretcher, fixed an oxygen mask over her face, wrapped blankets around her, and carried her down the staircase to the ambulance.

"We'll take her to Mother of Mercy. That's the closet. Do you want to follow us?" a medic asked Rosalind.

"I'll be right with you. I have to talk to the housekeeper first. I'll get there. You hurry!"

Scrunching Jessica's note into her jeans pocket, she flew to the kitchen. She hugged Rob and told him what a good boy he was, before telling Binkie she'd call as soon as she knew anything.

"Pray, Binkie! Pray!"

The startled, frightened woman nodded. "I'll pray, Miss Rosalind. Don't you worry 'bout that! I'se already been prayin'!"

As Rosalind jumped into her car, she heard the ambulance sirens in the distance and floored the accelerator. The Corvette screeched as it rounded the curve onto the street.

She didn't care where she parked, maneuvering the car into a stall designated for "Doctors Only".

"Give me a ticket, you fuckers!" she challenged as she dashed into the emergency ward. She grabbed the first nurse she saw." I'm here for Jessica Bothwell! She was just brought in! Attempted suicide!"

"She'd be in the Intensive Care Unit. They're probably working on her. You'll have to...Hey! You can't go in!"

"The hell I can't!" Rosalind snapped, sprinting down the hall.

"I'll have to call security!" the nurse called after her.

"Go ahead! Charge me with treason! It's my friend who's dying!"

Where the hell was the ICU? All the closed doors looked alike. She asked another nurse, who pointed out double doors.

"But you can't go in!"

"Says who?" Rosalind hurled over her shoulder.

She burst through the doors. "I'm here for my friend, Jessica Bothwell," she explained to the startled nurse, who was cutting away Jessica's nightgown, while another attendant set up an IV in Jessica's arm.

"You aren't supposed to be in here, you know!" the nurse snapped, pursing her lips into an angry pout.

"So everyone tells me," panted Rosalind. "But she's my best friend. She'd never forgive me if I let her die alone."

"If you want to, you can fill out this form. It'll help. Please don't get in the way. Sit in that chair over there."

⁂

From somewhere, a voice was telling Jessica to open her mouth. The same melodic voice said, "We're going to put this tube down your throat. We'll tell you when to swallow. We want to get that stuff out of your stomach. Can you hear me?"

She nodded. God! Where was that wretched disgusting odor coming from? She opened her mouth. The tube made her gag. Whoever it was kept pushing the tube down. Try as she might, she couldn't open her eyes, which seemed to be glued shut. Why didn't they just let her sleep?

"Swallow!" the voice demanded. She swallowed.

"Again! Again! Again! That's good. Now we're going to pull the tube out. It won't hurt. We've just pumped your stomach." That must be where the horrible stench was coming come. Yuk! It smelled like excrement. She seemed to be covered in it.

Someone else gently told her they were cutting her nightgown to remove it. Her eyes seemed stitched shut. A needle jammed into her wrist.

"That's an IV." A sweet, soft voice spoke. "My name is Cathy and I'm your nurse. Donna's helping me. We're looking after you. You don't have to worry about anything. Your friend, Rosalind, just arrived and you can talk to her later. We're going to give you a bath and wash your hair."

She felt loving hands lift her and place her in a chair. She was sitting up, but all she wanted to do was lie down, curl up, and go to sleep. Freezing, she shivered. She was wearing nothing.

"Let me put this blanket around you," purred the sweet voice.

With a slight jolt, she felt the chair being wheeled along. When it stopped, the soothing voice told her they were going to lift her, chair and all, into a bath. All she had to do was relax and stay seated. Someone removed the blanket. Soon she felt warm water caress her feet and then, while the water level crept upwards, it embraced her ankles, her calves, and her buttocks, right up to her breasts. While one set of hands shampooed her hair, another washed her body.

Did these hands belong to angels and were they preparing her to be brought into the presence of God? That must be it. She knew she had killed herself, but maybe something had gone wrong, and she had fallen into a tar pit. Maybe the angels did this for all people before they were received in God's presence. But why was Rosalind here? Rosalind wasn't dead! Well, heaven worked in mysterious ways, and perhaps the angels had borrowed Rosalind's spirit for a few hours to comfort her.

The water level crept down, and warm, fuzzy towels rubbed her all over. They put a fluffy, cuddly shirt on her; that must be the shroud, she smiled to herself. She hoped she looked beautiful.

Someone wheeled the chair again, and once more loving hands lifted her, this time onto a soft, clean mattress. Perhaps it was her very own cloud, the one she used to sit on when she daydreamed at home. The wicked, foul odor was gone.

"Don't lie down yet, Jessica," crooned the melodious, hushed voice. She was more convinced than ever that she was at the doorway to heaven. An angel, with a voice that chimed, sang, "You have to drink this. It's charcoal, and it'll help rid your body of toxins."

If this was heaven, she certainly hadn't expected this. They might serve charcoal in hell, but heaven was an entirely different matter. Heaven was for angels and white shrouds and haloes, although hers would be very tiny, and harps, and golden wings.

Jessica's eyes flew open. This wasn't heaven! This was a god-damned hospital room with enough wiring, enough computer screens, and enough things that went "blip" to lift a rocket off the ground! And she was staring into a very large glass of what looked like sludge from the bottom of a settling pond in a water treatment plant.

"I have to drink that!" she croaked, her throat raw and painful. She looked into the blue eyes of a tiny pixie dressed in white and pink. The pixie nodded.

Warily, Jessica reached out a hand, then both hands, to clutch the glass of very black brew. Holding it to her lips, she forced herself to swallow, swallow, and swallow. She knew that to stop swallowing would mean she would never get it back to her mouth. It was like drinking very thick, black clay from the bottom of a swamp.

"You might like to wipe your mouth with this," suggested the nurse with "Cathy" on her nametag.

Taking the wet cloth, Jessica smeared it across her mouth, scrubbing her lips, wiping her tongue, and cleaning her teeth. When she looked at the cloth, it was grimy with charcoal.

"Lie down, Jessica," said Cathy. "We'll cover you and give you something to help you sleep. Would you like to see your friend first?"

She nodded and Rosalind jumped from the chair, where she had been anxiously watching the proceedings. Trying not to entangle herself in the tubes and wires that extended from the body of her friend, she clasped Jessica's free hand. "Oh, Jess, you scared the hell out of me! What do you mean, trying to check out like that?"

"I guess it wasn't like in the movies, huh?" Jessica whispered, her throat scalding from the stomach tube.

"It wasn't one of your most glamorous moments."

"Sorry, Roz, I didn't really want to leave. It seemed like the only thing to do. I guess heaven didn't want me," Jessica groaned.

"Thank God!" Rosalind murmured, as she leaned over and hugged Jessica's slender form. "I'll come back later. Is there anything I can do? I'll check on Rob and Binkie."

"Please come back!" She strained to get the words out. "I love you, Roz...Thanks for my life!"

"Binkie deserves the thanks. She called me," Rosalind told her.

They both wept as Rosalind left the room. With a tiny pinprick of a needle, Jessica floated back to her cloud.

⁂

He strolled into the room as if he owned the place. Handsome, with an engaging smile, great teeth, a virile specimen radiating health, and an "I-swim-five-miles-a-day" aura. A doctor—but a hunk.

"I see you've been enjoying our charcoal cocktail," he grinned at her. "How does it taste?"

"Like shit!" she spat.

"Well, it does the trick. Works better than anything else. How are you feeling?"

"Like shit!"

"Limited vocabulary, Jessica?" he asked, his eyebrows raised.

"No! But what I said is true! That stuff tastes like I said, and I feel God-awful!"

"After that little escapade last night, I don't expect you to feel like performing on a flying trapeze. However, after a day or two in here, you'll be in fine shape."

"But I can't stay! I have a young son at home!"

"And exactly who was going to look after him if you'd completed your mission?" he ventured, daring her to respond.

"Oh, my God! Not his grandmother!" she gasped.

"No!" he laughed. "I've already talked to Rosalind Rodgers, and he's with her. So stop worrying. And get well."

"Thanks," she smiled, "for helping to save my life."

"My pleasure, Jessica. Now go to the bathroom and clean that black stuff off your lovely face," he advised with a mischievous grin.

As he left the room, she dragged her aching body to the bathroom, carting the IV apparatus with her, and was dismayed at her reflection in the mirror.

"Dear God, I never knew I could look so bad!" she cried.

Black smudges beneath her eyes met her scrutiny. Opening her mouth, she was stunned to see her tongue blackened, and her teeth streaked with charcoal. That people had actually seen her in this condition shamed her. My God! What must she have looked like when Rosalind had found her? This was the high price of suicide. You figure you're going to end up in heaven, and you wind up in a hell of your own creation.

*

A huge bouquet of red roses with feet beneath it padded into the hospital room. Jessica drew herself from the window to stare at the enormous arrangement, wondering who had sent it. A bright smile peeked around the blossoms—Rosalind!

"How dare you spend so much money on me!" Jessica

squealed with pleasure as Rosalind plopped the flowers into a vase near the bedside.

"They aren't from me, honey child; they're from Julian."

"Who told him I was here? I'll kill Binkie!" Jessica shrilled.

"No, you won't! No one told him. They were delivered to your house. You're worth three dozen red roses, dearie!"

"And no place in heaven! Give them to the nurses! I don't want the damned things in here!"

"Want to look at the note?"

Curiosity compelled her to utter, "Why not?" Tearing at the tiny envelope, she slid out the small white card. It read, "You're the best! J."

Jessica looked into Rosalind's eyes. "Do you know one of the last things he said before he left? 'You're a good fuck, bitch!' Now he says I'm the best! Oh, God, Roz, I wish things could go back to the way they used to be!" She sank onto the bed, despair in her eyes.

"Jess, what can I say?"

"What is there to say?" Jessica sniffled, dabbing at her eyes with a tissue.

"Well, while we're on the subject of notes," Rosalind said as she sat beside her friend and put an arm around her. "I found this little gem in your dressing room the other morning." She opened her purse and, withdrawing a crinkled piece of paper, handed it to Jessica.

Tentatively, Jessica took it and slowly uncrumpled it. As soon as she saw the first violet, she gave a startled cry and, as though the paper were a live coal, flicked it onto the floor.

"Oh, my God, Roz, that awful note! I forgot about it!"

"What should I do with it?"

"Burn it! I'm not saving that for posterity! Just burn it, Roz!

Take it and burn it!"

"Anything you say, honey child." Rosalind hugged her, and stooping down, retrieved the note and popped it into her purse.

"Now that we have two unpleasant tasks attended to," said Rosalind in that matter-of-fact-way of hers, "I have some good news to report. Dan Kennedy phoned, and Binkie took the message. I called him back, and he says you're supposed to be in Glenora on Sunday."

"Holy Mother of the world! That's in six days!"

"That's lots of time. You can pack in five minutes. I'll help. Oh, Jess, I'm thrilled for you. This'll be a brand new start!"

"If only I had a brand new Julian," she sighed. "But maybe with me gone for four weeks, he'll have time to think. Maybe Lydia will say something to him. You know, at lunch the other day, when he was haranguing me, she put her hand on mine and patted it. I think she might be on my side a little bit."

Rosalind gave her a sour smile. "Don't count on it. She cheats at bridge."

⁂

Home! It felt so good to be home! Binkie welcomed her with a hug, and Rob danced and jumped around her legs with Cuddles yapping and leaping, her toenails clicking on the marble foyer floor as she pranced around her mistress. It was comforting even to hear Cuddles. Binkie hung Jessica's coat, and took her bag to her room, while Jessica hugged Rob close, and received his slurpy kisses.

"Are you still sick, Mommy?" asked Rob. "Auntie Rosalind said you were sick."

"I'm better, sweetheart," she crooned into his ear, smiling at

Rosalind who was divesting herself of her fur jacket.

Rosalind, playing Mother Hen, wasn't going to leave Jessica alone for a second. The doctor had entrusted her with just enough Valium to ease Jessica down to a level where she wouldn't peel paint off the walls with her fingernails. If Rosalind had to, she'd stay overnight. But Jessica knew something Rosalind didn't. Stashed under her mattress were enough pills to blast her to Saturn. She had no intention of trying to check out again; she'd stay on Planet Earth, but once her guardian angel was out of her hair in the morning, she'd have her last fling with the pills. After Glenora, she'd be off the rotters forever.

Her last night at home. She set the alarm for 5:00 AM, which would give her plenty of time to shower, dress, and phone Rosalind to pick her up. Binkie was staying overnight, so she'd be there for Rob in the morning. Thanking God that Julian was still on his business trip, she took her last four Seconals and flushed the remainder down the toilet. Swallowing four Valium, and withholding eight, she dropped the rest into the toilet as well, and watched as they swirled from her life forever. It was her last night to float off and dream without anxiety and turmoil. She felt brave with a belly full of artificial serenity. How would she ever manage without the pills?

She was grateful that Julian was still away. Alone in her king-sized bed, she looked around the room, noting its lavish décor: the heavy oak furniture; the frosted French door to her dressing room, and the colonial oak door to the bathroom; the alcove with its plush, pillowy chairs and sofa and fireplace; the fully stocked bar in the corner. God! she thought, we have been blessed with so much. She knew any woman in Bangladesh, Bosnia, or Somalia would be happy to trade places with her and might even tolerate Julian's violent abuse. We live in such a crazy, basket case world. We have so much, while others have so little. And neither of us is content. I have money and want happiness and harmony; the poor would be relieved just to know the rent was paid or to be able to scavenge a cardboard box in which to sleep. I have more than enough of everything and live in opulent desolation. I never want to live in abject poverty, not knowing if I'd be able to feed and house my son, but living in this luxurious lunacy isn't my idea of how I want to spend my life.

What, she wondered, was she afraid of? Was it life itself that terrified her? Was she afraid of herself? Was it God that she feared? She wasn't even sure about there being a God anymore. She didn't want to die without finding out what living was supposed to be like. Her brush with death had acquainted her with her desire to live. She didn't want to die without discovering what it was that intimidated and emotionally crippled her. Julian certainly contributed to the terror that held her in its clutches, but underneath that obvious instinct for self-preservation, there was a dragon breathing fire in her psyche, and she intended to unearth it and invite it to leave.

Jessica used to have all the answers; now she didn't even have the questions. It seemed the older she became, the less she knew. At this rate, she calculated, by the time I'm fifty, I won't know anything at all. Are we born knowing who we are, only to forget as we become "civilized", trying to live up to other peoples' expectations and standards, other people's rules and regulations? Do we learn not to trust ourselves? Are we conditioned to become less than we really are? Oh, God, she didn't know why she was so screwed up! Surely, if life was so awful, and people needed alcohol and drugs to take the edge off their daily anguish, they would have been born with artificial support systems built right in—push your belly button and receive a shot of serenity.

This philosophical floundering was borne of drug-induced flights of fancy, but these were questions that Jessica often pondered when pills were not a part of her life. In quiet moments in her garden, watching a butterfly, studying an ant, admiring a dragonfly, or thrilling to the songs of birds, she marveled that their lives, while difficult, were simple. They obeyed the laws of nature. Not so with humans. She was confident that, somehow, the way humans lived was contrary to nature's dictates; and that someday we would all pay a great price for our arrogant disregard of the rules. Mixed up in this, she could understand the despair, anguish, and pain that resulted from our greed and selfishness; and how much the struggle for power and control over others had to do with the deteriorating state of affairs on Mother Earth. In her own life with Julian, she could see how much his desire to control her had created a nightmare that threatened to destroy her.

Her brain was thoroughly muddled from the strain of trying to figure everything out at once. She turned off the lamp, rolled over, and pulled the covers snuggly over her shoulder. Digging her head into her favorite pillow, she hugged it and lay awake in the dark.

This was the last night she would sleep in her bed for twenty-eight days. This was the bed where she and Julian used to love each other and talk the night away. This was the bed where they used to hope, dream, and plan for the future. This was the bed where Rob was conceived and where they used to watch him grow and kick inside her. This was the bed where Julian used to comfort her and brush away her tears. This was the bed where Julian learned to shut out her anguish and where they learned not to listen to each other. This had become the bed where she slept alone, even with Julian beside her.

☆☆

The alarm startled her awake. Dragging herself to the side of the bed, she sat up, hair tangling over her eyes, her brain fogged. Forcing her eyelids open, she squinted into the gloom.

Then she remembered, this was it! This was the first day of the rest of her life! Well, not quite. She still had a few pills to see her through the trip to Glenora. But *tomorrow*! That would be the grandest day of her whole life. Today was only semi-grand.

Shuffling into her dressing room, she blinded herself by turning on the light. A splash of cold water on her cheeks and forehead revived her. Now she could tolerate the day. Into action! Brush teeth, phone Rosalind, take a quick shower, lotion her body, get dressed, apply makeup, brush hair and tie it back.

Racing down to the kitchen, she danced on feet that were feathers. On with the coffee. Back up the stairs to awaken Binkie. Into her dressing room, pop two Valium, put the other six into her change purse, and check around for anything she'd forgotten. She had packed her suitcase the night before, so all she had to cram into her tote bag were the last minute things: makeup, shampoo and conditioner, body lotion, toothbrush and paste, hairbrush, and ribbons.

Back down the stairs she tap danced, excited, jubilant, anxious, terrified, hopeful, and sad, but filled with life and the love of it. Yessirree! She was going to set Glenora on fire when she got there, by God! She was going to be the most successful client that institution ever had. Were they going to be impressed with her!

As she dashed to the door to let Rosalind in, she felt the Valium kick in. Not enough for others to notice, she hoped, but she could feel it tug slightly at her feet, slowing her down, like a low gear. She'd lost a few cylinders. Rosalind puffed in, blowing steam into the frosted air that billowed through the open door.

Jessica lugged her suitcase, tote bag, and purse to the Corvette, which was hidden in the fog of its own exhaust. It was a ghost of a car, tail lights and head lamps casting an eerie glow on the skiffs of snow that swirled in the early morning darkness. Jessica felt as if she was walking in a time warp as she shivered in her jacket, bracing herself against the cold. The icy air seared her face and she stumbled into the passenger seat. As Rosalind wheeled the car away from the house, the last thing Jessica saw was Binkie peering out a foyer window, the chandelier ablaze above her.

The depot was quiet. She was the only passenger from Riverbend. No one in his right mind would travel in such a February cold snap. She and Rosalind pulled the suitcase to the baggage door of the bus. With a last embrace and Rosalind's wishes of good luck, Jessica tore herself away and escaped onto the bus, afraid that if she started to cry, she would never stop. Rosalind watched and then waved as she saw Jessica peer at her from a window near the front. Confident that her friend was all right, with a last wave, Rosalind fled to the warmth of her car.

The bus had only a few passengers. Jessica chose a seat where she could be alone with her thoughts. The sun wouldn't be up for hours. As the bus whined out of town, she watched the familiar sights: the drugstores and clothing shops, the Talisman Hotel, the restaurants and beauty salons, the barber shops and gas stations, the Mayfield Hotel, the Second World War Memorial, the new housing development on the outskirts, the lights of Sherwood Park twinkling on the distant hills. Then they were on the open highway. She was cutting herself off from the familiar, from her security, and from her old life. The bus was carrying her toward a new life, infinitely better than the old one she was discarding. She had once heard someone say that we can't go back and make a brand new start; but we can go forward and make a brand new ending. More than anything, she desired the rest of her life to be worthwhile.

The temptation was too great, as she knew it would be when she had dropped the Valium into her coin purse. Foraging for them in the dim light, she found the six promises of floating, drifting tranquility. She put them on her tongue and swallowed them dry, not appreciating their acrid taste, but craving their effect. Pulling a stick of Doublemint from her purse, she relished the burst of flavor as she chewed it to disguise the caustic sensation the Valium had produced in her mouth.

Resting her cheek against the icy window, she watched the snow banks sizzling past in the lights of the bus and fantasized about becoming a bus driver, flying through the snow swept landscape. And then she thought how she'd love to drive a semi-trailer. Right across the continent, she'd wheel all that power, sitting high above the rest of the traffic, with her spirit free and only the rig for a home. She'd live in, sleep in, and dream in her truck. She would know where she came from and know her destination. She would have no worries except driving, driving, driving. She closed her eyes, and drove her semi toward the scurrying swirls of snow, which she never seemed to catch. No matter how fast she drove, the snow drifted always out of reach, always beyond the grasp of the lights. She awoke with the driver shaking her.

"Look, lady, this here's the end of the line. You have to get off!"

"My God!" She jerked herself awake. Wide-eyed and confused, she stared out the window and saw buses lined in their stalls.

"You okay, lady?" The bus driver squinted at her quizzically.

"Huh? Yeah. Sure. Guess I dozed off. I'll be OK in a second." She stood up and lurched into the aisle, wiping dribble off her chin. Her gum was snarled in her hair. With her knees buckling one way, her ankles the other, she sagged against the armrest and yanked her jacket shut.

"I'm fine," she slurred, her tongue pasted to the roof of her mouth. "Jus' a li'l fuzzy. 'Sthere coffee in the...shtation?"

The driver shepherded her to the front of the bus and stepped down to take her arm, while she struggled not to stumble against him. Her tote and her purse felt like dead weight over her arm, and threatened to pull her to the ground.

"Coffee shop's inside. You sure you're okay?"

"Fine, thangs. I'm shtarting to come to now." She blinked her eyelashes unstuck.

"Don't forget your luggage. That must be yours." He pointed.

"Oh...Yeah. Sure. My bag." She eyed it stupidly. It certainly looked familiar. How in the name of God was she going to heave that sucker into the station?

"Here," offered the driver. "I'll get it for you. You want it inside?"

"Tha's ever so kine. Thangs so much." Her lips and tongue were functioning on their own timetable.

Gradually, her head started to focus. God! Why had she

taken those damned pills?

The driver deposited her suitcase outside the coffee shop. "I think it'll be all right here. You can have coffee and watch it through the window."

He peered at her for a second, and she wished she could have vanished into a puff of smoke. With a crooked smile, she turned and careened through the door. The clatter of dishes, clanging of pans, and the pungent aroma of frying bacon and eggs stung her senses into reality. This was the start of her new life. She thought she'd be sick on the spot.

Stumbling to a stool at the counter, she ordered dry toast and coffee; the coffee to get her juices flowing, and the toast to soak up the poison in her veins. The waitress bustled off to fill her order, casting a suspicious glance over her shoulder. Jessica caught the unsavory glimpse. Maybe she should go to the rest-room and assess the damage.

As she sagged against the grimy sink in the foul-smelling bathroom, the cracked and spotted mirror told the story. If it were true that a picture was worth a thousand words, Jessica confirmed it. Her mascara had mixed with tears as she slept, and two large semi-circles of black bloomed under eyes. Her hair had slipped its ribbon and was straggling across her fore-head with a wad of chewing gum clinging to the end, making a clump of it. No problem. A pair of scissors would take care of the gum. It was the rest that was the nightmare!

With bits of toilet paper from the near-empty roll in the stall, she scrubbed at the mascara. It was the brand that wouldn't come off in a cloudburst. Well, it had come off her lashes, but the manufacturers were partly correct—the damned stuff was welded to her skin. She begged a dribble of soap from the never-empty pump clinging to the splintered wall, and with the soap, scratched and clawed at the black, which slowly sur-rendered. Then instead of two black circles, she now had two angry red ones.

Digging in her purse, she found her comb and dragged it through the tangles until she had it under control, except for the gum. Avoiding the gummed strands, she pulled the rest of her hair back, securing it with a tornado-proof knot. Now for the gum. She was armed for combat, her purse containing all the essentials in the event of an emergency. It was crammed with everything—except scissors. But she felt triumphant when she discovered a nail file. Straining to see in the feeble light and filthy mirror, she slowly sawed and hacked off the offending hank of hair, dropping the hairy wad of Doublemint into the overflowing wastebasket. She surely wouldn't dare enter a beauty pageant, but she looked presentable enough for a bus stop coffee shop with its odd assortment of travelers in transition.

Shoulders back, she marched out of the washroom and tripped onto her stool. Her automatic pilot still wasn't operat-ing. However, her vision was no longer double, and she found her coffee cup with no difficulty. Maneuvering it to her mouth was slightly more problematic, but she managed to sip some of the now cold, thick brown brew. The toast tasted like saw-dust, but determined to be at her very best when she arrived at Glenora, she gagged her way through it. Her original game plan was a little off base, but she'd get there, by God!

With a few more drags on her cigarette, she drained the remaining coffee to the dregs. Still unsteady, she wavered to the glass door that led to the street. A half-dozen taxis idled at the curb, their exhaust fumes misting the chilly air. Waving, she indicated to the first driver that she required his cab. The car leaped to life and screeched to a halt beside her.

"I have a suitcase in there!" she yelled above the rattle of the engine. "Can you get it for me?"

While the cabbie stomped off grudgingly to retrieve her bag, she slid into the back seat. Slamming the trunk shut, the driver, fifty-ish, graying, wrinkled and grossly overweight, heaved himself into his cab and turning, asked her destination.

"Glenora Treatment Center," she replied.

"Where's that, ma'am?" he asked, and her anger was invoked.

"How the hell should I know? *You're* the taxi driver! *You* live here! I don't! Don't you have one of those location gadgets that help you find places?"

"No, ma'am, I don't!"

He radioed the control office, asking for directions to Glenora. Jessica eyed him. Anyone who didn't know where Glenora was shouldn't be driving a taxi. It was the most important place in the city, next to city hall. Any idiot should be able to take her there. She slumped against the door as he eased the car into traffic.

"It sure is hot in here!" she complained. "Any chance you'd turn off the heat?"

"Open the window!" he shot back.

"Mind if I smoke?" she asked, breathing in the crisp, cold air.

"Yes, ma'am, I do! I don't smoke and my passengers can't smoke either! I have a big sign on the dash, and there's a bigger one behind my seat." He had an irritating twang she was unable to identify.

"Oh, yes, I see them now." There they were. Huge signs. Funny she hadn't noticed them.

Slumping into the corner, she rested her head against the window, the wintry air cooling her flushed cheeks. Perspiration

She wasn't wearing an identification bracelet, so that ruled out a hospital or asylum. God! The place was as quiet as a crypt.

Rummaging in her purse, she dug for cigarettes and examined the walls for "No Smoking" signs. None. No ashtray either. She opened the night table drawer, which held a puny tin ashtray and a Gideon Bible. It had to be a hotel. Puffing on her cigarette, she strained her mind to remember the taxi trip, but a totally blank screen met her inquiring inner eye. Lord love me, she thought, this is creepy.

She sat smoking, deep in dazed thought, when suddenly a powerful wave of nausea swept over her. Her insides roiled and seethed and she clamped a hand over her mouth as she dashed to the toilet. Over the commode she heaved, the contents of her stomach dribbling into the water. The tile floor chilled her knees and she gagged, her stomach wrenching, while she choked with each spasm. Dear God, she thought, I'm going to die here. Head resting on her arms, hugging the bowl, she sobbed. This was the end of the line. She'd never again twinkle and sparkle; laughter breathed its last in her heart. She didn't even have the strength to flush the toilet. Sagging against the cold ceramic bowl, she prayed she'd somehow find the strength to die.

A soothing female voice behind her said, "Jessica, Jessica, it's okay. You're going to be fine. Right now, I know it's frightful, but soon you'll feel well again. I know you don't believe it, because I didn't believe it either....but you will recover. May I touch your shoulder?"

Convinced it was the Angel of Death coming to claim her, Jessica didn't care if it touched her shoulder or anyone else's. She managed a low grunt. A hand tenderly touched her back, stroking it lovingly.

"I know how terrible you feel, and you think it'll never

improve. But it will. Hang in there, and things'll get better."

Jessica couldn't believe her ears. Hang like this over a toilet bowl and things will get better? Things sure as hell couldn't get much worse! Tears, unbidden, streamed down her face. They flowed from a place where she had never been before. They gushed from her heart, saturated with devastating despair, crushing sadness, and shame.

Cramps in her legs caused by kneeling on the unforgiving tiles, encouraged her to stir. Slowly, she unwound herself from the commode. As she struggled to her feet, a hand helped her and led her to the bed. She sank down on the blanket, squinting through her tears at a gorgeous brunette with creamy skin, a vibrant smile, and penetrating eyes. She also saw in those eyes empathy and understanding.

"You didn't believe you'd be okay?" wailed Jessica. "What was wrong with you? A hangnail?"

"No," the woman said, "I'm an addict too. I was hooked just like you are. My name is Caroline, and I'm the night nurse. This is Glenora, and people get well here."

Jessica hunched over, hugging her pain to her, and wept. The whole cosmos vibrated to her keening for the loss of her life, her hopes, her dreams, and her soul. Anguish swathed her, while terror coursed through her veins. She hurled herself to the floor, cringing in the fetal position. It was her moment of deepest psychic distress. She wept for every ant she had ever crushed, every flower she had ever plucked, every word she should never have uttered, and every hug she had never given. Her horror held her fast, clutching, pinching, squeezing, and twisting every nerve. Myriad veins of torment tangled with the ganglia in her brain, short-circuiting every cell. Agony hissed through her head and, like lightning, slashed through her soul.

Despair suffocated her and hopelessness clung to her flesh as she thrashed, screamed, and begged to die. So deep was her desperation, she never heard the young woman repeating, "You're going to be okay. You will recover."

Exhaustion wavered its way through her sobs and whimpers escaping her lips and replaced the wailing of her distress. Her rasping hiccupping and tremors ceased, and she lay flat on her stomach on the cold tile, hiding her tears of shame in her hands, while they seeped through her fingers and puddled on the floor.

When she lifted her head, reality thunder bolted her to attention. She wasn't dead; she wasn't in chains; she wasn't being judged. And she was sick! She faltered to her feet, every cell of her body screaming for mercy.

"Dear Christ!" she gasped. "I never thought it could be this bad! Why am I so sick?" She tried to brush her hair from her forehead, where it clung like wet tissue paper. "I wasn't like this at home, even when I overdosed...I've never been so sick in my life!"

"Part of it's from the pills you took on the bus," said Carolyn. "Some of the illness is definitely drug withdrawal; your body would like some more to maintain the equilibrium it developed while you were abusing substances. Some of it's the fear of the unknown, and part of it is from the release of all the distress you've been experiencing. You've been through a lot in the recent past."

Jessica frowned, her head throbbing. "How do you know what's been happening?" she mumbled.

"You muttered some of it when you arrived, and your friend, Rosalind, called to see if you showed up. She filled in a few blanks for us."

Jessica was outraged. "How dare you pump my friend? If you

want to know something, you come to me!"

"She wasn't ratting, and we didn't pump her. We asked her general opinion...She loves you very much, and she's concerned."

"I still feel betrayed...*by you!* How dare you ask my friend about me? This is supposed to be private!"

"As private as the spectacle you created when the staff had to drag you from the taxi? You were quite a sight for sore eyes, let me tell you, Jessica! You created quite the scene, fighting with the taxi driver over the fare! As private as the exhibition you created when you overdosed? We got that from the hospital records. Now stop this bullshit and get real, lady! This is where we cut the crap! Grow up! Your life's on the line! You could be dead if not for people who care about you!"

Jessica was astonished by the nurse's burst of anger and deeply ashamed of her behavior. Had she really been scrapping with the taxi driver? She knew that under the influence of drugs, anything was possible.

"Sorry," she sniffled.

"Forgiven," Carolyn smiled. "Now why don't you have a shower and get ready for bed? I'll bring you some tea and a muffin."

Warm in her flannel pajamas, Jessica huddled on her chair, trying to focus on the papers Carolyn had given her along with the tea. The nurse had told her the papers contained information regarding the treatment program, a time-table of activities, a list of rules and standards, and also information on Alcoholics Anonymous and Narcotics Anonymous meetings, which she was obliged to attend.

It was no use reading the pamphlets; Jessica couldn't concentrate. Eating the muffin and drinking the tea provided enough of a challenge with her trembling hands and quivering body.

Glancing at her watch, she found it was almost midnight. This was going to be one long night! What had she been doing all afternoon and evening? The bus arrived at noon. She remembered being furious that the taxi driver didn't know where Glenora was; after that, one big blank screen.

Jessica had no idea that during the next few hours, she would be so busy that time would fly. Nor did she suspect that at the end of the night, she would want to make copies of her horror and tape them to her bathroom mirror at home, to the fridge, and to every wall of the house, so she would never forget the mischief and havoc that abused drugs can wreak on their victims.

Sleep eluded her while her head cracked open. Unable to lie down, stand up, sit down, walk around, or to simply be still, she paced the room, a lion snared in a cage. Up and down, around the room, back and forth, in and out.

Her mind wouldn't stop; on and on it chattered, making her wonder if her busy brain ever tired itself enough to simply shut up. The damned thing was so tightly wound; it crawled in her skull, firing thoughts like an AK-7 gone mad. Not one notion hit the target before it exploded into a new one. She couldn't make out the trace of the last image, before it zapped and zinged her with another. A dull electric current surged from her toenails to the very ends of her hair. Her nerve ends frazzled and sizzled, every cell snapping and crackling.

A projector in her mind, short-circuiting, hurled images against the walls of her mind: Julian battering her; Rob wailing; her mother and father; Lydia; pills; Julian raping her; her stinking, rotten life; death; hell; dead people; rotting corpses;

burning crosses; gargoyles with eyes melting down their cheeks; dragons breathing flames; screaming animals with their insides hanging out; bloody snakes writhing together; demons and vampires devouring screaming victims; skeletons reaching for her; witches cackling; human sacrifices smoldering on altars. The torture never ceased as she tore her hair and begged the universe for mercy.

May I never forget this, she thought. May I never have to endure another moment of tribulation because of drugs. She was in a vise, a prison from which escape was hopeless. She wanted to go home, she wanted to stay. She desired death, but yearned to live. If she had to tattoo a reminder of this agony on her chest in order to remember it, she would. Her ordeal of terror and anguish made the anxiety attacks resemble a Sunday school picnic.

⁎⁎

The morning wakeup call found her shivering in her chair. She hadn't slept a wink and knew she'd paced five hundred miles. No muscle in her body was free from pain, and every cell throbbed and pleaded for attention.

She scrubbed her face in the sink, brushed her teeth, dragged a brush through her tangled hair, yanked on her jeans and a white pullover, and laced up her sneakers. Grabbing her cigarettes, she directed her shaky legs to the cafeteria. The night nurse had shown her around the center during the wee hours when Jessica was on the prowl so she was familiar with the layout. Unable to face breakfast, she longed for a cup of coffee.

The dining room was as jammed as a bar on Saturday night offering free booze. She stood in line, positive in the knowledge that every eye in the room was on her, and poured half a cup of steaming coffee. She would never be able to carry a full cup in her fluttery hands. While she stumbled to the first empty chair, she prayed herself invisible.

"I hope you don't mind my sitting here," she apologized to the single occupant at the table.

"Suit yourself," he mumbled around the spoon he was shoveling into his mouth.

Friendly sort, she thought, as she lit a cigarette and tried not to look at him. He certainly was eye-catching. A big, bushy black beard partially covered his face, and his eyes burned like black coals. Black hair matted and curled over his ears and crawled on his sweaty neck. Dirty, broken, and cracked fingernails protruded from his scabby fingers. A shirt, that apparently hadn't seen the laundry in a month, was open at the neck, revealing black hairs that wiggled on his chest.

Why had she ever sat here? He looked like a pirate, if she ever saw one. Probably an escaped convict. He slurped the porridge from his bowl, dribbling milk into his beard. Grabbing the sugar bowl, he poured more sugar into the concoction and swirled the mush around and around and around until it resembled creamed vomit. As he slopped the gruel into his beard, bile filled Jessica's mouth. She couldn't stand the nauseating sight.

"Will you excuse me? I have to make a phone call," she spluttered and fled to her room where she cowered until the first lecture, which was scheduled for eight o'clock.

The first lecture was wasted on Jessica, whose concentration was at an all-time low. It concerned the nature of addiction and how family members, partners, friends, co-workers, and employers become locked into the same denial mechanisms with which the addict/alcoholic operates.

In the addict, denial says: "I don't have a problem." "I can quit anytime." "I'm only enjoying myself." "It helps me unwind." "Who can live without drugs in this crazy world?" "If you had my problems, you'd drink too." "I need something to help me sleep." "You think I have a problem? You ought to take a look at Joe." And the classic, "I haven't been drinking!"

In the non-addicted person, whose life is touched by an addict, the denial says: "He has such potential." "She is such a capable person." "He works twice as hard as anyone else." "I'm sure it's just a stage he's going through." "With her problems, I'm sure I'd drink, too." "He's quite shy and needs a few drinks to break the ice." "He only gets buzzed on weekends." "His drinking probably isn't as bad as I think it is." "She can quit anytime."

All Jessica did was pray to God she wouldn't throw up on the beige carpet in front of all the clients. She spotted the black-bearded guy who was sitting in the front row, legs stretched out, and ankles crossed, with his grimy black boots ready to trip anyone who walked by. He had his arms folded across his chest, and his black beard moved to the rhythm of his chewing. Probably chewing tobacco, she thought, shuddering at the idea of any woman curling into his arms. Why hadn't the police or narcotics squad picked him up?

Class over, she escaped to her room. Silence enveloped her, and she hugged herself, praying to make it through the day. The clock read 9:00 AM.

⁂

She was fifteen minutes late for occupational therapy. And what would she like to do? There were dozens of hobbies to occupy her busy little mind and nervous fingers. There was pottery, tie dying, leatherwork, knitting, crocheting, carving, macramé, decoupage, woodwork, oil painting, embroidery, and model shipbuilding. If she wanted to pursue a hobby, and it wasn't available, they would try to get it for her. In a cranky temper, Jessica wanted to ask if they had any class on constructing a birch bark canoe. Instead, she asked if they offered a class in basket weaving.

The little, crumpled, mauve-haired lady in charge smiled sweetly. "No, hon, is there anything else you'd like to do?"

"Not right now. I'm much too wrecked to do anything." Maybe macramé would be a good idea, she thought. Then I could hang myself.

"I understand, hon, but don't leave it too long. It's best for us to find a way to relax and get our minds off our troubles. A new hobby can distract our minds and open up new avenues to us."

"Are you an addict, too?" Jessica asked.

"No, hon, I'm not," the little lady sighed patiently.

"Oh, I thought it was a prerequisite to work here."

"No, hon, it's not."

Feeling as if she'd escaped her mother's clutches, Jessica made her way to the cafeteria for coffee, since she wouldn't be stuck in that busy little dungeon. She remembered her mother trying to teach her how to knit. It wasn't the knitting and the tangling of the wool that drove Jessica crazy. It was the way her mother always wanted to keep her busy, busy, busy. She was a confirmed believer in frenetic behavior to keep one's mind from paying attention to the world crumbling around her. And, of course, there was always Satan lying in wait for idle hands into which he could sneak his mischief.

Her mother used to clean closets, weed the garden, rake the yard, string beads on safety pins, and do anything! Jessica was unable to summon a single memory of her mother when she didn't have a needle, broom, hoe, rake, vacuum cleaner, dust rag, crochet hook, mop, shovel, scrub brush, knitting needles, paint brush, glue stick, or dish rag in her hands. Her mother never sat down to relax unless it was to knit a sweater, hook a rug, or crochet a tent.

Jessica preferred to unearth what was amiss rather than spend her life cleaning out closets or braiding rugs in order to escape. Valium and Seconal had been her perfect escape. Unfortunately, they sucked her life-blood from her veins and cooked her brain. The time of reckoning had arrived. She was damned if she was going to spend her time constructing little ornaments as mementoes of her despair.

⁂

Jessica hated group therapy. While she was willing to concede that first impressions aren't always accurate, she was convinced that her particular group deserved the Cracker Jack prize. She found it amazing that with so many clients in the center, the powers that be had arranged to have all the eccentric lunatics in *her* group. How they were going to share, relate, and recover seemed outside the parameter of possibility. It might have been a good idea to listen to Lydia, or perhaps, even to Julian.

Dan was their therapist, and he presided over the group as they individually introduced themselves, each offering a brief account of their problems. There were seven shattered souls, including Jessica, in various stages of withdrawal from their chemical of choice.

First to introduce herself was Irene, who looked like someone's spinster aunt in a Charles Dickens' novel. She had a prim, proper, starchy personality, and she spoke with carefully measured words, which she uttered with perfect enunciation. Jessica was convinced that Irene had ice water in her veins and probably didn't know a word of profanity. Irene stoically refused to say what had brought her to Glenora.

Jessica was sure she emitted a silent scream when the blackbearded guy strolled in and slid into a chair beside hers, leaning his head around to give her a nasty grin while he chewed on a toothpick. Dear God, it lent full credence to Julian's warnings. "There'll be criminals in there, you know!" he'd said, during one of their less argumentative conversations. "You'll *never* sleep... the *entire* time!"

The buccaneer's name was Mac, and he wore his squalid clothes like a suit of armor. He had worked on the pipeline in Alaska and had been involved in extinguishing the oil well infernos in Kuwait after the war with Iraq. His deep booming voice thundered in the room, and Jessica knew he had tied down oil wells with his bare hands.

"I'm here," he announced, "to get off the sauce and back to work as quickly as humanly possible."

Ray was diminutive, about sixty, shaking, and timid. He looked like a mouse caught in a jar; he was simply terrified. He wore little spectacles and had a bald head with fringes of white hair over his ears. He was an executive for a distilling company. It was probably a minuscule company, which distilled minimum alcohol level liquor, according to Jessica's assessment. Caught sampling one too many batches of product and reprimanded for tippling too copiously in his executive office with the secretaries after hours, he had been put on suspension until he had his problem under control.

Red was big, well muscled, tall, a loudmouth, and a cop. He was there to get himself off booze and back in his patrol car. He'd been suspended for stopping drunken drivers, confiscating their liquor and beer, and polishing off the bottles himself. He had been turned in for drinking and driving and resisting arrest. The arresting officer was still in hospital with a smashed-in face and two broken ribs. Red was in a pile of trouble and wanted to go straight and return to his job.

Then there was Molly, fat, and not very jolly, who wore her frizzled brown hair cropped close to her head. Her eyes bulged and her dentures clacked as she recounted her tale. Her husband ousted her from the family farm when she drove his tractor off the road in a drunken stupor, tearing out several yards of new fencing, and barely missing a prized bull which, seeing an opportunity, had escaped the pasture. To make matters worse, the bull made his way into a neighbor's meadow and bred nine of his prime cows. Unfortunately, the bull was a Holstein and the cows were Jerseys. All poor Molly did was weep while Irene passed her fresh Kleenex.

Montana sauntered in twenty minutes late, making quite an entrance in her leopard-patterned mini-dress, her breasts bursting over the top. Her legs never seemed to end and were tipped by black, four-inch spiked shoes. Her dish-water-blonde hair was arranged in scores of slender braids, with beads of wood and glass woven through each, African style. Tattoos adorned almost every inch of her body not covered by the dress. She had more tattoos than Dwayne, the Rock, Johnson, and no one would have been surprised if Arnold Schwarzenegger was her bodybuilding coach. Her fingernails, like claws, were bright neon orange and her eyes were hidden by lashes globbed with mascara. Huge gold dangle earrings completed the picture. Jessica thought it was safe to assume that Montana was neither an undertaker nor a missionary.

Apologizing for being late, Montana crackled her gum as she spoke. She was there, she confided, to get off the drugs and the streets and to become clean and sober very quickly. She had recently signed a movie contract, valid only if she showed up for rehearsals, which were scheduled to begin in six weeks.

Some rehearsal, speculated Jessica, as she watched everyone's eyes fixed upon the colorful apparition. She was, admitted Montana, a hooker.

"I'd never have guessed," muttered Jessica.

"What did you say, Jessica?" interrupted Dan. "I didn't quite catch that."

"Nothing," she replied, her face reddening and hot. Damn her mouth!

"No, I can't accept that," pressed Dan. "I want you to repeat what you said. It's important that we all interact, and if you have something to say, I'd like to hear what it is. Now, please repeat it."

Ray shriveled in his suit; Molly stopped crying, her eyes bulging more than ever; Red guffawed and slapped his leg; Mac hid a grin with his fist; and Irene looked like she just might say "shit".

Montana glared at Jessica from her caves for eyes, burning her to a crisp on the spot.

"I said...I said that I'd never have guessed," Jessica choked.

"And what exactly do you mean by that?" hissed Montana.

Before any blood was spilled, Jessica said, "Contrary to what some of the people in this room and the rest of the world might think, I'm very glad you got paid for it. Most of us women give it away for nothing!" And then she wished her fairy godmother would whisk her away to where Peter Pan lived.

"Thank you for clarifying that, Jessica," said Dan. "Well, I guess we can end this session. See you all tomorrow."

As Jessica rushed from the room, speeding to the safety of her bed, Montana caught up with her. Montana's legs were much longer than Jessica's, and she could probably have won an Olympic gold medal for the hundred-yard dash, even in high heels.

"Hey, woman, I wanna talk to you! Hold on a minute!" she called.

"I have nothing to say," pleaded Jessica as she hurtled through the hallway.

"Well, I have somethin' to say to you! I wanna thank you for what you said back there! That was wunna the nicest things I heard in a long time! Thanks!"

"You're very welcome," replied Jessica who stopped and looked into Montana's eyes. "What I said is true. Now, please excuse me. I want to go to my room."

"But I was gonna ask you to have lunch with me."

"Not today, Montana. I'm too sick to eat. I'll catch you later."

"When?" demanded Montana as Mac strolled by, eyes rolling, beard concealing what Jessica was confident was a lecherous smirk.

"I'm not sure, Montana. I'm too sick to even think. Maybe sometime this afternoon."

She turned and fled to the shelter of her room, wishing she had chosen to go to the Ford Clinic instead. Glenora was more colorful than she was able to handle.

✳

"What do you mean, Jessica? He *can't* come, or he *won't* come to participate in the family support program."

"Both reasons!" she snapped at Dan, who was her one-on-one therapist.

Dan leaned over in his chair and folded his hands. "What I want you to do is look at real reasons, not the way you want them to be or think they *should* be. When you see the truth in issues, then you know what you're dealing with. When you color them with your own desires or wishful thinking, it clouds and distorts things, leading to confusion. Now, let's start again. Tell me why your husband won't come."

"First of all, he hopes I'll fail here. Secondly, he won't lift a finger to help me. Thirdly, he's a snob and thinks the people here are lowlifes."

"How do you feel about that?"

"Terrible! I didn't expect him to take time from his precious hotels, but he didn't give me one word of encouragement." She picked at her cuticles while her stomach churned.

"I don't know if this will help or not, Jessica, but I like you. Sometimes it's nice to know others like us, no matter what we've done or how we feel about ourselves."

She squirmed on the sofa in the therapy room. "I...I, uh, like you too."

"How do you feel telling me that?"

"A bit uneasy...uncomfortable."

"Why?"

"Well, I guess telling a man I liked him always meant something more."

"Like you wanted something from him? Maybe to go to bed

with him?"

"Sort of," she whispered, wishing he'd shut up. This was a weird conversation. No wonder Julian preferred to discuss money, hotels, and the weather.

"Do you know why?" Dan was relentless.

"I guess I wanted to be close to someone. I hated the sex part, but I wanted to feel loved." How in hell had she become involved in this discussion? All she had said was she liked him.

"Did a man love you if you went to bed with him?" he probed.

"I don't know. I guess he did. Probably not." She stared at the wall, wanting to put her fist through it.

"Why did you do it?" he hammered.

"Dan, I didn't come here to discuss my sex life! I came to get off drugs! I don't even know who you are, and you're asking me all this personal stuff! What does this have to do with therapy? I think you're sick!"

"Addiction is only a symptom of deep emotional problems. You seem to need love from other people to justify your existence. Let's find out why, and let's find where it came from. Now, can you tell me why you did it?"

"Because I wanted love, acceptance, and approval!" she sobbed. "I don't want to discuss this anymore! I came here to get help, not to be crucified!"

"Remember when I told you therapy can get tough? This is it!"

"I've only been here one day! Can't I even get oriented first?"

"We have only four weeks, Jessica. It took you a whole lifetime to get here; a whole lifetime of warped values and beliefs and skewed thinking that made you sick and dependent on men for love and on pills to cope. Now let's get down to it! Did you love yourself if you went to bed with someone?"

"No!" she screamed. "What do you expect me to say? I hate this whole rotten conversation! I hated myself when a guy took me to bed, and it turned out all he wanted was sex! I felt used, ugly, and ashamed!"

"Would it be a fair assessment to say you slept with some men to get from them what you couldn't get from yourself?"

Lights came on in her head. Connections sparked in her brain. She nodded. "Oh, God, Dan, I don't know. I never wanted to think about it. I mean, it was so awful! But that was probably the reason. But Julian wasn't like that! He didn't use me! He loved me! We got married! And I loved him, too!"

"Do you love yourself?" he asked quietly.

"Not a whole lot," she whispered, intent on picking a Kleenex to bits.

"That's what you're going to learn here," he smiled as he put his hand on her shoulder. She looked at him but was unable to smile back.

She straggled back to her room. Confusion and despair winged their way through the skies of her mind when she thought about going to bed with men, hoping for a shred of love. Hating herself, she cursed Dan for dredging up those memories from the scrap heap where she had buried them. How was it possible to love herself if she had committed acts that filled her with guilt and shame? Where did Julian and her marriage fit into this morass? She wished she had a Valium to shut up her head, to deaden the feelings, to brush away the memories, and to transport her to open meadows where she could run tirelessly through fields of daisies.

Her father! Was he a connection? Did those shameful secrets from her childhood launch her on the roller-coaster ride to this hell?

Now she had two things she'd be unable to share with Dan and the group—her disgraceful childhood secrets and Julian's violence and threats. But she knew there was an association between her loveless early days with their incest and her relationships with the men in her life. To her, that insight solved the riddle of the destructive way she related to men.

Throwing herself onto the bed, she wept. Intense emotional pain wracked her body as she sobbed for her lost childhood and the wasted, empty years when she had depended on men to give her the applause she needed to feel alive and validated. She had to learn to love herself, but where was she to start? I'm here, she thought. I loved myself enough to want to live.

⁂

Group therapy was no better than *Monty Python's Flying Circus*, Jessica decided, as Red expounded on how he used to stop people for drinking and driving, confiscate their booze, and let them go. Then he'd enjoy their liquor for the rest of his shift.

"What did you think of yourself for doing that?" Dan asked, leaning back in his chair, relaxed and unruffled.

"A great deal for me! I saved a pile of money on liquor, and I got them to quit drinkin' and drivin'."

Irene glared at him. "Your attitude needs adjusting!"

"What in the hell is that supposed to mean?" he exploded.

"You're a smart law officer! You figure it out!" she shot back.

"I agree with Irene," Jessica interjected.

"Who the hell do you think you are, Miss Fancy Pants?" he snarled, fixing her with a defiant stare.

"I'm nobody, Red, just a nobody, trying to get to know the person I am underneath the layers of self-deception. But I think what you did was *sick*! Your job was to get drunks off the road, and you were worse than they were! You used your power and authority to intimidate others for your own selfish purposes! You're sicker than anyone in this room! And what about that officer in the hospital? How do you feel about that?"

Group erupted into a frenzy as Molly howled about her shattered dreams and how unfair life was and now law and order was ripping people off too. Mac cheered Jessica onto victory over Red's shouting. Ray held his head in his hands, dismayed to find himself seated in a room with such flagrant corruption. Montana calmly chewed her gum, one leg crossed over the other, swinging one high-heeled shoe as she gazed from one frantic client to the other with complete indifference.

Dan, unperturbed, viewed the antics, occasionally glancing at his watch. When the hour and a half was up, he walked to the door, opened it, and hollered, "Time!" Circus was over for the day.

Jiminy! thought Jessica as she skittered to her room. This is supposed to help? It was looking more and more like *One Flew Over the Cuckoo's Nest!*

⁂

There was a tapping at her door, and an attendant announced there was a long distance call for her.

Straightening her sweater, her fingers brushing back her hair, she ran down the hallway to the telephone.

"Hello?" she said and was startled to hear the familiar voice.

"Darling, how are you? I didn't interfere with anything, I hope."

"Only my peace of mind. I thought you weren't going to call."

283

"I'm concerned, and I wanted you to know I think you're doing the right thing...being there, I mean."

Suspicious, she asked, "What changed your mind?"

"I've been thinking about my abysmal behavior. Please get well and happy, so I can see that beautiful smile you always used to have."

"Well, all I can say, Julian, is we need to make some major changes between us. Rob deserves better than me being sick and you beating me up."

"I know, my precious sweetheart," he agreed. "Just get well and remember how very much I love you. Bye, Princess." He hung up.

Jessica stared at the receiver as if she expected to see a spider crawl from it. Now that is a tactical change, she mused. I wonder what he'll do next. No use worrying and hoping. I'll do whatever's put in front of me to do instead of engaging in wishful thinking.

⁂

Jessica headed for occupational therapy where she was making a belt for Rob, one with ponies galloping with the wind. Montana, who was knitting a sweater, spotted her, and sauntered over to the bench where Jessica was hammering the damp leather.

"Can I ask you somethin'?" queried Glenora's main attraction, conspicuous in her leopard-print dress as she attempted to disengage a strand of wool from her orange claws.

"Sure. Go ahead," replied Jessica.

"You sure are a pretty lady. You got some class too. How can I start lookin' more like you, than bein' what I am?"

"Well," answered Jessica, putting down the hammer and turning to appraise her admirer, "there isn't too much you can do about the tattoos, but you might trying wearing something other than that skin-tight dress that reveals everything you own and shoes that are stilts. You need to tone down your makeup and wear earrings that don't clunk like cowbells."

"But I don't have no other clothes 'cept others like the one I brung," whined Montana.

"Go out on the weekend and buy something," Jessica advised.

"Like what?"

"How about jeans that don't look like you've been poured into them? Find some small earrings and a top that doesn't have 'hooker' stamped on it. Wearing a bra might help, too. And pick up a pair of sneakers or sandals and buy some socks."

"What about makeup?"

"Don't buy any more! All you need is a giant jar of cosmetic remover. Then come down to my room and we'll do a make-over."

"How about my hair?"

"Leave it. It's great! I love it!"

"You do?" Montana beamed.

"And stop selling yourself and advertising sex. Just be Montana. Maybe in three weeks or so, we'll know who we are. And by the way, you'll have to ask the office for a pass to leave this place for any reason. Since we're the new kids on the block, we need passes to leave, and we have to check it out with our therapist. We can't leave if there's a mandatory activity happening. In our third week, we'll have more freedom as long as we check it out with staff. I read all about this stuff my first night here when I couldn't sleep. I'm sure the office will understand when you explain you need a new wardrobe. They've probably already noticed you're a mighty great distraction in that dress."

Montana stared at Jessica and burst into laughter as she hugged her new friend.

⁂

Group continued to be *Saturday Night Live*.

Molly received a call from her husband's lawyer, saying he had filed for divorce. It seems the neighbor with the prized Jersey cows was suing for damages, and Molly's husband could no longer afford to keep her. Hysterical, Molly screamed that her life was over, ruined by a horny Holstein bull.

Red contributed to the furor with, "Oh, shit, here we go again!" while Jessica flared at him, saying he was "nothing but a rotten bastard, an insensitive, typical man!"

Holding his head, Ray mumbled there was nothing but pain and misery in the world, and if someone didn't do something fast, everyone would wake up some morning to find the entire planet buried in an avalanche of disposable diapers!

Mac offered his two cents worth. "Your husband sounds like he's meaner than a junkyard dog! Forget him, Molly. He's not worth it."

Irene consoled Molly, and Dan handed out Kleenex to the two women as they clutched hands and wept about Molly's fate. Montana blew giant bubbles with her bubble gum, while Dan observed his fledgling sober and straight addicts as they battled for life. He thanked God they were confined to a treatment center. Letting such a cluster of misfits loose on the world would jeopardize social order. But he knew that within a short time, his savages would be quite civilized—provided they didn't make a break for freedom over the weekend.

⁂

Saturday. The center was a morgue. Many of the clients who were near the end of their treatment time had gone home for the weekend or were out enjoying a few hours of liberty. There were no counselors or therapists on site, and with only a skeleton staff to keep things going, Glenora was almost quiet. Gone were the weekday hustle and fervor and the pumped energy of the newly clean and sober.

Jessica meandered down to the cafeteria. She hadn't trusted herself to go home, and she and Dan had decided she was better off staying at Glenora. While there were no pills left under her mattress, the liquor cabinets and bars in the house offered ample opportunity to silence the chatterboxes in her head. Besides, she didn't feel like dealing with Julian.

Glancing around, she saw that no one from her group was at any of the tables. In fact, there were no more than a dozen clients in the room. She didn't see it as a problem that she had no one with whom to talk. She had brought *The Golden Spruce* for company and poured a cup of coffee. With her book and cigarettes, she had plenty to occupy her time. Spotting a window table, she was just about to pull out a chair when she heard a man's voice call out to her.

"Hey, Jessica, come and join me. It's lonely here."

Looking around to find the source of the words, she saw a man wave. "Over here!"

Curiosity often defeating caution with Jessica, she walked to his table, while he stood to draw out a chair for her. Puzzled, she sat down, spilling a dribble of coffee as she placed the cup on the table. Gallantly, he mopped it up with a serviette. As she lit a cigarette, she stole a glimpse at this dark-haired, dark-eyed stranger. He was definitely easy on the eyes in a rugged sort of way. His shirt was open at the neck to reveal a brilliant gold eagle pendant and chain. There was something about him that was vaguely familiar.

"I hope you don't think I sit with strange men as a rule. I don't like to see people lonely, especially in a treatment center," she explained. "Are you a client here? I haven't seen you before."

"Sure am. I've seen you around. How's your therapy going?"

"I don't know how anyone is supposed to get well here," she shrugged. "Locked up with a bunch of crackpots! I've seen some really wrecked cases walking around here. Do they actually expect to get back into the mainstream of life?"

He smiled at her. A dazzling smile. Capped teeth, no doubt. "I'm not sure. I know the hard-core cases can stay here for six months...tops. Then they go upstate for long-term care."

Those eyes. That voice. Jessica's mind strained to place him. She looked at him quizzically. "Do I know you from somewhere?"

He laughed, a deep, warm, resonant laugh. She wished she could laugh like that.

"You sure didn't want to sit with me the first morning you sat at my table. And you sure seem disgusted with me in group."

"My God!" She was aghast. Her cheeks flushed with embarrassment as recognition dawned. "Mac! I don't believe this! What happened to you? You look terrific! What I mean is...you look so...so different!"

"I certainly hope so," he chuckled. "I got a pass and went out this morning and had a shave and a haircut and picked up a few clothes."

"What a transformation!" she gasped, still feeling the heat of a blush on her face.

"A great social appearance is not one of the requirements of my job. Last Sunday, when I came here, I came straight from the rigs in the middle of nowhere in Alaska. I'd been out there for months. I was into the sauce pretty bad, and my boss said it was either my job or treatment. Came straight from the ice and cold to here. Guess I threw a scare into everybody. Smelled worse than a grizzly bear and looked like I'd been denned up in a coal mine."

"It's absolutely remarkable what a week of being sober can do," she said, sipping her coffee. "Amazing!"

"Thanks," he smiled, leaning closer to her. His eyes were beautiful. She could lose herself in those eyes.

"Do you like it here?" she asked. "You don't say much in group."

"Who the hell can with that crew? It's kinda interesting though…watchin' people get all riled up. Never saw anything like it. It's almost as much fun as freezin' my ass in Alaska."

"Something I've noticed is we've all been clean and sober for almost a week. Maybe group is working in spite of the yelling and arguing and hysterics. I know I'm here to find out what I'm running from."

He grinned at her, crinkling his gorgeous eyes, as another blush crept into her cheeks.

"And, Jessica, what is it you've been trying to escape? You seem in control, except the times you hollered at me in group. The first few days you were bouncing off walls, but you seem to be in control now."

"I do? Well, I can assure you I'm not! I have some renegade brain cells in need of a major overhaul."

"Doesn't seem to me you have any reason to be unhappy. You're a good-lookin' woman. You're intelligent and well spoken. That you came here shows you've got courage."

She sighed. "You know, Mac, I used to make lists for myself about the reasons I should be happy. The only thing the lists achieved was to make me feel guilty about not being contented. Then I was dealing with my misery plus guilt! And that was before I dove into the damned pills! Don't you ever feel like you're drowning in a swamp?"

"Sure. Lots of times." Dragging on his cigarette, he pushed his chair back and stretched his legs out, the gold chain winking and gleaming on his chest. She could see the dark hair and muscles of his forearms as he shoved his sleeves up. "Yeah, Jessica, I do, but I don't worry too much about it. I know as long as I stay off mind-altering substances like booze, things go along pretty smoothly. I've been through this place before, Jessica, and another one up North in Canada."

"Well, at least you're consistent. You keep drinking and going to treatment centers. Are you married?"

"Not any more. My wife couldn't handle my lifestyle."

"Don't you ever get lonely?"

"Now and then I do," he replied, twisting the empty coffee cup in his hands. "But a guy like me is always movin' around. Of course, I get lonely. Don't you?"

"Yes," she admitted. "I think I was born lonely. Scared, too. Sometimes I get so lonely, I think I'll die."

"You're married, aren't you?" He leveled his eyes at her.

"Yes, but it doesn't help. Especially when my husband doesn't understand and won't even talk about it."

He looked straight into her eyes and then allowed his glance to drift down her neck to her chest. A hot flush stole along her throat. What was she doing talking with this guy?

"You know, Jessica," he said in a low rumble, which was barely audible, his eyes gazing into hers, "if you were *my* wife,

I'd see to it that you were never lonely. Your husband's a fool."

What was she supposed to say to that? She felt herself drawn to him. What lonely woman out of her right mind wouldn't be attracted to such a man? He was terrific looking, virile, and intelligent. He had a captivating smile, fabulous eyes, and his husky voice sounded sexy. To add to his obvious charms, this man even had a job.

"Mac," she said, looking him in the eye as well as she could in her flustered state, "I can't handle the man I have. What would I do with someone who drank all the time and was never home? I have that now, and I can't stand it."

She knew she should leave that instant, run like hell to her room, and never look back. But the delicious sensation of being hustled by this man was too tempting.

"Jessica, with a woman like you, drinking would never enter the picture, and I'd make damned sure I was home every night!"

Where were her senses? Where were the brains Mac said she had? Where was the control she seemed to exhibit? She tapped her cigarette in the ashtray, her eyes darting around the cafeteria, avoiding his face. "Mac, I think I'm going to my room for a while."

"Look, Jessica," he smiled, then took her hand gently, "I'm just telling you I think you're special, and I find you attractive. Even though you scream at me in group, I really like you."

"Thanks for the visit," she said, disengaging her hand and picking up her book. "I'll see you later."

As she sauntered down the hall, she savored the flavor of his flattery. Julian never said things like that to her anymore. Damn me! she thought. I'm here to get well, not hung up on some drunk from the frozen North. She looked at the hand he had held and could still feel the warmth of his flesh. I may never wash this hand again, she grinned to herself.

⁂

Saturday night and nowhere to go. With only the newest clients who hadn't been granted passes on the premises, or those who chose to stay in for the weekend, Glenora's hot spots on the weekend were the TV room, the poolroom, and the cafeteria with its non-stop coffee, pop, and juice. Jessica strolled down to the TV room where several clients, including Ray, Irene, Mac, and Molly were watching a movie. Strategically, she seated herself on the sofa beside Ray where she had an excellent view of Mac, but made neck craning necessary to see the television. Stretching his legs out, Mac folded his arms across his chest and winked at her. God! Everything he did was so sensual. He rippled with it. He'd make tearing an engine apart look sexy, she thought.

"How about going for a coke in the cafeteria?" he asked Jessica. "This movie's the pits."

"Sounds like a good idea," she answered, saying goodnight to the others in the room.

"Well, now," Mac grinned, as he carried two glasses of pop to the table and pulled out a chair, "this is more like it. Maybe we can continue the conversation we started earlier."

Her body registered high alert when he draped his arm over the back of her chair. She felt the warmth emanating from him, and the scent of his cologne wafted through the air.

"Your hair is really beautiful," he said. "It looks very soft and silky."

"Thanks," she said, inching away from him.

"I'll bet you wake up in the morning without a hair out of

place," he smiled.

"Not exactly. I'm usually declared a disaster area early in the day."

"Do you think I'll ever have a chance to see you in the morning when you wake up?" he asked, not a trace of humor in his eyes.

This was leading somewhere; she would have bet her last dollar on it. It felt delectable, but also very wrong.

"Sure. Meet me for breakfast right here tomorrow," she teased.

"That's not exactly what I meant."

She shifted her chair to face him. "Mac, I know precisely what you had in mind. I'm not stupid. Look, I'm going to level with you. I find you very appealing. Any woman with hormones would find you enticing. But I don't think this will benefit either one of us. Another time, another place, perhaps, but not here!"

"Jessica, I'm sorry." He was contrite.

"I don't want you to be sorry. I'm saying I can't be interested in you. I'm very married, and what I came here to accomplish is much too important to allow myself to get sidetracked." Tears brimmed in her eyes.

"Hey, Jessica, I didn't mean to upset you. Please don't cry."

His arm encircled her shoulder, and his hand brushed her hair. He offered her some serviettes for her tears. Suddenly, Dan's words exploded in her mind. 'Why did you go to bed with men?'

Diving for her cigarettes, she lit one, puffing on it as if it were her last before execution.

"Mac, you don't know me at all!" she whimpered, as she dried her tears with the napkins. "I don't know you either. I think we're both lonely, and we're both coming down from mind-bending crap, which is no small feat. Sobering up is enough of a problem without throwing a fling into the mix. I'm in the middle of something I don't understand...myself and my relationship with my husband. Two weeks ago, I attempted suicide. That's how unhinged I am! And my attraction to you isn't any kind of answer for me."

He leaned against the back of his chair, and smiled at her as she peeked at him through the napkins and her tears. "You know, Jessica, you're one hell of a woman. And you're absolutely right. This isn't going to help either of us."

She sniffled. She was trying to release something from her heart, struggling to extricate it from her very soul. "I'm going to tell you something, Mac. I've never shared this with a living soul, except my counselor. Even my husband doesn't know. You can hate me if you want to or treat me with contempt. I came here not to hide myself, but to expose myself! I've had a few affairs in my time, but I never got involved for the right reasons. When I did, it was because I was lonely, and I needed closeness and love.

"Mac, can you understand that? I needed love, and the only way I knew how to get it and feel I mattered was to go to bed with the guy I was involved with at the time. He wanted sex, and I needed love. He had his needs met, but I never did. The reason was this: I didn't love myself! Sex has never, ever been just a roll in the hay for me. It has always meant something deeper, a kind of spiritual communion. When I went to bed with those others, I was being used. They weren't looking for a spiritual communion any more than the devil himself!"

He didn't say anything, and the silence clung to her like wet newspaper. She felt him looking at her, thinking about her, and *judging* her! He was probably going to say something she had heard before from a man who'd been rejected: "You gave it away to everyone else. How come I don't get any?" or "It's your fault I have this hard-on, so do something about it!" or "You know you want it as badly as I do, so come across!" or "You are the only one I ever get this way with!" or the classic, "Baby, you don't want me to suffer from lover's nuts do you?"

Mac reached over and, with the tip of his index finger, traced the path of a tear on her cheek. "You really are something, lady. Do you know that?" he whispered. "I can't imagine you not loving who you are. I can't imagine anyone ever hurting you. Jessica, I want to thank you for sharing what you said about relationships. Believe me, I don't hate you, and the last thing I'd feel for you is contempt. You've given me a few things to ponder." He lit a cigarette and played with his empty glass. "So what does your husband do?"

"He's into hotels. He has three of them."

"Oh, so he has a few bucks?"

She nodded. "We get by a lot better than some people. It's a good living."

"And he doesn't treat you right."

"Not exactly. He's whacked me around a few times."

"And you're intending to stay with him?"

"I'm not sure." She couldn't bring herself to tell him how terror stalked her footsteps and how torment corroded her insides. How could she tell him that Julian would surely murder her if she ever left him? How could she share that Julian would kill their child in front of her before he pulled her to pieces? Who would ever believe hideous stories like that?

"Jessica, I want to ask you something. I've never asked a woman this before...I would like it if you would do me the very great honor of being my friend."

"Nothing would give me more pleasure," she smiled, putting her hand in his. "Being your friend is a privilege."

He lifted her hand and kissed it. "Thank you," he said, his eyes serious but warm and caring. "If you ever need help, I want you to know you can count on me, no matter what."

He walked her down the hall to where the dorms were located. At the entry to the women's section, he lifted her chin and gently and softly kissed her on the lips. "You have a wonderful sleep. I'll see you at breakfast."

As she crawled into bed, she hugged her pillow, pretending it was Mac she was embracing. She could hear his heart beating.

※

On Sunday evening, urgent pounding made Jessica open her door. In breezed Montana, laden with boxes and bags and packages from various department stores and boutiques. In amused amazement, Jessica watched as Montana squirreled and dug her way through bags and tissue paper, ripped open boxes, and piled her purchases on Jessica's bed.

Montana proudly displayed her new wardrobe: four pairs of jeans, two of them designer style with pockets all over and flashes of beads at the hip; a jean jacket with an eagle hand-painted on the back; a black sweat suit with "Always A Lady" embroidered in magenta thread on the front; three modest white silk blouses; a pair of sneakers; two pairs of sandals; two T-shirts; three sexy but functional bras; five pairs of undies; two G-strings which, she explained, were for wearing under jeans so the panty line didn't show; a huge jar of makeup remover; six pairs of button earrings; and a silver bracelet watch.

"Good grief, Montana, you certainly shop when you shop!

You must have spent a small fortune!" Jessica laughed.

"Had to turn a few tricks to buy all this stuff, but it wasn't no big deal."

"I thought you wanted to get off the street!"

"Well, I have to have the right clothes to get offa the street, and I didn't have no money, so I did what I had to do. And I told the guys...they're real regular customers...what I was doin', and they thought it was great, so they all gave me somethin' extra, kinda like a goin' away present. And I gave them extra special service! I made a bundle, Jessica!"

"You're priceless, Montana!" hooted Jessica. "But don't breathe a word to anyone else around here about what you did. If you drink or use drugs while you're a client here, you get tossed out. God only knows what they'd do with you for your little caper. These are great clothes! You're going to look sensational!"

"You said to buy cosmetic remover, and you'd help me with makeup."

Jessica pointed. "Into the bathroom and take off that gunk."

When Montana emerged, Jessica saw a woman she would never have recognized. Montana's skin was flawless and radiant; her eyes brown and clear. She had the face of an angel.

"Okay," said Jessica, "here goes. Get your stuff, and I'll give you directions."

When they were finished, Montana, except for her tattoos, which were mostly concealed by her new clothes, looked as if she was ready for choir practice.

"God Almighty!" she squealed as she looked in the mirror. "I can't hardly believe that's me! You know, Jessica, my own mother never took the time with me that you have."

"I just noticed, Montana, where are your orange fingernails?"

"Oh, them. I pulled them off. They were only fake. I used

them on the stroll 'cause they were as good as weapons. If a guy's gonna get weird, I can claw his eyes out! And I'm thinkin' about turnin' down that movie contract."

"Are you sure about that? You might make some serious money."

"Yeah, the money ain't so bad, but I'd end up on some kinky guy's TV. It was for porno flicks, and I got higher standards now. Money ain't all that counts."

"You've got that right," Jessica agreed, surveying her ex-hooker pal. Wouldn't Lydia just swallow her dentures!

⁂

"How are things going, Jessica?" Dan asked, as she sat down in his office.

"I still feel like I'm rearranging the deck chairs on the *Titanic*! My mind won't stop for a second. It's noisier than an automobile assembly plant. And I'm not sleeping very well."

"That's normal, Jessica, normal."

"Isn't anything ever abnormal around here?" she complained. "Every time one us of has a problem, wants to commit suicide, wants to drink or wipe out with drugs, feels like selling the family heirlooms to move to Fiji, or wants to run away and live in an abandoned mine, you people says its *normal!*"

Dan nodded patiently. "Considering what people are here for, what they're experiencing *is* normal."

"So all the crap I'm feeling is normal," she sighed. "That's comforting! Will I ever sort this confusion out, so that I'll know which thought matches what feeling? I'm worse than a five year old having to match a picture with a word. I just despair at times!"

"What's the despair about?"

"Oh, mostly my marriage. I'm scared about things at home."

"What concerns you?"

A mouse skittered through her insides and pushed the terror button, her stomach churning in response. A second mouse tripped the guilt switch, and tension snaked through her being. She simply couldn't tell Dan about the terrible violence. How could she tell him that she feared for her life, that Julian was capable of skinning her alive? How could she say that Julian had threatened to murder his own child? Who would ever believe that about Julian? No one! And who could help her, if the police wouldn't? Who would even believe her about her missing call on the police log and her missing medical file after that beating?

"I'm not really sure," she said in response to his question. "I think I'll have that sorted out by the time I leave."

"Your husband is quite wealthy, isn't he?"

She nodded. "Very! He knows it, too!"

"I haven't met too many wealthy people who didn't know they had money."

She laughed. "I guess what I mean is...well, he uses his money and power as a coat of armor. It buffers him from life. He can always hide behind his money and status when things get uncomfortable."

"If it comes down to a separation, would you be able to make it on your own?"

He skewered her to her chair with his questions. They were finally getting down to the issue: could she live poor again. It was always, always the money. The whole planet was in trouble because of the bloody stuff.

"I'd survive, Dan," she managed, swallowing hard. "I did it

before, and I can do it again."

"I'm sure there'd be a settlement."

"Oh, Julian would be more than generous!" She picked at a cuticle to avoid his eyes. She loathed the lies, but she was unable to tell him she'd be lucky to escape with the hair on her head, let alone the skin on her back.

As she left his office, she knew she really could survive without the cash. It was her life's blood she couldn't survive without.

⁂

Down to occupational therapy, she marched. Pounding the leather belt might stop whatever was cooking her insides. There was something churning in her head and invading her right to privacy. Montana waved at her, grabbed her knitting, and strutted over to Jessica's table.

"You don't ever take a break from the stroll do you?" Jessica observed sourly as Montana pulled up a chair.

"What d'ya mean?" Montana asked, tossing her head full of braids and beads.

"Even when you wear sneakers, you look like you're cruising the street and trolling for men."

"I suppose I have to take walkin' lessons next!" snapped Montana.

"You sure do!" Jessica glared at her. "When you walk, you have what my grandmother called 'a hitch in your get-along'! The way you walk draws men like sewage draws flies!"

"I don't know what you mean." Montana could be as thick as a plank at times.

Irritated by her own problems, Jessica declared, "Your brains must be in your braids, Montana! Look, I'm going to demonstrate two ways of walking for you! Let's just see if you can spot the difference!"

She swung away from the bench and, swaying her hips and grinding her thigh muscles, sashayed to the end of the room, where she did an about face, and walked with a normal gait back to Montana. "Do you get it now?"

"Yeah, I see what you mean," conceded Montana.

"If you want to get off the street, you better stop acting like you're still on it! Now, smarten up!"

"Christ! You sure are snippety and grumpy today! What's eatin' you up?"

"Nothing!" Bang! She pounded the hammer onto the stamp.

"You sure got your undies in a twist!"

"I'm working on some personal stuff."

"Mind if I ask what? Maybe I can help."

"No one can help me! I have to help myself!" Bang! Another pony on the belt. Bang! Bang! She smashed the hammer down onto the table. "I'm sick of living in shit!"

"Well," observed Montana, "it's gotta be one of the three M's—Momma, Money, or Men. In your case, it's probably some man. Women always feel rotten when they're tangled up with some man who ain't treatin' them right."

"You're better than a psychiatrist!" clipped Jessica.

"I earned my degree the hard way," Montana stated flatly. "There's no better way to get an education than on the street and on your back."

"No, thanks."

"What's eatin' you alive, woman?"

"I'm worried about my marriage and my husband. That's all I can say." Tears swam in her eyes.

"Oh, I see, it's not really all that important. Just a small chunk of your life, is all. Hell! That don't look like no problem to me!" Montana's words oozed sarcasm.

Tears blinded Jessica. Damn it, she didn't want to cry! She buried her face in her hands and sobs wracked her shoulders. Montana threw her knitting aside and leaped to throw her arms around her new friend. Jessica slumped against her.

"Hey, woman, you better start talkin' about what's makin' you so sad," Montana crooned, as she held Jessica tenderly in her arms. "Your eyes always look so afraid. You look like you're bein' hunted."

"Sometimes I feel like I am," Jessica sniffled as she pulled away and dug through her purse for a tissue.

Montana stepped back. "Look, Jessica, I don't know much 'bout your personal stuff, 'cause you don't open up that much in group, but don't sell your soul to no man. If you do, you're no better'n me sellin' myself for a few lousy bucks. You'd still be prostitutin' yourself. I know your husband's got money, but it ain't worth it if you always feel sad and feel like slop in a back alley."

Jessica stared at her with reddened eyes, her face contorted with despair. "Oh, God, Montana, I don't know what to do! I want things the way they used to be."

"You love someone who puts all that sadness in your life, who makes you feel like shit? Woman, you better take a good look at what love is! I don't know much, 'cause I ain't got an education like you, but I know I ain't gonna stick to no man who gives me grief! And nothin' stays the same, Jessica. Look at me! Look at how much I changed since you met me. I might still walk like a whore, but I'm gonna learn to walk right, with my head up and cruisin' for my *own* life!"

"Montana, I'm not with Julian for money! I truly loved him! I didn't marry him because he was rich and important. I married him because he was my best friend, and we had fun together. But everything has gone wrong, and it's pathetic the way we live. We rarely speak, and he's hardly ever home...And I miss my son so much! I wish I could snuggle him and kiss him and hear his laughter."

"Sounds like you better get strong for yourself," offered Montana. "Stay off the drugs and heal."

"I know you're right, Montana," Jessica sniffled and tried to smile. "Sorry I was such a witch a few minutes ago."

"You wanna hammer the table some more or do want me to whip your ass at badminton?"

✻

The group therapy bunch was certainly not like the crowd that drank at "Cheers" of TV fame. Jessica was convinced that between group and individual therapy, she would never use drugs again because she'd be in lock-up somewhere, having been driven totally insane by the antics of her group-mates. Why had she been so anxious to come to this stinking place?

"Well, if it isn't Merry Sunshine," quipped Dan when she tiptoed in late.

"I don't think much of your sense of humor," she sizzled, plopping herself into a chair. "Sorry I wasn't here on time."

"What's wrong?" asked Red. "You seem glum."

"Not much. Just me, my life, and this place for openers. Then we can say the city's a mess, the country's going to hell in a hand basket, and world tensions are going to explode at any minute and blow us all to smithereens."

"I sure like optimists, Jessica," commented Dan. "That's

what's so easy about your case. You always look on the bright side of things."

"Jessica," interjected Ray, who was still quaking in his chair, "I have to point out to you that the world's not going to blow up. We're going to bury ourselves in a mountain of garbage first."

"Thanks, Ray, that's encouraging," said Jessica.

"I'm glad I can help you feel better," sighed the little man. "Thoughts about nuclear holocaust and terrorism alarm us so much, we don't realize how we're raping the planet. Don't you worry any more about mass instant annihilation. We're all going to die a slow, agonizing death from pollution."

Moments later, Molly and Mac tangled with their opposing views on marriage and the causes pertaining to its breakdown. Irene rushed to a blubbering, whimpering Molly to defend her against Mac's "mean and nasty, typical man's attitude!" while Dan chided Irene for her willingness to console Molly when she remained steadfast in her refusal to be forthright about her own reasons for seeking treatment.

"You're hiding behind a smoke-screen of dedicated altruism, Irene, but none us knows one thing about you," noted Dan. "I suggest you stop helping Molly and concentrate on what brought you here. Otherwise, you'll be the first one to end up on drugs again when you leave the program."

If looks could have killed, Irene was the one to pull the trigger as she glared with lethal intent at Dan. Ray, shriveling into his suit, muttered he was lucky to have been spared marriage, and that he intended to mind his own business from then on. Montana sat quietly in her own corner, eyeing the proceedings with intense disinterest, while she crackled and popped her gum.

"Montana," remarked Dan, "I'm not here to criticize, but

would you please not chew that stuff in here!"

With her brown eyes registering total boredom, she looked at Dan pensively, chewing away in her open-mouthed manner. Then without warning, she protested. "Christ! Somebody's got to do somethin' constructive in here! God! I ain't never seen such a pack of whiners! Be grateful you ain't on the drag!"

With snarling distaste, Irene attacked Montana. "What a disgraceful, shameful thing to say! I'd never for a second consider that as an alternative! You're nothing but an illiterate tramp and a filthy slut!"

Montana eyed Irene with disdain. "You'd never make it on the drag, honey! Ain't no man crazy enough to give you one lousy dime for a trick! But I'll tell you somethin', woman. If you get hungry enough, you do 'bout anythin' to feed yourself. But you'd bloody starve! And I wasn't on the street 'cause I liked it! I was there 'cause there weren't no other place to go. I'll tell you somethin' else, woman. I ain't never goin' back!"

Chapter Seven:
Life on Life's Terms

Attending films and lectures was mandatory for all clients, and the film on the modern, drug-laced North American culture was no exception. Jessica sat with Montana and Mac at the front of the room, where Red and Ray found them. In a stage whisper, loud enough for the entire assembly to hear, Red announced that Irene and Molly were boycotting the rest of the group because of Montana's "unsavory attitude" and "inflammatory remarks".

"Tell them to call the President," Montana sighed around a wad of bubble gum.

The film, they all agreed later, was informative but alarming, and Jessica recorded its message almost verbatim in her head.

"From the time we're born, we're taught never to suffer discomfort of any kind. Modern medicine has a pill, powder, or liquid for everything. It is interesting to note that doctors and the pharmaceutical industry contribute to the drug culture with their seemingly harmless medications, and that their attitudinal impact on North American society is considerable.

"We graduate from children's medicines for the relief of the physical discomfort of teething or upset stomach to the subtle 'adult soothers' to quell our emotions. With no need to tolerate even the mildest form of physical pain, why on earth should we have to endure something as stressful as emotional turmoil? Instead of investigating the underlying causes, which may be contributing to our physical or emotional distress, we turn to the local pharmacy, neighborhood bar, liquor store, or friendly drug dealer.

"It doesn't matter what the condition is, we treat it with a pill, a liquid, a suppository, a powder, a needle, an eyedropper, or a spray. If we don't find relief from these remedies, perhaps we require surgery.

"Don't tolerate one more minute of sniffling with that cold! Just mix up some concoction from the drugstore with hot water. Its special lemon flavor and magic combination of chemicals—everything from sedation to help induce sleep to a drug to counteract drowsiness—will have the system so utterly confused that no human being will even notice or care he has a cold! Some over-the-counter medications are so powerful that warnings are included with the packets, indicating one should not operate a vehicle or use machinery while taking them. Some labels say side effects could include DEATH!

"Don't consider the stresses in your life that may be triggering your heartburn, your ulcers, your headaches, your sleepless nights, that knot in your stomach, or that 'on edge' feeling. After all, it's easier to swallow a pill than change your job, go for counseling, alter your lifestyle, or get a handle on increasing debt.

"Is it any wonder that when our living problems overwhelm us, and our emotions are short-circuiting, we pour a drink, puff a joint, pop a pill, snort cocaine, or shoot up with something else? If we can't swallow it, pop it, shoot it, or snort it, then life isn't worth living.

"We are indoctrinated from the cradle to the grave not to deal with discomfort meaningfully. We avoid it all costs and at a terrible price. We spend billions of dollars on easy solutions to alleviate the frustrations of everyday living problems. Instead of learning to deal with life's challenges, we avoid them as we have been taught and encouraged to do by advertisers, unwitting doctors, the pharmaceutical companies, the liquor vendors, and the street-corner drug pushers. Many of us have learned the seductive lesson so well that we languish in hospitals, and some of us lie, forgotten, on the back wards of mental institutions. Some of us die on skid row. Some overdose in our homes and some in back alleys. We develop incurable diseases from the ingestion of bottled serenity and chemical peace of mind.

"And some of us—the lucky ones, about one in ten—make it to treatment, where we learn how to deal with life's challenges in new positive ways. In treatment, we learn to break the addiction to the substance, and then we have to break the *idea* that emotional stress and turmoil are somehow bad for us. We learn that emotional stress is a part of the human condition, and that there is not something wrong with us when we experience it. It is how we deal with it that separates the men from the boys and the women from the frightened little girls.

"We learn how to grow up and deal with life on life's terms."

Jessica was fascinated with the information and identified with many of the comments. She vowed to clean out her medicine cabinets as soon as she arrived home.

✳✳

Dan flipped through the pages of the reports, while Jessica

fidgeted in her chair.

"I'm reading the gossips sheets on you," he muttered.

"Gossips sheets?" Fear slithered through her heart.

"Yes! The reports that the staff here make on clients."

"I had no idea I was being spied on!" she declared indignantly.

"We're not spying! We're interested in your complete recovery. I know you haven't been to group for three days, because you're in *my* group! You haven't been to the gym. You've missed three out of four lectures this week, and occupational therapy hasn't seen you in days. You haven't been in the cafeteria for one meal, except to buy sandwiches from the dispenser, and your light is on until three in the morning. What in hell is going on with you?"

"I've been out walking!" She settled back in her chair.

"Walking?" His voice went up an octave.

"There's a beautiful world out there, Dan. There's a driveway leading to the main road and a gorgeous trail through the bush. I've been out walking to clear my head, and at night I've been reading and doing some writing."

"Look, Jessica, you're supposed to be participating in here! Not blazing trails out there!" he scolded, not too gently.

"I know that, Dan, but group is too overwhelming, and I loathe occupational therapy. I've made five belts for Rob! And I *have* been to the gym. I've been pumping iron when no one else is there."

"All right, but from now on, you participate in lectures, films, and group. It isn't my business what you do with your free time. Go and build snowmen and shovel the drive, for all I care! But you get to group and other mandatory activities! Now, let's get down to what's happening in your life. We haven't discussed the attempted suicide."

"I had a bad day," she mumbled. "I don't want to discuss it."

"You can't just brush that off, Jessica. An attempt on your life is a very serious, very desperate act. Why did you do it?"

She couldn't tell him the truth! That Julian had beaten and raped her and shattered her desire to live. That could lead to more questions and more revelations until the whole sordid nightmare was laid bare. Who would believe her? Who would help protect her and her son from Julian's murderous rage? Playing for time, while she unjumbled her thoughts, she begged Dan for a glass of water. When he returned with a paper cup of tepid water, she was composed.

"I was in a very bad situation, and I thought it best for everyone if I wasn't around anymore. Since my recovery, I've had some time to ponder my actions, and I realize it was a very selfish thing to do. My thinking, at that time, was skewed with drugs, and I know that suicide is no longer an option. My son would be devastated for the rest of his life if his mother took her own life. I have a very important job to do, Dan, and that is to raise my son with all the love, care, and guidance I can give him...Oh, God, Dan!" she sniffled. "I miss my son so much. He's mine to love and protect. I'm so anxious to get home and see him and get his sloppy kisses. For me to think of doing what I did is unbelievable. Thanks, Dan, for your concern. I think that's all I want to say about it, if you don't mind."

"I see," he said. "Well, if you ever want to share more deeply about it, I want you to know that I'm here for you. That includes when you go back home. You have Glenora's number and e-mail. I'm always available if you need to talk."

"I appreciate that, Dan. Thanks."

"What's going on with your marriage?" he ventured.

"That's interesting," she said, squirming slightly. "I've been giving it a lot of thought. You know, Dan, I've been hanging from a cross in that situation. Julian helped me build the cross, then he helped me climb up on it, and when he handed me the nails, I pounded the damned things in myself."

"You certainly have a flair with words, Jessica," Dan told her in exasperation. "Get to the point. What are you going to do?"

"I'm not sure. Just pulling out the nails is going to be a bitch! I've also come to the conclusion that women are expected to love someone who thinks they are inferior. Somewhere in all this mess, I have to figure out where I fit in. I'll have to wait until I get home to see where I have to build a bomb shelter to keep myself safe."

"A bomb shelter?" Dan's eyes widened and his eyebrows shot up.

"Figuratively speaking, of course. What I really mean is Julian and I have to find a place where we can be on level ground together. I know he has to work, and he has many community commitments, but we need a time and place just for us. I'm positive we can do that." She was nodding as she spoke, assuring herself of her statements.

"And in the meantime, are you going to avoid the group as if we all had a social disease?"

"In the meantime, I'll be at lectures and group," she conceded.

Dear God, she thought, as she left Dan's office, I may, literally, have to build a bomb shelter. Julian is my own personal holocaust.

The cafeteria was full. Meal times were more than nourishment for the body; a lot of socialization and "underground therapy" occurred over food and coffee. When she entered the hectic room, Mac and Montana waved.

"Where have you been for the last three days?" they both wondered aloud, as Jessica seated herself with her first hot meal of the week.

"You sure have missed a lot!" Montana seemed to be bursting with news and gossip. "You'll just die when we fill you in!"

While Jessica enjoyed her roast beef, mashed potatoes with gravy, fresh sliced tomatoes, and fried zucchini, Mac and Montana eagerly shared the group's adventures.

Montana had secured a position at a halfway house, where girls and women from the streets could go for help if they wanted a better life. She had also applied to go back to school.

Jessica squealed with delight. "Montana, I'm just so proud of you! I think you'll be a fabulous example for young women enmeshed in that way of life. God! I can see you now, helping them get straight, and then showing them how to walk, what to wear, how to put on makeup, and how to get free from that life. I'm thrilled for you, Montana!"

"You helped, Jessica! If it wasn't for you that first day, I mighta walked outa this joint! See what you've done! Now every woman who gets processed at the shelter and makes it because I help her, will really be helped by you!"

"Julian will love the plaque you're going to give me, I'm sure!" Jessica laughed. "It'll put him off his oatmeal for a week! You are one heck of a woman, Montana! I'm so proud of you!"

Mac delivered the news that Red had been fired from his job and was facing imprisonment for his unprofessional behavior. All was not lost, however. One of Red's buddies operated a private investigation service and was willing to hire Red once he had his act together and got out of jail.

Sadly, Ray had been expelled from the treatment program. Horrified about the burning of the Amazon rainforest, the poor man was so overcome with despair and grief, he had left Glenora on an afternoon pass and returned plastered. The staff had quietly suggested he leave.

Molly and her husband were reconciling. After reconsidering the situation, Molly's husband decided she was worth more than the Holstein bull and had given it to his neighbor in lieu of cash for the mischief the animal had caused. The two neighbors had agreed to split the future breeding fees the bull would provide. The critter had his own private pasture away from the Jersey cows.

Red had told an amusing story about one of his police-days adventures, and Mac simply had to share it with Jessica. A man, down on his luck and on welfare, had held up a bank at gunpoint and escaped with over ten thousand dollars. Several days later, the robber tried to deposit the money in his own neighborhood bank. The manager, knowing the man was unemployed, grew suspicious at the large amount of cash this fellow wanted to deposit, so he called the police, and Red was one of the investigating officers. Sure enough, the man had the money from the other bank. And why did he want to put it into an account? He was reluctant to have that much cash around because most of his pals were no better off than he was, and he didn't want them stealing it!

Laughing so hard when Mac finished the tale, Jessica agreed with Montana's assessment that she'd "just die"!

Irene, the mystery woman, had a story to tell and had done so under duress in group. When she had lost her job as a nurse because she was stealing drugs from the hospital dispensary and using them on the premises, she had gone home, determined to commit suicide. Distraught and desperate, she stole some more pills before she went home. Once home, she washed down as many pills as possible, knowing that too much of anything can probably cause death. When her husband arrived home, he discovered Irene unconscious and rushed her to emergency at the hospital. The staff did all the usual things to rescue someone from the jaws of death. The next day, her physician visited her in her room, where she was recovering from her attempt. He said he had seen many methods of suicide in his career, but this was the first time he had seen anyone try to pee herself to death. Irene, in her confusion, had taken a fistful of diuretics!

"Irene has, by the way, changed. She's climbed off her high horse," Mac assured Jessica. "I think telling her story leveled her, and she knows she's no better and no different than anyone else."

"She even apologized to me! Can you believe that?" Montana laughed. "I'm still in shock!"

"You comin' to the action in the assembly hall tonight?" Mac asked.

"I saw something on the notice board. What's happening?" Jessica inquired, pushing her plate aside.

"A few of us are puttin' on a bit of a show," he replied. "Strictly amateur. It should be fun."

"Only if you're doing something," she teased, grinning at him.

"Might be. Might not be," he responded, searching her face.

"Please come, Jessica! Please!" Montana pleaded. "You just have to be there!"

Red stopped by the table, interrupting Montana's pleas. "You guys better hurry up. Lecture's in five minutes. This one's on spirituality. Guess now we're going to learn how to walk on water!"

✵

The group sat together in the front row, Jessica between Mac and Red. The ex-cop shifted restlessly, while Mac lounged comfortably in his chair, with his arms folded across his chest. Montana was enjoying snapping her bubble gum, until Irene politely asked her to stop—and wonder of wonders—the ex-street-walker wrapped it in a tissue and tossed it into a waste-basket. Bubbling in anticipation of this wonderful lecture, Molly extolled the many blessings she had received because of God's Grace.

"Just think," she said, "if I had stopped praying, my husband and I might never have kissed and made up. Oh, prayer is so helpful! See, what did I tell you? Everything always works out for the best! If it wasn't for that awful bull, I might never have stopped drinking! This lecture is just what we all need!"

Jessica, feeling trapped into sitting through the oration, just as the Jehovah's Witnesses had trapped her on her porch on that freezing morning, leaned over and whispered to Mac, "If there's a God, I pray this is the shortest speech on record. And I pray Molly shuts up before I stick a rag in her mouth! And since when did she tell us that things work out for the best!"

Mac put his arm around the back of her chair. "I know how you feel, Jessica," he murmured. "But let her be happy. She's cried for the past three weeks."

"Sorry," Jessica murmured. "I'm cranky and don't want to be here. You're right. Molly deserves to be happy."

A tall, slim man in a navy sports jacket, gray slacks, and a pale blue shirt open at the neck, strode to the front of the room. Jessica's heart sank deeper than it had when she'd talked to Reverend Babbitz. It promised to be one long lecture! This man appeared to be too healthy, too perfect, and too young ever to identify with all hers sins of commission and omission. Her watch-face was infinitely more interesting than anything this young man might say. Jessica scowled and, beside her, Mac sighed.

"...and so I realized religion was not the answer," the young man said, as he stood, strong and clean-cut, in front of the assembly of drunks and addicts. "It seemed there was something I'd missed in life because I had this empty, dead feeling inside. I didn't understand it, because I had followed to the letter all the rules, regulations, dogma, and traditions of my church."

Jessica was bored. The hands of her watch stood still. Red grunted. Behind her, someone snored. She heard much coughing and shuffling of feet. She craved a cigarette. In her non-listening state, against her will, she heard the words "addict", "suicide", "life-support system", "reason for going on". Was this guy for real? This good-looking, young man of the cloth had been an addict and tried to kill himself?

"Slowly I became aware that all my knowledge of my religion had failed me utterly. I had a job, but no purpose. I had a church, but no home. I had a family in the church, but no friends. I had a future with the church, but no direction. I had rules to follow, but no convictions of my own. In short, I was empty inside. There was nobody home."

He could have been reading Jessica's mail. She had gone to Sunday school and church, but never felt she belonged. The rules were too hard, and she was guilty of every sin in the book, including admiring her reflection in the mirror when she was five years old. Her mother had caught her and told her she was "nothing but vain"! She was never able to live up to all the sanctimonious preaching, which guaranteed she'd live in guilt, misery, and eternal damnation if she didn't measure up. Her list of transgressions was long: nasty thoughts, mean actions, terrible words, hating her sister, fighting with the other kids, desiring material possessions, wishing for a good life, arguing with Julian, disliking Lydia, shrieking at Rob, and using drugs!

Why would God want such a sinner? If she did get to heaven, her halo would be rusted, her wings would be missing feathers, her gown would be patched, her harp would be out of tune, and her cloud would have a hole in it big enough for her to fall though. And for sure, God would never, ever speak to her. She'd be the Cinderella of heaven, with no Prince Charming!

"It seems to me," he continued, "that long before we take a drink, pop a pill, smoke a joint, or use a needle, our spiritual lives are in poor shape. Life lacks luster; it seems purposeless, and we despair. Of course, once we discover chemical peace of mind, our lives shine...for a while. To keep that high, we continue our habit, all the time destroying our spirit, which is too delicate and too fragile to withstand the constant assault with chemical substances. Our spirit wants to show us the way, but we've discovered an instant fixer. We don't want to go through the hard work of getting on track. Because of the nature of addiction, we aren't even aware we've de-railed. If we're lucky, our chemical dependency backfires, and we're in trouble—with ourselves, with loved ones, with our employers, with the banks, and perhaps with the law. Then we have to take a look at ourselves and what we're doing.

"Most of us...and I fall into this category...aren't even aware that there's a spiritual aspect of ourselves, which has never been nourished. We've been force-fed rules, commandments, and dogma, all of which we find distasteful, so we stop paying attention to them. Nourishment means something necessary for growth, but rules are confining. Our spirits need things to make us grow, to give us joy, and to expand our horizons. When we run from the rules, we often run from the nurturing as well because we've put it in the same basket with the things we find distasteful. And so our spirits die of starvation.

"We take it for granted that once we're no longer staggering and no longer frying our brains, we're fine. We're not! That nagging restlessness, that free-floating fear, and that rudderless idea that there is something more to life is none other than a malnourished spirit begging for a bit of recognition. I've heard it referred to as Divine discontent.

"Call it what you want—your inner life, your inner self, your Divine spark, your life-force, the spirit within, or your God-spark. It's the real you, and it wants to be acknowledged! Some people call it conscience, or that still, small voice. Whatever you call it, start listening to it. It's a gut feeling about things, people, places, or situations. All you have to do is start paying attention to it. Start doing things that bring you joy. Follow your bliss. Your spirit will recover when you start to nourish it. Remember it's the first to suffer from addiction and the last to recover.

"Feed your body, and exercise it. Think with your brain and stimulate it with books, lively conversation, and ongoing education. But above all, don't forget that aspect of yourself that is your ultimate reason for being—that wonderful, delightful, and enchanting spirit that lives, laughs, and loves inside of you.

"In parting, I wish to leave you with two thoughts to ponder. I can't remember where I heard them, but they mean a great deal to me. The first is: 'Your destiny depends upon what you do about what your soul becomes aware of.' The other is: 'The one for whom you are looking is the one who is looking.'"

That said, he walked from the room, smiling and confident, exuding an air of goodness and joy. Against her will, Jessica had clung to every word. Something within her had stirred. It was something strange, yet vaguely familiar.

"Coming for coffee?" Mac intruded into her thoughts.

"Huh? Oh...sorry, I was lost in space," she spluttered. "No, thanks, Mac. Not now, maybe later."

He looked at her for a long moment, and she shook her head. As the rest of the clients filed out the door to make a dash for the cafeteria, Mac joined them, leaving her alone.

Something flickered deep, deep within her soul. It felt warm and very comfortable, like a cozy fireplace in the dead of winter. Sitting there alone, Jessica looked at the sun streaming through the partially opened window and felt a fragrant breeze caress her face. The young man's message had somehow mingled with the breeze, and she breathed in both, filling her lungs with fresh, clean air, and her heart with fresh, new hope.

Jessica glanced at her watch. It was six-thirty and time to go back to her driveway, to walk along the snowy mile to the main road. As her boots crunched through the ruts and bumps of the drive, she breathed in the frosty air. A few stars winked at her, tiny zircons flickering, mimicking the spark in her heart. Maybe it was true that everything in the universe had a cause-and-effect relationship. "Thou canst not pluck a flower without the trembling of a star."

She remembered other winter evenings when she and Julian had walked through a fresh snowfall at the cabin and then cuddled on the polar bear rug in front of the blazing fireplace.

Maybe they could do these things again. Maybe the tenderness would still be there. Surely it wasn't too late. Their marriage was scarcely four years old. But something frigid whispered that nothing would ever be the same again.

A cool breeze kissed her cheek, and she smelled the scent of spring; a mid-March night with spring hinting its promise. She sensed the fresh season, even though it was weeks away. Was it primordial instinct? Pausing, she lifted her face to the zephyr, breathing in the promise of things to be re-born, of life with a new beginning. And then the breeze wafted away, leaving her with hope. Listening to the silence, she embraced the darkness and watched as the wispy clouds partially veiled a blushing full moon. She felt the snow like packed talcum beneath her boots and heard the snapping of a branch as the frost worked its mischief. Tucking her chin into her jacket, she turned and headed for the warm lights of Glenora.

⁂

The assembly hall was jammed. It was five minutes to show time. Montana snared Jessica as she entered.

"C'mon," the transformed Montana urged, "this way. There's a special place for us up front."

"The front row is becoming a regular spot for us, isn't it?" Jessica laughed, as Montana pulled her along.

"Nothin' but front-row center for us, Jessica. The best for us from now on. You taught me that I deserve the best and to expect it!"

"I did? That must have been in one of my other lifetimes!"

"Here! You sit here!" Practically pushing Jessica into the chair, she rushed off.

Jessica looked around. Yes sir! She, Molly, and Irene were all front-row center.

"I think we're in for a treat!" giggled Molly. "Montana's been excited all day. I don't know what they have planned, but there's been some scheming going on for days! We have to save these two seats for her and Red."

"Where's Mac?" asked Jessica.

"I think he's part of the plot," said Irene, who was actually rather pretty with the touch of makeup she had applied.

Someone dimmed the lights, and a rigged up spotlight flashed on over the makeshift stage, which boasted only a high stool and a microphone on a stand. Then, from the front door of the hall, Red ran in, hopped onto the stage, and grabbed the mike.

"Ladies and gentleman, Glenora is pleased to present its new discovery, a singing sensation flown in from Alaska—the land of the wild and free—especially for tonight's performance...Mac Traynor! Actually, I caught him singing in the shower, and he admitted he used to sing professionally, and he's graciously consented to entertain us all! I know you're really going to enjoy his music! Mac! You're on!"

Red stepped off the stage and seated himself beside Irene as Mac entered with his guitar and took his place at the mike. He grinned into the crowd.

"Red nearly broke my arm to persuade me to sing for you tonight, so whatever goes wrong is his fault. I haven't been singing in a while, and my guitar's a bit rusty, but we'll see what comes down here. I want to thank everyone for my sobriety, especially the group I've been with for the past three and a half weeks. And a very special thanks to a very special lady, who has set an example to me of courage, honesty, and humor." He looked down from the stage and smiled into Jessica's eyes, the luster and joy in his eyes warming her heart. "Montana and I have a little something for her."

Montana emerged from the same front door, carrying an immense bouquet of tiger lilies, and put them into Jessica's arms while the crowd clapped, whistled, and cheered. Through her tears, Jessica saw Mac blow her a kiss. Montana sat down beside her, grabbed her hand and said, "Thanks, woman! I would be nuthin' without you!"

Mac thrummed his guitar, and rich chords reverberated through the hall. The acoustics were perfect. Mac looked down at Jessica and then grinned and winked. "First song for you, Jessica," he said softly.

Embarrassment flushed her cheeks. She recognized the song immediately: "You Are the Wind Beneath My Wings". Mac's voice was full and deep. She couldn't believe the beauty, passion, and love in his singing. My God, she thought, he's wasting his time on the rigs. He was a trained, very gifted professional. He sang Glen Campbell's songs, some by Johnny Cash, others made famous by Neil Diamond. And Mac sang to her. He looked at her as he sang "Help Me Make It Through the Night", and a painful ecstasy tingled in her soul. When the words to "Take the Ribbon From Your Hair" graced her ears, she felt her soul reach for his, but consciously, she felt anger rising.

Oh, Mac, she thought, what a stunt to pull! I'm so weak and vulnerable, so in need of strong arms to hold me, so in need of a man's love and tenderness and warmth, and you sing songs like that! Damn you for doing this to me! Despite her mixed emotions, she loved every moment, abandoning herself to the poignant love and exquisite sadness of the lyrics.

The audience cheered Mac on. For two hours he sang, until

his voice was hoarse and he begged off. Two hours melted into nothing. Those hours were etched on Jessica's heart forever. Mac's talent was, without a doubt, a gift, and he had freely shared it with everyone, giving them all a fragment of the love that went into his singing.

"Before you all leave," he said, as he wound up the evening with "Amazing Grace", I want to tell you I wish you all the best. Glenora is a mystical, wonderful place where we have felt safe and loved and cared for, even though group gets tense at times." At this, the clients all laughed and clapped. "But some of us will be leaving the day after tomorrow. I hope we can all take with us some of the magic we've shared within these walls. We're all miracles because we've stayed clean and sober for the time we've been here. It's up to us now to continue to be miracles in the outside world, where we won't feel as safe and loved and cared for. May you all enjoy successful lives because you learned to deal with your inner demons, and live life on life's terms."

Watching him, Jessica was touched by his words, and she felt proud to know him and grateful for having shared in a tiny moment of his life. He was a delicious-looking man with a talent and personality to match. He had brains, humor, and honesty, and displayed a leashed sensuality that she found electrifying.

Montana squeezed her hand. "I'm gonna run ahead to the cafeteria and get us a table. Please come!"

As the last echoes of the guitar faded, Mac left the stage and, in one stride, was beside Jessica.

"Mac, what can I say?" she murmured through her tears of joy and sadness and love. "That was the most splendid performance I've ever seen. My heart says thank you. And thank you for the tiger lilies. They are my most favorite flower."

Putting an arm around her waist, he murmured, above the

din of people scrambling to beat each other to the cafeteria, "Anything for you, dear lady. That gave me the greatest pleasure. Will you come for coffee?"

"Sure," she smiled, brushing a tear away, "but I'll let you know right now that I consider you armed and dangerous."

"What do you mean?" he asked, pretending innocence, while mischief danced in his eyes.

"Don't hand me that!" she laughed. "You know very well what I mean! Singing all those beautiful songs, looking into my eyes..."

"Oh, that! You're the only one I cared enough about to sing to. Didn't you enjoy it?"

"Mac, that's not fair! Of course, I liked it...I loved every minute! You have such a marvelous voice."

"C'mon." He gently took her hand. "I need some coffee."

In the cafeteria, amid clients shaking his hand, slapping him on the back, and thanking him for the evening's entertainment, Jessica gleaned some information as Mac answered their questions. Yes, he'd been on the pro-circuit. No, he hadn't been with Johnny Cash or any other major star. He quit because he saw no other choice at the time. Yes, he regretted it.

As the crowd thinned, Jessica leaned over and asked him the reason why he had given up such a promising career.

Looking into her eyes, he sighed, "My wife hated that life. Never knew where I was, never knew when I'd be home...at least those were her complaints. I called her nearly every day when I was on the road, but that wasn't good enough for her. She's a very jealous, insecure woman. She thought I had a girl in every town I played in."

"And did you?" she asked.

"Not every town!" He winked at her. "Jessica, I was into

music back then, not into women..."

"That's noble. How come you quit?"

"Couldn't handle the pressure of her crying and nagging, and from trying to please her. The combination of dealing with her emotional meltdowns and trying to get a career going was too much for me, so it just seemed easier to pack in the music."

"So you quit to please her. Went to work in a damned oil field, and she still isn't happy, and then she leaves you anyway? What a waste! Mac, you *have* to get back into music!"

"Maybe..." he sighed, as he rubbed an imaginary spot on the table. "Maybe..."

Sleep eluded her as she tossed and turned. She hugged her pillow, pretending it was Mac, and feeling guilty because she wasn't dreaming about Julian. Loneliness and frustration vied for attention, as she sat on the edge of the bed, trying to enjoy a cigarette. Damn Mac and damn his singing for dredging up feelings she had buried and covered with concrete.

Suddenly, she had an idea. Flipping on the light, she grabbed a pen and notebook and scribbled the first things that came into her mind. As she read over what she had written, she smiled at the words. Then she ripped out the page, folded it, and tucked it into the pocket of the jeans she'd be wearing in the morning. Satisfied, she turned off the light, slipped under the bed covers, buried her head in the pillow and dreamed about a man she could never have.

The wake-up call at six-thirty jolted her into fuzzy consciousness. She remembered Mac and lay with her eyes closed, relishing the delicious thought of him. God, tomorrow was the last day! Julian invaded her reverie. As well, he should, Jessica! You're married and don't you ever forget it!

The icy sting of the shower jolted her into reality. A blast of hot water to melt her blood and she toweled herself dry. With clothes and makeup on, hair brushed and tied back, she was ready to face the morning.

Steaming down the hall, she headed for the cafeteria. Mac was leaning against the corridor wall, waiting for her.

"Mornin', friend!" Sultry smile, eyes with that come-hither look.

"Good morning," she smiled back. She had the greatest urge to flirt. "Of course, I don't know if I ought to thank you for keeping me awake half the night!"

"What's that supposed to mean?" he wondered with an impish grin.

"You and your music did a number on me, and I got all lonely and sentimental."

"Well, you'll be with your husband soon, so he should be able to fix you right up!" His words had a brittle edge.

"Sorry. That wasn't what I meant." She dug in her jeans pocket and withdrew the paper she had scribbled on. "Here. This is for you."

"Should I read it now or later?"

"Whenever. It's yours, so you can do whatever you want."

Trays laden, they found a table in the corner of the dining hall. The table was a small one to discourage others from joining them. Shoving his tray aside, Mac carefully unfolded the paper Jessica had given to him, while she busied herself with prying sections out of her half grapefruit. Every now and then, she stole a glance to see if anything was registering on his face, but she could read nothing in his features that might betray his thoughts. It took him a long time to read what she had written, and she hadn't written that much! Perhaps he couldn't read! She broke her toast into pieces and drank her coffee. She had eaten half her breakfast before he had finished reading her humble offering. God! Why had she ever given it to him? This was embarrassing!

Finally, he folded the paper into his shirt pocket, but he didn't look at her. With his index finger, he traced along the scars on the tabletop.

"I don't know what to say, Jessica," he said softly, after a long moment. "It's exactly what I needed." He took her hand and gently squeezed it.

"It's from my spirit to yours," she murmured. "Maybe we can both do something about the dreams we let go of."

"If what you wrote means anything at all, it hits me where I live. I've got a gut feeling I have to mend some of my broken dreams, or I'll never be truly happy. Last night, when I was singing to you and the other clients, I was happier than I've been in a long time."

"I knew that...I knew that last night. That's why I wrote that for you."

"Did you write this? Or copy it from somewhere? It's beautiful!"

"I wrote it, so it's an original," she assured him, reveling in the praise.

"I love it! I'll treasure it forever," he told her, and then took it from his pocket and read it aloud to her.

"Where do broken dreams go when they die?

Do they flee the way of shattered hopes and lie
In the murky, shadowed tombs
Of the graveyard in my mind?
Are they lost, and then forgot,
Or are they ever after sought?
Dare I hope, and I dare I think that I might find?
Are those whispering, gnawing yearnings
Just the ghosts of dreams returning,
To haunt and taunt the soul that cast them out?
As fragile as a moonbeam,
And elusive as a night dream,
Their murmuring echoes cry me all about.
Their gentle tunes relentless,
Assault my heart's defenses,
And I yearn, and ache, and pray to make them mine.
Betrayal, lies, deceit,
Fall crumbling to my feet,
My spirit sings the song of blood-red wine.
The childhood hopes and dreams had never flown,
Just misplaced, forgot, they really were my own.
And now I surely see,
That I must be true to me.
There's none like me, my soul is all I own."
With tears in his eyes, he put it away.

"Eat your breakfast," she suggested softly. "Group's in about fifteen minutes."

∗

They all sat together, laughing over lunch about their misadventures.

"Yes, sir! I thought they were all heroes when I was a kid!" boomed Red. "Where I come from, they were known as the town drunks, but I thought they had a great life! They carried wine in their topcoats and drank it through straws, and they slept on park benches. I used to think they were lucky to be so free and independent. Never occurred to me that people left them alone because they stunk so bad and were so obnoxious!"

"Phone for you," whispered one of the center's attendants into Jessica's ear.

Excusing herself from the table, she took the call in the lounge.

"Darling, how are you?" Julian's words flew from the receiver, assaulting her ear. "I have a big surprise planned for you. I'll be in to meet you at the Embassy Hotel. I've made reservations. It'll be that special time we always planned to have, but never did. I've missed you so much, in more ways than you can imagine. I can hardly wait to get my arms around you, and show you how much you mean to me! Here's a big kiss to hold you until I can give you the real thing, and all the rest I've been saving up just for you!" A juicy smack into her ear and he hung up. All she had said was "Hello". He hadn't even mentioned Rob.

As she returned to the table, Molly was finishing her tale about pouring vodka into a hot water bottle to conceal it.

"If you think booze tastes bad," Molly giggled, "you ought to taste it when it's flavored with rubber!"

Everyone laughed except Jessica, and Montana, noticing that her friend seemed stricken, moved closer to her.

"Hey, Jess, what's wrong? Is everything okay at home? Was that call bad news?"

"That's one way of putting it," Jessica mumbled.

"Nothing's wrong, I hope," offered Irene.

"Let's put it this way," Jessica said, an edge creeping into her words, "nothing's right. Julian's coming to the city tomorrow to meet me at the Embassy Hotel. We're going to spend some time together."

"Whoopee! Second honeymoon!" cheered Red.

"That's more or less the idea!" she snapped. She looked at Mac whose eyes were blank, watching her over the rim of his coffee cup.

"Oooo! Have a wonderful time!" gushed Molly.

"Yeah. Sure. Thanks." She stabbed a cherry tomato, and it splattered on her plate. She wasn't hungry any more.

⁂

They picked out sandwiches—ham and cheese, turkey, and tuna—and stuffed them into their jacket pockets. Mac held the heavy glass door open, and the crisp evening air tingled Jessica's cheeks. Snowflakes skittering out of the black sky, tickled their noses. Mac unwrapped a sandwich and offered her half.

"Nothing like a picnic in the snow," she laughed. "This is a first for me!"

"Me, too," he mumbled, his mouth full of tuna sandwich.

"What a great idea! Thanks for suggesting it," she said, as she nibbled the bread.

"Time's so short," he said. "We're leaving tomorrow, and I had to have some time for us to talk...alone. That place is a fish-bowl. I couldn't handle supper with the group...not that I don't like them...I needed to be with just you."

They walked a little distance in silence. Jessica felt her hands trembling.

"So, what do you have on your mind?" She was curious. She

thought she knew what he might say. Please don't let it be, she prayed. Don't make it hard for me. It's too difficult already.

"Well, I have so many things to say. Time's running out. I may never see you again." His voice cracked. "You see," he stumbled on, "let me put it this way. I like so much having you for a friend. You've made my time here come alive for me. I care a lot about you."

The blood rose in her cheeks and warmth flooded her body. "I care about you, too, Mac. You've made me see things about myself I'd never have seen in a million years," she told him quietly. "The most important is that I have to live my own life. I can't live in spite of, or under the control of, other people. I love having you for a friend too. You are very dear and very special to me."

"Do you have any dreams for yourself? I mean, beyond staying off drugs and beyond your family?"

"Not really," she admitted. "I did have a big dream once, but my father discouraged me."

"What was it?" he asked.

She looked at what she hoped were his eyes. Damn the darkness! "Gee, it's so dumb, I don't even like to talk about it. I forgot about it so long ago."

"I'd like to know what it was, Jess. I'd like to know things like that about you. You know things about me." It seemed important to him. There was urgency in his words.

She shrugged and then hunched slightly to gather inner strength. "Promise you won't laugh? Okay, here goes," she smiled sadly. "I wanted to be a writer. God knows what I'd have written about. I wrote all the time as a kid. I even won contests at school and once won a citywide writing competition. But my father said that writers starved in garrets, and that I should concentrate on a real career—one with meaning and direction and a built-in retirement plan. So I just gave up and forgot about stories and poetry."

"Don't you ever write at all?"

"Sometimes I jot down a thought or a poem. I used to keep a journal, but that's all, and now I don't even keep a diary." Defeat mingled with her words.

"Why don't you do something about your singing?" she asked quietly, almost whispering the question into the night.

"Maybe because I'm scared...Scared that I can't make it happen."

"Mac, you can do it! I know you can!" she cried. "You're so talented! Give yourself that chance! Never give up! If you weren't terrific, I'd tell you to forget it, but you have so much to offer!"

"I'm giving it serious thought. We'll see."

They walked along in silence, munching their sandwiches. Then he stopped, and said, "I don't really know how to say this, but...Jessica, I know you're going through a bad time at home, and I know you're very married. And I also know you have a deep sense of honor. But I want you to know this...I have very deep feelings for you. I...Christ!" His voice cracked again. "I hate the thought of you going back to that house...with *him!* I get sick every time I think about it!"

Grabbing her arm, he pulled her to him. She didn't resist. She wanted him to hold her close, to touch her, and to kiss her. She never wanted him to let her go. His arms encircled her, and it felt as if she had never left them, that she'd been in his arms since the beginning of time. He kissed her gently, then more deeply; and more gently and firmly he held her. It seemed he couldn't hold her any closer, but his arms were loving and strong. She felt he could never hurt her, no matter how closely he folded her against his body. Tears washed down her cheeks and mingled with the snowflakes until their faces were wet with her tears and the snow. He pressed her head into his sweater and touched her hair.

"Lady," he whispered, "you'll never know. You'll just never know what it is I feel for you."

"I do know, Mac," she sobbed. "I've known for a long time. But it can't be like this! It can't be like this at all!"

He unzipped her jacket and put his hands under her sweater. His hands were ice, and she knew she'd have a difficult time explaining to Julian how she had contracted pneumonia the night before she left the center. But Julian belonged to another world. Her world, at that moment, was Mac, and she longed to have his hands touch her flesh. Extending her arms through the front of his jacket, she wrapped them around him, cursing the cold, and their bulky sensible clothes. Standing there in the snow, they clung together, and she had never felt so loved in her life. In spite of her tears, she chuckled.

"So, what's funny, lady?" he murmured into her neck, teasing her with nibbles.

"Making out in a snow bank! Julian and his dear mother would be so proud of me!"

"You have a wicked mind for one so nice," he whispered into her ear. "What do you take me for? A dirty old man who'd do it in a ditch? If...if we ever get together, you'll be in satin pillows, satin sheets, and satin comforters, the works."

"Plain cotton would be fine. All the silk and satin in the world wouldn't matter if I were with you! Oh, God! What am I saying?" she sighed. "We're in a big enough mess with ourselves without entertaining the thought of sleeping together." But she didn't let go. It felt too delicious to be close to him and to hear his heart beating beneath her cheek. He kissed her neck, her ears, her face, and her hair.

"C'mon, let's walk a bit," she murmured, stirring in his arms.

They untangled themselves, and she placed her arm around his waist. Putting his arm over her shoulder, they trudged through the snow, heading for the lamp at the end of the drive. The night was peaceful and black. Only the sound of their boots scrunching through the snow broke the stillness.

"Mac, please listen carefully to what I'm going to say. It's important."

"Mind if I hold you while I listen?" he asked, as he wrapped her in his arms, kissing her forehead and brushing her wet hair.

"Dearest Mac, I've had warm feelings for you for a long time. Not the first week. You were a disgusting grunge at times. Belligerent and deliberately offensive."

"I like a woman with taste," he laughed. "You recognize quality. Sorry I offended you."

"You didn't really offend me. You astonished me more than anything. But once I got to know the man behind the filthy beard and under the ratty clothes and arrogant swagger, I found a delightful human being. I like you even better now. But, Mac...I don't know what I'm going back to. I don't want to go back, but I must. But I'm not going to dream and hope that if my marriage falls apart, I can run from Julian to you. I'd love to run to you, but that's not fair to you or me. I'd be setting myself up for something starting right now. I can't live with hidden agendas and ulterior motives any more. I'm sick of playing games with my life, and I won't play one with yours."

"Jessica, I want to be there for you!"

"Please don't make this any harder for me than it already is! I have to forget I ever knew you! The issues I have to contend with are muddy at best without my complicating them even more!"

He kissed her lips, her cheeks, her forehead, and her throat. As he held her, she longed to lose herself, pressed to his heart, forever. She had never felt before the intensity of yearning that surged through her soul. It was deeper than mere emotion; it was her spirit. She felt it in her heart. They held each other, listening to the snow crackle. She longed to have him make love to her because she knew that with Mac it would never be simply lust. It would be a tender, loving communion. More important than the communion was being with him. Just to be with him!

"You know, lady, I'd love to hold you like this until the end of my life. Making love to you would be the most joyous thing I could ever do. It's a loving thing, loving you."

"Mac, I can't stand this! I can't live with hope for us. I have to leave here tomorrow with no hope of ever seeing you again. But Mac, you have to do your music! Promise me! Promise me you'll do it! Not for me, but for yourself! If you meet someone else, go for it! Right now, we have nothing to offer each other but problems. You hate your wife; I'm frantic about Julian. We haven't been clean and sober long enough to make life decisions like the one we're tampering with right now. You're separated; I'm still married. And if Julian even suspected that I was less than loyal in my thoughts, he'd carve me up for breakfast!"

"Without hope? God, I need to have hope, Jessica! I've never felt like this in my life!"

"We've known each other for only four weeks," she sobbed. "There's so much you don't know about me, and there's so much I don't even dare tell you!"

"What we've been through and what we've shared in this place, people who've been married for twenty years don't know as much. Most people don't ever go as deep as the stuff the group's argued and cried over." He kept cradling her, and she drank in the faint camphor scent of his woolen sweater, never wanting to forget it.

They walked the rest of the way up the drive, holding hands and kicking the new fallen snow into tiny showers of crystals. Where the drive met the road, they stood under the lamp. Mac held her face up to the light and kissed her so tenderly that she thought her heart would shatter.

"You really are lovely, Jessica," he murmured. "You're a lovely woman, and I love you."

"All teary, and skin splotched from the cold, and hair wet, and eyes red," she sniffled, trying to smile.

"Jessica, listen to me...I love you because you're you. And you have never looked more beautiful than you do now."

Blinking her eyes to free her lashes, which were clogged with slush and tears, she peeked up at him. He had such a marvelous face, strong and kind, fierce and beautiful, yet soft and inviting. His eyes were coal-black pools, fathomless, but warm. Someone was at home behind those eyes. And that someone, she thought, is an enchanting, passionate man with a zest for life.

They stood there under the lamp, cherishing the moment, as snowflakes melted in their hair, and droplets of water trickled down their faces. When at last they made their way back to Glenora, Jessica shuddered at the sight of the front door. At that moment, she didn't want to share Mac with another person, and they had to go to an A.A. meeting in the lounge with one hundred and twenty-seven other clients.

∗⁎

In spite of Mac's presence beside her at the meeting, the two speakers held her rapt attention. They stressed sobriety above all else. Without it, nothing else matters. Loved ones, jobs, money, and freedom can all be forgotten, if we don't get clean and sober and maintain a lifestyle free from mood-altering and mind-bending substances. Without sobriety, we might not have even the lives we thought we had, because alcohol and drugs rob us of everything, demanding our sanity, and sometimes even the breath of our bodies.

The last speaker finished by speaking these words: "God didn't open up the gates of heaven and let me in; He opened up the gates of hell, and let me out." Then he sat down amid enthusiastic clapping and many thanks for sharing his experience, strength, and hope.

As people drifted out of the lounge after the meeting, Mac signaled to her not to leave. "Wait until everyone's gone. We can sit in here and talk, if it's okay with you," he recommended.

The stragglers finally left, after putting the extra chairs away. As the door hushed shut behind the last person, they sat on the sofa in front of the unlit fireplace. Mac put his arm around her shoulder, and she rested her head against his chest. She didn't care if anyone came looking for her; she was sitting with her special friend for what might be the very last time. They had found a tiny corner of comfort in each other, for that tiny fragment of time. She wanted to savor it, treasure it, and tuck it away in her heart, where she could cherish it forever.

He put his cheek against her hair and stretched his long legs out. He talked about his job, and his dream about going back to his singing career. She loved his tales of traveling with his group, his stories about the oil fields, and about the fires in Kuwait. She told him about her childhood, her teaching career, the travel agency, Rob, her shooting lessons, and how she wanted to carve out a life for herself, in spite of Julian.

They talked for hours, touching each other and holding hands. Caressing her arm, he kissed her forehead and brushed her hair with his fingers. As she snuggled closer, his fingers brushed one of her breasts through her sweater. Even through the material, his caress electrified her, and she uttered a moan. It escaped before she knew it was there. He smiled at her, as she lifted her face to look at him.

"Touchy, lady?"

"Only with you," she whispered.

"Someday, lady, if we get together, I'm going to love you so much for so long, you'll beg me to stop."

A luscious fantasy. She knew she should stop it, but she was starved for affection and love, and she pursued it, weaving more tantalizing gossamer into the fabric of her dream.

"Mac, it'll never happen with you."

"What will never happen? That we'll never get together or that you'll never beg me to stop?" He looked at her intently, caught in the web of her silky pipe dream.

"Maybe neither will ever happen. But if we ever see each other again, I'd never ask you to stop," she murmured.

"I don't think you'd have to anyway," he whispered into her hair, as he brushed her cheek with a kiss. "I just want to love you. I'd love to watch you live, and see you well, strong, and happy. God! I'd love to see you get what you want from your life."

"Mac, I want the same for you. If I've learned anything from this hell I've endured, it's to let the other person *be!* Why do we get into relationships and try to control the other person or allow them to control us? It seems to me, people become involved in relationships so they can both benefit from sharing their lives, but they both end up diminished and the relationship becomes larger than life. Pretty soon, the relationship is so important that they sacrifice themselves and the other person to keep it going. That's what's happening to me...I'm less important than Julian and the marriage. It doesn't matter if I crack up, swallow pills, or am so unhappy I want to die—don't let the marriage end. Let Julian live as a widower because I overdosed, but don't let him live divorced."

"Please don't ever overdose again, lady. It'd break my heart to know you did it, and it'd break my heart to know you were so unhappy." He stifled a yawn. "I think we should try to get some sleep."

Hand in hand, they approached the entry to the dorms.

"Jess, if you're ever so sad that you want to do something desperate..."

"I'll find you, no matter what. And I can find you, too. My shooting instructor's a detective. He's the very best of the best."

As she looked up at him, she found his eyes searching her face. "Don't worry, Mac. I have too much to live for. And I want to be the first one to buy the first recording you make."

"I love you, lady. Meet me for breakfast?"

"You're on!" she smiled.

He watched her as she walked down the corridor to her room. Such a beautiful lady, he thought. I wish her eyes weren't so haunted.

✳

Six-thirty came too early it seemed, as she listened to the wake-up call. This was the last day! She was barely catching on to how much she had to learn about life, and they were tossing her out. Perhaps she could pretend to have a serious relapse, and they would let her stay for another month, maybe for the rest of her life. Julian! Dear Mother of God! What was she ever going to do? Had he really thought about things while she was away? Perhaps the nightmare was only that...a nightmare. For sure, she was capable of dealing with it, now that she was off the pills. Don't worry about that now, she thought. I'm having breakfast with Mac!

He was waiting at the same place in the corridor, where she had met him the day before.

"Mornin', lady!" Mischievous grin, eyes twinkling. "Sleep well?"

"You'll never know!" she teased, grinning up at him.

With his hand on her shoulder, they fell into line at the steam table of the cafeteria. He pointed to the table in the corner. "Same place as yesterday?" he asked.

"Why not? I'd rather be alone with you than having to share you with everyone."

"The other day," she said, adding milk to her coffee, after they had settled themselves in their corner, "the day of your show, you seemed rather glum a few times, and your eyes looked empty...I wanted to ask why."

"Thinking about leaving here, I guess. I know what I'm going back to up North...I think it was mostly because I wouldn't be seeing you again."

She fell still, gathering her thoughts, and it was a long moment before she spoke. "Mac, I don't know where my life is headed. I haven't a clue what's going to happen at home. But I'm going to be the best Jessica I can possibly be."

"I admire your enthusiasm and your courage," he told her softly. "I love the way you bubble with your convictions and rambling thoughts. I'll miss you every minute. But I'm going to do what I have to do, too."

"Time is against us, Mac," she said. "It's the last day of summer vacation, and I've fallen in love with the lifeguard and have to leave for school in a few hours."

"Only," he reached out to touch her hand, "I'm not the lifeguard, and you're not going back to school. This, whatever it is, is real life, and it's for keeps."

"Please remember what I said about hope, Mac. I want to hope we'll see each other again, but if I do that, I wouldn't do what I have to do for myself...This is the first time in my life I've finally understood what it means to look after myself. You do what you have to do for yourself, too, Mac, and good things will happen for both of us. The one thing I have to look forward to when I go home is seeing my little boy. I can't tell you how much I miss him. But he needs a strong mom, so I need to heal for myself and ultimately him. You, too, have to do your own healing."

"I know deep down that you're right," he said, his eyes intent on her face. "I also know I'll never forget you."

As they walked to the group session, she wished with all her heart that she wasn't right about saying goodbye to Mac. All her life, she had fought tooth and nail to be right about something, and now that she knew she was doing the right thing, it left a caustic taste in her mouth.

⁎

Group was exquisitely heartrending. Dan surveyed his civilized savages. "One of the most rewarding aspects of my job," he said, "is watching people like you recover. Most of you arrived frightened, lonely, feeling hopeless, and filled with despair and shame. Watching you heal from the devastating effects of your substance abuse and experiencing your growth through the days, and then seeing you bloom with vigorous life and new hope, has been like watching a garden burst into blossom. The saddest thing is saying goodbye. You're on your own to shape your lives as you will."

Members, in turn, recalled how he or she entered treatment and what they had learned. All were positive that without each other, none would have recovered and grown. In spite of all the turmoil, hysterics, arguing, and tears of the last four weeks, it had been a time to be remembered and treasured forever. They had grown closer together in four weeks than a family does in a lifetime. Each had been willing to share pieces of his or her life because the others had willingly opened their own storybooks. They had learned to live clean and sober in Glenora in order to live clean and sober in the real world.

Flamboyant to the end, Montana vowed to visit Riverbend to "see how you rich bitches live!"

Jessica didn't disappoint anyone by not crying. "God knows you probably wouldn't recognize me if I wasn't weeping or tearing my hair or throwing a fit. But my tears now are ones of joy because I've learned so much and those of sadness because I'm leaving all of you. And," she challenged Montana, "I can assure you that us 'rich bitches' aren't quite as rich as you think! However," she conceded, one arm around the slightly more demure ex-street walker, "I'm wealthier in wisdom because of you."

Hugging Dan, she said, "The first time I met you, I liked you. You never told me what to do, but you phrased things so I answered my own questions. Because of you, I learned I could think and trust my feelings, no matter how crazy they might be. God bless you for the gift of myself."

He smiled at her. "Treat yourself well, Jessica. You don't know it yet, but a whole new world is waiting for you when you discover who you are...And remember, this is not a dress rehearsal; life is in session. Live each day to the fullest."

⚜

After lunch, the members of the group said goodbye again. Everyone promised to phone and to write or e-mail everyone else. Within herself, Jessica knew that once away from Glenora, the real world would hit each one, and the only envelopes they would be mailing would contain checks in payment for bills.

Mac helped carry her bag to the front door. Her cab was already waiting and the driver took her suitcase. The moment she had been dreading had arrived. She looked up at Mac, trying to be nonchalant, but it was impossible. His face was a mask, revealing nothing. No emotion glimmered in his eyes. She touched his cheek, brushing it lightly with her fingers.

"I can't say goodbye," she choked. "It's too hard."

"Then don't say anything at all," he whispered, encircling her with his arms and crushing her against him. His kiss was tender, strong, sweet, and filled with such love, she felt her heart bursting with longing for him. When he released her, he gazed into her eyes with ones that were filling with tears.

"My most precious Mac!" she gasped, "I love you more than words can say." Turning, she fled through the front door and down the steps. The cabbie held the door for her as she bolted into the back seat. She prayed Mac wasn't watching.

She never looked back as the car sped down the driveway.

She wouldn't allow herself to look back, knowing that a piece of her life was still within Glenora's walls. Touching her heart, where she knew Mac belonged, she closed her mind to what might have been if it had been another time, another place, and another world. She had too much to deal with. But she couldn't stop crying, because even though Mac was in her heart, he wasn't holding her in his arms and laughing beside her.

Chapter Eight:
Scrambled Eggs for Breakfast

THE BELLBOY UNLOCKED THE DOOR FOR JESSICA, AND SHE STEPPED INTO THE SUITE. He deposited her bag and tote on the luggage shelf. Digging in her purse for tip money, she thanked him as she handed him a generous gratuity, and then waited until he had closed the door softly behind him as he left. She glanced around the suite. It was luxurious and lavish; probably the most expensive the hotel had to offer. As she stepped onto the lush carpet, she realized Julian hadn't yet arrived. Good! That gave her some time to unwind and prepare for the real world, which held a real husband, who was really wealthy, and who had a real problem.

Hanging up her coat, she wondered how she should play her role when Julian entered the suite. Should she be coy, flirtatious, understanding, happy, terrified, solicitous, upfront and honest, intense, serious, or light-hearted? Should she be delighted to see him or pretend she didn't know him? Why worry? she thought. Whatever strategy I use will be the wrong one, so I'll let him take the lead. I'll let him think he has control while I take a reading on the situation.

She explored the suite, the main color theme of which was

French blue, a hue easy on the eyes and senses. The living room had massive sofas with pillowy cushions, and the enormous bathroom delighted her with its immense Jacuzzi tub. The gorgeous bedroom had a king-sized bed, and tiny twinkling lights, set into the carpet, were reflected in the totally mirrored ceiling, lending a touch of fantasy, romance, and slight perversion. She had never before been in a bed with mirrors on the ceiling.

When she heard the knock at the door, she jumped, as startled as a deer at the snapping of a twig in the woods.

"Who is it?" she squawked.

"Darling, it's me!"

As she opened the door, her heart leaped into her throat, her knees turned to slush, and her stomach lurched against her rib cage. He swept into the room with a suitcase and three huge boxes, which were wrapped in silver gift paper with bows and streamers fluttering as he tossed them onto the floor, before he gathered her into his arms.

"Oh, my darling, at last!" His kisses covered her neck, her lips, her hair, and her hands, while his arms twined around her like Virginia creeper. If she hadn't known better, she'd have thought an over-zealous chimpanzee was mauling her.

"Let me look at you!" He stepped back, his face glowing with pleasure, making him look like one giant smile. "Dearest, you look more ravishing than ever! You'll never know how much I've missed you!" And he embraced her again. "My love, my love, my love! It's so good to have my arms around you! I can't believe you're here!"

Considering their last encounter, she decided to be guardedly friendly and to take it one step at a time. Cautious, the doctor had said about the pills. She hadn't been, and it had landed her in serious trouble. Well, caution might be most prudent in this situation.

As gleeful as a child with a new Nintendo game, he released her. "I have a few things for you!" He stooped and picked up the boxes. "Here, let me put them on the sofa so you can open them."

Sitting down with the gifts, she suspected she was being bribed. On the other hand, it was possible he was being sincere. The parcels were large, and the biggest one was the heaviest. She selected that one to open first. As she untied the ribbon, he perched on the armchair opposite her, as eager as a child on Christmas morning. She ripped the paper, opened the box, and stared at a silver mink coat, trimmed with silver fox.

"Julian, I don't know what to say! It's...gorgeous!" she gasped.

"Put it on! I had it made especially for you! The furrier still had your size on file, but he said if it doesn't fit, he can adjust it."

He helped her as she slipped it over her shoulders, and she ran to the bedroom to admire it in the full-length mirror. Stunning was the only word to describe that treasure of a coat. Silently praying for the creatures that gave their lives for it, she spun around the room in the furrier's creation.

The second box revealed a black lace and satin peignoir and nightgown. The coat, long-sleeved and full, was trimmed with marabou on the cuffs and along the hemline. The gown, what there was of it, was simply cut, much like a loose slip, and had a slit up one side—Julian had a fetish for nightgowns with slits—tiny straps, and a lace bodice which, Jessica calculated, plunged to her knees. This probably means he'd like to screw me, she surmised.

The third package contained a favorite dress style, a straight-cut, tailored, simple cream-colored linen cocktail dress, with short sleeves and a round neckline. Also within the third gift-box, she found a small black velvet box. Opening it, she gazed at a heart-shaped diamond watch, with heart-shaped diamond earrings, and a pendant to match. These gifts, she thought, probably mean he's very sorry for his abhorrent behavior and now wants to take me out to dinner. And I can't say I have nothing to wear.

"Shall we go out and celebrate our reunion?" he suggested, as he nuzzled her neck and nibbled her ear, while she checked out her new dress and jewelry in the bedroom mirror. Julian had exquisite taste.

"That sounds like a smashing idea!" she agreed readily, thankful he hadn't suggested a brief bedroom skirmish. She needed time to adjust to his enthusiastic welcome. After all, their last scuffle had left her with such shame and anguish that she had attempted to take her life.

⁂

"Thank you for such a marvelous welcome," Jessica smiled at her husband. She paused as the waiter removed the remains of their chateaubriand and asked if they would care for more Perrier.

"Thank you, no," replied Julian, looking into his wife's eyes and reaching for her hand. "God, Jess, I love you," he said softly. "I love you so much that my heart is filled only with you."

"I can't tell you how happy I am!" she breathed across the table, studying his handsome face.

"Sweetheart, this is a new beginning for us. We can forget the last few awful months, my precious Jessica. I know it's because I drank that I behaved so abominably."

You weren't drinking when you raped me before you left for Germany, she thought, and tucked the information into the back of her mind.

"I haven't had one drink ever since you went to the treatment center, not even a glass of wine with meals. And do you know what? I really enjoy not drinking."

Should she throw caution to the wind and accept him at his word? Deciding to wait and see, she encouraged the conversation to continue.

"I'm very happy right now, and I adore being with you when I see the man I married, instead of the maniac you become when you drink. But I paid a terrible price for the joy I have now."

"You'll never have to pay that price again." He kissed her fingertips. "I know how horrifying it was for you, because I've experienced what I put you through. I've never told you this before, but my dad was a brutal man."

Binkie had told her she'd seen Lydia bearing the bruises of old Mr. Bothwell's wrath. It hadn't occurred to her that perhaps Julian was also a recipient of his father's rage and abuse.

"Was he cruel to you?" she asked.

He stared at the tablecloth, brushing a few crumbs into his hand and dropping them onto a sideplate. "Yeah...It...it was God-awful at times. He laid beatings on me many times."

"Julian, why didn't you tell me this before? I'm your wife for God's sake!"

"I just couldn't, Jess! I was too ashamed! And it's a family secret. Don't breathe a word to anyone! Mother would kill me! Dad was a whiz at making money, but a holy terror at home. Mother took a lot of whippings too. He scared the bejesus out of me! I grew up with the kind of hell I put you through. It isn't right, and it isn't fair. I never want to see you or Rob suffer like that again. My darling, can you forgive me? My apologies come from the bottom of my heart." His eyes swam with tears as he

349

held her hand tenderly.

He had won her sympathy. Champion of the underdog, the first to go the aid of a suffering animal, she was a woman who sobbed through sad movies. "My poor, sweet Julian. I'm here for you if you ever want to talk about it. That must have been terrifying for you!"

He continued, now toying with a knife, the edge of which he ran along the creases of the cloth. "I'm considering seeing a psychiatrist. Not in Riverbend, of course..."

"Of course, I'm in full agreement. Tongues will wag. You need the anonymity. You need to feel safe." She gave him the reasons he need not seek professional help in his hometown.

"I need to root out some of those old tapes and messages my father drilled into me when I was just a little kid. I've been busy while you were away," he announced proudly. "Don't ever let it be known," he said, lowering his voice conspiratorially, his eyes darting around the dining room as if there were a secret agent behind every potted tropical plant, "but I've watched a lot of talk shows recently—even Dr. Phil—and some of them have dealt with spousal abuse. It was agonizing for me to sit through them, but I concluded that the pain held some truth. I even went so far as to pick up a book about it, and I know how sickening it's been for you. Jess, I'm going to spend the rest of my life making it up to you. Please, please forgive me."

Tears glistened in her eyes and, in the candlelight, she saw that his face glowed with sincerity and love. So intent was she on listening to his petition for pardon, she never noticed that, not once, did he ask her about Glenora.

⁂

Stretched out on the king-sized bed, Jessica gazed up at the mirrored ceiling to see their reflections, seemingly afloat in black space, with stars dancing and flickering around them. Julian was sprawled face down on the sheet, smothering himself in his pillow, while she lay beside him, enjoying the flavor of a cigarette after passion. It had been delightful, she decided, to watch in the ceiling mirrors as Julian did what he was a master at doing—making wild, scrumptious love to her.

Pulling the blankets around herself and covering Julian as well, she lay back and contemplated her day. One thing Dan had cautioned her about was tempestuous mood swings. Saying goodbye to Mac had been excruciating, and her heart had wept her lament as the taxi had whisked her to the hotel. And now Julian had proclaimed his intention to seek therapy for himself, to aid in his own recovery from parental brutality. It had been, all in all, a day of seething emotions. She was glad it was over, and that she was safe, secure, and sober.

Dan had been right; something wonderful would happen when she found out who she was. As she listened to Julian's gentle snores and rhythmic breathing, she thanked God her dreams for both of them were going to come true after all.

She thought of Mac, his laughter, his sparkling eyes, and his passionate music. Mac knew about Julian. But Julian must never learn about Mac! Her husband might be considering psychiatric therapy, but she knew that if he suspected anything amiss, he would have her head on a platter, served with scrambled eggs for breakfast. Her husband deserved her loyalty and fidelity forever. By bringing his monster to the surface...his father's sadistic aggression...she now knew what the enemy was. She was no longer shadow boxing in the dark with a phantom.

Rising from the bed, she flicked off the carpet lights, bathing the room in blackness. Walking to the window, she pulled the curtain aside and peered out at a city alive with neon, halogen, fluorescent, and incandescent lights, shimmering, sparkling, twinkling, flashing, and ironically, some glaring and offensive to the eye. Insulated from the noise in their suite, she heard no sounds from the street twenty floors below, although traffic was snarled at two intersections, and a gang of teenagers danced down the sidewalk. She watched as an old man, tattered and limping, struggled down the street, dragging a small cart.

She raised her eyes to the sky, finding a few faint stars above the city's garish reflection against the atmosphere. The plump, but waning moon, with no clouds to obscure it, hovered in a sea of wispy exhaust fumes from the streets. Glenora seemed only to be a fantasy from another world. It was a beautiful, timeless, and mystical mirage.

"May God keep you safe, Mac. I'll never forget you," she whispered into the night.

⚜

"It's great to have you back, Jessica. How're you feeling? You're looking good."

"Casey, you've no idea how glad I am to be back. You missed me?"

"You bet! Any teacher would miss his best student. You done any dry firin' to keep in shape?"

"Guns weren't exactly welcome at the center, Casey. But I've practiced for the last day or two. Is it okay if I try some target practice? I'm not into the crouch position yet, but I'd like to make sure my sighting's still on."

"Anything you say!" he grinned.

"By the way, how did you find out where I was? I loved the card you sent, but I was mystified about how you knew what happened to me."

Holding up his hands, he stepped backwards. "Uh, uh, darlin'. I never reveal my sources!"

"Please!" she implored. "My curiosity will kill me!"

"Your curiosity can have you embalmed! I'm not saying a word! I'll give you a hint, though. It isn't anyone you know. By the way, how's my buddy, Julian?"

"Casey," she said, as she clicked the cylinder open and loaded it, "if you're such great pals with my husband, why don't you know yourself? Don't you ever see him?"

"Yeah, of course, I see him. Guess I like to hear myself talk. Habit mostly. I always ask about people I'm thinkin' about."

She narrowed her eyes at him, as she clicked the cylinder back into the revolver, checking the safety. "I don't know about you, Casey. You're cunning, baffling, and devious."

"That I am, Jessica. That I am. Way of life. Now, c'mon, I want to see if you can still shoot straight. You're sure you're feelin' better?"

"Honest, Casey, I *am* better! I'm grateful I went to Glenora, but things were a little dicey before I left..."

"Yeah, I know. I was concerned about you."

"Why on earth would you be worried about me?" Wasn't she the consummate actress? Didn't she look good on the outside, even when she felt like a nest of centipedes on the inside?

"I could tell," Casey said. "Mostly your eyes. I can tell a lot by readin' faces. You changed. You weren't the same lady I first met. You started to look lost and haunted."

"I did?" No Academy Award this year!

"Yep! Now c'mon. Let's see you shoot!"

It felt exhilarating to pull the trigger, hear and feel the BAM! and know that the bullet hit target zero. Every shot blasted into the "x" area. A half hour was all she able to handle; her arms and wrists ached.

"Ever thought of getting a semi-automatic?" Casey wanted to know, as they sat sipping Cokes in the coffee shop at the range.

"What's that?"

"It keeps firing as long as you hold the trigger. No need to cock it."

"No," she replied, scrounging in her jacket pocket for cigarettes.

Casey leaned over and lit the one she pulled from her package. "Just a thought, Jessica. You know, Sherwood Park is a swanky part of town. You've already been broken into once. A semi might be worth considering."

"With all the security we have now, it's a wonder we can even enter our own home without a police escort. Besides, I'll never use the damned gun. I can't kill anyone."

"Perhaps if it came down to the wire, you'd have to," Casey said quietly.

She shivered. The coffee shop was warm, but she suddenly felt a chill.

❄️

"I don't know how you talked me into this, Rosalind, but if I don't kill myself, I swear I'll get even!"

"Uh, uh, Jess, that's not part of the deal. You said if I went skating with you, then you'd come skiing with me."

"How in hell do you fasten these stupid things?" Jessica whined, as she pretzeled over, fumbling with the clips on her boots with mittened hands.

"God, Jessica, you're worse than a kid! Here, let me help!" Rosalind snapped in exasperation.

Snap! Snap! Click! Click! In five seconds, Jessica was earthbound in her gigantic ski boots.

"Now slip your boots into the bindings like this." Rosalind demonstrated. "They're safety bindings, which'll open if you take a tumble...and you're not going to do that!"

"What do I do if I lose my skis? Run down the hill after them?"

"You won't lose them! Nobody loses skis!"

"That's only because I haven't been here before."

"Okay, here's the plan," advised Rosalind. "We're at the lower parking lot now. All we have to do is ski down to the chalet to meet your instructor. It's only a short distance."

"Roz, I haven't been on skis since I was a kid! And that was skiing in ditches! These are bloody mountains! I didn't mean that promise. I lied!"

"I've told you a hundred times, you'll be on the bunny hill, Jess. The bunny hill is perfect for you."

"I wish you'd stay with me," Jessica complained as she faltered after Rosalind, tangling her poles around her skis.

"Just follow me, Jess. You're doing swell. Don't forget, we meet at the chalet at four after your lesson. You're doing fine."

"We haven't left the parking lot yet, Rosalind, and it's *level!*" Perspiration beaded her forehead.

When they arrived at the turn to descend to the chalet, Jessica's eyes popped in horror. "I'm supposed to go down there? I'll never make it! This is the highest peak in the Swiss Alps!"

"Jessica," mothered Rosalind, "this is a *small* hill. Don't worry about it. You'll be all right."

Digging her poles into the snow, Jessica cursed her friend

under her breath. "One broken neck coming up!" she hollered after Rosalind's hot pink jacket.

"Look how easy it is," pleaded Rosalind. "Flex your knees and shift your weight from leg to leg to make your turns."

Gingerly, Jessica followed the instructions and wiped out with her first shift of weight. "I should've brought a toboggan," she muttered as she struggled to untangle herself. Heaving herself to her feet, she maneuvered behind Rosalind, who waited patiently, silently whistling under her breath.

It was a glorious late-March afternoon, with sunshine glinting off the snow. A southern breeze tickled the senses of the skiers enjoying the slopes beneath a spotless blue sky. In midweek, there were only a few people on the hill. With five inches of powder at the top of the mountain and packed snow near the chalet, Rosalind was anxious to attack the black diamond runs. Ski season was almost over, and she wanted to cram in as much action on the hills as she could.

"Here I come!" yelled Jessica, as she directed her skis, shifted her weight, and forgot not to nail her poles into the snow in front. Another wipeout. "I'll never make it!" she grumbled as she rolled herself up onto her feet.

"Sure you will!" encouraged Rosalind. "After one lesson, you'll love it."

"Why do I need an instructor, Roz? Why can't you teach me?"

"Did your best friend teach you how to drive? Is Julian giving you shooting lessons? Need I say more?"

Five minutes later, Jessica was away from the gentle slope, punctuated with pines, and on the bare, hard, packed snow of the descent leading to the chalet. For the first time in her life, she wished she were a fly, with its natural ability to stick to inflexible surfaces. She felt her skis take on a life of their own, sliding and slipping on the hard snow.

Rosalind coached her. "Bend your knees, and shift your weight...Take your poles out of the snow, Jessica!"

"Can you ask the instructor to come up here, *please!*" bleated Jessica.

She could hardly wait to get off that mountain and onto the bunny hill. Maybe she could pick her way down this incline, by keeping her skis parallel to the hill. Carefully, carefully, she inched her way to the chalet.

Rosalind stood by to keep her company and to coax her, beg her, encourage her, and to make petitions to heaven for her, while Jessica's one thought was that once she made it safely to the bunny hill, she'd be off this suicide run.

It took twenty minutes to achieve the lower chalet. Triumphantly, Jessica turned to view the mountain she had descended at the risk of life and limb. To her dismay and discouragement, the parking lot was only a few yards away.

"You stay here, and I'll go find your instructor." Rosalind skimmed off, returning with a blond, gray-eyed, vitamin-packed parcel of gusto and vigor. "This is Mark," she declared. "He's going to show you the ropes. I'll meet you in the lounge at four."

"Do they serve morphine cocktails to people who are injured?" wondered Jessica.

Mark laughed over his shoulder as she followed behind. She was a whiz on flat ground so the bunny hill should pose no problem as she was positive it would be no more than a small knoll. They must be close to the bunny hill now, she thought, as she swished over the packed snow, keeping her eyes to the ground to avoid any small bumps. In no time, she looked up to find herself in a lineup for the chair lift.

"Why are we here, Mark?" she asked. "I'm a beginner, and I thought we were going to the bunny hill."

"We are," Mark replied. "We're taking the chair."

"The chair?" she squawked. "*No one* said anything about any *chair!* I'm supposed to be on the bunny hill! There's some mistake! Chair lifts don't go to bunny hills! They go the tops of mountains!"

"That's where the bunny hill is. Up near the top."

"And how do I get down from up there? Is there a chair to bring me down after my lesson?"

"We ski down, Mrs. Bothwell. You'll be fine. Trust me. I'll be with you every inch of the way."

Jessica reckoned it was millions of thousands of inches to the bottom. "Is there any other way down?"

"We have a ski patrol to take injured people down on toboggans, and we have rescue helicopters. Or you can always walk. But the best way is to ski. My job is to teach you how to do that."

Jessica eyed him. Smug little bastard, she thought. He's probably Scandinavian and has been on skis since he was in the womb.

"You better stay close to me," he said. "We're on the next chair. Here. Just stand here. When the chair is directly behind you, sit down, and the chair will grab you."

Anxiously, she kept her eye on the approaching chair. At what she judged to be perfect timing, she sat down. The chair brushed over her. As she gathered herself from the snow, Mark dragged her away from the following missile, helping her to her feet.

"Don't worry about that, Mrs. Bothwell. That happens all the time. Just stay calm. Here comes another chair. Now...sit!"

The chair lifted her and lifted her. She was airborne! Not

daring to look down, she clung to her poles and Mark's sleeve. Realizing she was safe, she glanced over the side. A little boy, about five years old, was flying over the moguls, while behind him, a youth flew down the slope on a snowboard, like a surfer. Cringing ever so slightly at the height, she looked around and gasped at the beauty. The chair was silent as it glided over the pine trees, their branches tipped with the overnight snowfall.

"It takes about five minutes to reach the top, so you can relax and enjoy the scenery." Mark's smile revealed orthodontic perfect teeth. "Isn't this fabulous, Mrs. Bothwell?"

"I never realized how wonderful this was. My husband skis, but I never got around to joining him. Now I'm determined! That little boy back there inspired me! I'm going to learn a lot today, Mark. I'm not giving up until I can ski!"

"That's the spirit, Mrs. Bothwell! We like to hear enthusiasm! Okay," he said, pointing ahead, "there's where we get off. Now when you get off, just let the chair nudge you."

"What happens if I don't get off?"

"You *have* to get off!"

"Yes, but what happens if I don't?"

Mark wet his lips and gazed at the slopes, squinting thoughtfully. "If you don't get off, the safety switch will stop the chair, and you'll have to wait for the ski patrol to take you down. Okay, here we go!"

Jessica catapulted from the chair, barely feeling the crash as she scrambled after her skis, which slithered down the incline. Mark was at her side instantly with her poles.

"Don't worry about that, Mrs. Bothwell. That happens all the time. Just stay calm."

Snapping her boots into the bindings, she thanked God she couldn't see the bottom of the mountain. God had, with mercy, obscured the bottom with a million pines.

"Okay, Mrs. Bothwell, watch me, and I'll show you how to shift your weight...See? Isn't that easy?"

To her, it looked as easy as mastering calculus, but her spirit was determined. She longed to fly over the snow, skim through the trees, dance over the moguls, and glide around the drifts. Positioning herself as one does when lining up a golf ball, she was off, sailing, twirling, zooming, and picking up speed. This was freedom! Until she hugged the branches of her first tree.

"That was wonderful, Mrs. Bothwell, for your first attempt. But we do have to be careful of the trees. You can really get hurt by colliding with trees. Don't worry about it. That happens all the time. Just stay calm."

Digging her way out of the bush, she was ready to tackle the hill. No bloody hill was going to keep her from the bottom!

"Maybe just a wee bit slower, Mrs. Bothwell. And if you find you're going out of control...here, I'll show you how to stop."

With a graceful turn, he dug his skis into the powder, sending up a shower of crystals.

"Has anyone ever asked you where the white goes when snow melts?" she asked.

"Not yet, Mrs. Bothwell. And I don't know the answer. Now let's get you to the bottom, so we can come up again."

"Sure!" she agreed, aiming for that gentle curve.

"No! No! No! Mrs. Bothwell! That's the black diamond run! That's only for experienced skiers! We're doing the green diamond run! See the sign on that tree? That's for us!"

"Okay!" she grinned, breathing in the cold, crisp air. God! This was fun!

Eyes front, she slid into position, and gradually the skis gave way to speed as they hissed through the snow. How was she supposed to stop these damned things? She couldn't crash into another tree. Shifting weight was the game plan, but she couldn't turn the way she wanted to. Desperate, she shifted her weight the other way. It worked. She flew up the black diamond run as skiers whizzed past her, waving, yelling, and screaming. Her speed didn't decrease; she was going up at the same velocity as she had been traveling down the hill. She couldn't stop! But the trees would interrupt her hurtling up this bloody run. With the shift of weight that had worked to propel her onto this spine-tingling mission, she headed for the trees and six feet of powder. Her landing was silent as the pine dumped its burden of snow on top of her. Spluttering the slush from her face, she felt around for her skis.

"Wow, Mrs. Bothwell, that was great! I've never seen anyone do that before!"

"You're telling me this is something that doesn't happen all the time?" She wiped the melting snow from her face. "Thank God I did something original!" she muttered as she snapped on her skis.

"The only problem with what you did, Mrs. Bothwell, is that it's very hazardous. If anyone hit you, you'd both be injured, perhaps fatally. Remember, we're going *down* the hill!"

Ten falls and six trees later, Jessica was searching through the lift lineup for Mark. God! Where was he? He whooshed to a stop beside her, his skis creating a small blizzard.

"You really should stay with me, Mrs. Bothwell, at least until we get things together. I lost you in that last clump of trees."

As she hurtled off the chair at the top, she knew she'd have to take landing lessons. Once again, Mark helped her retrieve her skis and poles, and coached her to the bottom. Only five tumbles this time and no trees.

The third crash landing from the chair was discouraging.

"Don't worry about it, Mrs. Bothwell. It takes time to learn how to get off these things. Just stay calm. Do you see your skis?"

"No. They went into the powder, I think...Oh, there they are."

Halfway down the hill, she was tired and hot and knew that if she heard one more "Don't worry about it, Mrs. Bothwell", she wouldn't stay calm, and she'd strangle her instructor.

"Look, Mark, you've been wonderful. But I'm a bit tired, and I think I'll call it a day. You go and have fun, and I'll go and sit in the bush for a while."

"Are you sure, Mrs. Bothwell?" His eyes registered surprise. "I thought you weren't going to give up?"

"I'm not! Just for today, I am. I'll be fine."

"Okay," he grinned, and he was off, hot-dogging down the slope, pelting the air with snow.

Taking off her skis, she trudged across the hill pulling a ski in each hand, with the packed snow squealing and groaning beneath her boots. Two skiers swished to a stop beside her.

"Ski patrol ma'am," said one. "Is there a problem? Do you want us to get a toboggan?"

"Thanks, no." She flashed her brightest smile. "I'm a little tired, and I thought I'd rest over there." She pointed to the pines, inviting her with their peace and tranquility.

"Well, please be careful and watch out for skiers coming down. Have a nice day."

"You too," she sang as they whisked away, and she continued to trudge across the hill into the bush.

A cigarette would be nice, she thought. I'll just sit on the fallen tree and have a smoke, and then ski down to join Rosalind.

But no one had told her about the bush without skis or snowshoes. In less than an instant, she found herself up to her waist in powder. It was much like falling into a white coalmine. Floundering, gasping, and astonished at the sudden descent, she burst into laughter. So this is skiing, she mused. I'll never make it to the Olympics, but I love it.

She struggled her way to the tree and pulled herself onto the fallen trunk. Lighting a cigarette, she watched from her haven as skiers whooshed and whizzed by. She might not be a professional, but at least she was a beginner. She was proud to be an amateur because it was better than not skiing at all.

Glancing at her watch, she saw that it was almost time to meet Rosalind. Alone in the hush of the trees, a sparrow scolded her for disturbing his corner of the world. She blew the indignant bird a kiss. "Bless you, little one. Thanks for lending me your tree."

Clambering through the powder, she dragged her skis behind her and climbed out of the loose snow onto the packed run. From this lofty pinnacle, the bottom was visible, and she knew she could make it on her own.

Spring! How Jessica loved it! Digging in the loamy earth to make beds for her plantlings, she tucked them in and watered the soil. If the weather stayed warm, in no time, she would have an impressive display of floral delight.

"Really, Jessica, you ought have a gardener do that," sniffed Lydia, as Jessica proudly showed her the fruit of her labor. A few tiny plants hinted a promise of the splendor to come by winking flashes of color at them. "I must say, Julian really does let you have much more say in things than his father ever did with me. You're certainly a headstrong young woman. And why on earth would you ever plant marigolds? They're such common things with such a repulsive odor!"

"I think they're glorious," replied Jessica. "Such vibrant colors! And their blooms are enormous. Last year, I had plants that bragged about their health with blooms as big as roses."

"And that atrocious birdbath! What a silly idea! One always has so many droppings around when one has those things. All you're doing is encouraging birds to dirty your patio."

"It's certainly nothing worse than the sewage and pollution we're dumping into our rivers, lakes, and oceans. Please loosen up, Mother Lydia. I love doing this, and you don't have to clean up after the birds...I do!"

"Well, I'll have coffee with you, and then I really have to leave. I must get home because the girls are coming for bridge this afternoon."

"It was thoughtful of you to stop by," Jessica smiled as she followed Lydia into the kitchen where coffee was ready. Holding her temper with Lydia was becoming more and more difficult, but she didn't want to upset the applecart by being downright rude to Julian's mother. Besides, she had scarcely seen the woman since her return from Glenora. This impromptu visit would come to an end soon, she silently prayed.

"And how are you feeling, my dear?" Lydia asked as Jessica scoured her hands at the sink, using a small hand brush to remove the soil from her fingers.

"I'm doing much better, thanks for asking, Mother Lydia," she answered, drying her hands, and reaching for coffee mugs.

"Well, personally, I can't see a bit of difference in you... Maybe a bit more intractable," Lydia said, seating herself at the table.

"You didn't have me throwing up on your carpet." She poured

the coffee into the mugs and passed one to Lydia, fighting the desire to dump the steaming liquid into her mother-in-law's lap.

Lydia daintily dropped a sugar lump into her coffee. "Well, I see no reason for you to have taken those silly drugs in the first place. You have so much more than you did when you married my son."

"Yes," grimaced Jessica, twisting her mouth into what she hoped was a smile. Montana was right; this was how wars erupted. "Without Julian, I suppose I'd be living in a tar paper shack."

"Exactly!"

"Mother Lydia, I don't know if you're aware of this, but did you know that Julian has beaten me within an inch of my life? Not just once, but on several occasions? Did you know the conditions I was trying to contend with?" Dear God, cut out my tongue! she thought.

Lydia fixed her with that special squint reserved for errant daughters-in-law. "I can't say I'm surprised. What did you do to prompt his doing such things? I'm sure Julian must have had good reasons for disciplining you!"

Jessica couldn't believe what she was hearing. May God cut out Lydia's tongue!

This conversation was going nowhere, its major accomplishment being to frazzle Jessica's tolerance level. The day had started out so sunny, but thunderclouds were beginning to form on the horizon of Jessica's emotional weather-screen. She prayed Lydia would finish her coffee in short order and leave before any more of a storm brewed. The best way to deal with Lydia was not to deal with her. After all, Rosalind had said the woman cheated at bridge.

Glancing at the kitchen clock, Jessica said, "Oh, my, I see the time is running on. You said you had to be leaving soon, and I don't want to keep you from your engagements." She whisked Lydia's mug from under her nose, dumped the contents into the sink, and hustled the stunned woman to the front door. She stood on the porch, holding Rob's hand as both she and her son waved goodbye to Lydia who was climbing into her car.

"You're welcome to visit whenever you wish, Mother Lydia," she called, "but make sure you can stay longer next time!"

Chapter Nine:

Upping the Ante

RATIONAL REASONING MADE IT SEEM SO LOGICAL.
One evening, curled with Julian on the sofa, watching TV, she asked, "Have you given any more thought to seeing a psychiatrist?"

"Yes, I've been thinking about it. But it's not at the top of my list of priorities any more. You and I are getting along famously, and you're happy. I think I was making too much of it. Besides, all that hell was in the past and Dad is long dead and gone. Time to forgive and forget."

His kisses, and his arms around her, the charity garden parties where he hovered around her with attentive displays of affection, his exquisite love making, his generosity with surprise gifts, and his not drinking, lulled her into responding, "Well, it's an avenue that's always open to us."

⁂

A few evenings later, at supper after a movie, Julian asked, "Why don't you order wine with your chicken, darling? You always did enjoy white wine. Go ahead. Just because I'm not drinking doesn't mean you can't have a little something."

She thought about it before answering, "Well, yes, sweetheart, I think I'd like that. It'd be a treat...but only a half bottle. I can't drink a whole bottle by myself."

"Oh, we'll order the full bottle," he insisted. "I can always help you finish it."

"Are you sure?" she asked, as a finger of fear touched her spine. "I love you not drinking. No, I don't think I will have any wine after all."

"Yes," he said to the wine steward, "the California white Chablis will do. Bring a full bottle and two glasses."

"Julian, do you really think this is a good idea?"

"Princess, I hope you aren't going to start badgering me again. I'll be fine."

⚶

One night, lying in his arms in bed, she asked, "Can't I please go to some of those charity meetings? I'd love to get involved with the 'Relief for Children' organization or raising money for the new wing of the Civic Hospital. I'm sure I can think of oodles of ways to make money."

"Precious," he replied, with a kiss on her forehead, "the only thing I want you to do is be a good wife and mother. Charities demand far too much time. That you attend the functions is sufficient. I'm only thinking about what is good for you."

⚶

Helping him pack for a trip to England, France, and Germany, she wondered again why she wasn't able to accompany him.

"Sweet Jessica, you'd be bored stiff. All I do is attend to business. I'd feel uncomfortable leaving you alone to fend for yourself...but when I get back, let's plan a holiday...maybe Fiji.

"Promise?" she asked, as she looked into his eyes.

"I promise."

It was a glorious morning by the pool, and Jessica and Julian were enjoying morning coffee on the patio.

"Julian, I'm becoming scared and worried."

"Why?" he asked, as he read his morning paper over coffee.

"Well...you seem to be drinking again."

"Darling," he smiled around his paper. His smile held all the cheer of a January blizzard. "Don't worry your sweet little head about it. I learned my lesson about booze. I can control it. Besides, I may never drink again. Who knows? The hangover I have right now might be the last I'll ever have. And, Jessica, don't start your nitter-nattering again."

Jessica kept herself happily occupied every day: She spent joyful hours in activities with Rob, doing laps in the pool before breakfast, going to lunch with Mary-Beth and Rosalind, practicing at the range with Casey, attending her aerobics class, playing tennis with Rosalind, taking drives to the lake, reading by the pool, dabbling in her garden, and puttering in the house. But the nights were becoming long and lonely again. Julian was always busy with the hotels, out of town, attending

Town Council and hospital board meetings, and devoting time to charities.

"Can't you come home early?" she asked, "Rob and I never see you!"

"I can't be home early every night."

"But you're never home early any night!"

"Jess, leave it alone! You live in the lap of luxury! What more do you want?"

"You! I never see you anymore! For a while, you managed to be home for Rob and me, but now you seem to think we no longer exist. And I'm so lonely without you."

"You don't seem to be too lonely when I'm not here. You seem to be keeping someone pretty busy when I'm away." His eyes glittered at her over the rim of his coffee cup.

"Yes! Rob!"

"From what I hear, it isn't Rob."

"Julian, please stop that outrageous accusation!"

"Right, sweet stuff." Rising from the table, he folded his paper, and kissed her cheek. "By the way, please don't bring home any unpleasant social diseases. Why do you think I haven't touched you in weeks? God only knows what you could be infected with!"

As he walked to the front door, she scurried after him. "Julian, this in insane!"

"Maybe your illness is getting to you. I hope you aren't back on those pills again. That would be such a pity." His voice was devoid of emotion as he stroked her hair and then closed the door in her face.

Leaning against the oak door, she wept.

***

Shooting lesson at two. After showering and tying her hair into a ponytail, she pulled on her clothes. As she climbed into the Mustang, a note under the wiper blades caught her eye.

"Listen to the CD, sweetheart. Love, J," she read.

She flipped on the CD player as she whirled the car down the drive. Recognizing the song immediately, she was curious why he had chosen for her to listen to *"Every Breath You Take"* sung by Sting of the musical group, The Police. She had always liked it because of the beat, the arrangement, and the passion. But now as she listened to the words, they took on an ominous, sinister intent. This wasn't a song about love. These were the words of surveillance!

Every breath you take, every move you make,
Every bond you break, every step you take,
I'll be watching you.
...Oh, can't you see, you belong to me?'

"Dear God!" she screamed, her cries drowning out the music. "He's going to drive me mad! He's driving me crazy!"

Her knees gelled, and she gripped the steering wheel, perspiration dribbling down her forehead. As she stumbled from the car at the range, Casey was there to meet her.

"What the hell's goin' on, Jessica?" he asked, as she sagged against the Mustang, gulping in huge gasps of air. He touched her shoulder. "You have an accident or something?"

"I almost hit a kid!" she lied. "He jumped in front of my car! Holy shit! Look at my hands!" They shook and trembled under his gaze.

"Maybe practice isn't a good idea today," he suggested softly.

"You're right!" she smiled through her tears. "If I almost hit a kid, I might end up shooting you!"

⁂

She refused to let him see her fear. As he read his paper and enjoyed a light breakfast by the pool, she leaned over and kissed him.

"Good morning, darling," she smiled. "I hope you slept well."

"I always do. How about you? You seemed restless."

"Oh, I was a bit warm, couldn't get comfortable. May I have the front page of the paper?"

"When I'm finished with it. Where's Rob?"

"Binkie's making him breakfast."

"You know, Jess, I've been thinking. I really should let Binkie go. We put out a lot of money for a housekeeper, and that job really is yours. You seem to have too much time on your hands."

"Let her go?" she asked in shock and dismay. "Julian, she's been with the family for years! She'd be devastated! That really isn't fair!"

"Oh, I'd give her excellent references. It's just a thought. Here you can have the front page now."

⁂

Jessica knew it wasn't her imagination as she watched the bluish-gray Sebring pull in behind her and then blow past her on the freeway. Dear God, she thought, what is Julian up to now? She had seen that car several times before. It was a new menace in her life, as if she didn't have enough threats to her peace of mind already.

That Julian was drinking again unnerved her; that he was staying out later and later each night frightened her because it could lead to him battering her again. His threats to let Binkie go were designed to keep her off-balance; and his accusations about her infidelity were demoralizing and hurtful. But all those ploys were old games. That hideous CD was something that came out of left field, completely ungluing her. But she was certain now, right in this moment of time, that he was upping the ante to drive her over the edge with that car.

She would never have paid it the least attention when she first became aware of it a few days ago. As she had pulled out of her drive onto Sherwood Boulevard, a bluish-gray Chrysler Sebring with tinted windows had slid from a driveway a few doors up and across the street from her home. Meandering down Sherwood Boulevard, she watched in the rearview mirror as the blue car glided behind hers at a discreet distance. It was just one car of many that drove through the neighborhood, except that when she pulled onto the crescent where Rosalind lived, the car followed. Parking the Mustang in Rosalind's driveway, she watched as the Sebring cruised by.

Even that encounter would not have aroused her suspicions, but the next day she drove to the lake with Rob. While they sunbathed and played on the sand, Jessica saw the Sebring whisper past, slow down...and *stop!* Breathless, she peered through the bushes lining the road and separating it from the beach. Whoever was driving that car was faceless because of the tinted windows. With a roar of the engine, the car vanished.

The following afternoon, as she left for her shooting lesson, there was no sign of the car. Not until she was at the end of Sherwood Boulevard, did she spot it. As she wheeled onto the street leading to the thoroughfare, the Sebring pulled in behind her. On the freeway, she gunned the Mustang, weaving in and out of traffic, leaving the freeway by one off-ramp, cruising around a non-descript neighborhood, doubling back to the freeway, and continuing on to the next ramp that led to the range. The blue car followed, seemingly effortlessly. As she parked at the range, the Sebring sailed by.

"I still can't shoot, Casey. Can we just have coffee?"

"Sure. You buyin'?"

"Why not?" She gripped his arm as they entered the snack shop. It felt reassuring to touch a man's muscles, wishing she had her own.

But she didn't tell Casey about the car. How could she possibly tell one of Julian's best buddies that Julian was having her followed?

⁎

The first call came early in the morning as Julian was leaving for the day. No one answered when she said, "Hello...Hello?...*Hello!*"

"Wrong number?" Julian wondered.

"Probably," she purred as she kissed him.

She registered five more hang up calls that day, including two when Binkie answered. But the last call, the one that sent her spinning into the old horror, was the one late that evening when the song "*Every Breath You Take*" responded to her "Hello". She threw the receiver down as if it were an asp.

Not one word did she say to Julian. Not even when the answering machine recorded heavy breathing and that horrid song. Not even when all the calls came from a number that blocked the number of the caller.

Not even when she was unable to sleep.

⁎

Jessica was sure that the calls came from someone deliberately spooking her, and she would have bet her last dollar that Julian was the mastermind behind that miserable mind-bending game. But the car following her was quite another matter. There was real danger involved in being followed by a car. Accidents. Being forced off the road. Kidnapping. Things like that only happened to people on *20/20* and *Investigative Reports*. But wait! That reporting was about real people! She was a real person! Again, Julian sprang to mind as the root cause of this new threat.

To test her suspicious mind, she drove to the Green Tree Mall. No sign of the car. Around and around the mall, she drove, parking here, parking there. Going in and out of the mall. No sign of the Sebring. Where was that car? Maybe she'd take a leisurely drive to the Terrace Lodge Hotel and relax at the wheel.

Lined with pines and spruce, the Lodge Road was pristine and peaceful. When the Sebring suddenly appeared in front of her as it exited a service road, she slammed on the brakes, almost skidding into the ditch. She clung to the steering wheel, unable to breathe.

As she calmed, she knew what she had to do. The Sebring turned onto the Lake Road, and she continued to the hotel. She parked in the "No Parking" zone in front of the Terrace Lodge.

"Hey! You can't park there!" a bellman yelled, rushing over.

"Says who? I'm Mrs. Bothwell! I can park in the goddamned lobby!"

"Who's Mrs. Bothwell?" He was impertinent.

"The wife of the man who signs your goddamned paychecks! And you'd better watch your step or you won't have your goddamned job!" She had never sworn at an employee before, but this was a goddamned emergency!

"Gee, I'm sorry, Mrs. Bothwell, I didn't know."

"That's all right," she said, softening. Maybe this young man with pimples could help her. She smiled at the embarrassed employee. "Have you seen a bluish-gray car with tinted windows go by?"

"No, ma'am."

"If you do, I'm supposed to meet the driver in the lounge. If he stops, please tell him I'm here. It's important. And, by the way, he can park in the no-parking zone too."

"Sure, Mrs. Bothwell!" Eager. So young and eager.

Swinging her purse and trying to look more confident than Hilary Clinton, she sauntered into the lounge, sat at the empty bar, and ordered a soda and lime. If she ever needed a Valium, it was now. If she ever needed her wits about her, it was now.

Twenty minutes, three cigarettes, and two fingernails later, she was still the only guest at the bar. Signing the tab...her goddamned husband could pay for it...she sauntered out, her heels clicking on the slate floor of the lobby.

"Did he come?" she asked the bellman.

"A car of that description drove by twice, Mrs. Bothwell," he said. "It slowed down, but didn't stop."

"Thanks a lot for your help," she smiled, crushing a twenty dollar bill into his surprised hand. "Have a drink after work."

Strolling to her car, as if she was about to take her grandmother on a Sunday afternoon drive, she knelt down at the front bumper, walking her fingers up and down the underside of the metal and chrome. Nothing! Now for the back bumper. She stretched her arm as far she could beneath the undercarriage and felt a tiny round piece of metal. Aha! Success! Why hadn't she thought of this before? Idiot! Not for nothing had she taken that course in undercover work. She smiled to herself when she recalled ripping the house apart trying to find a bug Julian may have planted in their home. With the changes in technology, she wouldn't have recognized a listening device to save her soul, but this one was easy.

The tiny spy came off with a jerk; its magnetic seal broken. It wasn't quite an inch in diameter and a quarter-inch thick, but it was capable of ultra-mischief.

"Come on," she whispered to herself, dropping the gadget into her purse. "Now that I know you're here, maybe I can flush out whoever owns you!"

Her appointment with her hairdresser was for the next day at twelve-thirty. Seating herself in the front window of the shop, she had a clear view of the street while she waited her turn. The blue car skimmed past on the one-way street. Pretending to read a magazine, she flipped through the pages, pondering her next move.

Three times the car circled the block. And then! The driver parked it! He maneuvered it into a spot halfway down the block on the side opposite the salon. And the driver emerged! Jessica saw him! She couldn't get a really good look at him because of the traffic and the people on the sidewalk, but she saw that he was short, rotund, and bald. Not the bone-crusher type. With a slight touch of insanity, she was faintly disappointed to see he was so insipid compared to *Magnum P.I.*, but she felt relieved to know that she could run faster than he could. He disappeared into a restaurant.

Glued to the window and clutching the magazine, she was

377

startled when Harriet called her to the sink.

"Your turn, Mrs. Bothwell!" Harriet called a second time. "What's yo'all lookin' at through that window? You bin sittin' there rippin' up my magazines just starin' outa that window!"

Jessica looked at her hands. Sure enough, the magazine had shredded pages, and tiny scraps of paper littered the floor. She had thought herself so cool.

"Sorry, Harriett. Too much coffee this morning. Can I use your phone? And cancel my appointment for now. I'll re-schedule later."

"Rosalind, I have to see you! Now! Right this minute!"

"Where are you?"

"Chez Francois! I had a hair appointment, but I've just cancelled it."

"You want me to meet you there?"

"No. Meet me at the Diplomat! Can you be there in fifteen minutes? In the lounge?"

⁂

The maître d' met her at the Diplomat's entrance.

"Mrs. Bothwell, how nice to see you! Your friend is waiting for you in the lounge. Let me take you in. How is your husband? And that charming little boy of yours? My, he's so good-looking; he'll break a lot of hearts when he grows up!"

"I certainly hope not!" she laughed. "If he does, I'll break his neck!" Light-hearted conversation. Normal. Amusing. Even in the midst of terror, she was the accomplished actress.

Jessica huddled into a chair opposite Rosalind.

"What's eating you? What's all the mystery? You look as calm as a blender on purée speed. What's happening?"

Rosalind queried.

"I'm being followed," Jessica whispered. "Keep your voice down!"

"Jess, this isn't your imagination working overtime, is it?"

"Don't play Julian with me! Have I ever lied to you?"

"Yes! When you took all those pills on the damned bus!"

"Look, this is life and death! I'm not kidding!" She slapped the electronic device on the table. "Look at that if you don't believe me!"

Rosalind leaned over the table and squinted at the device. "What the hell is that?"

"It's a bug! Goes on cars. It lets the person following you know where you are. He has the equipment to monitor this nuisance in his car!"

"Why are you carrying it in your purse? Smash the damn thing!"

"Not on your life! I want to hand it back to the owner. We'll probably have a visitor in here. I made sure he saw me leave the hairdresser's shop and drove slowly enough to enable him to keep tabs on me. He's short and chubby and bald. What're you drinking?"

"A double scotch on ice."

"Soda with lime," Jessica told the waiter. "Lots of ice." To Rosalind, she whispered, "I'd love to get pleasantly plastered to do the number I have planned for the little gremlin if he arrives."

Rosalind frowned at her dithered friend. "Are you okay, Jess?" she asked softly.

Jessica shook her head, "No, I'm not, Roz. You know who's doing this to me, don't you?" Rosalind nodded. "I'm so bloody frightened. But I don't know what to do!"

"I thought things were better. Can't you talk to him?"

"Can you talk to a wolverine? All I can do is act brave and strong, as if this isn't getting to me!"

Ten minutes later, a short, fat, bald man waddled into the lounge and hoisted himself onto a chair in the corner. He placed an order with the waiter, and Rosalind and Jessica quietly watched as the waiter delivered something in a giant snifter, loaded with cracked ice.

"You stay here," Jessica whispered to Rosalind, taking the bug from her purse.

"You be careful!"

Jessica sauntered over to his table, as confidently as her watery knees would allow. Giving him her most dazzling smile, she held her hand over the snifter, letting the device plunk into his drink.

"What the hell are you doing?" he spluttered.

"Returning your property to you," she smiled. "May I sit?"

"Sure, sure," he blathered. "Be my guest. Bring your girlfriend over, too. I like female company."

"I'm sure you do," she purred. "You seem to like stalking them, too."

"What's that supposed to mean?"

"Well, I'm Jessica Bothwell. And what's your name? Tom? Dick? Harry?"

"Hank. My name's Hank."

"Well, Hank...my, my...I haven't met any men called Hank before. You're the first!" she warbled. "Hank, you and I have something in common."

"We do? What's that?"

"Julian Bothwell. I'm his wife, and you're his snoop."

"Who's Julian Bothwell?"

"Look, Hank, I'd hate to think you're dense as well as being fat and bald," she said, adding an unfriendly edge to her words. "You and I both know what that little device in your drink is, and we both know you've been following me for over a week, maybe even longer. At this point, I don't know and I don't care. I just want you to know you really are a nuisance! But I have a proposition for you."

"What's that?" His beady eyes stared into hers.

"How much is my husband paying you to tail me?"

"That's confidential."

"As confidential as your being dim-witted enough to get caught at your miserable little game?"

"A hundred and fifty a day, plus expenses."

"So...is my husband paying for your drinks, too?"

"Absolutely. That's an expense if I have to watch you in a bar."

She leaned over the table, her face so close to his she could smell garlic on his breath. "Look, Hankie Baby, I think I can make you an offer you can't refuse."

"What's that?" His eyes glittered. Perspiration beaded his forehead and his jowls. "I'm always open to offers."

"I'll bet you are! I'll double what Julian is paying you to follow me, to follow him instead. That's three hundred bucks a day. I can tell you this, Hank; I'm not nearly as interesting to follow as Julian is. I think he's screwing around, and he does some pretty nasty things that I'd like to have documented. Three hundred a day, Hank. That's big money! Much more than Julian is paying you."

Leaning back in her chair, she surveyed his sweaty brow, his polished head, and his acne scars. I'll bet you're a humdinger in bed, she mused, as he twirled his drink in his chunky hands, thinking, thinking, thinking.

He brightened. "Yeah, sure, Mrs. Bothwell. I can do that little favor for you. In fact, I'd consider it an honor working for you. Sure!"

She leaned across the table again so he could see the fire in her eyes. "Listen to me, you obese, over-cooked marshmallow," she hissed. "I wouldn't hire you to babysit a sea slug! You're as brainless as they come! And you don't have any scruples, ethics, or loyalty! You trot your ass back to Julian and tell him you were stupid enough to blow your cover! That I know who you are! And if you don't tell him, I will! He's wasting his money, as well as *mine*, paying flotsam like you to spy on someone who's as interesting as Betty Crocker! And order a jug full of martinis! You look like you need them!"

She pounded back to her table. "Come on Rosalind! The Diplomat will have to be fumigated after serving a cockroach like that one!"

⁂

Julian was home early that evening. It was eleven when he stumbled into their bedroom, where Jessica was watching *Investigative Reports*. He smashed the off-button, plunging the TV into a blank screen, and whirled to face her.

"You're nothin' but a smart-assed bitch!" he slurred. "Christ! What a black day in hell it was when I met you! You're worse than a boil on the butt! If something's got tits or tires, it's sure to cause trouble!"

"It's nice to see you, sweetheart." Her blood congealed in her veins. "Did you have a bad day?"

"Shut your fuckin' mouth, bitch!"

"Julian, if you'd rather have the bedroom to yourself, I can sleep in the nanny's room." She picked up her book, edging toward the door.

"Yeah! Get the fuck outa my bed! I'm sick of the sight of ya!" He slammed the door shut.

She stood at the top of the stars, empty, stunned. Perhaps Hank had admitted to Julian that he had blown his cover and that Jessica had confronted him. A cigarette and a drink might help. She crept down the staircase and pouring a glass of sherry, took it and sat in her plush rocker that overlooked the pool and patio. Dear God! Would this hell-on-earth never end? Tears, unbidden, washed down her cheeks, and she wiped them away on the sleeve of her robe. As she took a swallow of sherry, feeling it burn its way down her throat, she heard someone creeping down the staircase. It was Julian come to slaughter her, of that she was certain. There was no escape! Mother of Mercy, why had she sat in this corner? She was trapped!

A tiny shadow appeared at the living room entrance. Rob! He swished across the carpet into her open arms.

"Don't cry, Mommy!" he pleaded. "Don't cry. I love you."

"My sweetheart, I love you too." She crushed his little body against hers and covered his head with kisses.

A scraping sound and faint whimpers drifted through the air.

"That's Cuddles, Mommy. Can I let her out?"

"All right, but don't make any noise. We don't want to wake Daddy."

The small white poodle bounced into the living room with Rob. For the first time ever, Cuddles bounded onto Jessica's lap, giving her eager, sloshy slurps on her cheeks and chin. Rob giggled.

"Cuddles loves you, Mommy. We both love you."

She laughed through her tears. "I'm so lucky to have so

much love!"

As she sat in the rocking chair, with two little bodies vying for attention on her lap, she knew, beyond any shadow of doubt, there were two living beings in that house who loved her—her son and a nerve-wracking poodle.

⚜

The sun streamed onto the patio. Another glorious day. Rob and Cuddles were already playing on the grass, while Julian studied his newspaper at the table under the umbrella by the pool.

Not daring to sleep all night, she shuffled around the kitchen, feeling as if she and death were kissing cousins. The entire nightmare was duplicating itself, and she knew it would never end. Maybe if she talked to him, she could convince him to let her leave with Rob.

God! What had happened? Things were so wonderful after Glenora, and now they were back to square one minus a hundred. She dribbled coffee into her cup and dragged herself out to the table under the umbrella.

"Julian, we have to talk." The words stuck like tar in her throat.

"Not today, my love. I want to read the paper."

"This is important, Julian. It can't wait. I must talk to you!"

"All right!" he snarled, slamming down his paper. "You have two minutes!"

"Can't we talk indoors? I don't want Rob to hear this?"

"He can't hear what we're talking about, for Christ's sake! He's playing with the dog! Now you have one minute!"

"Julian, I think we should try a separation. Maybe get a

divorce. I don't want a dime! I'm not happy. You're not happy. And it's horrible for Rob. We're living in a concentration camp here. I can't stand it anymore."

"Jessica, we've been through this before," he said, in a voice that was scarcely more than a whisper, and it sounded as if he was invoking Satan himself. It sounded as if he were trying to explain something as rudimentary, yet frustrating, as tying shoelaces. His voice was as menacing as the hiss of a cobra. Her heart stopped in mid-beat, and every cell in her body ceased functioning. She felt as if she'd been thrown into a pit with a million tarantulas with no escape.

"One of your qualities that I found most attractive was your intelligence, but I'm beginning to think I was sadly mistaken. Maybe that's why you're having such trouble getting this through your head. We've discussed this before, or is your memory as short as your intelligence? Please listen and try to remember it this time, because I find repeating myself tedious. We are married! You are my wife, and I am your husband. We aren't *ever* going to get divorced. We will *never* separate. If you decide to leave, I will hunt you down and kill you. Simple as that. And Rob will die first."

"Why are doing this to me?" she sobbed.

"I'm not doing anything to you, Jessica. You're doing this to yourself. I'm perfectly contented with our marriage. You're everything I've ever wanted in a woman, except for your constant insistence on discussing what you see as problems. Sure, I drink a little bit and get edgy, but if you'd just leave me alone, there wouldn't be any friction. If I've ever struck you, it's your fault because you won't stop harassing me. Your incessant complaining is tiresome. I'm not sure if you can understand what I'm telling you, but for your sake, I hope you can. You're young, gorgeous, and in good health, with so many things to be grateful for, and yet you're utterly miserable. I think you need an attitude adjustment."

"Why won't you let me go? Why would you kill me? Why would you kill Rob?" Tears streamed down her face and her whole body vibrated.

"Jessica, Jessica, Jessica," he sighed. "That's so fundamental that I can't believe you haven't figured that out. I love you and couldn't bear the thought of another man having you! As for Rob, I just want you to suffer before I slice you to ribbons, too. Now, sweetheart, why don't you take it easy today? Think about how you can help yourself feel better. This really is your problem, you know. I have absolutely no difficulty with our relationship. If you're having problems, it's up to you to change your own thinking. It's entirely up to you whether we live happily ever after or not."

Shell-shocked, she shriveled into her chair as he gathered up his newspaper and stooped to kiss her. "Julian, please..."

"Princess, I do have to run..."

"Why did you have that awful man follow me? Why the hang up calls?"

"Why, sweetheart," he smirked, "I want to keep you on your toes."

⁂

The telephone rang at noon.

"Is that you, Jessica? It's me, Montana."

"Montana! What a treat to hear your voice! Where are you?" Dear God, she thought, the last thing I need is Montana as a houseguest.

"I'm still in the city."

Jessica relaxed. "How sweet of you to call! How are you doing?"

"I'm working at the halfway house, and I'm goin' to school. Haven't hit the street since we left Glenora. How're things with you?"

"About the same. I'm not taking pills, but I'd like some strychnine about now."

"For Julian, I hope. Not for yourself."

"Things aren't good, Montana."

"Jess, I have somethin' to tell you," Montana said gently, "and it's gonna hurt. But I wanted to tell you before you read it somewhere, or heard it on TV. It's about Mac. There's been an accident, Jessica. Mac...Mac's dead."

"Not Mac!" she screamed. "Not Mac!"

"Jess...Jessica," Montana urged her to listen, "a well exploded. He and another guy were workin' on it. It was over real quick, Jessica. Mac didn't suffer."

"How did you find out?" she choked.

"He and Red kept in touch, and I guess one of Mac's friends told Red. Anyway, Red checked it out, and then called me, and asked if I could phone you. He thought it'd be better if you found out from me."

Holding the receiver, she sank to the floor, cowering against the wall. Anything for support.

"D'ya wanna talk about it, Jessica? I know you two was real close, and I know how much he cared about you."

"No...no, Montana...I don't want to talk. Thanks for being so kind to call. Thank Red for me. That was thoughtful of him to remember me. I'd better go, Montana. I need to cry."

"Please take care, Jessica. And if'n you need me, you know

where I am. God bless, Jess. I love you."

"I love you too, Montana. Thanks for telling me."

She fumbled the receiver onto its cradle, and with tears gushing from her heart, she tore up the stairs two at a time, and threw herself sobbing onto the bed. It wasn't true! It couldn't be true! But it was.

With a soft tap on the door, Binkie asked," You okay, Miss Jessica?"

"Oh, Binkie," she wept, as the little gray lady shuffled into the room, "it's so awful! A good friend of mine is dead! There was a terrible accident! The most awful accident! Oh, my God!"

Binkie sat on the edge of the bed and cradled Jessica in her arms, as her cries tore at the silence in the room. "I'm so sorry," Binkie said over and over, as she patted Jessica's shoulders. "I'm so sorry."

At last, she pulled herself from Binkie's arms. "Can you look after Rob? I have something I'd like to do. I won't be gone long."

After splashing her face with cold water to clear her head, she dashed into the garden with a bag and a pair of scissors. Roses. That's what she needed. Roses! To hell with Julian and his precious roses! Swiftly, she chose twenty-eight of the choicest blooms, and clipping them from their thorny home, dropped them into the bag.

Rob trotted over to investigate. "How come you're taking Daddy's flowers, Mommy?"

"I have a very good reason. Don't tell your father. They're for a sick friend who likes roses." She couldn't discuss death with a three year old. Not now.

"Can I come?"

"No, darling. Not now."

"I hope your friend feels better soon," he said solemnly as she hugged him.

Out the front door and into her car. She screamed the car down Sherwood Boulevard, heading for the bend in the river about twenty minutes outside of town. With tears blinding her, she arrived at the spot she knew to be perfect for her purpose. Parking the car on the shoulder of the road, she strode onto the concrete and steel bridge, watching as the river rushed and swirled beneath. Opening the bag, she tossed the roses one by one over the railing into the dark water below. The blossoms floated and danced on the waves, the current carrying them away.

"One rose for each day I knew you, Mac," she whispered to the wind that ruffled her hair and caressed her face. "You are so dear to me, and I will never stop loving you, no matter what. You are in my heart and my mind and my soul. Bless you for the precious gift of your friendship and for touching my life in such a special way. I shall cherish your precious memory forever. God must have loved your music so much that He called you to sing for Him."

With her face to the wind, she stood and watched as the roses, one by one, twirled and bobbled out of sight in the bend of the river.

⁎⁎⁎

The two men, both well-dressed in slacks and sports jackets, closed the door as they left Julian's office.

"That guy is one sick son of a bitch," said the shorter, stockier one of the pair. "Where does he get off doing shit like this?"

"I guess that's how he gets his rocks off!" said the other, tossing a key into the air, and catching it in his hand. "Who gives a shit? He's paying us well enough. You got the map of the house?"

✻

Julian was home when she returned from the river. It was only three-thirty in the afternoon.

"You're home early," she commented flatly, walking into their bedroom where he was changing his suit.

"You're always complaining about my late hours," he smirked, "but please, don't get your hopes up. I'm leaving for France and Germany. Lincoln's been traveling too much so we're trading off."

"How considerate of you," she quipped. "And when can I expect you back?"

"In a week or so. Maybe never. I might meet some dish on the Riviera."

"It'd be my luck you wouldn't!"

"No, I probably won't. I much prefer tormenting you."

"Are you putting your dogs on me again? Or should I keep a logbook? That might save you some expense."

"You really are angry, aren't you?" He embraced her. "There you go, over-thinking and worrying again."

"I'm no more to you than a prisoner! I'm a bloody hostage!"

"Tut, tut, tut. And what a beautiful hostage! And how well cared for. Of course, if you're not grateful, I can arrange for someone to pick up the Mustang, and I can empty your bank account, cancel your credit cards, fire Binkie, and cut the phone lines."

Yanking herself from his arms, hatred bubbled in her blood, and disgust diced her soul. "I'm going to tell you something,

Julian!" she spat. "I may never be rid of you, but get this straight! Don't ever get sick or have a heart attack around me, because I'll wait until you're cold before I call an ambulance! I'll watch you die before I lift a finger to help you! I loathe you! You're the most contemptible bastard I've ever known! Next to you, Satan is the Easter Bunny!"

He laughed. "Satan? Thank you, my dear! Now go away and let me pack in peace. And...don't forget I love you!"

"Life might be fatal, Julian, but you're lethal!"

Chapter Ten:

Deadly Games

BAM! BAM! The bullets zammed into the target. It felt good to stand and fire, fire, and fire. Each bullet exploding from the revolver was another piece of the hatred and rage that beat in her heart. She had been at the range for five days straight, and her arms and back ached from the relentless practice.

She felt a tap on her shoulder. Dropping the revolver into the safety position, she turned and looked into Casey's eyes.

"Not bad," he remarked. "How come you haven't called me for lessons? You still have a lot to learn."

"Sorry, Casey, I wasn't in shape for lessons. But I've been practicing a lot."

"I can see that! You're doing swell! How about coffee?"

"Yeah, sure, I'm about ready to quit for the day anyway."

As they walked to the snack shop, he put a hand on her shoulder. "I still think you ought to go into undercover work. You're a natural. Quick mind. Great shot. Perfect actress."

"What do you mean 'perfect actress'?" She filled the Styrofoam cup with coffee.

"Let's take our coffee outside," he suggested. "Nice day. Too nice to be cooped up in here."

On the parking lot, they leaned against his car, breathing in the warm air, fragrant with the scent of drying hay in the fields surrounding the range. Everything was so peaceful, so picturesque out here, she mused, as she looked at a herd of dairy cattle, lying in the shade, chewing their cuds. The world could be so beautiful, but it was filled with pain, anger, hatred, and terror. There was nowhere to be safe, nowhere to be secure.

"Okay, Casey." She faced him. "What's this about my being an actress?"

"Come on, woman, who do you think you're talkin' to?" He looked at her, his eyes slate and penetrating, his face a mask of granite. "You're not the same person you were when I met you. Something's happening to you. Big chunks of your soul are missing."

Unable to bear his gaze, her eyes darted from the car in the lot, to the puffy clouds, to the fields, to a crow flying overhead.

"Everyone changes, Casey. You know that. I haven't been feeling all that well for a while. I did a number on myself with all those pills I was taking. It takes time to recover from the damage I inflicted on my body."

"Cut the crap, Jessica! I'm not buying that! Seems to me when you got home from the center, you were back to your old self. You were shining and happy. I've been watchin' you fold up and wither. I don't like to see that. But you pretend there's nothin' wrong. It might fool some people, but it doesn't fool me!"

"I've got a lot on my mind," she mumbled.

He chewed on the plastic stir stick. "Listen, Jessica," he said, his voice softening, "I want you to know I care about you, and I see something that bothers me. If you ever need me, just call."

He was so big, so strong, so tall, and so confident. He was a powerhouse. But he was Julian's friend. He'd never believe her, and if he did, he'd tell Julian. She felt as alone as a single fly stuck on flypaper.

"I think I'd better get home." She poured the rest of her coffee onto the gravel and crumpled the cup. "Binkie wants to leave early today."

He watched as she slipped her slim figure into her red Mustang and slowly drove off the lot. She doesn't even drive like a dynamo any more, he thought. What in hell was happening to his star pupil? He figured he knew the answer to that question.

⁂

Mornings used to be marvelous. In the not-so-long-ago past, waking up was delicious. When she and Julian were first married, it was a time to cuddle, laugh, and plan. Then after Rob arrived, it was enchanting to watch him nurse, kick, and smile. Even when she and Julian began experiencing difficulties, mornings were livable. The worst mornings occurred when the pills had taken over her life. At Glenora, she had learned to ask God, as soon as she awoke, to remove the pill temptation for that day, and to thank Him at night for doing so.

Now mornings assaulted her. Some part of her head stayed awake all night, perched on a bedpost, waiting for her to wake up so it could recite all the things she'd done wrong since the beginning of time, to remind her that life was a bitch at best, and to list all the things that could possibly go wrong.

"Your fairy godmother lives on a worm farm in Montana."

"Julian really loves you. You're expecting too much."

"Today's the day he'll cancel your credit cards."

"Why don't you shoot him and spend the rest of your life

behind bars?"

"In no time, Rob will be grown and gone, and you'll be alone."

"Your revolver's going to backfire and kill you."

"Someone is going to poison the world's water supplies."

"As soon as you get your act together, some idiot is going to start a nuclear war."

"You're ungrateful, mean, and selfish."

"That little blemish on your shoulder is really skin cancer."

"Julian is going to send you on a two-week cruise on a torpedo."

"Lydia is the wicked witch in *Snow White*."

With all these cheerful little messages awaiting her, she dreaded opening her eyes to face another day. Dragging herself from the bed, she shuffled to the window and opening the draperies, peered out. Another glorious day smiled at her. Groaning at the sight of the sunshine pouring through the sheers, she pulled on her robe.

As she pitter-pattered down the stairs to the kitchen, her mind was on letting Cuddles out of her kennel and making coffee. The fuzzy white bundle of energy bounded from the basement, yipping, yapping, jumping, and wiggling. Jessica opened a can of dog food and plunked the contents into Cuddles' dish. Turning to pour water into the coffee maker, she saw that it wasn't there. A note, in black Magic Marker was in its place: "We told you we'd be back!"

Hysteria exploded in her brain. Up the stairs two at a time, she burst into Rob's room. He was still curled up in his blankets, but the teddy bear was gone! She flew to her room, fumbled with the phone. Dead! Dead as a mackerel. Down the stairs. The kitchen phone was dead too. Into the study. The phone was useless. Where was her cell phone? Buried somewhere. Out to the garage. The phone in Julian's car. Panic pounded in her heart. 9-1-1! Crying, screaming, trembling, she pleaded with the operator to send help. "Please tell them to hurry! Please hurry! They're going to kill me!"

She called Casey. His deep, gruff voice answered after the first ring. "Casey, I need you! Please hurry! Something terrible is happening! They're going to kill me! I know they're going to kill me!"

Up the stairs again to make sure Rob was safe. Down the stairs. From room to room, her feet didn't stop flying. She heard the sirens and flung the door open before the two police officers had a chance to ring the doorbell. Grabbing one of the officer's hands, she dragged him into the foyer. Gibberish was all that came out of her mouth. She might as well have been babbling Portuguese. Crying, shivering, shattering, she led him to the kitchen.

"Here's the note! This happened last year! They left a note! They said they'd be back! And they did! They came back! They came back! They're going to kill me I know!" Her words pelted the air.

In a frenzy, she paced the kitchen, out to the patio, back to the kitchen, into the living room, around the house, up and down the stairs, leaving cigarettes burning in every ashtray. One officer, trying to keep pace with her, asked questions. When had she gone to bed? Were the alarms activated? Had she heard anything? Was anything missing? Had she locked all the doors and windows?

She answered every question ten times. "I can't remember! I don't know! I didn't hear anything! They took the coffee maker! They stole Rob's teddy! Why would anyone take a teddy bear? I can't remember! I don't know? I can't remember! There're going to kill me!"

When the doorbell chimed, one of the officers opened the door. Casey filled the foyer, and Jessica flew into his arms.

"Casey, they came back! They came back! They said they'd be back and they did! They were in the house, and I didn't even know it! They're going to kill me! I know it! They're driving me crazy!"

Casey held her as she sobbed onto his shirt. "Jessica, you're safe. I'm here. You're safe." He stroked her hair and rubbed her back, but she was trembling, and he knew she was almost beyond hearing him. "Jessica! Do you have anything to drink in the house? Like bourbon or something? We've got to get you calmed down."

She pointed to the bar in the living room and crumpled onto the bottom step as Casey went to pour her something. The officers stood by helplessly as she clung to the banister.

Rob pattered down the stairs, inquisitive about the commotion and the police. Hugging him to her, Jessica showered him with kisses. One of the officers suggested she give him some breakfast to keep him occupied.

"Mommy, my teddy's gone. Are the police going to find him?"

"Yes, sweetheart," she smiled through her tears, as she gulped the bourbon Casey handed to her. "They're here to find teddy. Why don't we get you something to eat, and then you can play with Cuddles."

A search of the house revealed nothing missing except the coffee maker and Rob's teddy bear. Both surfaced in Jessica's dressing room, in the cupboard under the sink.

"Oh, my God, Casey! They were in my bedroom, too!"

"You heard nothing?" he queried.

She shook her head. "I sleep like the dead sometimes. I'm

exhausted lately, and if I fall asleep, I'm completely out of it. I've slept through hurricanes and earthquakes. What kind of sick mind would do this? And to cut the phone lines! I'm completely vulnerable! They can come in anytime and blow me away!"

"Where's your revolver?" Casey was brusque.

"Locked in my car."

"I want it in your bedroom! On the double! Loaded! Safety on! Does Rob ever rummage in your drawers? Some kids do."

"Never!"

"Okay! That gun stays in your night table!"

He left the kitchen where Jessica was brewing coffee now that she had the maker back. The police had dusted it for prints, but it was cleaner than the day it was manufactured. Returning, Casey heaved his huge bulk into a chair at the table.

"Okay, listen. I've told the police everything I know," he said, fixing her with his granite eyes. "With nothing missing, this was a set-up. Is there anyone you know who'd try to spook you, keep you off-balance? Have you ever met anyone who might get kicks out of scaring you to death?"

Julian! whispered her head, but who'd believe you?

"No one," she sniffled, wiping her eyes with a tissue. "There isn't anyone who's this sick! Casey, what if they come back?"

"That's why you keep that revolver in your room. I've got a hunch about somethin', but I need time to work it through. Don't mention to a single living soul that I'm working on this. Not even to that Rodgers woman."

"What about Julian? He's in France. Should I ask him to come home?"

"If you phone, don't mention me at all. By the way, your phones will be on soon. The police already called the company for you."

"Why not tell Julian you're helping? You're such good friends."

"All the more reason for not telling him. He'll expect me to pull rabbits out of hats. Friends always expect more than we can deliver. Promise me. Don't tell *anyone!* Don't even mention me in your prayers!"

"I'm terrified, Casey! Something terrible is after me! I know it!"

"Jessica, I've gone over the alarm system. There isn't a thing wrong with it. Those guys knew exactly how to get in here and disarm it. But I can promise you this! They won't be back! They've had their fun! It was probably the same guys who broke in before doing it for the adrenaline rush. They won't chance it again."

"How can you be so sure?"

"I'm the best of the best! Remember?" He grinned at her. "Not for nothing did I get commendations all the time. You've got the best detective working on your case. Just don't tell anyone.

"One more thing; I want you to change every lock on every door that leads into this house. But make sure when you tell Julian that he knows it was your idea to have it done. Get it done today!"

"I don't understand."

"Jessica, I told you I had a hunch. Part of that hunch means you change the locks!"

At the door, Casey hugged her. In his arms, she felt fragile, innocent, and helpless. But he knew she had molten steel in her veins.

It was hours before Julian returned her urgent call.

"What's the emergency?" he asked the instant she said, "Hello". "Has anything happened to Mother? Are you okay? Is Rob all right?"

"Julian, please come home! I need you! The house was broken into last night!"

"Again?" he hollered into the phone. "What's wrong with the goddamned alarms? Are you okay? What did they take?"

"Nothing!" she cried. "They cut the phone lines and put the coffee maker and Rob's bear in my dressing room. They left a note. Just like they did last year! Oh, Julian, I'm so scared!"

"How awful for you! Keep the gun beside the bed. They wouldn't have the balls to come back again. I'll have things wrapped up by Friday."

"That's four days! I'm terrified out of my mind!"

"Darling, I love you, and I miss you. Make sure you look beautiful when I get there. I want to love you to death."

As she hung up, something ominous clung to her. Julian might be doing exactly that—loving her to death.

⁎⁎

Sleep was a luxury of the past and nothing but a scant memory. She paced the house. Every room held its shadows, phantoms, and things that went bump in the night. Cuddles paced with her, keeping her company until Julian came home.

Midnight! The witching hour! Why had she ever read *The Silence of the Lambs?* She felt like Little Red Riding Hood with a wolf ready to pounce from every dark corner. She cruised the house again, turning on every light and every lamp. The foyer chandelier blazed. With a flick of the switch, the floodlights on the front lawn bathed the house like the noonday sun. If

Riverbend was on anyone's bombing run, her home would be the target. It was lit up brighter than the Griswold's in *Christmas Vacation*.

⁂

She phoned Casey. "I've had all the locks changed. What did you find out? Do you know who broke in? Do you know anything? How long will this take? I'm coming unstuck! I haven't slept a wink! I won't let Rob outside alone! I'm considering ordering a pack of Dobermans!" The words staccatoed from her lips.

"Patience, Jessica, patience...one of the most important things in an investigation. I don't have anything concrete yet. Give it a few more days. Julian's home tomorrow, isn't he?"

"Yes. Do you want me to give him your regards?"

"Please do, but don't breathe a word about what I'm doing. I don't need him breathing down my neck."

⁂

Rosalind called. "Sorry I wasn't home, Jess. Mary-Beth told me what happened. What bad timing that we were at the cottage. Do you want me to come over and stay with you? Or how about you and Rob coming for a sleep-over?"

"No, thanks, Roz. I've weathered the worst of it. I'll be all right. It's only for one more night. Binkie's been good company during the day. The poor soul is just as spooked as I am. We both dive for our bunkers every time the phone rings. Yesterday, a deliveryman brought flowers to the house. Binkie wouldn't open the door and made him leave them on the porch. By the

401

time she and I had snooped through every bloom looking for a bomb, we'd shredded the whole bouquet. When we finally read the card to see who had sent them, we discovered they were from Julian. I'll have to tell him the florist must have used a bunch of old flowers because he'll wonder what happened to them."

"Are you going to Mary-Beth's party on Saturday night?" Rosalind asked.

"You bet! I'm looking forward to meeting this Orville, who seems to have stolen her heart."

"It'll be a great party. I'm glad you'll be there. Maybe you and Julian need to have some fun. It helps make life sparkle."

She never mentioned the discussion she and Julian had on the afternoon before he left on his trip. It was so venomous that she didn't think anyone, even Rosalind, would understand. There wasn't any problem with her friends believing her. Rosalind, even Mary-Beth, would believe her. The crux of the matter was, no one would *understand* why she would stay in such a lethal union. Some men really did stalk their mates and, having ferreted them out in their precarious sanctuaries, slaughter them. There was no doubt in her mind that Julian was one of those murderous few. On the other hand, maybe he wasn't.

⁂

The limousine pulled up to the curb at seven-thirty in the evening. Rob, who had been eagerly waiting at the foyer window wriggled with glee and squealed with delight as Julian swung him into the air.

"How's my tiger?" Julian laughed as Kenneth carried the luggage into the foyer.

"The police were here," Rob informed his father gravely. "I

was scared. A bad man took my teddy bear."

"I know," Julian said, hugging his son to his chest and glancing at his wife. "You don't have to worry. They won't be back."

Lowering the child, Julian embraced her, crushing her to his lithe, firm body. "And how are you, my sweet? You look just as scrumptious as the day I met you!"

She gave him what she hoped was an enthusiastic hug in return, but tiny footsteps of fear left their trail of foreboding in her heart. Eyeing the suitcases, she said, as she slithered from his arms, "You brought more bags home than you left with."

"I did some great shopping in Paris," he replied. "Bought a couple of new suits and some shirts. The latest styles. But I can hardly wait to show you what I picked up for you!"

Probably a caged scorpion, she thought, or maybe a pet black mamba.

⁂

As a special treat, Julian bathed his son. She listened to their laughter and the splashes, and Rob chattering a mile a minute about what he had done while his father was away. Later, she heard Julian read Rob's favorite book, *Cars and Trucks and Things That Go*, with her son giggling when Julian was unable to find the gold bug on every page. He can be such a fabulous father, she thought, as she mindlessly watched *Mayday* in their bedroom. Her head, busy with entertaining itself, couldn't have come up with an answer to a skill-testing question about either the program or its own thoughts if anyone had bothered to ask.

With Rob tucked into his bed, Julian joined her in their room, and grinning with mischief, handed her a package wrapped in gold paper.

"Especially for you, darling, straight from Paris with all my love."

Sitting on the side of the bed, she carefully untied the gold ribbons while he sat beside her, one arm around her, nibbling her ear. She wasn't sure if the shivers rippling through her were from pleasure or terror. Gingerly, she lifted the top off the box to reveal something wrapped in tissue. Pushing the fragile paper aside, she saw a delicate, translucent black nightie, which lay on top of more finery. She held up the gown, which appeared to be made of cobwebs, so fine and frail were the tiny threads holding it together. Putting it aside, she reached in and pulled out a transparent two-piece red panty and bra ensemble. With dismay, she observed that the nipples and crotch were missing, and that the finest black lace trimmed the areas surrounding the absent material.

"This will certainly raise the dead!" she tried to laugh.

"It'll raise more than that!" He pulled her hand to his crotch, where his erection lurked under his trousers. "Take a look at the last one. It's enough to make an impotent priest horny!"

It certainly is, her mind muttered, as she lifted out a black and red contraption. It seemed to be a kind of corset, made of soft black lace, with little frills of red lace dribbled over it. The top would certainly not cover her breasts. The idea was to push them up to her chin, while the rest of the lace-up front trapped her with heavy boning. It extended to mid-hip and garters dangled from the bottom. A pair of black fishnet stockings and black elbow-length gloves completed the ensemble, which included a tiny black lacy G-string.

At the bottom of the box, were tubes and jars of jellies and lotions to be applied so that one's partner could lick them off. A pair of black, backless, gold-spiked shoes, adorned with red marabou puffs over the toe, was the icing on this sex-drenched cake. She was outfitted with the finery of a strumpet on the stroll. Of course, the strumpet would be wearing considerably more.

"I don't know what to say, Julian," she whispered, breathless.

"Don't say anything, darling," he breathed into her ear. "Why don't you bathe and put on the nightie and bra set first. Maybe put some jelly around your nipples and other yummy spots so I can nibble it off."

"Those sound like easy instructions." She hoped she was smiling and wondered if this was how hookers felt. Sex was the farthest thing from her mind, but she was too fearful to reject the plan he seemed to have entrenched in his mind. She suspected that if she suggested a game of Scrabble instead of this bedroom bash, she'd be eating marabou feathers, while Julian strangled her with the G-string. To the marrow of her bones, she believed Julian to be capable of ruthless, lethal savagery, and if he wanted sex, who was she to argue?

Gathering up her equipment, she vanished into the bathroom, wishing he had been a little more modern in his ideas about this necessary room. It was an old, sixties-style, tub/ shower, sink, toilet affair; granted it was lavish, but it was not contemporary. She had tried in vain to talk him into a Jacuzzi with a separate shower stall, but he was adamant in his refusal to upgrade.

Running the bath, she opened one of the tubes, which had a juicy strawberry on the label. The instructions were in French so she had no idea if this was strawberry-flavored arsenic or jelly. Oh well, he was the one to slurp it off her body.

After toweling herself, she squeezed some of the jelly onto her hand. With a liberal slathering over her breasts, she spread a generous amount on her midriff and abdomen, and a tiny dribble on the front of her thighs. He might want it in more private places, but she refused to humor him any more than she had already. The gel had a glue-like consistency. Speculating that it might take a few minutes to dry before she donned her brothel attire, she sat on the toilet-seat and smoked a cigarette, testing the gel on her breasts to see if it was drying. With her cigarette now only a memory, she knew the gel wouldn't dry if she remained in the bathroom until Christmas. Warily, she stepped into the crotch-less panties. Now here's a Chinese puzzle, she thought, as she maneuvered them into place, only to discover that she had one leg in the waist of this maddening creation and the leg part around her middle. One more attempt.

"Hurry, Princess! I can't wait to peel those little treasures from your gorgeous body!"

"Coming!" she sang, thinking, if this stuff acts like glue, it could mean a surgeon's scalpel.

The bra wasn't too complicated, but she was right—the gel stuck like crazy glue. The nightie clung to her flesh like flypaper.

Opening the door, she saw that Julian had champagne chilling in an ice bucket, candles lit, and soft music playing. With her papier-mâché apparel, she put her hands behind her head and did a few bumps and grinds into his eager arms.

He grabbed her hungrily, like a dog after a bone, fondling her breasts and shredding the nightie as he peeled it from her body. As he stripped the panties away, she wondered if the gel was really supposed to be used for a wax-job; she was sure she'd lost all her pubic hair. In a feeble attempt to respond to his passion, she tried to purr, moan, and groan at the appropriate moments. Somehow she was unable to muster her sexual appetite. But she knew what to do...like riding a bicycle or sorting the laundry, one never forgot. Within minutes, it was over, and Julian lay panting on top of her.

"You're the best, baby! The best!"

Compared to whom? she wondered.

"Julian," she gasped as she shifted under his weight. "I have to get up. The jelly is still all over me, and I'm cementing myself to the sheets."

"Why don't we shower together?" he suggested. "Then you can put on the corset and heels and do a strip for me?"

Montana, where are you when I need you? her head pleaded silently. Maybe he'd wear out soon.

In the shower, they lathered each other with soap and shampooed each other's hair. They laughed and played like children under the eaves in the summer when it rains. But through the gaiety and laughter, teasing and caresses, her vibe detector told her she was toying with a lethal weapon.

Toweling each other, he offered to blow-dry her hair. What a luxury. While he dried her hair, he massaged her scalp, nibbled her ears, and kissed her neck and shoulders. He was as loving and charming as the man she remembered. When he finished with the blower, he brushed her hair until it glistened. With a longing, famished kiss, he left her to put on the corset outfit so he could watch her wiggle out of each tantalizing morsel.

The corset was tricky. There were dozens of tiny holes for the laces, and she had to suck in her stomach to achieve the full benefit of thrusting her breasts up to her ear lobes. With the gloves, mesh stockings, G-string, and shoes, she knew she was worth at least a thousand dollars an hour for her time and effort.

To the raunchy music he provided, she twirled and strutted, wriggled and writhed, thanking Providence she didn't have to earn a living as a stripper, knowing she'd have ended up on a corner with a little tin cup. Piece by titillating piece, she shimmied and shook, and squirmed out of the costume.

As Julian mauled her on the bed, her mind wandered back to the way their lovemaking used to be. What they used to do all night now seemed, to her, to take all night to do. She thought of the long years ahead, and what she would have to endure to save her and her son's life. She looked back wistfully to her dating days when sex was simply "Wham! Bam! Thank you, ma'am!" How appealing that seemed right now. How much torment and humiliation did she have to tolerate with this capricious madman? He was more difficult to predict than the weather; a gentle sea breeze one minute, a hurricane the next.

At last, Julian shuddered and trembled with his orgasm, while she gasped, moaned, and faked hers. He rolled away to refill their champagne goblets. "This is a celebration of our love," he murmured, raising his goblet to hers. "May our lives always be as happy as this moment."

⁂

The next morning, Jessica poured a glass of orange juice and was carrying it onto the patio to join Julian and their son, when what she witnessed jolted through her body like a thunderbolt. Her knees gelled, and her stomach knotted. Her first instinct was to scream, but she willed herself into a deadly calm.

"Julian," she crooned, her eyes wide with horror. "Julian... Julian...what are you doing?"

"Showing Rob how to use a gun...in case he ever has to shoot a burglar. I borrowed yours. Mine's locked in the trunk of my car."

Rob grinned at her. "I can kill people, Mommy!" he announced. "Now we don't have to be scared!" He was sitting on his father's lap, while Julian spun the cylinder. "Daddy showed me a new game!"

"Let me guess," she whispered. "Is it Russian roulette?" Stay calm. Don't scream.

"You're clever for so early in the morning." Julian directed his gaze, granite and cold, at her. "Here, Son, you spin it and show Mommy how this works." Rob struggled to turn the cylinder, while Julian held the revolver. "Now let's see if this is the one with the bullet. Sit down, Jessica. And take it easy...Relax!" He pointed the gun at her. She sat. "Okay, pull the trigger, Rob." Click!

"Julian, don't you think this game is a little mature for a three year old?" Whatever you do, don't start screaming.

"No!" he laughed. "People of all ages are thrilled by it!"

"Please, just give me the gun, and I'll put it away."

"Jess, I'm playing a game. Either you sit and watch and shut up, or I'll find the chamber with the bullet in it. Okay, Tiger! Spin it again!"

Perspiration ran down her back and between her breasts. She never knew anyone could feel such terror and live. Eternity hung suspended in the air.

"Spin it! Pull the trigger!" Click! "Spin it! Pull the trigger!" Click!

Caterpillars crawled on her flesh; stomach acid devoured her insides; bullets ricocheted off the walls of her skull. And Julian and Rob reveled in the new game. She was sure it was sunset before Julian tired of his new torment for his wife and shooed Rob off, telling him to get a ball and play with Cuddles.

"I'll give you a swimming lesson later!" he called, as their child romped and rolled on the grass. "Great kid, isn't he?" he asked no one in particular.

Putting the revolver on the patio table, he relaxed, resting his head on the back of the chair and relishing the sun on his face. He appeared as satisfied and peaceful as he would have had he just read the Saturday newspaper comics to the little boy. Jessica sat paralyzed, her orange juice glass welded to her hand.

At last she ventured, "I think I'll take this into the house," and slowly reached for the revolver. Then snatching it, she flipped open the cylinder. Empty! Not one bloody bullet, thank God! She wished she had a machine-gun to fire at this psychopath sunbathing in her back yard.

"You abhorrent bastard!" she hissed through clenched teeth. "How could you do this to me? And to Rob? You're nothing but a despicable bastard!"

He laughed, eyes closed to the sun. "Come on, Jess! Where's your sense of humor?"

"I should call the police. I'm sure they'd love to arrest you for endangering the life of a small child and your wife," she snapped, pocketing the weapon in her robe.

"Speaking of police, Jess, darling," he said conversationally, still enjoying the sun's rays, "I thought I made it clear to you before when I told you I had lunch with the chief. So go ahead and call the cops, Jess. Just try to prove it was me playing with the revolver and not you. With your history of anxiety attacks, drug abuse, and going to a treatment center, *plus* that suicide attempt you thought you could keep a secret from me, it seems to me you could end up at the wrong end of this call to the police. Think about things before going off half-cocked."

"Like I said before, Julian, don't ever get mortally ill around me! I'll wait until you are stone-cold before I lift a finger to help!"

She left him laughing at the sun while she fumed her way to their bedroom to stash the revolver in her night table drawer. Dear God, she thought, when will this nightmare end? Helpless frustration and terror washed over her as she recognized that all the corrupt chips of this deadly game were in Julian's hands.

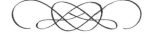

Chapter Eleven:

Thou Shalt Not Kill

ULIAN STAGGERED AND STUMBLED INTO THE MUSTANG, WHILE JESSICA HUGGED THE BRIDE-TO-BE. She vowed to herself that this was going to be the last of her keeping up appearances bullshit with her husband. If he needed her to accompany him on any other social engagement, he could bloody well go alone. She had wanted to attend Mary-Beth's party alone, but Julian had threatened to crash the party if she didn't bring him with her. How childish! But he was capable of unimaginable chaos if he didn't get his way. Rather than risk it, she caved in to his whim.

"Thanks for inviting us to your lovely party, Mary-Beth," she said. "Orville's a treasure. You were absolutely right about him, and I'm so happy for you. Sorry about some of Julian's colorful comments and offensive jokes."

She embraced Rosalind.

"Will you be all right, Jess? I mean...he's had a lot to drink. Do you want me to follow in my car in case you need help?"

"I'll be fine. Once he's in bed, he'll pass out. I may have to drag him out of the car when we get home...Perhaps I should let him sleep it off in the car, and let him wake up in the garage."

Her face looked haggard and drained, and her words dripped with disgust.

She climbed into the car, closed the door, and waved to her two friends who stood anxiously on the curb. She turned the key in the ignition, and the car hummed to life. Gracefully, the Mustang maneuvered its way around the driveway and onto the street. Checking in her rearview mirror, she saw Rosalind and Mary-Beth still waving.

Julian's head lolled against his window as he tried to focus.

"I'm gonna puke!" he gagged.

"Not in my car, Buckshot!" Dumping its contents onto the floor, she threw her purse at him. "Here use this! And don't miss!"

Stepping on the gas, she careened around curves and crescents to Sherwood Boulevard. If she was stopped for speeding, Julian could puke on the cop. She squealed to a stop at their front door and dashed up the stone steps to unlock it for her husband, who was gagging and choking, with spittle drooling down his chin. God! she thought, I wish the Town Council could see him now! Flying back to the car, she yanked open the passenger door and grabbed Julian by the arm.

"Leave me alone, bitch!" he snarled. "I can get outa this tin can without your help!"

Rolling himself out of the front seat, he stumbled onto the curb, lurched across the walk, and faltered up the steps into the open doorway. As she locked the car, she watched his brilliant performance, then followed him into the house, and shut the heavy door with just the right amount of push that she didn't slam it off its hinges.

Fury simmered in her veins, and she felt as if she could dismantle the arch and foyer with her bare hands. Julian slid and dragged himself up the staircase and made it to the bathroom in the nick of time. Jessica heard him heaving and retching. Maybe he'd rupture his esophagus and bleed to death.

She smiled wearily at Binkie who came out of the living room, where she had been watching television.

"Everything's fine, Miss Jessica. Rob hasn't made so much as a peep since I put him to bed. Sounds like Mr. Julian had quite a time for himself at the party."

"Oh, yes, he had quite a time. I don't think anyone there will ever forget him... Listen, while I think about it, could you wait an extra minute? I want to park my car in the garage. It'll take just a minute or so."

She dashed back to her car, unlocked it, and spun it around the drive, opened the garage doors with her remote, and pulled her car in beside Julian's. Lowering the garage doors, she flew up the flagstone steps and into the house.

"Thanks so much Binkie. With all the action we've had around here, I don't want my car stolen."

"Well, I'll be getting on home then... that is, do you want me to stay? I mean, Mr. Julian oughta go right to sleep."

"We'll be fine, Binkie. Listen, why don't you take tomorrow off? He'll probably stay home...sick! You don't need to deal with that. Thanks for looking after Rob for us tonight."

"You're sure you don't want me to stay?" Binkie asked as she opened the front door.

"Absolutely sure." Jessica watched from the step while Binkie got into her car and then stepped back into the foyer as the car's taillights disappeared down the drive.

Checking the alarms, she saw that everything was in order, and turned off the downstairs lights before she made her way upstairs to peek in on Rob. As she pulled Rob's covers over him and kissed him lightly on his forehead, she heard Julian's snorting, mumbling, and snoring. With stealthy, silent steps, she made it into her bedroom and tiptoed across the plush broadloom carpet to her dressing room, deciding to change into her nightie and sleep in the nanny's room. She didn't want to make the slightest sound to disturb her husband. He was in an ugly temper, and God only knew what might come unraveled in his head. He was sprawled naked across the quilt, and his clothes were strewn where he had dropped them.

Stepping into her dressing room, she closed the door with a hush, before flicking on the light. Her face stared back at her from her mirror. Who else did she expect? She was dismayed at her appearance: eyes that looked disturbed, with dark circles under them; a pallid complexion in spite of makeup; and a deeply furrowed brow that no cream seemed to ease. She leaned forward on the counter and slumped down, braced on her arms. When would this nightmare end?

Sitting down on the chair, she removed her makeup. Any task drained her strength these days and even preparing for bed seemed daunting. At last she had on her nightie. Carefully, she switched off the light, and with all the stealth of a cat burglar, she opened the dressing room door, planning to creep from the bedroom into the hall, and inch her way to Rob's room, and then into the nanny's room. She slid around the doorframe, slipping into the bedroom, silently, furtively.

Steel fingers clamped themselves around her arm just as she entered the hall.

"Where are you sneakin' off to?" Julian hissed from the shadows.

"Leave me alone!" Panic rose in her throat, as she pried his fingers from her flesh. "I want to check on Rob! I'll be right back!"

His icy grasp hurled her into the bedroom. Carpet burns scorched her thighs and she staggered to her feet. He tackled her as she struggled to maneuver herself into a position of power, which was to flee from the room. In a blind rage, he ripped her nightgown, which became part of her torment, acting like a hobble as it slid down her body. She was tangled in it. A sharp cry pierced their grunts, pleas, and curses. Rob was awake, alarmed. "Mommy! Mommy!"

Jessica tore herself from her bonds. "Let me go to Rob!" she begged. "He's scared, Julian! Let me go to him!" she pleaded through her anguish.

His strength was mind-boggling, and as a drunk as he was, he had the expertise of a wrestler.

"Why are you doing this? Leave me alone!"

Dragging her to her feet, he threw her onto the bed. She flailed at the blankets, the pillows, the air, anything to give her leverage to pull herself from his maniacal rampage.

"I'm gonna check for pecker marks!" he panted, his hands wrenching her legs apart. She felt her tendons squeal with pain as she tried to kick for freedom. She tore at his hair and thrashed her torso in her attempt to escape his iron strength. "You were fuckin' all the guys at that party! And I'm gonna prove it! Then I'm gonna fuck you like you've never been fucked before! And then I'm gonna kill you! I shoulda done it long ago! And then I'm gonna kill that little bastard! That kid's not even mine!"

Screaming, gasping for breath, writhing, and struggling, she felt as if she was drowning. God! I'm going to die here! She knew it! The scent of death flared her nostrils. She knew she was dead as his fingers found her throat, squeezing the breath from her body. Thrashing, she heaved to obtain a gulp of air to relieve her bursting lungs. As though from under water, she heard Rob scream his fear. In her last fragment of life, her thought was of her son and his terror. Something snapped in her brain. She relaxed. She was putty in Julian's hands.

With a body starved for oxygen, frantic for air, her insides grew hard and cold. From a place deep within her psyche, there swirled up a deadly determination to survive. She had to live. If this demented creature killed her, Rob would have no chance at all! Her survival and Rob's meant this lunatic's death.

Every fiber of her being strained for air, for life. Desperate for survival, she ceased her struggle, and he miraculously released her.

"Come on, stud!" she gasped, her lungs craving to heave in great gulps of air. "Show me what you've got!" Instinct demanded that she claw her way to freedom, but her mind told her the only freedom she would ever have would be when Julian was dead. It was kill or be killed. Eat or be eaten. The Law of the Jungle.

"Shut up, bitch!" He thrust his head between her legs, and his tongue found its mark. "I love fresh cunt!" he mumbled, as he thrust his fingers into her.

Pain sliced through her pelvis. Relax, she said to herself. Relax and breathe. Just stay alive. Don't scream. Don't inflame him. Go along with his shit. It's your only chance. It's the last chance you have. It's Rob's last chance.

"Mmmm!" she moaned, wriggling ever so slightly, so that his ramming hand didn't explode her vagina. "That feels so good, Julian! You're the best, darling! Just give it to me!"

He threw himself onto her, fumbling with his erection, jamming it into her. He groaned as he entered her. And she knew she had him! The fury was gone. He'd forgotten his rage. She raised her hips to meet him, swinging her legs up around his back. She heard her son sobbing. Wait, sweetheart, she pleaded in her head. Mommy will be there. Please just wait until I can save our lives.

She writhed to meet his pounding with her back aching and every muscle of her body screaming for mercy. Would he never orgasm? With all the drinking he'd done at the party, she knew it could take until sunrise. Melding her body to his and hugging him, she willed him to orgasm. Her fingers longed to scratch his back and tear his flesh open with her nails. But she caressed him, soothing him. Every fiber of her being hated him, loathed this moment, despised this life. Would he never come? Please, she pleaded, begged, and petitioned in her head, have your orgasm, and relieve me of this never-ending hell! Her lungs screamed for air as he ground her into the mattress with his pounding weight. At last, he came in a blaze of glory and hellfire!

"That was the best yet, darling!" she gasped into his ear. Anything to keep his mind off killing her. Anything to keep him from snapping into the kill-your-wife mode. "I'm going to freshen up a bit," she teased, as she nibbled his ear. "How about a nightcap?"

"Sounds like one hell of a good idea!" he mumbled from his corner of the shadows.

She scampered into the bathroom as fast as her trembling, aching legs would allow. Safe within the locked room, she leaned against the sink, and greedily gulped air into her lungs, and willed herself to be strong. Would this night never end? Running hot water over a cloth, she cleaned herself. She thought about Rob and his softening cries. I'm saving us, she hoped. We'll never have to live like this again.

Gliding back into the bedroom, refreshed, she headed for the bar, and flicked on the dim lamp over it. The tiny icemaker was full. She zipped a few ice cubes into a tumbler, and poured Scotch up to the rim. That'll do it, she hoped. If he drinks this, he'll be out cold. The way he pushed them back, he'd love her forever with this generous offering. Usually, she was niggardly with her measures, thinking she was helping him to cut down on his alcohol intake. She splashed a little over ice for herself, just to be neighborly.

She slithered across the carpet to the bed and handing him his glass, she sat beside him and winked at him. Raising his head for a swallow, he gave her a lop-sided grin, and in that fleeting moment, he resembled the real Julian, the one she cherished and loved. But this brute in her bed wasn't Julian. It was someone who hated her, despised her, wanted to destroy her, wanted her insane, and desired her death.

She leaned over and kissed him, her tongue playing with his lips, and tickling his nose. She nuzzled his neck. As she straightened up, she sipped her Scotch. The taste exploded in her head. She peeked at him from under her lashes, making a toast "to us". She was the vamp, tempting and tantalizing. She pretended to savor the Scotch as she choked on it. Her life and Rob's depended on it. Julian raised his head for another guzzle. She observed that it wouldn't be long now. His glass was almost empty.

"Can I freshen it for you, darling?" Fake a perky voice.

"Tha'd be reeeeal nice...if you would," he slurred.

She sprang from the bed, ran for the bottle, splashed the glass full, and had it back in his hand before he blinked. Gently, she cradled his head so he could force another swallow. His eyes were unfocused, leering into space. With another generous swig, maybe he'd be out. She held his head as he slurped the Scotch, draining the glass.

"Tha's the best…loving…I've ever had…" His hand swung up to caress her breast. It stuck there. His lips curled into a pucker as he whooshed her a kiss. "G'night, swee…"

A statue, not moving, she sat there, as he slipped into unconsciousness. Stealthily, she slid away. Leaning over, she whispered into his ear, "Julian, can you hear me?" No response, except for a feeble grunt. Louder, "Julian!" Nothing. Louder still, "Julian!" Not a murmur. She heard his breathing change from alive and awake to blitzed and out cold. She raised his arm and let it drop. Not a quiver.

She flew to the dressing room for her robe. Pulling it on, she ran to Rob's room, where she found him tangled in his quilt, one arm clutching his teddy bear and sucking his thumb. He had cried his terror to sleep. Carefully, she re-arranged his blankets and kissed his damp cheek.

"I love you," she whispered. "Everything will be fine. You'll see."

She tore from his room and padded down the staircase. The marble was ice on her feet. Refreshing. Running into the kitchen, she ripped open a cupboard and grabbed three huge, heavy-duty garbage bags. She knew she had to do it. It was either this or do nothing. To do this meant she would live; to do nothing meant her certain death at the hands of this capricious madman. Her choice was simple; either live or die. She chose to live. These bags would do the trick. Snatching the scissors from their hook, she snipped the bags down one side and across the bottom. She opened them wide. Perfect! They rustled in her fingers.

She glanced around for the ashtray, the big, white, heavy, onyx one that Lydia had brought as a gift from Mexico. She needed the damned thing! Where was it? Holding the bags, she ran into the living room, switching on a lamp. She scanned the tables; it wasn't there. Into the family room. Another lamp. Her eyes fell on the ashtray. Right where Julian had left it, full of butts. She grabbed it, scurried back to the kitchen. Butts and ashes into the trash. Rinsing it off under the tap, she dried it with a paper towel. Towel into the trash.

She flicked off the lights as she made her way back to the foyer and up the stairs, carrying the ashtray and the black garbage bags. In their bedroom, the dim bar lamp gave her enough light. But...she had a problem. Julian was heavy and she doubted very much that he'd oblige her and move to a more convenient place for her. Never mind, said her head; we'll figure out a way.

"Julian!" she said. "Julian!" she yelled. "Wake up, you shit!" she hollered. Not a murmur indicated he'd heard her.

She set the ashtray on the night table on his side of the bed and turned on the light. Thank God he slept on the side nearest the bathroom. Taking off her robe, she tossed it across the room. She didn't want it soiled. He was sprawled on his right side, buck naked, snoring and slobbering in his sleep. With pains-taking, tender, breathless care, she worked one of the plastic sheets down and under his right shoulder. She couldn't get it down quite far enough without his help, and she wasn't about to ask. Spreading the plastic up and over the high headboard, she covered as much of it and the pillows as possible. She didn't want blood on them. It was messy enough without having to do laundry as well. In case of blood splatter, she covered up her side of the bed with another plastic sheet. The third sheet was there for unforeseen technical problems. She had never commit-ted murder before and one just never knew what might crop up.

Looking at him, she wondered if he would feel it. She picked up the ashtray. Her emotions were dead; no anger, no joy, no fear, no guilt, no shame, no mercy.

Wielding the ashtray in both hands, she brought it down full-force on the side of his skull, catching him near the crown, on the left. There was a dull, crunching thud. He never twitched a muscle, but she heard a gurgling escape of air from his lips. She stood there, paralyzed, holding her weapon. Blood oozed from the wound and matted with clumps of hair as it trickled down his skull in little rivers, into his ear and onto his neck... She examined the ashtray. Red blobs glimmered on the onyx in the dim light.

Down to the kitchen. In the dark. No lights. Into the dishwasher with the guilty secret. Who cared if there wasn't another thing to wash? She wasn't about to start practicing energy conservation now. She was amazed at how clear her head was. It was operating like a computer, telling her what to do.

Back to the bedroom. More blood, but not too much. She stooped over to listen for his breathing. Shallow gasps. Her luck! He was still alive! Never mind. His skull injury was surely enough to make him expire. Continue with this hare-brained plan. She picked up his legs and lifted them off the bed. They sagged like broken tree trunks over the side. Now came the hard part...getting the rest of him off the bed.

First, she checked for blood splatters on the headboard, the blankets, the pillows, the lamp, night table, and the sheets. Nothing. Don't screw this up. Lifting one of his eyelids, she saw only white with a hint of the iris. She wanted to know what that meant, wishing she had taken some kind of medical course. She wrapped the garbage bag around his shoulders and up over his head. The idea was to lower him to the floor, while containing the blood on the plastic sheet. How was she to prevent it from slipping off? Scurrying to her dressing room, she rummaged through a drawer. Huge safety pins would do it. She worked fast. Ten pins did the job.

Her mind raced, pushing her body into over-drive, as she hauled, pulled, lifted, and tugged the limp body of her husband off the bed. At last, he tumbled onto the carpet. She had never before considered what "dead weight" meant, but she knew now as she dragged him by the ankles, her feet sliding and slipping on the carpet, as she strained and struggled to gain the bathroom. The bag started to slip off, and she had to stop every few inches to secure it, and then scuttle back to the slow, laborious task of heaving and pulling him another few inches. The bathroom tiles were easier; they offered less resistance than the broadloom. Her struggling exhausted her, but she pushed her body beyond its endurance on adrenalin alone. She couldn't give up until this monster was in the tub.

Panting and perspiring from the effort of hauling him into the bathroom, she sank onto the toilet seat, considering how best to maneuver him into the tub. Feet and legs first or upper body? Get the heaviest, most strenuous part over with. The upper body won by acclimation.

My God! He was heavy! Why hadn't she starved him for days before this? And the way he had gobbled down Mary-Beth's delicacies had not helped her cause one iota. Grunting and sweating from the exertion, she heaved with all her strength, but it was impossible to lift him. What was she going to do? She couldn't leave this job half-done!

She stepped into the tub. Her bare feet offered some resistance, and she tugged until she thought she'd pull his arms from their sockets. But she was doing it! She had his shoulders, arms and head over the edge of the tub. Another good yank pulled another inch of his upper body over the rim. Jumping out, she put her arms under his rib cage and grunting, groaning, and straining, heaved most of his torso up over the edge of the tub. With a mighty lift, she managed to get the rest of his pelvic area to follow. Thank God she had been pumping weights for months in the exercise room. Without that extra muscle strength, her efforts would have been useless.

Now for his legs. Compared to what she'd accomplished, the legs were a snap. Julian lay slumped in the tub, crumpled and broken. But he was still breathing—shallow gasps, but he was still alive. How long did it take a person to die? She undid the safety pins and unwrapped her grisly package. A few smears of blood around the lip of the tub made it appear that he'd fallen and smashed his head while showering. Thank God they hadn't remodeled the bathroom as she had suggested; there was a lot to be said for old-fashioned things—especially lethally slippery bathtubs.

There was so much to do! Would she ever get finished? Did people who killed people plan things better than she had? Perhaps she should have thought things through more thoroughly. No time! He would surely have murdered her! And Rob! Perhaps not today, but soon! Stop thinking! Just do! She scoured her hands in the sink, every trace of blood swirling into the drain.

Into the bedroom. Drag marks on the carpet. Down on her knees, scrubbing her fingernails through the pale blue wool. She jumped up and surveyed her work; no one would ever know.

Now for that bloody garbage bag in the bathroom. Down the stairs again. She should have remembered the damned scissors. Oh well, one can't think of everything. Turn on the dishwasher. Another cycle for the ashtray. One can't be too careful. Up the stairs to the bathroom. Down beside the toilet with the bag. Warily watching Julian. He was an awful color. She raised the toilet seat. Snip! Snip! Flush! Flush! Her legs ached; her whole body was one giant cramp from her night's mischief. God, what time was it? Hurry! Hurry! Snip! Snip! Flush! Flush!

Was there anything else to do when this wretched chore was done? The cursed pins! What was she to do with those miserable souvenirs? She had tossed them onto the floor. Reaching over, she scooped them up. Examining each one, she was satisfied they were fine; not in mint condition, but no one would question them. Pins got used. Sometimes they were in top condition; sometimes they became bent. Scrambling to her feet, she padded into her dressing room, and tossed them into her junk drawer.

Back to the bathroom for more snipping and flushing. She never realized how much cutting it took to reduce a garbage bag to tiny snippets. At last she watched the final fragment of her awful secret swirl into the whirlpool and vanish. She waited and flushed the toilet ten more times; just to make absolutely sure no vestige of the bag remained in the plumbing.

With a cloth around her fingers, she turned on the shower spray to make things appear "authentic". Julian's skin glistened with water droplets as she turned off the tap, but he was a ghastly gray. He had never looked better.

Once more she scrubbed her hands in the sink, allowing the water to wash from her flesh the tales of this horiffic night. There was enough of a story in the tub. Grabbing the scissors, she scoured them off with a washcloth. No trace of blood on the scissors or cloth. She'd take them both down to the kitchen and give them a whirl in the dishwasher. Leaving the light on and locking the door by pushing the button in with a fingernail, she pulled the door shut on the madness behind her.

As she glanced around the bedroom, she saw that it appeared as if a wonderful couple had spent a few delightful hours together—except for the two unsoiled black plastic sheets, and Julian's clothes in a heap. She carefully folded the sheets and dashed to the Mustang in the garage and popped them into the trunk of her car "for picnics to keep the table cloth clean and dry". Ripping back to the bedroom, she picked up her robe and stepped into her dressing room to check her body for any tattletale signs of blood. All clear, except for the purple finger marks on her throat. On with the robe. Scissors and washcloth into a pocket. Back into the bedroom. The pillows looked slept on; the quilt was rumpled; two glass tumblers were on his night table. Detail. She moved her glass to her table. The Scotch she had barely touched was watered down with the melted ice. She gagged at the stench. Then she picked up Julian's jacket, trousers and shirt from the floor, and hung them neatly over a chair. Nothing gave the impression of being out of place, odd, weird, or "arranged".

Turning off Julian's lamp and the one at the bar, she tiptoed into Rob's room. He had stirred in his sleep and was flung on his back, his blankets twisted. She didn't disturb his slumber.

Down the cold marble steps to the kitchen. Open the dishwasher. Ashtray still warm. Dry. She lifted it out and turned on the washer for one more cycle to remove any evidence from the scissors and cloth. Details were important. It was still dark. What time was it? Five thirty! It had taken over fours to end her nightmare.

She took a fresh package of cigarettes from a drawer and, with the ashtray, she shambled into the living room to curl up in her favorite chair by the window. Flicking her lighter, she picked up the ashtray to examine it. Not a crack, not a hair, not a drop of blood. She lit her cigarette and rocked and smoked in the shadows.

Her mind was numb, beaten, and wasted. Her body slumped in the chair. My God! What a horrid night! But she was free! Julian could never injure, threaten, or terrorize her again. He'd never play Russian roulette with her life or Rob's life again. What if that gun had discharged? What if there had been a bullet in it? Maybe there wasn't one this time, but he was insane enough to load the gun the next time.

Her only fear was that she had left something undone, that she might have left a clue. And then that fear faded as well; if she was charged with murder, prison was preferable to living on a precipice, never knowing when the earthquake would strike.

Dawn stole in through the curtains. She lit another cigarette. She'd smoked half a pack. She might as well eat the damned things! She wished she had a Valium. She wished she had a whole bottle of Valium. Her nerves twitched, skipped, tingled, and frizzled through her body. Was there a group she could join for husband killers, she wondered, where they could compare notes and help each other deal with the horror of it? Probably in prison. She felt so alone and desolate. God was probably not in her corner any more either.

The sun rose, sending its rays through the sheers, heralding another day of splendid weather. Stirring in her chair, she knew Rob would awaken soon. She'd check on him in a while. Then she would see what was happening in the bathroom where Julian lay in the tub. Rob liked to use their bathroom rather than the main one off the hall. He considered himself to be much more grown up if he was allowed to use his parents' private bathroom.

The sun rose higher, and she decided to see if her son was waking up. Sure enough, the moment she stepped into his room, he turned his blond, curly head to look at her, a wide grin dimpling his cheeks.

"Hi, sweetheart," she smiled. "Time for breakfast. Let's get up."

"Bathroom," he giggled, holding himself through his pajamas.

"Let's use the other bathroom this morning," she suggested. "Daddy's in the tub."

"Daddy's home?" he asked, yawning and rubbing his eyes.

"He sure is! Let's not disturb him."

Agreeing wholeheartedly, as the young and innocent will do if they are manipulated skillfully, he did his duty in the other toilet and played jump, jump, jump, down the stairs as he held onto his mother's hand. Letting Cuddles out of the basement, he scooted into the family room with the dog to watch Sunday cartoons, while Jessica prepared toast and juice and made coffee. She was dying for a steaming cup of plain, old-fashioned, ordinary coffee. She loathed all those fancy designer brands, which Julian had recently discovered were tantalizing to his taste buds.

Waiting for the toast and coffee, Jessica admired her kitchen. It was such a wonderful, friendly, cozy place, with a crystal sun catcher in one window sending rainbow sparkles swirling around the walls and cupboards. Walking to the wide window, she hugged her shoulders and delighted in the view of her lawn and patio and garden. Such a tranquil place of beauty. The birdbath was full of early risers, splashing and twittering their joy of life. A robin bounced across the lawn, stopping and cocking his head to listen for breakfast. The trees were alive with sparrows, chirping and squawking. What a glorious morning. Not a cloud marring the sky. A great day for spending by the pool. Also a great day for an autopsy, she thought bitterly.

The aroma of coffee blended with the fragrance of fresh toast, and she turned from her reverie to buttering the crisp slices and pouring juice and coffee. Rob galloped into the kitchen for his toast and jam, begging to take it with him to eat in front of the TV.

"No jam on the furniture!" Jessica warned. "And you can't take your juice. You have to drink that in here. I don't want a mess!"

She had to go and see what was happening with Julian. Have a cigarette and coffee first, she deliberated. No, I have to do it now!

Trembling, she climbed the staircase. She willed herself to be brain-dead so she didn't have to think about it, didn't have to feel anything. This was the most terrible moment in all of eternity.

Creeping to the bathroom door, she put ear her against it. Horror consumed her when she heard a faint scraping sound, a low moan, and Julian rasping, "Jes...si...ca." Realizing he was scratching on the door, her knees gelled with her alarm. She leaned against it and slid to the floor. What was she supposed to do? Her heart thumped against her rib cage, threatening to pound its way into her hands, which she held clutched to her breast. Closing her eyes, she willed herself not to panic. What about her vow to let him turn blue and have rogor mortis set in before she lifted a finger to help him? With perspiration drenching her forehead, she called to him.

"The door's locked. Can you open it?"

"Can't...reach," came his gasping reply.

Damn! Struggling to her feet, she ran to get the small tool

that fitted the tiny hole in the doorknob and released the lock. Twisting the knob and pushing the door, she discovered that his body was blocking it.

"Julian, I can't get in...Can you move a bit so I can open the door? I need a few more inches."

She heard him claw himself away from the door. With enough space, she squirmed through the doorway. There were no words to describe what met her eyes, other than to say it was a gruesome mess. He had defecated and urinated in the tub and on the floor. Blood smeared the walls, tub, toilet, and tiles. He was far from bleeding to death, but what blood there was went a long way.

"What happened?" What if he knew?

"Dunno," he slobbered and gasped. "Woke up...here...I...was."

Frenzy tormented her mind. Panic knifed her heart. Hysteria gripped her vitals. Keep calm! Guilt whispered in her ear, "Now you've done it!" Fear intoned, "You're going to hang for this!" Terror screamed, "Julian will murder you for sure now!" Shut up! I don't have time for any mental acrobatics! Keep calm!

"Oh, Julian, I told you not to shower in your condition last night!" She knelt down beside him. "Oh, my God! Here, let me get a cold cloth!" She ran cold water over a face cloth, and wringing it out, applied it to the wound. "I'll call 9-1-1.... Hang on! We'll get you looked after!"

She scrambled to the phone in the bedroom. "My husband's badly injured!" she gasped to the operator. "I think he fell in the shower! He's barely conscious!"

The dispatcher told her to wrap him in blankets and not to move him. Standing in the middle of the bedroom, she couldn't remember where the blankets were. She didn't know what day it was. Her brain was fogged, her thinking obliterated. Blankets?

It didn't matter. Grabbing the quilt from the bed, she tucked it around him, pushing it under him to keep the cold tiles from his body. With a shallow gasp, he lapsed into unconsciousness. With one last look at his limp, lifeless body, she flew down the stairs to the family room.

Rob was mesmerized in front of the television.

"Sweetheart, Daddy's feeling a little sick. Some people are coming to help him. Be a really good boy and stay here with Cuddles. I'll be back soon. I'm just going upstairs to be with Daddy."

Instantaneously, "Daddy! Daddy! I wanna see my daddy!" he wailed. Exactly what she didn't need.

He tried to push past her, but she gripped him gently by the shoulders. "Rob, please stay here. Daddy needs us to help him, and the very best way for you to help is to stay right here. Daddy will be so proud to know you helped. I'll tell him as soon as he's feeling better."

His sobs stopped while he thought things over. "OK," he agreed.

The whining of the siren reached her ears, and she bolted to the door to open it for the paramedics. She led the way upstairs with them following with the stretcher.

"What seems to be the problem?" asked one, as she pointed to the bathroom.

"I think he fell in the shower. Will he be all right?"

"We'll check him out."

His partner called from the bathroom. "We need an IV. This guy's pretty messed up. Radio the Civic that we're on the way with a massive concussion."

Gently, they placed Julian on the stretcher, while Jessica watched, wringing her hands, anxiety gnawing at her insides.

Within moments, he was in the ambulance.

"I can't go with you...I have a three year old, and I need someone to care for him. I'll be there as soon as I can." She spoke in a monotone, willing the words to come out.

"The Civic is where he'll be," one medic reassured her. "We're doing all we can for him. We'll let the hospital know you'll be there soon."

Running back to the family room, she checked on Rob in front of the television, cuddling with the poodle.

"Will Daddy feel better soon?" he asked.

"Yes, sweetheart, Daddy will feel better soon. I have to go to the hospital to be with him, but I'll get Binkie to come and stay with you."

An immediate reaction. Fresh crying. "I wanna see my daddy! I wanna go with you! Daddy! Daddy! Don't leave me, Mommy!"

Dear God! This was a disaster! "Rob, please! You have to be a big boy right now! We both have to help Daddy! Please don't cry, because then I'll cry and that won't help Daddy!" Putting her arms around him, she held him close. "I really need you to be grown-up, Rob. Just for a little while. If things are okay with Daddy, I'll take you to the lake for a picnic."

"Promise?" He was suspicious and grim.

"I promise." She squeezed him. "I'm so proud of you!"

She couldn't think. Her head refused to function. Who was she supposed to call? Binkie...to look after Rob.

"I knew somethin' like this would happen," Binkie sympathized when Jessica told her what had occurred; a modified version, of course; the story about Julian's falling in the shower. "I'll be there as fast as I can."

She phoned Rosalind.

432

"Hang on, Jess." Rosalind was always calm, always organized. "I'll be right there. Don't do anything stupid like drive to the hospital yourself. Harry and I'll be there in ten minutes."

Jessica raced upstairs to dress. Tearing open her closet, she yanked out a pair of jeans and a T-shirt. On the front of the shirt, it said, "I'm 49% Pussy Cat and 51% Tiger. Don't push me." It hardly seemed appropriate under the circumstances, but who cared? She pulled on her clothes, slipped on her sandals, and twirled an elastic band around her hair to hold it in a ponytail.

Looking in the mirror, she saw circles under eyes. Her skin sagged on her face. There was no way to repair that mess without a plastic surgeon. Worse, angry purple marks stained her throat. Julian's finger marks! She scrounged through a drawer and found a silk scarf, which she knotted around her neck. Perfect. Another guilty secret covered up. My God! This whole nightmare was one long cover-up, an endless string of lies. Was there a Commandment that said, "Thou shalt not lie"? Yes, there was, come to think about it. "Thou shalt not bear false witness." For sure, God was out for vengeance.

The doorbell chimed.

"Come in!" Jessica shrieked from the landing.

Binkie emerged through the front door.

"Rob's in the family room! I'll be down in a minute! I've got to get to the hospital! Rosalind's coming to pick me up!" Jessica's words sliced the air.

She was out of breath, her heart pounding in her throat. My God! My God! Why didn't she leave well enough alone? She could have hung on a little longer with Julian and his shit. Now she was in this apocalypse. Forget it, her mind told her. You can get through this.

Rosalind hollered from the foyer. "Come on, Jess! Harry's in the car! Come on! This is an emergency, not a beauty pageant!"

"Here I am!" Jessica called out, bolting down the stairs. "I don't care what I look like! Let's get out of here!"

In the back seat of Harry's Continental, she reached for the tissue that Rosalind offered. Then she shrank into the leather corner, her arms folded over her purse, and stared out the window, thinking nothing and feeling everything.

⁂

The emergency ward was as crowded as a Turkish bazaar. Gurneys plugged the hallways. Orderlies scuttled from one stretcher to another. Chairs filled with the sitting wounded lined the corridors. Nurses threaded their way silently, cat-like, on thick-soled shoes, among the sick and injured, checking IV's, feeling for pulses, taking blood pressures, whispering comfort, nodding sympathetically, and pleading for patience.

Leaving Harry to park the car, Rosalind wound her way through the choking, coughing, moaning, retching, bleeding, and the few suffering-in-silence patients to the admissions desk. She dragged Jessica along with her. Pounding on the counter, she demanded attention. Now! A nurse's head bobbed up from behind the counter, which was littered with medical questionnaires.

"Yes? May I help you?" A happy, bright munchkin.

"We're here to see Julian Bothwell. He was brought here a few minutes ago by ambulance. He has a concussion. This is his wife. We want to know where he is, and what's happening."

"Oh, yes," the energetic young woman in pink and white snipped efficiently, "he's in surgery now and his condition is critical, but we will have a brief report in a while. The doctor can talk to you in the family lounge. This way."

She led the way down one corridor after another, through sets of double swinging doors, up a flight of stairs, down another hallway. "This is the lounge," she said, as she held the door open. "Please observe the "No Smoking" signs. Dr. Landry will see you as soon as he's finished. He can fill you in on all the details regarding Mr. Bothwell's condition." And she flew off in a puff of pink and white.

"Christ! I hope Harry can find us!" Rosalind snapped. "We're miles from civilization here!"

Jessica folded herself into a chair, clinging to her purse, her legs wound around each other, her arms holding her insides in place. She was numb. No sounds. No tears. No breathing. No heartbeat.

Rosalind sat beside her, reached over, and took one of Jessica's hands. "Hon, your hand is as cold as ice. Are you sure you're okay? What happened?"

"He fell in the shower." Silence.

The door through which they had entered, whooshed open, and a head popped in. Harry. The rest of him followed his head.

"Wow! That was some tour I had getting here. How're you doing, Jess?"

He was a kind man. He was slightly plump and had a florid complexion due to high blood pressure. On his balding head were a few wisps of graying hair. He patted Jessica's arm. "Did they say anything about how Julian is?"

"He's critical, Harry," Rosalind informed him. "They're operating now."

"D'ya wanna pop or something, Jess? There's a pop machine in the hall. Maybe a Coke?"

"A Coke would be fine, thanks, Harry," she whispered.

He returned with three Cokes, and they sat and sipped in silence. Jessica's distress hung in the air, shrouding them. The minutes ticked by. Four hours and still they waited, Jessica either huddled on her chair or pacing the floor.

The double swinging doors at the end of the lounge opened, and a tall man strode through them. He was garbed in hospital greens and walked toward the trio as he pulled down his facemask.

"I'm Dr. Landry. Which of you two ladies is Mrs. Bothwell?"

Couldn't he tell? The one who was trashed was Mrs. Bothwell.

"I am," Jessica muttered as she paused in her pacing to shake his hand.

"Your husband is alive. He's in critical condition, but stable." Dr. Landry looked very gentle, and the sound of his voice was comforting. "We did a blood test which revealed excessive alcohol in his system, so anesthesia was a bit tricky. We operated to relieve some pressure. Just to drain off some fluid to ease the brain somewhat. We also had to remove some tiny bone splinters. He's in the recovery room right now, but we'll put him into intensive care to keep a close watch on him."

"Can I see him?" asked Jessica. "I'd really like to."

"Sure, I guess that'd be fine. Actually, it's just down the hall. I'll take you, but you can't stay. It'll only be for a minute."

That's fine with me," she whispered.

"We'll wait for you right here," Rosalind announced as the doctor led Jessica away.

"Actually, he looks a lot worse than he is, with all the bandages and tubes and machines," Dr. Landry explained as he guided her down the hall. "I'm not underestimating the severity of his injuries, but his appearance can be quite intimidating to someone not in the medical profession...especially if that person is a loved one, like your husband is."

"I can handle it. I can handle almost anything now."

The doctor opened the recovery room door for Jessica. She had no trouble picking out her husband; he was the only one in there. The sides of his bed were up, and if it's true that all roads lead to Rome, in this room, all the tubes and wires led straight to Julian. Machines and lights surrounded his bed and computer screens blip, blip, blipped his vital signs.

Jessica inched up to the form lying there, wrapped in white, packaged in white, bound in white. With the white sheets tucked tightly around him, he was swaddled like Lazarus. A huge bandage surrounded his skull, almost to the bridge of his nose. The little flesh on his face that was visible was pasty gray.

"Thank you, doctor," whimpered Jessica. "I appreciate all you've done. I'm very grateful." And she collapsed in tears on the floor beside Julian's bed. "Oh, my God! I'm so scared! I'm so scared! What will I do? What will I ever do? What's going to happen to me? What's going to happen to my son?"

"Mrs. Bothwell!" The doctor was alarmed. "He's going to be fine! You don't need to be frightened! Now come along with me! You can't stay in here! I'll take you to your friends! Come along now, Mrs. Bothwell."

Gently, with hands under her arms, he tugged her to a standing, but crumpled position. Tears washed down her face as he guided her into the hallway. Rosalind, hearing her howling, dove through the double doors, rescuing her from the doctor.

"Sometimes it's difficult to see a loved one in such serious condition," the doctor explained. "She'll be fine. I've tried to reassure her that her husband will make a full recovery."

"Thanks, doctor," Rosalind said, as she held her weeping friend.

"Oh, dear God, Rosalind! I'm terrified! I'm so scared! I've never been so terrified in my life! What's going to happen to me? And to Rob? What about him? What's going to happen to us?"

"Jess, everything's going to be fine." Harry patted her back as Rosalind led the way through the maze to the exit. "I can safely say," continued Harry, "that Julian will pull through this with no problem. He's strong and healthy."

"Oh God! What am I ever going to do?" wailed Jessica.

"Cry it out," Rosalind instructed. "Get rid of all those tears, and you'll feel better. You can't keep all those thoughts and feelings bottled up inside. Come home with Harry and me, and you can cry all you want."

⁂

"Jess, I need some more tea. Lots of sugar," Julian ordered from his court in their bedroom. "Maybe bring me some cookies too, while you're at it. And what about the TV guide? I can't find it. And I want that newspaper, too."

She stomped into their bedroom where Julian reclined on plumped up pillows. "I'm trying to read Rob his bedtime story," she hissed. "I am *not* your personal maid! I told you to hire a private nurse! If you want tea and biscuits, get them yourself!"

"Maybe I should go home to Mother," he smirked.

"That's the best idea you've had in a long time! Should I call her to pick you up? Maybe pack a lunch with a polished apple to take with you?"

⁂

Jessica called Casey two days after Julian's accident to tell him what had happened and that she would be unable to join him at the range until Julian had made a complete recovery.

"Gee, that's too bad, Jessica. Sorry to hear Julian got hurt. Man could kill himself fallin' in a shower. Make sure you look after yourself. I have nothing to report from the range, but as soon as you can get down here, I have some juicy gossip to tell you. Keep in touch."

His tone was light-hearted, but Jessica knew there was a message for her in those words.

⁂

Frightened? She was petrified. Her one bid for freedom had failed. Would the concussion make him worse, more volatile? Despair sank into her pores like body lotion. Rob's laughter cheered her, but his smiles and innocence alarmed her. How was she to save her son from this nightmare?

With Julian back at work, she had a break from his constant demands for anything that popped into his head. And she had Binkie back. For the three weeks he was at home, Julian preferred that the housekeeper not come in.

"I don't want that old busy-body with her dusting feathers in this house! I want to be sick in peace!" Then he turned up the volume on the television to tune out Jessica's voice.

⁂

Her home was charged with foreboding. It dribbled down the windowpanes as the summer storm swirled through the trees in the yard, hurling the rain against the house in angry gusts. Jessica stared outside from her chair in the living room, a cup of coffee, now grown cold, on the side table along with an ashtray, bursting with butts and ashes. It's hard to believe, she thought, but on the other side of that vicious sky, there is actually a shining sun. To her, it appeared the world was one giant mud puddle.

The phone jangled and she leapt to her feet, breathless and rattled. She was losing her grip, she knew.

Binkie called from the kitchen. "It's for you, Miss Jessica."

It was Rosalind, chuckling. "I read something in the morning paper and thought it would tickle your fancy."

"Okay, shoot. I need a good laugh."

"Scientists say one possibility is that someday the universe will collapse back on itself in a reverse of the Big Bang. We hope that doesn't mean we have to relive all of this, only backwards."

"Right, Rosalind! I'm glad you found that funny. This life is bad enough forwards. I can't imagine it in reverse."

"Come on, Jess, I thought you'd like it."

"In another lifetime, maybe. Not today."

"Mary-Beth and I are doing lunch today, and we're going shopping at the new mall. Why don't you come? It'll get you out for a while."

"No thanks. I think I'll go to the range. I haven't been there since Julian's accident, and today's the first chance I've had to go."

"Aren't you becoming obsessed with this shooting thing, Jess? Are you sure that's healthy?"

"I need to protect myself. The next time anyone breaks in, I'll splatter his brains all over my walls!"

"Liberated at last, Casey!" she said into the phone.

"Great stuff, darlin'," he laughed.

"Can we meet this afternoon?" she asked.

"I'm pretty sure I can fit you into my busy schedule. Like I told you before, I've got some interesting gossip. I think you'll be fascinated with what I have to tell you. I'll see you at twelve-thirty."

***

Rain pelted the car, the wipers barely able to clear the windshield from the torrents gushing from the tormented, blackened sky. Jessica hunched over the steering wheel, squinting to see the road through the streams of water sluicing down the windshield. Anxious to meet Casey, Noah's flood wouldn't have kept her from venturing out to satisfy her curiosity. She and Casey had an agreement that he not phone the house about "business" regarding the break-in. She feared that with a psychopath like Julian, the phone might be tapped. Even though Casey was a family friend, she wasn't willing to leave herself open to what Julian was capable of deliberately misunderstanding. Casey had said that once he had the information he needed, they could tell Julian. The police had come up with a big round zero. Maybe Casey would have something to tell her when they met. He had certainly hinted that he had some "interesting gossip" from the range, and she concluded it was definitely information regarding the break-in.

Casey's car was parked right at the entrance to the building housing the range. Few cars were in the lot. There were many more sensible people in the world than she was, she mused. As she pulled in beside his car, she saw that he was still in it, and through the rivers of water rushing down the windows, she was able to see him motioning for her to join him. Dodging raindrops, she jumped onto the front seat beside him.

"How's Julian?" he asked as she lit her hundredth cigarette of the day.

"Recovered."

"Here. I want you to read this. No lessons today. We have to talk. Like I said, I have some interesting gossip for you, only it isn't gossip. These are facts."

"How about the break-in? Did you learn anything?"

"All in good time, Jessica. Read this first." His voice was gruff, and his face wore a worried expression. He handed her a beige file folder. "Take your time. I want you to understand what it says, and the repercussions. It took me a while to get this information. I had to grease a few palms, and kiss some asses...I'd heard some scuttlebutt about this years ago, but I didn't pay too much attention to it. For a great detective, I loused up royally on this one—but it seemed too far-fetched, too beyond the realm of possibility. It's not that these things don't occur. They do! And this incident did occur! I remember reading about it in the papers years ago. But to personally know a participant was too wild for even me. Instead, I filed it in my head, and then when things looked like you might be in big trouble, I decided to snoop—mostly for my own peace of mind. It mighta been better if I'd checked this out long ago, but sometimes we don't take things seriously enough; especially something like this. It does something to your heart and spirit to know that people are capable of such malevolence. Go ahead. Read it."

Warily, she looked at the folder, and then back at Casey. Dear God! She didn't know if she had the strength for any more spiders in her life. Was this folder a Pandora's box of tarantulas and black widows? She opened it. Inside were several Xeroxed copies of hand-written reports. The letterhead was "Homewood Sanitarium". The patient's name was "Julian Bothwell". Age of patient: 16.

Every word stunned her brain and stopped her heart. This made Pandora's box look like a Christmas stocking stuffed with gumdrops. Don't think. Don't feel, her mind screamed. Stay calm!

"Are you scared?" Casey wanted to know when she closed the folder.

She nodded. "Why didn't you tell me? Why didn't you let me know about this?"

"I didn't receive this until a few days after Julian's accident, and I didn't even want to phone you for a lesson because we don't know what he's been up to. I sure didn't want to remind him of my existence even though he thinks we're buddies. With a slick bastard like him, I wasn't willing to take any risks. Too bad he didn't die from that goddamned fall in the shower."

"That break-in was a set-up, wasn't it?" she asked quietly, her voice barely audible above the din of the rain hammering the car. "Like you said when you came over, it was a set-up, but it wasn't those guys coming back. This was Julian's doing, not those guys from last year." She didn't cry.

"I'm sorry, Jessica."

"How do you know?" She stared at the rain.

"I'm not one hundred per cent sure, but I was able to track a check for five thousand dollars that someone cashed the afternoon before that day that you called the cops and me. The check was made out to the Fenwick Paper Company. There is no such company. The check was Julian's, and it was made out on his personal account. He left for France the afternoon the check was cashed....It looks bad, Jessica. It might be a coincidence, but I don't think so. Here..." He pulled a slip of paper from his jacket pocket and handed it to her. "That's a copy of the check."

She held the copy and stared at it. "I don't understand this, Casey. I thought you and Julian were friends."

He directed his gray eyes at her. "There's a lot you don't know. And Julian doesn't know this either. Did he ever mention anything to you about his girlfriends from his younger years?"

"Not much." Don't volunteer a thing. Casey and Julian conspiring to flip you over the brink is not beyond the realm of reality at this Mad Hatter's Tea Party.

"I had a kid sister who came out to work at one of old man Bothwell's hotels. Julian romanced her, and she fell for him. He bedded her, and she got pregnant. Julian's father paid for the abortion. He also gave my parents twenty thousand dollars to forget about it. They were dirt poor. That money silenced them. It also killed my baby sister because she bled to death in her sleep just after the back-alley abortion. Julian doesn't know I'm her brother."

Rain pummeled the roof of the car. Inside, the air was thick with the acrid smoke of their cigarettes. They sat in a toxic bubble; toxic with the contents of the folder; toxic with the smoldering tobacco; toxic with the memory of a young woman's life oozing onto the bed sheets where she died.

"Jessica, I can help you if you want to get out...I've..."

"I can't leave!" she screamed. The leash on her emotions snapped, letting loose her terror. "I can't leave! He'll kill me! You know that! I'm nothing more than a blood sacrifice! And he'll kill Rob! My God, Casey, you hand me that shit from that hospital, and you think I can simply disappear? For a goddamned smart detective, you are sure one stupid cop! He's told me time and again, drunk or sober, that I have nowhere to hide! He'll find me! I know he will! And you might be working for him! He can buy anyone off! Why not you too? He's my worst nightmare come true! He's depraved and SICK! I hate him! I hate him!"

"Jessica...Jessica." He reached over and put an arm around her. She collapsed against him, shuddering and trembling, sobbing her terror onto his chest." I really can help you. I know you don't believe me, but there is a way out..."

"How?" she shrieked, pulling away, her face grimaced into an accusation, a challenge. "A rocket to Mars? A submarine in the Dead Sea? A space station?" Tears poured in rivers onto her jacket. "Do you really believe that shit about women leaving abusive partners and surviving if those men threaten to kill them? Casey, those guys stalk their women! They're as relentless as wolverines! Those women have nowhere to hide! With Julian's network, he can find me in no time! And he's threatened to kill Rob, too! You just don't understand! Oh, God! Oh, Jesus! I can't take any more!"

"Jessica!" he barked, jolting her out of her hysteria, "do you really believe that staying is better than leaving?"

"No," she hiccupped, "but why bother running, when I might live longer by staying? Maybe I can keep Rob alive!"

"I'm going to tell you something that'll show you he can kill with impunity. He murdered two people in this town."

"I suppose you're going to say he did in Tiffany and Jack. Come on, Casey..."

"Jessica, how could you have read that report, learned the truth about my sister, and not believe he's capable of cold-blooded murder?"

"If he did, why wasn't he convicted?"

"Rich daddy! I followed that case with a great deal of interest, especially since my sister had been involved with that crew. There was plenty of evidence pointing in Julian's direction that he had arranged that accident. Broken battery cable, my ass! But much of it was lost or destroyed or tampered with. Julian's father was a rough, tough old bastard who'd buy off anyone to get his way and to save his son and the family name. There was big money at stake, not to mention a reputation. As sure as I sit here, Julian left them to freeze to death, while he maintained to the end that he'd been trying to save them. I did some checking on the police file investigating the deaths, and it's still open as they never were able to establish guilt beyond doubt. The inquest was inconclusive."

"My days are numbered, aren't they?" she sniffled, rifling her purse for tissues. She yanked them out, and blew her nose.

He nodded. "The problem is, Jessica, we don't know how many days he's given you."

Suspiciously, she eyed him. "How do I know you're not lying to me? You could be setting me up. You could be working for Julian." She twisted the tissues in her hand. "I don't know who to trust anymore! You could blow me away, and no one would know the difference!"

"You might have to trust me," he said softly, taking her hand. "I can get you and Rob out. I can set the whole thing up and have you out within a few days. I know some people who can help. Is Julian going out of town soon? That'd be the best time to do it."

"He's not planning another trip until October, thanks to his ever-loyal manager who's volunteered to do more overseas jaunts...probably to get away from all his kids and Roxanne. Julian can murder me and have Rob and me on meat-hooks in cold storage fifty times between now and then!"

"Then we'll be working under more difficult conditions. Do you want to hear what I have in mind? Or would you rather take your chances with Julian?"

"Can I think about it? I mean, if I know what the plan is, then I can decide if I want to do it or not."

"Yes, we can do it that way...but...you do not tell a living soul about this! No one! The only person you discuss this with is me! And you don't say goodbye to anyone either! I know you and that Rodgers woman are best friends, but you don't breathe a word of this to her. The only way to keep a secret is not to tell anybody! If one word leaks out about this, it could put us all in serious jeopardy, most especially you and Rob!"

"But Rosalind wouldn't tell anyone! She'd be thrilled for me!"

"Jessica, if you tell the secret, then it's no longer a secret. Get that through your head! This is your life and Rob's we're talking about!"

"If I vanish without a trace, the first person who'll raise the alarm and go to the authorities will be Rosalind! Millions of people will read about Rob's and my mysterious disappearance in the morning newspaper over their coffee, and it'll hit the six o'clock news! It'll be all over the Internet. How's that for a secret?" Jessica protested.

"I'll get word to her that you're safe once we have you out of harm's way. Don't worry about that," Casey reassured her.

She nodded as she looked deep into his eyes. They were blank.

"All right," he said, "here's what I have in mind."

Mesmerized, she listened to his plan. Eyes widening, she couldn't believe her ears. This outrageous idea resembled the Scarlet Pimpernel's feats to rescue unfortunate souls during the French Revolution. She'd never be able to do it. This was a

James Bond scheme. Totally ludicrous. Her shooting instructor was offering her a madcap solution. He had once accused her of watching too much TV. That was a laugh in comparison to this scheme.

"What's the price tag on this? I have money in my account, but not enough for something as elaborate as this."

"Not a dime. These men do this as a kind of hobby, keeping their skills honed. I'm calling in some favors on this, Jessica, so don't you worry about the cost. I've already talked to them about this assignment and they're willing to help us. All you're going to need is the price of a couple of airline tickets for you and Rob."

"How do I know they won't sell me into white slavery? They might nab Rob! Kill us!"

"You can trust them with your life, Jessica, which is what you'll be doing. If they rescued political prisoners and hostages from tight corners in hostile countries, they can free you from your impossible, potentially fatal situation. You can compare it to the FBI Witness Protection Program, only this is totally unofficial and probably a lot safer. The only thing I need to ask you is are you willing to go up North?"

"Will I need to wallpaper an igloo?" she sniffled.

"The North covers a lot of territory. I was thinking of some place in Canada...maybe British Columbia...a city or town in the interior. I'll arrange for new identities and passports for you and Rob."

She narrowed her eyes at him. "Cross-border trafficking in battered women? Come on Casey! This is preposterous!"

"Think about it, Jessica. It's the only chance you have."

She sat frozen to the seat, staring at the rain as it pummeled the windows. Her heart jack hammered against her chest, threatening to explode into her hands. Fear gripped her vitals. Her head stopped working, thoughts congealed into white-hot terror. She threw herself into Casey's arms, against his massive chest.

"Hold me tight, Casey!" she pleaded. "Hold me as tightly as you can! I'm so terrified! I shall fly into a zillion pieces if you don't hold me! I'm so scared! I'll never be safe again!"

She dug her hands and nails into his doeskin jacket, burying her face in his shoulder as her held her. For two cents and one bullet, he'd have dropped Julian where he stood, probably in his bar at the Terrace Lounge. If ever a guy deserved to die, Julian did. Casey vowed he'd bring Julian to justice. One way or another, Julian was not going to get away with murder, and he'd never harm Jessica again. Casey held the sobbing Jessica for what seemed like hours while her sobs died to whimpers, and gradually she came back to her senses.

"You're right Casey. I can do this. I just need time for this plot to sink in."

✳

"Binkie," she asked, when she arrived home from her "shooting practice", how long did you say you've worked for the Bothwells?"

Binkie had taken the stove apart for cleaning and was scouring the burner linings. "Almost thirty years. Long time, Miss Jessica."

"Julian was a teenager when you started. What kind of kid was he?"

"Oh, he was wild! Most kids are at that age. Good kid, though. Of course, his daddy kept him in line."

"Did he have lots of friends?"

"Good golly, Miss Jessica, that was a long time ago. I can't hardly remember."

"He was in high school when you started?" Jessica wanted to know.

"That's right. Miss Jessica... the next time you burns somethin' on the stove, could you please soak the liners? I can't get the scorched stuff outa this one, and I bin scrubbin' it for a hour."

Jessica took a Coke from the fridge and snapped the tab, sucking the cold fizzy pop from the can. Lighting one of too many cigarettes of the day, she sat down and watched Binkie. "Do you remember if he went away to school at all? Or did he always go to a local high school?"

Ceasing her frantic scrubbing, Binkie stepped back from the sink and looked for the answer written on the ceiling. "You know, that's right...I almost forgot about that. Yes...Yes, he did go away to school! His daddy sent him to a boardin' school for two years. Somethin' about Mr. Julian getting mixed up with the wrong kids or something. But you know, Miss Jessica, I always knew that the 'wrong kids' wasn't the real reason."

Jessica's adrenalin level soared. "What was the real reason?" She almost whispered the words. Binkie might corroborate what she had read in the file.

"Old Mr. Bothwell was a real snob. A very uppity man. He always thought hisself better than everybody else. He sent Mr. Julian to that boardin' school 'cause he wanted him to mix with high-class folks, not with what Mr. Bothwell thought was rubbish."

Jessica's heart pounded. Maybe the report was phony. Maybe Casey was in cahoots with Julian. What was in the file didn't match what Binkie had said, other than the time frame.

Julian hadn't gone to boarding school. He'd been locked up in an institution!

"Did he ever come home during holidays when he was in the boarding school?"

Binkie was busy scrubbing again. "Lordy, Miss Jessica, I can't remember! I never paid their business much heed. I had troubles of my own a-plenty. A person who minds someone else's business, ain't got time for their own. And besides, they wasn't talkin' that much to me. Mr. B. hardly never said nothin' to me, and Miss Lydia never paid me much attention neither. If you tells me somethin', fine. If you don't, ain't none of my business."

"You're one in a million, Binkie. You ought to work for the CIA. Not even torture would persuade you to tell any tales."

Stopping her attack on the liners, Binkie squinted at Jessica. "I knows what I knows, and I'm tellin' the truth! I'se loyal to you because I like you. If I knew somethin' about Mr. Julian, I'd tell you, and I have. I don't carry tales that ain't true, and I don't go pokin' in people's affairs. And I don't think Mr. Julian is treatin' you right. He's downright nasty, if you ask me."

That's putting it mildly, thought Jessica.

That night, after tucking Rob into bed, Jessica readied herself for bed, determined to watch a movie and concentrate on it rather than allow her mind to terrify her. But it was no use. Casey's words haunted her. Her own mind haunted her.

Julian was all the people Jessica's mother had warned her about as a child rolled into one grotesque bogeyman. Everything added up! And, of course, the wife was the last one to know! No one suggested she not marry him, because it was "suspected" he may have murdered Tiffany and his best friend—or to put it more precisely, left them to freeze to death. Even Rosalind had been ambivalent about Julian, one time saying Jessica should leave before Julian killed her, and then saying it would be nice when Julian came home from a trip so Jessica wouldn't be lonely. And of course, Julian thought Jessica was unfaithful; with his brain burned by electric shock treatments and drug therapy, he'd revert to the Tiffany-mode. Rosalind had said she thought that Tiffany had been afraid of Julian, that something she had heard about him had frightened her. Now Jessica understood why. Perhaps she had tried to call off their wedding, and rather than lose her, he killed her. Accusing his women of infidelity was a malicious way of keeping them de-railed and defensive and undermining their confidence. What that young woman must have endured boggled Jessica's imagination.

With Julian's sadistic streak, coupled with his involvement at an early age with a cult with such evil tendencies, the synergistic effect had created a fiend. Lydia's warning was packed with truth: Julian's women came and went because he murdered them, either directly or indirectly. Casey's hideous file terrorized her. Things like that existed, but never in her wildest dreams did she suspect something so repugnant would touch her life. One read about it in *National Enquirer,* or tucked into the last page of the last section of a newspaper, or maybe in *True Detective.* It didn't happen in one's own life.

How could she corroborate Casey's story and the file? Dear God! What was she going to do? Participate in Casey's preposterous scheme? Fly off to a foreign country, for God's sake? Maybe she should shoot Julian and pretend she'd mistaken him for a burglar. Perhaps she should level with Julian, tell him her concerns and suspicions, ask him to confess, accompany him to the sanitarium, and have them confirm that he was cured when he was discharged, and that this was all simply one big mistake. She knew where that trail would end—with her at the bottom of the river!

Her eyes were riveted to the television, but she was tuned to the station in her head. This program was sure to win an Emmy Award. Thoughts winged their way through the cavern of her mind, like bats with a new batch of mosquitoes. But her bats had defective radar; they kept colliding with each other. She was unable to pin her thoughts down and unable to think things through. Every idea ended up in a no-escape labyrinth, a mangled maze. If there was a God, she wished He would materialize right here in her bedroom and issue a summons that Julian take an early retirement from life.

⁎⁎⁎

Her eyes ached, her head throbbed, and her mind was in major over-drive. With yesterday's storm only a memory, the sun had risen this morning eager to make up for the rain. The problem was, the fervent glare almost blinded Jessica as she drove to the range. Not having slept a wink because she was overloaded with terror and anxiety and because she had kept a wary eye on Julian all night, she found driving into the sunlight an aggravation. But it didn't slow her down. She had to get there!

Jerking the car to a halt amid a spray of gravel, she fled into the building and raced to the pay phones. Fumbling coins into the slots, she prayed Casey would be home. His phone rang and rang, as her panic escalated. If there is a benevolent power in the universe, please let Casey be home! Seven rings and

453

he answered.

"It's me, Jessica! I'm at the range! I need to see you! I dug into the old newspaper archives this morning, and read all their accounts about the accident in the blizzard. I also researched that outrageous incident that Julian was allegedly involved in, and I know now it's true! It's all true! Oh, Casey, I'm so scared! Please come!"

"I'll be there right away. Relax. You'll be fine. We'll get you out!"

✻

Casey thought she was demented when she told him. "You're nuts! I cannot believe I'm hearing this! You're either courageous, know something I don't, or you're a total fruitcake! I will not allow you to do this!"

She begged, pleaded, and remained adamant. "I need to do this, Casey! I'll have only one chance to do it, and if I don't, I'll regret it for eternity! I want to betray him, the way he deceived me! And I want the power he stole from my life back in my own hands! Besides, then we'll all know where he is. We don't know what he's been cooking up. He could have the place surrounded for all we know, waiting for me to make a break for it. He's more unlikely to do anything, and he'll suspect less, if he's in my tender, loving embrace. He'll think all is forgiven and forgotten, and that I've learned my lesson to be subservient to his capricious whims."

Casey was infuriated with this woman he was trying to help. God, females could be exasperating! He could just picture her becoming unglued at a crucial moment and the whole plan having to be jettisoned. With a madman like Julian, they could be hauling her out in a body bag. "Christ, Jessica, I don't think you have the nerves for this! You told me yourself you shied away from undercover work because you were scared of what might be under your bed at night! And the way you've been panicking lately, you're going to unravel! When you called me a few minutes ago, you were ready for a straightjacket, and now you're as smooth as James Bond! Sweet Jesus, Jessica, you're a loose cannon! You're going to get us all killed!"

She narrowed her eyes, looked straight at him, and quietly said in a matter of fact manner, "Casey, you are looking at a many-faceted woman. That little tumble Julian took in the shower? That was no accident. Yours truly intentionally clobbered him with a heavy object and then hauled him into the bathroom. I had the moxie for that, and I was all by myself, in the middle of the night, with a man with his mind on murder. Don't worry about me when I have you and three other professionals backing me."

"Tell me how you nailed him!"

"Oh, no, Casey," she said, with a touch of mystery in her tone. "I don't give away my trade secrets. But just because you're such a good friend, I'll tell you all about it over a cup of coffee sometime. I might have been unglued yesterday, and this morning, and for the better part of sixteen months, but that was because I was trapped and living in hopeless despair. Now I have a goal, Casey, and it's only a few days away. Complete freedom from that unmitigated monster! See these hands, Casey? Ice water flows in their veins! You told me I might have to shoot someone someday, and I never believed you, and I never thought I could do it. I know now I can. Julian better not mess with me!"

Whatever doubts Casey may have had vanished as he stared at this woman who could appear so fragile and even hare-brained. Her apparent weaknesses were her greatest strengths. No one would ever suspect the tiger that lurked beneath the surface. This woman had invisible stripes!

Chapter Twelve:

Keeping up Appearances

TWO DAYS LATER, THE AFTERNOON WAS EVENTFUL. First, Jessica visited the lingerie boutique, where she picked up a few items guaranteed to tantalize her husband, and then she stopped at the sports shop for heavy-duty fishing line. One never knew when it might come in handy.

Adorned in a red, orange, and yellow floral full-skirted sundress, toeless pumps to match, and a red Coach tote over her shoulder, she sailed into the bank, swished into the manager's office, begged him for a private audience, and confided in him. She was planning a wonderful surprise for Julian—a cruise—and needed to empty her account to pay for it.

"You know how good Julian's been to me, Sam. Remember that cruise he took me on to Hawaii, just after we met? Well, he took his Mother on a three-week Caribbean cruise before that, and he raved so much about it that I thought I'd surprise him with another one for our fourth wedding anniversary. Only this trip is going to be more extravagant. Nothing but the absolute best for my man, Sam! First class all the way! And I'm certainly not going to put it on any of my credit cards because all those bills go straight to Julian's office. I don't want a paper trail on this because that would just ruin the surprise. Do you think you could do me that one little favor, Sam?" She batted her eyelashes at him, and pasted on her brightest, most sincere smile. "Of course, leave enough money in the account to keep it open, but I wanted to talk to you because the tellers are so persnickety about anyone withdrawing large amounts of cash."

"I don't see that as a problem, Jessica." He rose. "I'll go and get that for you right away, if you'll just sign this withdrawal request."

As she signed the form, she said, "Oh, Sam, before I forget, Julian and I are having a patio party on Saturday night. We'd love to have you and Dorothy join us. It's casual, of course, and bring your bathing suits."

"That sounds swell, Jessica, but Dorothy's parents will be here for the weekend."

"Oh, bring them, too! The more the merrier! In fact, why don't you ask the bank staff to come? I'm sure you don't have more than thirty people working here, and they all know Julian. Thirty people is a drop in the bucket at our place. I think that would be grand. Julian will just love to see everyone!"

"Gee, Jessica, that's a generous invitation."

"My pleasure!" she beamed.

As he counted out the fifty thousand dollars, he cautioned her to be careful with that much cash.

Shoving it into her shopping bag, she said, "Oh, Sam, I'm so thrilled to be doing this! I'll keep you posted about all the arrangements. Don't breathe a word to Julian. This will be our little secret, right?" She hugged him and gave him a peck on the cheek. "Don't forget Saturday night!"

Then she sashayed out of his office, giving him a sly wink over her shoulder as she closed his office door. She could picture an embarrassed and flummoxed Julian—if he was still alive or not hospitalized after her confrontation with him that night— explain to the crowd arriving for the pool party on Saturday night that no such party existed. She had already invited dozens of Riverbend residents to the social gathering and knew nearly everyone would show up because people just loved revelry at the Bothwells' mansion. The puzzling non-party would be sure to cast some focused attention in Julian's direction. The nonexistent festivities plus his obnoxious behavior at Mary-Beth's party would be sure to arouse some nasty speculation about Julian's stellar reputation. With Rob and Jessica missing, what would people say?

On her way home, she stopped at five automatic tellers and withdrew her cash limit on all her credit cards, plus made a sizeable withdrawal from her and Julian's joint account. The transactions wouldn't be accounted for until the next day, and by that time, if any of the credit card companies or the banks took note of her large withdrawals, it would be far too late. My, my, my, Julian was not going to be a happy little hummer when he received his new credit card statements. If he lived long enough to be unhappy, that is.

Her second-last scheduled appointment was for three-fifteen at her home. Because it was such a private affair, she let Binkie leave early.

"Binkie, why don't you take the rest of the afternoon off? You've been working so hard lately and deserve time to yourself. I don't think I'll need to have you tomorrow either because the girls are coming for lunch. But I've put a little something in this envelope for you to make up for those hours, plus a bonus for your loyalty and service. You needn't tell Julian about this. It's just between you and me. You know...girl secrets." She winked at her old friend and devoted helpmate and embraced her warmly at the door. "I love you, Binkie; please take really good care of yourself. I'll see you in a day or two."

Binkie smiled at her. "You're a good woman, Miss Jessica. I love you, too."

Jessica watched as the little gray lady chugged to her car and climbed into her old beater. As Binkie drove away, there were tears in Jessica's eyes. I may never see Binkie again, she thought, as she hugged herself and prayed for strength.

Her callers arrived promptly at three-fifteen. All were dressed in black trousers and black turtle-necked, long-sleeved sweaters. They were efficient, professional, impassive, and silent.

Systematically, they disabled or rigged the telephones in the house, the alarms, the electrical supply, the cars, Julian's revolver, and his car phone. The house phones and anything powered by electricity still worked so that everything appeared normal, but all Jessica had to do was push a remote device button to render them useless. The men also changed every dead bolt lock in the house, with both sides of the lock requiring a key. None of Julian's keys would work, meaning that if the doors were locked, Julian would be housebound. Even the garage door leading to the house had a new dead bolt, so that was not an avenue open to him either. The only doors that did not have a dead bolt on them, the sliding doors to the patio, were fastened shut with screws. His only means of getting out would be to break a window, but by then they would have a major head start. And with no alarm system with which to alert security people, no phone with which to summon help, and no car with which to follow them, Julian would be in a bit of predicament for a considerable length of time—if he survived. She prayed *she* would live to tell the tale! Both their lives were at stake.

While the three men were immersed in their assignments, Jessica, following their advice, emptied the disaster drawer in the kitchen, removing all the candles and flashlights that they kept there in case of a power blackout and placed them in a cardboard box. She also searched out and removed the candles and flashlights they had in their night tables for the same purpose. The scented candles in their fancy holders, as well as any lighters and matches she found, she tossed into the same box filled with the emergency sources of light. She packed the carton out to the garage where she added the hurricane lamps and other flashlights they had hanging on hooks. Satisfied that she had collected anything that might help Julian light his way in the blackened house, she buried the container in the garage under a pile of storage boxes.

As the three men left, the oldest one said, "You'll do fine. Just don't forget to leave that front door unlocked for your husband when he comes home, and lock it on your way out. If you need us, use that two-way radio. We won't be far away. Otherwise, we'll see you at 3:00 AM. Good luck!"

With little time to spare, she hurriedly packed a few necessary clothes for Rob and herself. Casey had ordered her to take only two small suitcases. "Christ, woman, you don't need a steamer trunk! Take what you need and leave the rest!"

Giving Rob his supper, she happily announced to him that Casey would be picking him up for a night out with the boys.

"Isn't that exciting, sweetheart? Casey thought you might like to have some fun without Mommy tagging along. Make sure you take teddy with you, and Casey's going to take some of our suitcases, because after you and Casey have fun, Mommy has another big surprise for you!"

On the dot of seven, the time of the last appointment, Casey was at the door. Rob stared in awe at this huge man with whom he was supposed to have fun.

"Do you remember Casey, sweetheart?" asked Jessica, stooping to hug her son. "He's the man who found your teddy bear."

"That's right," Casey grinned as he squatted so Rob didn't have to crane his neck to see his face. "Just between you and me, Tiger, I was more interested in finding that terrific bear, than I was in looking for that coffee pot."

"Yeah," pouted Rob, "I can't sleep without my teddy bear. Mommy doesn't need her coffee pot to sleep."

"Well, I know the importance of bears, Rob. I used to have one that slept with me, too."

"You did?" Rob stood in wide-eyed wonder.

"Yep," Casey assured him. "Now, why don't you and I go and do some good stuff, while we wait for your mom. Where would you like to go?"

"Chuck E. Cheese's," giggled Rob, taking the big man's hand, as Casey picked up one of the two suitcases. Jessica carried the second, and they walked down the steps to the black car, with one of her rescuers at the wheel. Casey loaded the bags in the trunk. With a last wave to his mother, Rob climbed in, hugging his teddy bear.

Jessica stood on the porch until the car disappeared from sight, asking Providence to watch over her child and for the strength she needed for the hours ahead.

Now for her secret weapon! Grabbing the bag in which the store clerk had put it, she snatched her kitchen scissors and a roll of scotch tape and ran up the staircase with her equipment. Sitting at the top of the staircase, she ripped open the package of fishing line and unraveled several feet. Carefully, she chose the third spindle of the railing, the one that stood by the second step of the staircase, and painstakingly wrapped one end of the line around the wooden spindle, knotting it several times about twelve inches above the step. She tugged on it, to make sure it was secure. Then she strung the other length across that step, so that it was a foot above the stair, and cut it, leaving enough to enable her to knot the end around the spindle opposite the first. She tied it, tugged on it, and cut it. Then she carefully rehearsed what she had done several times, to make sure she knew exactly what to do, especially with the second knot, because that was the crucial one. Over and over she practiced the knots, her eyes closed, as if she was working in the dark.

Satisfied that she was an expert with fishing line, she cut the last length from the spool and carefully tied her first knot on her chosen spindle. With the correct measure to stretch across the step, plus enough to secure it on the opposite spindle, she cut her last length. But this length she did not tie across the stair. Instead, she secured the line along the inside of the row of banister spindles with scotch tape. All she required were a few pieces of the invisible tape, so that the line wasn't dangling in empty space. She stepped back to take a look at her simple idea. The clear fishing line was almost invisible, and would definitely escape the notice of anyone in general, and Julian, in particular. The beauty of the scotch tape was that it gave her immediate access to the loose end of line.

With that task completed, she gathered up the cut pieces of line, the spool, and the empty package, and thrust the litter into the store's bag and into the attaché case, which held her cash and valuables. She wasn't about to leave that trash behind her. She'd think about what to do with the line tied around the spindles later, if she had to.

After putting the tape and scissors back in their places, she returned to the staircase. She ran to the top and walked to the bedroom door. Walking backwards, with the railing to steer her, she counted the steps along the landing/hallway required to reach the stairs. Then without looking, she stepped back onto the staircase and descended it backwards, sliding her body along the railing, which she used as a guide. Back up she ran and repeated the procedure. This she rehearsed over and over with her eyes closed, just as if she was operating in total darkness. Lastly, she practiced her movements, holding her revolver as if she were in a defense stance and carrying the attaché case. She had no idea if she would be required to exit the house in this manner, but she wanted to be prepared and to be confident in her ability to maneuver in darkness. With Julian's unpredictable nature, she was unsure what to expect, but she wanted to be prepared for the totally unexpected. Of one thing she was certain: This house would be as black as the ace of spades.

All she needed to do now was make that all-important phone call, the one guaranteed to have Julian where they wanted him. It was 9:20 PM, and if Julian was as unpredictable as the weather in his home-life, he was more than reliable about his non-working hours at the hotels. Right about now he should be in the lounge at the Terrace Lodge Hotel more than likely listening to good old Amber singing up a storm.

"Darling," she breathed into the phone, when he took her call, "I hope you're not too busy for me. This is Jessica. Remember me?"

"What is it, Jess? For Christ's sake, I'm busy!"

"Too busy for a woman craving your body? It's been a long time, sweet stuff. Too long," she crooned. "Do you think you might be able to come home a little early tonight?"

"I'm not sure."

"Please try, sweetheart. You have a woman at home who's weak at the knees just thinking about you and how delectable you are in bed."

"Look, Jess, if this is your idea of a joke, cut it out!"

This was not going well. "I have champagne chilling for us, your favorite Scotch is on the bar, the lights are dimmed, and soft, sexy music is playing."

"What the hell for?"

"Well," she cooed, "it's been a long time since I've shown you a good time, and I thought we might get re-acquainted with some new tantalizing moves I've been practicing that are guaranteed to drive you into ecstasy."

"Let me see what I can do about cutting out early."

"Remember the sexy outfits from Paris? Well, I found a little number today that will make your eyes pop and get your body all hot and bothered. I'm going to wear it for you, and peel off piece after tempting piece, until all I have on is my passion for you. It'll be the sexiest and most alluring strip you've ever seen."

"Listen, Jess, I'm probably going to be able to leave around midnight. That won't upset your plans too much will it?"

"Midnight will be fine, darling. In the meantime, I'll shower, and have myself all silky and satiny for you and your gorgeous body."

"What about the strip-tease?"

"I'm practicing now. Bye, sweetie."

＊＊

She glanced at the clock again. Midnight. He'd promised to be home soon, when she called with that little invitation for a night of smashing sex. She hated to use all her feminine wiles, but there wasn't much else that would lure him away from that damned lounge. And she wanted to say goodbye in a way he would never forget.

Restless, she had to keep moving. Checking her outfit in the mirror, she knew it would whet his appetite. Made of red shimmer satin, it was a provocative corset, with a flounce skirt attached. The skirt was tiered so that it was nonexistent in front, exposing the entire leg, but it fell in ever-increasing lengths from the waist until, at the back, it reached to mid-calf. The top was scandalously naughty and her breasts burst over the black lace trim. Tiny shoulder straps held the rig in place. The panty was crotch-less and the skirt was adorned with black lace along the hem. To complete the ensemble, she had donned the shoes, stockings, and gloves, which Julian had brought from Paris; and she had purchased a red feather boa for more pizzazz and a black ostrich plume for her hair. If she didn't look like Saloon Sally, she'd eat the feathers.

Having pulled on her terry robe over her costume, and kicking off the shoes, she prowled the house, turning lights on and off as she said goodbye to this dwelling, which had been her home for over four years. Cuddles trailed along with her. The minutes ticked by. Everything was set. The only thing missing in this drama was the star attraction—Julian.

He was late! It was almost 1:00 AM. Please come home, she thought. Unlocking the French door with her new key, she let Cuddles out for bathroom detail. She walked onto the patio, while Cuddles bounced off to her corner of the yard, lost in the shadows. Jessica had turned off the garden lights and crickets chorused in the gloom. She looked into the night sky. Black. A sliver of crescent moon. A million stars winking and glimmering. A perfect night to work mischief. A good night for a cat burglar. An ideal night to put an end to Julian's counterfeit life.

After locking the French door behind her, she picked up the poodle tenderly and scratched her ears, gazing into her trusting eyes. Poor Cuddles! What would become of her? "I pray you will be alright. Thank you for being such a good friend to Rob...and to me." Gently, she put the small poodle on the top step of the basement stairs and softly closed the door.

She turned off the downstairs lights, leaving only a few nightlights burning, and tramped up the stairs for another inspection. Champagne chilled in the ice bucket. Where was he? Damn him anyway! She checked her clothes in her dressing room. She had laid out everything she needed for a quick change. Shoving her fingers into her jacket pocket, she reassured herself that the penknife and penlight were there. One never knew what one might need when the lights went out. The revolver was in her junk drawer. Loaded! She wasn't fooling around! She patted the attaché case with her cash and valuables.

Hanging up her robe, she surveyed her reflection. Sexy, sensuous, desirable, perfumed, and deadly. After tonight, she would never have to wear outrageous finery again.

Scurrying into the bedroom, she scooted around, turned off the bright central light, and switched on the bar lamp, which lent a lovely dim glow. Next, she turned on the stereo, which she had loaded with soft, romantic, making-out music. She put on her fancy shoes and tapped her way down the staircase, deciding to wait for him in the foyer. That way, he wouldn't be suspicious of the front door being unlocked. Sitting on the foyer bench, she smoked and waited in the shadows, with the only light coming from the front porch lanterns, which cast an eerie radiance as their beams crept through the windows and trickled on the soft gray marble, and the small night-lights they had installed in the foyer and upper landing.

She was devoid of feeling and thought. All she wanted was for this night to be over. *What do we do if he doesn't come home? Leave anyway, I guess. He'll have one hell of a surprise when he can't get in!*

And then she heard it. The soft whine and hum of the limousine. She saw the headlights wash their beams over the foyer windows, and then listened to the sound of the car stopping, a door opening, Julian saying goodnight to Kenneth, the soft thud as the door closed, his footfalls on the walk, and his shoes hitting the steps. She swung the front door open, and he almost fell in, so surprised was he that he found it opening on its own.

Jessica stepped out from behind the door. "Hi there, sailor! Got a little time for me!" she said throatily.

Startled, he laughed. "Jess! You scared me there for a minute! Thought I had the wrong house! I mean, it's been a long time since you've greeted me quite like this! Wow! That's some flashy outfit!"

"Glad you approve," she smiled as she took his hand. "Why don't we just hustle up the stairs and let me make you comfortable?"

Only too willingly, Julian followed her up the stairs to their room. Once through the door, she flung herself at him, gave him a deep longing kiss, and slithered down his body until she was on her knees. "Let me help you undress," she whispered, undoing his pants zipper, then his belt buckle, and sliding the trousers to the floor. "Just step out of them," she breathed, slithering back up. She kissed him again, grinding her body against his, as she loosened his tie, unbuttoned his shirt, and slipped his suit jacket off. She could feel his cell phone in the inside breast pocket. Casually, she dropped the jacket to the floor and skillfully caught it with the toe of her shoe, kicking it closer to her dressing room door, all the while paying superlative attention to his delight with her invitation.

"Holy shit, Jess! You're going to have me coming before I make it to the bed!" he groaned, as he buried his face in her breasts.

"Oh," she simpered, "how selfish of me! Come and lie down! Get comfortable and I'll pour you some champagne...or would you like something stronger?" She grabbed his hand, playfully led him to the bed, and pushed him down against the pillows. Diving on top of him, she writhed over him, playing with his hair, and French kissing him.

"God! Men dream about this!" he moaned. "Where did you learn...?"

"At Glenora," she groaned, "from a genital technician."

"They teach stuff like this at a treatment center?"

"No...I met a hooker. She taught me all I know," she giggled. "I've been dying to try it out, but things interfered. How about that drink I promised?"

"Make it a triple Scotch!" he leered.

She splashed the Scotch into a glass. Much more generous than a mere triple. Then she trickled a little champagne into a goblet for herself. Peeking at the clock, she saw that it was 1:55 AM. This was going better than she planned, and she was glad now he had been late; she didn't feel like playing the trollop for hours. Handing him his glass, she knelt by the bed, and with her champagne goblet in her hand, she wound her arm around his and proposed a toast.

"May this be the night to end all nights!" she breathed into his ear.

Putting her goblet on the night table, she leaned over him, and pulled off his shirt. Flicking her tongue over his chest and belly, she worked her way down to his vitals, teasing him. Positive that she had him aroused and interested, she lifted her head to peek at him coyly. "Would you like that strip-tease?"

"Whatever you say!" he sighed with ecstasy, raising his head for a swallow of Scotch.

Slinking across the carpet, she changed the music to a raunchy, suggestive tune, and grabbed her red boa. To the beat, she twirled, gyrated, twisted, wiggled, bumped, swayed, and kicked. The red boa fluttered and the ostrich plume jiggled. The skirt swirled and her breasts quivered. Asking him to undo the back zipper, she slipped away from his eager hands and, in time to the music, peeled away the gloves, the corset, and the stockings. He watched with intense enthusiasm, while she strutted her stuff, and with one well placed sexy movement of her leg, she kicked his jacket so that it lay directly beside her dressing room door. She was about to blow him away with her expertise, both in bed and with a gun.

With all the prowess of a cathouse entrepreneur, she lured him to the brink of orgasm, then teased him as she shifted her attention to his face, his neck, his ears, and the back of his knees. She tickled him with the ostrich feather and titillated him with her fingers. And she kept her eye on the clock. At 2:30 AM, she felt him shudder, shiver, and tremble to orgasm. Exhausted, he collapsed against the pillows.

As she pulled herself away, she murmured, "I have one more surprise. You'll love it!"

"Can't it wait until tomorrow?" he gasped. "I'm wiped!"

"I've been waiting for this moment all day, darling," she

whined. "You can't spoil it for me now. It'll only take a minute. Here, drink some more Scotch while I change."

She whipped into the dressing room, snatching his jacket as she closed the door. God! She'd like a shower in disinfectant after that performance. No time! 2:32 AM. Into her bra, panties, jeans, sweatshirt, socks, sneakers, and black leather jacket. No time for her hair. Grab his cell phone. It wouldn't fit into her cash case. What to do with the damned thing? Throw it in the sink and drown it. Running water into the sink, she sang out, "Just freshening up! I won't be a minute!" She grabbed a washcloth, soaked it, and wrapped it around the cell phone, leaving them both to float in the up-to-the-rim sink full of water. Get the gun. Open the drawer. Don't forget the attaché case. Open the door. Into the bedroom. Gently, she deposited the brief case on the carpet.

He lay in the soft glow of the bar lamp, propped up on the pillows, his eyes half closed.

"Julian, darling!" she called.

He shook his head and stared at her stupidly.

"What do you think?" she asked, standing at the foot of the bed, with the revolver pointed at him. "Do you like my new outfit? Does it turn you on? Does it remind you of anything?"

"What the hell are you doing?" he mumbled. "Christ, Jess, come to bed!"

"I thought we'd play a little Russian roulette first. Like you played with me. I'd like you to know how it feels. Rather suspenseful, I'd say. Only this gun *is* loaded! Six slugs, Julian! *All* with your name on them!"

"If this is supposed to get me hard again so I can fuck you, forget it!"

"No, Julian, that isn't my idea! I want to say goodbye! I'm

leaving! Don't try to stop me because I'll blow your goddamned head off!"

Through the fog of his mind, he received the message. He laughed.

"You couldn't kill a housefly! You couldn't shoot me on a bet!"

With deadly calm, she cocked the .38 so that it was on a hair-trigger. "I can, and I will, and I've already tried to kill you! Remember your concussion? That Julian, was my attempt to send you to the great beyond, where you couldn't hurt anyone again! I smashed in the side of your head with the ashtray your mother brought back from Mexico. Of all her gifts, that was the most functional. If you thought I was crying because you were injured, you were sadly mistaken. I was crying because you weren't *dead!*"

"You dragged me home to listen to this shit?"

"No, Julian, I dragged you home so you could learn what it feels like to be led down the garden path by someone you trust and have that person turn on you and threaten to murder you! Feels good, doesn't it, you son of a bitch? There's nothing like the adrenaline rush of imminent death! That's what you've been doing to me for the last sixteen months!"

"You're nothing but a bitch!"

"I'm glad you noticed! And don't forget I'm the bitch with the gun!"

"You're fucking crazy!" he hissed.

"No, Julian, you are...I read the reports from Homewood Sanitarium. I know all about your involvement with that satanic cult. I know it was responsible for the sacrificial deaths of two babies, a ten-year-old boy, and three young women, whose remains were found half-burned and buried up on the Tanglewood Creek Ridge. You were lucky to have been as young as you were and fortunate to have had a father with tons of money to keep you out of prison and your name from being splattered all over every newspaper in the country. Your daddy bought off a lot of people to protect the family's good name. I *hate* you, and I *loathe* you! You are a despicable excuse for a human being! And your brain is cooked from the shock treatments and drug therapy they gave you in Homewood."

"Shut up, Jess! Just shut up!"

"Have you forgotten *I'm* the one with the gun, Julian? You *will* listen!"

He narrowed his eyes at her, and from a source deep within his being, he snarled, "I'll cut out your heart and eat it for breakfast, and it'll still be beating!"

"I think not, Julian! If anything happens to me, I have friends who'll leak that cult and sanitarium shit to the press. You'll have CNN and their investigative reporters breathing down your neck! Let's see what that will do to your precious reputation! Your life won't be worth two cents!"

"I'll hunt you down and strip every shred of flesh from your body and your brat's! And you won't be dead when I do it!"

"No, Julian, you won't, because underneath all your glitter and charm, lurks a coward. You run away from trouble and buy your way out of problems. Keep your stinking status as Riverbend's leading citizen. And while we're on the fascinating subject of you, I know now what happened to Jack and Tiffany. You weren't trying to save them! You left them to freeze to death! You deliberately *cut* the damned battery cables; they didn't snap on impact. Jack knew nothing about car engines, and you used that against him, you poor excuse for a human being. It was your screaming at me about Tiffany that started me thinking about you, you sick, slimy bastard!"

"You fucking bitch! You married me for my money! You women are all the same!"

"I wish I *had* married you for your money!" she hissed through clenched teeth. "I loved you, Julian. But I think you married me because you needed to hide behind a wife and a child. Maybe someone knew too much about your past, and said something, and you had to add us to your list of 'normal activities'. I think Rob and I are only a smoke screen to hide your evil past and your unsavory present. You're still involved in Satanism, only not here. Now I know why you never took me with you on your trips overseas. As far as your money is concerned, I don't want any of it, or your precious possessions. You can keep the Mustang, the furs, and all the rest of the shit you gave me. I don't want anything from you, not even a memory. I'll forget you ever happened!" She glanced at her watch. "My goodness! Look at the time! I do have to run. I hope you've found our little chat enlightening, Julian. If you try to stop me, so help me, I'll blow you from here to kingdom come! I'd love an excuse to pull this trigger!"

Her eyes never leaving him as he lay bathed in the dim lamp-light, she kept the revolver trained on him, slowly bending her knees and lowering her body so she could retrieve the attaché case. Slowly, she stood up, breathless, as his eyes skewered her with his venomous hatred. Little by little, she backed out of the room, hardly daring to breathe as she concentrated on her movements, never lowering her guard because she knew that, at any instant, he could charge. He might have had a bit too much to drink, but she knew he was now as alert as a cobra; he could strike at any moment. Inch by inch, she backed onto the landing and felt for the first step of the hallway behind her. Quietly, she lowered the case to the floor, felt for the remote device on the newel post, and pushed the button, rendering the house's communication and electrical systems impotent. The state-of-the-art alarm system was finished. The porch lanterns and night-lights died, and the entire house was as black as a cave. For Julian, his home was now virtually a prison. She stuffed the remote device into her jacket pocket.

There was a thud from the bedroom and then another. She knew he was coming after her. Her major advantage was her practice in the evening; she knew her way to the front door blindfolded and backwards. But that didn't stop her terror.

"You stay there, Julian, or by God, I'll ruin your social life. You know I'm a crack shot! I'd like a little target practice!"

"You stupid bitch! What good's a target if you can't see it?"

There was a crash and a curse as he stumbled into something. "You lousy bitch! What the hell happened to the goddamned lights?"

In the blackness, she heard him fumbling, bumping, and banging around the furniture, whacking his legs on tables, and stubbing his toes on chairs. Sooner or later he'd stumble through the bedroom doorway. She inched her way backwards to the staircase and stepped onto the first stair, then the second and third.

Cautiously, she squatted down, silently placing the revolver and the case on a step to free up her hands. She felt for the fishing line. With a quick yank, she snapped it from the tape and hollered, "I'm still here, Julian! One silly move on your part, and you'll end up with a hell of a lot more than a cracked skull!"

Quickly, with skillful fingers, she twirled the line around that second opposite spindle and knotted it. With one testing tug, she was satisfied her secret weapon was secure.

Swiftly, she felt for the revolver and her case and continued her stealthy, backward descent of the stairs.

Suddenly, a harsh swishing sound invaded the pitch-black air, accompanied by soft thuds. He was feeling his way along the hallway wall!

And then the unexpected! There was a flash of light. For one awful moment, they stared at each other, his face with glittering eyes lit by the feeble flame of his lighter.

"Shoot me, you bitch! I'll choke the life outa you before you get off one shot!" His words sizzled and echoed in the black void of the cavernous foyer. With a loud curse, he dropped the lighter, the heated metal burning his fingers.

In the darkness, Jessica wasn't sure what he was doing. All she could hear was his panting and muttered curses; and she said a prayer of thanks she had had the foresight to leave that line.

But she was certain that if she couldn't see him, he more than likely didn't know where exactly where she was. Darkness is totally disorienting. She had the advantage of being armed and dangerous; and of knowing that staircase intimately. Julian was simply dangerous. Silently feeling her way to one side of the stair on which she stood, she pressed her body snug to the railing, scarcely daring to breathe, while her heart hammered in her chest. She heard him place a foot on the first step and then the second. Then she heard a sudden gasp as he tripped on the fishing line and a loud crack as he hit the railing. A startled cry escaped his throat as he hurtled past her like an invisible disaster, the spindles and banister splintering and cracking as he bounced off them or tried to grab them to break his fall. With a nauseating crackle and thud, he crash-landed on the marble foyer floor. She hadn't fired a shot.

Swiftly, she dug in her jacket pocket for her penlight. She felt her way down the steps and, revolver in hand, flicked on the light, and fixed the tiny beam on Julian. He was sprawled naked on the marble, definitely unconscious, with blood bubbling from his mouth. Broken spindles lay around, and one he grasped in his hand. With no emotion, she uncocked the revolver, flipped on the safety, and tucked it into her jacket pocket.

Up the steps she dashed, the delicate beam lighting her way and, with the penknife, severed the line's knots from the spindles. Twirling the fishing line around her fingers in one hand, she shoved the tangle into her jeans pocket along with her knife. She didn't want anyone else tripping over it, and she wanted no evidence as to what on earth could have caused Riverbend's most prominent citizen to fall down his own staircase, for God's sake. Peeling the tape from the wood, she scrunched it in her fist and jammed that, too, into her pocket. Grabbing the case, she gingerly found her way to the bottom of the steps and tiptoed to the front door.

Just as she twisted the knob, she heard a soft whine. Cuddles! God! She couldn't take her! Casey had forbidden it! All she had to do was open the front door, and she'd be free! But she couldn't simply abandon the dog.

For one long moment she hesitated, listening to Cuddles whimper. But when Julian moaned, she made an instant decision. She dropped the case, and with the fragile shaft of light from the penlight illuminating the way, tiptoed to the basement door, opened it, and grabbed Cuddles. On cat feet, she tiptoed back to the foyer, transferred the penlight to the same hand that held Cuddles, opened the door with her free hand, grasped the handle of the case, and soundlessly slipped into the night.

The car was waiting, black, humming, no lights, a phantom in the shadows. The back door was open, and she handed the dog to Casey.

"Not one word!" she whispered to him. "I had to take Cuddles. I didn't have the heart to leave her. Here's the case. I have to go back and lock the door."

Scampering to the door, she quietly closed it, and with the key, locked Julian's lurid life inside the darkened house. As she scurried back to the car, she tossed the key into Julian's rosebushes.

She slid into the car beside Casey.

"I gather you didn't put a final touch on the proceedings," he rumbled.

"Not this time," she answered.

"Mommy, we're going for a helicopter ride!" Rob announced. "Isn't Daddy coming with us?"

"Not this time."

As silent as the hush of an evening breeze, the car vanished into the night's soft embrace. It was 3:03 AM.

The Beginning

Jessica's Song

My mother never taught me to
Be on the watch for men like you.
She never said the world is full
Of guys who really shoot the bull.
She always said be good and sweet,
But not to stand on my own two feet.
And so I wandered down the trail

That leads to where we women fail.
Raised was I to believe the dreams
That all is really as it seems.
Never think, and never act,
Just obey, use lots of tact.
Never argue, never shout,
Don't get angry, swearing's out.
Strict adherence to the rules,
God, but are we women fools.
I followed this good formula,
And knew I'd find my Shangri-La.
Down life's path I wandered 'til
I chanced upon a lonely hill.
Lost and frightened, all alone,
I gazed around, and saw a throne.
There you were, my savior sweet,
You smiled, and then our eyes did meet.
Protection, comfort, offered you;
You loved me on the morning dew.
Gone was hunger, gone was sleep,
You filled me with your love so deep.
Lost was I in Love's embrace,
I did not see the devil's face.
"Follow, follow," so spake you,
I never doubted words so true.
And so I clambered up the knoll,
And fell into a rabbit's hole.
Where were you to rescue me?
Perched up in your apple tree;
And from your lofty nest on high,
You laughed, and jeered, and scorned, while I

Killarney Greene

Straggled out, decided then
To hell with love. Will I try again?
Sad but wiser, now I see
That I must learn to count on me;
To depend on me, and God alone
And now *I* sit upon that throne.

About the Author

Tap Dancing on Quicksand is Killarney Greene's first novel, although she has been composing stories since she was old enough to write. In speaking about the birth of this novel, Killarney Greene  notes it grew organically from her experiences and imagination. "My inspiration came from the universe, and many times when I started my morning writing, I had no idea what would happen by midnight. Every day, new ideas tumbled onto the computer keys. Characters appeared as if from nowhere. They blossomed and bloomed, argued, fought, loved, hated, and sometimes triumphed."

Killarney Greene lives in a small town in the middle of the Canadian Rockies. There she reads, walks, bikes, studies university courses, and contemplates worldly matters in the serenity of her surroundings. She also enjoys spending time with friends and family and, of course, writing. Killarney Greene is working hard on her next book, which her fans will be delighted to learn is almost complete.

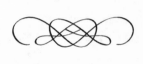